SOMEONE
ELSE'S
SHADOW

SOMEONE ELSE'S SHADOW

International Bestselling Author
MONICA JAMES

Cover Design: Perfect Pear Creative Covers
Editing: Editing 4 Indies
Formatting: E.M. Tippetts Book Designs

Follow me on:

authormonicajames.com

OTHER BOOKS BY
MONICA JAMES

THE I SURRENDER SERIES

I Surrender

Surrender to Me

Surrendered

White

SOMETHING LIKE NORMAL SERIES

Something like Normal

Something like Redemption

Something like Love

A HARD LOVE ROMANCE

Dirty Dix

Wicked Dix

The Hunt

MEMORIES FROM YESTERDAY DUET

Forgetting You, Forgetting Me

Forgetting You, Remembering Me

SINS OF THE HEART DUET

Absinthe of the Heart

Defiance of the Heart

DEDICATION

This book is dedicated to me. I thought I was broken.
But then, then I wrote this book...

ONE

Something about a thunderstorm in June is utterly captivating.

With the sunlight kindling across the horizon, one cannot be condemned for peering up into the heavens and believing we're not alone because only the hand of God could create something so perfect, so picturesque. But just beyond the skyline, an undercurrent of electricity soon overshadows the sun.

Before long, the sunshine surrenders to the darkness, disappearing to an untouched paradise because Mother Nature has no mercy when it's her time to shine.

The clouds emerge quickly but quietly, setting the stage for Act 1. The destruction lingers in the air minutes before you can hear it or feel it. One can taste it on their tongue. People scurry like mice, desperate to get indoors and safe in their houses because the roar of the thunder warns what's approaching from the distance.

Dark gray blankets the vibrant sky, and without warning, it's illuminated by a flash of lightning. By setting an ominous mood with the warmth still loitering, one can almost forget that the heavens will open and baptize us all with driving rain in seconds.

A thunderstorm in the summertime is such an oxymoron. The weather is stifling, yet the punishing downpour forbids basking in the seasonal heat.

But for me, I must be the epitome of an oxymoron—a smart fool—because all I can think about is breaking free from the suffocating confines of this car and dancing in the rain. My feet yearn to kick at the puddles, bouncing recklessly into each one like a five-year-old. I want to tear off my clothes—overpriced garments which could feed a small nation—and spread my arms out wide and fly. I want to feel the rain on my face trickle into my mouth as I scream in liberation.

I don't care what others think of me; let them ridicule me because I've always been utterly captivated by a thunderstorm in June or…so I think I have.

"Peyton, is everything all right?" Tearing my gaze from the storm just outside my window, I meet Stella Lane's hazel eyes.

I can see the resemblance. I have her large eyes, which are almost too big for my heart-shaped face. My locks are a deeper, darker orangey copper than Stella's, but we both wear our hair long. My lips are naturally full, tinted a rosy pink. Stella's are plump, thanks to her cosmetic doctor. Our builds are slim.

Yes, I can definitely see the similarities…but it's still so difficult to accept this stranger as my mom. "Yes, I'm fine. Just a lot to take in."

I know she wants me to say more, maybe explain why I've decided to move from her gated mansion in Myrtle Beach, South Carolina, to a small, secluded property forty-five minutes away. But I can't give her a reason because I don't have one. I have no idea why this less than luxurious home appeals to me. It just does.

Stella's pout slants downward, and I know what she's going to say. "We can always turn this car around and go home."

Home.

They say home is where the heart is, but the problem is, I've misplaced my heart, along with the memories that go with it.

When I look into the mirror, I don't recognize the person staring back at me because I don't know who I am. Snippets of information have been relayed to me over the past six months in hopes that it will jog some kind of memory, but all it does is leave me feeling empty; I'm a stranger in someone else's skin.

They tell me my name is Peyton Veronica Lane. I was born on October first. I'm twenty-seven years old. I have four siblings—two brothers, two sisters—and I'm the third oldest. I'm a marketing manager who loves water sports and having a glass of wine while listening to classical music. The small scar on the underside of my chin is from falling off my mare, Sabina, when I was nine.

It seems I've lived a full, rewarding life, one which many may envy, thanks to the blue blood running through my veins. Still, I would give it up, all of it, in a heartbeat if only I could remember who I was.

Six months ago, I woke up…woke up from a coma with no recollection of anybody, anything. The doctors told me I was involved in a head-on collision that almost claimed my life. On the outside, I look unscathed, a pillar of perfect health, but the unseen, like an iceberg submerged deep in the murky depths, has caused me the most harm. My mind is a blank slate. Every moment in time was wiped clean.

I'm told by my friends and family that I'm a good woman, that I'm loved, but I just can't remember any of it…any of it at all.

"Thank you, but I need to do this. I think."

Stella tugs at her mother-of-pearl earring—a sure sign she's annoyed I've said no, a word she doesn't hear too often. Augusto Lane, Stella's husband and my father, merely sits quietly in the driver's seat, occasionally glancing at me in the rearview mirror. He seems just as unsettled as I am.

It's disconcerting to have people you don't know but who know you trying to narrate your life. Every time someone details a memory, I see the hope flash before their eyes—they're hoping something will finally resurface. But nothing ever does.

Only time will tell if I'm forever broken. The doctors aren't even sure.

So I'm sitting in this Mercedes on the way to my new home because it's the first flicker of familiarity I've had in so many months. I'm drawn here, and I need to know why.

Stella said it's because we vacationed on the lake when we were kids. She has the photos to prove it. But those photographs may as well have been taken in another lifetime because I'm looking at them through the eyes of a stranger.

When Augusto takes a left, the lush vegetation becomes thicker and the location more remote as we journey down a quiet stretch of road. The bustle of Myrtle Beach has left me with a perpetual case of seasickness. The world moves faster down there, but here, the easygoing pace appeases my need for calm.

The wide road is unevenly paved, but it doesn't seem to bother the locals. Appearing to have been standing for an eternity, the weathered lake houses radiate warmth and love. The neighborhood is everything you'd expect a small community to be—private, tended, and still.

As the storm subsides, I rub a circle in the condensation and peer out the window, all but pressing my nose to the glass. The farther Augusto drives, the more secluded we are, but who needs civilization when a mysterious lake emerges from the isolation? I hold my breath.

Its size is considerable, almost daunting, and one can't be blamed for looking into the cavernous depths and wondering what secrets it conceals. With trees forking from within the water and low-hanging branches skimming the water's edge, it throws off a swamp-like feel.

The car decelerates before veering down a steep driveway. I know without looking that this is my new home.

Stella whispers something to Augusto, who turns over his shoulder, his thin lips slanted into a puckered line. I know they'd rather I live anywhere but here, but this isn't their decision. I've lived by their rules for the past six months, and I'm no closer to unearthing just who I was...who I am. Unsnapping my belt, I reach for my backpack, unable to leap from this car fast enough.

"Peyton! Use your umbrella. And dear Lord, put on some shoes!"

I pay no heed to Stella's requests because the moment I step foot outside and my bare feet connect with the recently showered earth, my lungs fill with air, and I breathe. The oppression gradually fades, and I take a moment to appreciate everything around me.

Spinning in a slow circle, I admire my quiet neighborhood. The two-story houses across the road are weather-beaten but well loved. Most are bright white or pale yellow with wraparound white balconies. Wooden rocking chairs sit on front porches for my neighbors to admire their perfect views. The manicured gardens are flourishing with not a blade of grass awry.

Small hybrids or compact cars are parked in all the driveways except one. A stunning two-story home a few houses down has clearly been renovated, but the addition of the floor-to-ceiling windows doesn't make it any less beautiful than the neighboring houses. If anything, I imagine the living areas glowing from the brilliant sunshine and warming the occupants all year round.

An enormous black SUV pickup in the drive towers over the adjacent cars. The flourishing rose bushes lined up like regimented soldiers along the paved pathway contrast the virile feel of the home.

My admiration continues when I look upward and marvel at the Spanish moss decorating the gigantic oak trees lining the road. The silver-gray strands sway gently in the wind, hanging like a trapeze, ready for her next trick. The soaring oaks arch over one another, the sunlight capable of breaking through only when the leaves dither in just the right way.

An undercurrent of enchantment is in the air, and when I turn, that magnetism amplifies tenfold when the lake comes into view. An unforeseen sense of déjà vu passes over me. My attention drifts to the towering oak across the lake. A well-loved wooden swing rocks lightly in the breeze. But that's not what I'm fixated on. I'm spellbound by the red ribbon tied to the weathered rope. It looks…familiar.

"I have no doubt that the roof will cave in the moment a wind blows." Stella's judgment is a sudden, welcomed distraction.

My home is an olive-green lake house; it may not be the prettiest of the bunch, but I envision the possibilities. With a fresh coat of paint and some TLC, both inside and out, I can see myself building a life—a life I will remember—here. Clutching the straps of my backpack, I can't wait to start.

However, all plans of moving forward are put on hold when a boisterous barking, followed by the wind being knocked from my sails, requires my undivided attention. Thanks to the wet ground and my bare feet, I lose my balance and end up very ungracefully tumbling onto my ass. The plush grass breaks my fall, but nothing protects me from the bouncing Golden Retriever who dives on top of me and assaults my face with his very affectionate tongue.

I can't stop my laughter as he pins me down and smothers me with kisses. "Hey, boy. Are you the welcoming committee?" In response, he licks my cheeks like I'm his new chew toy.

Reaching for his furry face, I gently coax him backward so I can sit up. He grants me my freedom, but only because I allow him to sit on my lap.

"Oh, shoo, you big, ugly mutt! Shoo!"

In the midst of an eye roll, I'm curtly incapacitated of any movement when a voice that can only be compared to molten honey materializes out of thin air.

"Mutt? Now, that's not nice. Empire, come here, boy." The bouncy pooch, aka Empire, barks once.

His tone is husky, laden with sinful promise, and I'm suddenly left breathless for an entirely different reason. Unable to stop myself, I peer to the left and appreciate the tall, dark, and handsome guy standing only feet away. The first thing that strikes me is the penetrating clarity of his hooded blue eyes. Brought to life by the stirring of gray in their bottomless depths, they have the ability to lure one in and completely hypnotize— just as they're doing right now.

His bravado suddenly dies when he sees me with my ass slathered in mud. I was hidden behind my mom, but now that I'm out in the open, he pauses, watching me closely.

A rigid, perplexed frown tugs at his pouty lips, and when they part slightly, I imagine they have the ability to whisper sweet nothings and vow empty promises to anyone within a hundred-mile radius. His face is chiseled and hard with a strong jawline. The peppered stubble only accentuates his cleft chin. His upturned nose enhances the air of arrogance radiating from his broad shoulders as he holds my curious gaze.

His light brown hair is mussed, kicked into a natural coif, the longer strands bowing forward lazily. The soft undercut is textured and groomed at the sides, but the style is far too long and wild to be labeled clean-cut.

But one would never mistake him for being anything but

trouble because his hulking, muscular build combined with his rugged, rogue looks all point to the fact that this man is the epitome of what every bad boy strives to become when he grows up.

A close-fitting light gray V-neck and ripped blue jeans hug his taut body. A pair of motorcycle boots completes the brutish look.

Once I've perused him from head to toe—twice—I swallow past the lump lodged in my throat.

I'm rendered speechless because he's eyeing me so openly, uncaring that my mother is about five seconds away from throttling him. Her sharp voice reminds me that we're in a deadlock, which is highly inappropriate considering I don't even know this handsome stranger's name.

"I don't care. Take him away this instant." Even I cringe at her insolence and am disappointed that someone of her social standing doesn't know better. The stranger doesn't seem bothered in the slightest and brushes past her, sauntering toward me.

I instantly release Empire's collar, afraid his owner will demand I unhand his dog and tell Stella and me to take the high road. I wouldn't blame him if he did. The only thing is, I live here now, and I have a feeling he does too.

Empire runs toward him, happily wagging his tail when the stranger ruffles the fur on the back of his neck. I believe he will turn away now that he has his dog, but I thought wrong. He continues ambling toward me, never breaking eye contact.

When he's a hair's breadth away, he comes to a stop. His wide shoulders block out the sun, but the blaze ignites his shadow, bequeathing an ethereal glow. I blink once.

Now that he's standing before me, I notice how incredibly tall he is. It could be, however, that he appears this way because I'm still sitting in the mud. Absolutely horrified, I attempt to arise, but a small gasp escapes me when he offers me his large hand.

I peer up at it and then back at him. I'm certain I resemble a cartoon character because a flicker of a smirk pulls at his curved lips as he examines me carefully.

Breaking from whatever this insanity is, I slap my palm into his because this is ridiculous. I'm behaving like a high school girl, smitten by her first crush. I'm a grown woman, and just because he's stupidly handsome does not mean I have to go goo goo ga ga all of a sudden. I'm here to find my independence, and a man will only complicate my plans.

That theory is all good and well for roughly three seconds because the moment he encloses his hand around mine, a smolder begins to kindle, and I'm certain I'm running a fever. The tips of my ears ignite, followed by every part of my body.

A strangled wheeze squalls past the floodgates, and although it's subtle, I know he heard me loud and clear. My cheeks blister, which doesn't help with the current inferno raging out of control within.

What is the matter with me? I have no idea if this is how I would usually respond to an attractive stranger because I can't remember. That thought is my saving grace—reminding me why I'm here—and I allow him to help me to my feet. The moment I stand, I feel dwarfed in his shadow. He's tall. I'd say six-foot-three. My small stature of five-foot-four has me feeling dainty and delicate in his presence.

I meet those mesmerizing eyes and am instantly rooted to the spot.

"You're dirty."

"I-I'm what?" I ask in a squeak, fumbling over my words.

"Dirty," he simply repeats.

My mouth falls open and dances in wordless animation. Can he read my thoughts? I'm beyond mortified. Heat creeps up my neck to unite with the flush painting my cheeks.

"I'm so sorry"—I clear my throat—"I didn't mean to stare. How incredibly rude of me."

A throaty chuckle slips past his full lips as he shakes his head. "No, I meant your clothes. They're dirty." To accent his point, he gestures with his chin toward my soiled dress.

I, on the other hand, wish the puddle of mud I'm standing in would swallow me whole.

Scrunching up my nose, I awkwardly tug at my ear. "Oh, right. Well, fuck me, that wasn't at all embarrassing."

"Peyton! Language," Stella scolds, but she's ignored.

He instantly makes me feel at ease when he chooses to ignore the fact that my feet aren't the only thing in the gutter. "Hi, Peyton." As our hands are still intertwined, he shakes them once. That draws attention to the fact that I'm still holding his hand, which is highly improper, but it never crossed my mind to sever our connection.

Regardless, I gently pull from his hold, missing the warmth instantly. "Hello. What's your name?" His eyebrows arrow upward, but I ignore his strange response. "I'm your new neighbor. If you live here, that is. Don't worry, my crazy isn't contagious." I hook my thumb toward my house. "By the way, I have amnesia. So don't be offended if I forget we ever met."

It was supposed to be a joke, a bad one at that, and clear the air, but when his mood sours quicker than curdled milk, I know he doesn't appreciate my humor in the slightest. I suddenly wonder what I said.

"C'mon, boy." He turns without delay, patting his thigh, gesturing to Empire it's time to go. "We won't bother you again."

My mouth parts as I'm totally confused. What just happened? "Do you want to stay for coffee?" I have no idea what just possessed me to say that, considering I don't have coffee—or anything, for that matter—to offer him, but I want him to stay.

However, when he sharply replies, "No," and takes off in a huff, I'm glad he didn't accept my invitation because we would be having a side order of awkward with our caffeine.

"It was nice meeting you. Both of you!" I call out, shielding the sun from my eyes with my palm to ensure I'm not seeing things. But it's clear as day. The stranger is practically running away, desperate to flee from a situation that clearly made him uncomfortable.

I stand on tippy-toes, hoping to catch a glimpse of where he's going, but Stella blocks my view. "Darling, please reconsider. You'll probably need a rabies shot after consorting with that beast." The sad thing is, I don't know if she's referring to the man or his dog.

This is exactly why I need to leave. I can't bear to live under her roof a moment longer. If I'm going to find myself, it most certainly won't be locked away in her tower. "No, I'm doing this.

I have to. You heard what Dr. Martinez said. I need to go out on my own and live my life and be self-sufficient. It's the only hope I have to remember who I was."

Stella purses her lips, not at all impressed with my constant need to challenge her. It makes me wonder what kind of a person I was. Have I not defied her in the past? Did I accept her judgmental ways because I was cut from the same cloth?

If that indeed is true, then this is my chance to make amends for all the wrongdoings of my past.

"You may have amnesia, but your constant need to defy me seems to have remained. You'll learn soon enough. Everything I do is to protect you. Come on, Augusto." My father is a man of few words. However, it could be because his wife does all the talking for him.

He treads forward and embraces me awkwardly. I stand with my arms rigidly by my sides. I don't think I was a hugger. With a firm pat on the back, he pulls away and gives me a look that can only be described as him bidding me good luck on my maiden journey. I'll need it. Stella doesn't bother with farewells.

Their expensive car leaves smoke in its wake as they speed away back to their cozy lives, hidden from the real world. It's no wonder I still have no idea who I am six months later. I know I haven't seen anything they haven't wanted me to see. Stella's comment rings loudly in my ears.

"Everything I do is to protect you."

For quite some time, I've had a sneaking suspicion that the Lanes are hiding a deep, dark secret…from me, but more so, *about* me. It lingers in the air whenever I enter a room; my siblings are too afraid to look at me in case their guilt shows.

Peering off into the distance, I'm hypnotized by the lake once again because it's why I'm here. I discount all the things I can't remember and focus on all the things, or *thing*, that I can. I haven't told anyone about this memory because, how do you describe something that doesn't make a lick of sense?

The familiar touch of helplessness overcomes me, and I submerge like a weighted rock to a bottomless depth, unable to breathe. I don't fight it because it's become a part of who I am.

Gasping, I attempt to break the surface, but I suddenly can't swim. The harder I push, the farther I sink. Invisible manacles secure my ankles, dragging me down. Muddy water fills my lungs, and before long, it's all I can taste. I stop fighting and surrender... surrender to death.

My chest rises and falls as I clutch at my throat, desperate for air. It takes a few moments, but eventually, I steady my breathing and return to the present. The aftertaste of the sullied water is on my tongue; it lurks in the air. The hair at the back of my neck stands on end because I know...I know the answers I seek lie buried at the bottom of the lake. That's why I'm here. The memory I have isn't mine...it's what I witnessed.

So I wonder what it would feel like to remember... remember who I was, but more importantly, remember what I did.

TWO

"The pictures really did not do this place justice," I mumble aloud as I spin in a slow circle. Sadly, that isn't a positive thing.

When the flickers of this location became more persistent, I knew I had to find out where it was. I started my search by scouring the internet, probing for any small scrap of evidence to confirm this place as being real.

Night after night, I dreamed of the tall oak, my attention always fixated on the red ribbon. What was its significance? As time progressed, the dreams turned into visions and cultivated into something more.

The lake was always the star attraction, the focal hub of what all of this meant. It started with a flickering mirage of me peering out over the still water, engrossed by the towering tree with the red ribbon flapping lightly in the cool breeze. But then darkness shrouded that stillness, and I was no longer looking—I was submerged.

I know I'm drowning, but there isn't a damn thing I can do about it because when I gaze at the surface as the ripples of water siphon off my life source, I'm staring back down at me from the dock. I call out for help, my arms desperately seeking something solid to hold, but it's useless; the other me turns her back and leaves.

I needed to find out what that meant, and I knew that the red ribbon and this lake were the keys.

After a fruitless search, I was ready to give up, but life worked in mysterious ways indeed. Stella, as usual, was intent on having me remember a past I had no recollection of, but I humored her anyway and sat through the endless parade of photographs.

After a while, everything starts to look the same—it's all foreign. Places, people, occurrences, they meant nothing to me; however, when Stella flashed a photo of the unmistakable lake with the tall oak and weathered swing, something struck a chord.

I all but leaped from my seat and grilled her for any information she might have. She revealed our family vacationed here when I was a kid, as our vacation house was by the lake, but she seemed reluctant to tell me more. My brothers and sisters confirmed her story, but something was askew, and that's why I'm here.

If no one will tell me, then I will uncover the truth myself.

My older brother, Lachlan, is a successful businessman in New York. Next in line is Ursula, who lives in Savannah, living the true Southern beauty life with her wealthy husband and three bratty children. I've seen my eldest siblings a handful of times. The two youngest, Blake and Isla, are twins. They seem to be more on my level . . . well, I think they are.

Blake and his fiancée, Sara, live about an hour away, but Isla, she still lives with Stella and Augusto, and apparently, before my accident, I did too. Isla is a nurse, much to the horror and disgust of her mom, *our* mom. She's the only one I have anything remotely in common with, but every time I try to talk to her and ask questions, she seems to have somewhere else to be.

I have a feeling she's frightened of Stella's wrath if she was to divulge something Stella wishes to keep under lock and key.

With that said, that only left me to fend for myself.

So with what little information I had, I checked the listings and found this house that had been on the market for quite some time. I breezed over the pictures, not at all worried about what was inside, because the moment the photo of the outside decking with the picture-perfect view of the lake flicked onto my screen, I knew this house was the key to unearthing everything.

Vehemently opposing the idea, Stella argued with me every chance she got, but nothing and no one would change my mind. I bought the house for a steal, and when a droplet of water backflips and lands dead center onto my forehead from the leak in the ceiling, I know why.

And that's my story. At least it's one I can remember.

Peering at my surroundings, I take in the small living room that needs so much more than a coat of paint. Burnt orange leaves litter the hardwood flooring, making me wonder if I have a hole in my ceiling or maybe a broken window. As I turn to face the brick wall, I find cobwebs decorating the corners and looping along the wooden mantel above the fireplace like tinsel at Christmastime.

The once pristine white panel walls are now more of an eggshell color, faded over time from exposure to the harsh elements. My bare feet leave footprints in the dust as I move from room to room, familiarizing myself with my new surroundings. I'm hoping each step will disclose a memory, offering a small piece of the puzzle, but that only seems to grow more ambiguous by the minute. So far, everything looks the same.

I'm almost done with the tour—not that there's much to see, considering each room needs more work than the one before. I exit the bathroom and amble down the narrow hallway and into the last door on the left.

I don't have high hopes that it'll look any different from any of the other rooms, but the moment I step inside, the beaming sunshine bouncing off the swelling water fills the modest space with a warmth that thaws out the constant chill in my bones. Stiffening, I turn my head ever so slowly from left to right as a spark of recognition barrels into me.

Taking a small step backward, I steady my breathing and clear my mind. I focus on the faded wallpaper, determined to hear these walls talk. I wait, desperate for something, anything, but all I get is a fistful of nothing. I blow out an exasperated breath.

My gaze swings to the lake, which is just outside my room. The double doors lead out onto a small balcony, so without further ado, I wrench down the stiff brass handles, both whining in protest as I push open the doors.

The first thing that hits me is how easy it is to breathe out here. I lightly test the bowed wood of the deck with my big toe, ensuring it can handle my full weight. The recent downpour has soaked the surface, but once I'm satisfied it won't collapse, I step out onto the balcony and take two deep breaths.

The white paint has chipped away from the railing, leaving behind a rough wooden texture, but it somehow adds rustic charm, complementing the simple paradise before me. The lake is endless, extending as far as the eye can see, and I wonder what is on the other side.

The soaring oak is a few hundred yards away from where I stand. Leaning my forearms against the top of the jagged railing, I sink low and turn to the right, surrendering to the racket inside my head.

I don't know why, but I correlate happiness with this tree and all that it represents. I can hear the joyous laughter of children as they beg their friends to push them higher, feeling invincible as the swing veers far above the ground and extends over the water's edge. One can wiggle their toes in the air and look into the heavens before screaming in excitement as they come back down, only mere feet from the rippling water. If one were brave enough, they could let go and dive into the depths, but there's only a small window before you're back on land.

I can almost feel the wind in my hair and taste the rich water as I take my leap of faith. The red ribbon flutters gently in the calm breeze, but it may as well be waving a red flag in front of an angry bull.

My attention drifts to the dock extending from my property line. It's hardly sizeable, but at the prospect of walking on it, I suddenly feel like my feet are caught in quicksand. The farther I'd advance, the harder it would be to breathe. I suddenly have the urge to demolish it from my acreage and send its remains to the bottom of the lake.

From the corner of my eye, a flash of red strikes, erasing these irrational fears which simply make no sense. "I'm losing my mind."

Running a hand through my hair, I begin to wonder if it'll ever be found.

Lost in blurred insights, I don't hear the floor creak behind me, which is a complete rookie mistake.

"Hi."

My heart lodges in my throat as I yelp. Spinning so quickly, I almost fall face-first. "Holy fuck!" Pressing a hand to my chest, I gulp in mouthfuls of air, attempting to breathe.

"Oh, my God. I'm so sorry. I didn't mean to scare you. I'm Lacey. Your neighbor." The friendly-looking brunette rushes over, homemade pie in hand, offering an olive branch.

The sweet smell of cherries permeates the air.

When I've calmed enough to speak without wheezing like a winded hyena, I attempt to smile. I hope I don't resemble a deranged freak show clown. "It's fine. I'm the one who's sorry." I wave off her concerns when she bites her lip guiltily. "It's nice to meet you, Lacey. I'm Peyton."

When the air settles, she smiles. "It's nice to meet you, too. I brought pie," she declares, holding up the plate with pride. "I thought it would be a nice way to welcome you to the neighborhood, but considering I just scared you half to death, I kind of feel like I should have brought coffee, too."

A laugh escapes me, which startles me because I don't think I've laughed since "waking up."

Lacey is quite pretty. With long, brown hair, sun-kissed freckles, and a kind smile, she radiates the girl-next-door vibe. She looks a little younger than I am, but I instantly feel like I could call her my friend.

I don't have many—well, any—friends, so if I'm determined to do this living thing, what better way to start than by making my first friend. "I literally have nothing to offer you. Not even a glass of water because I don't have any glasses." Peering down at the delectable pie, I regrettably add, "Or forks, for that matter."

Lacey's light laughter fills the room. "Lucky for you"—she hunts through her large brown handbag, tonguing the corner of her mouth in concentration—"I never leave home without them." Just as I'm about to ask what, she holds two plastic forks high in the air. "Ta-da!"

Another laugh slips past my lips, which surprises me. It feels so foreign yet so familiar, too. "I can offer you a view, though." We both gaze out over the lake, a mutual respect for our picturesque backdrop.

"Sounds perfect to me." She places the pie on the railing between us and hands over a fork. I gratefully accept.

"I thought this was a myth," I confess, pursing my lips in thought.

"What?" Lacey asks with her fork paused en route to the pie.

"Friendly neighbors coming over with baked goods to

welcome someone to the neighborhood," I reply, tongue in cheek.

She grins, the sight shedding much-needed light on my otherwise dreary day. "It's best to know one's neighbors, they say. You never know who's living next door to you. I wanted to make sure you weren't a serial killer." Her tone is completely playful, but a shiver racks my body.

Lacey reads my sudden withdrawal and gasps. "Oh gosh, I didn't mean you were a creep or anything. If anything, I'm the creep for wandering in uninvited, bearing a pie." She seems upset and genuinely embarrassed by her comment. But there is no need.

"It's completely okay. I'm glad you came over. Before you did, I was debating whether I'd lost my mind."

"And the verdict is?"

"The jury is still out," I reply honestly.

This would be the time Lacey says welcome to the neighborhood and runs from this madhouse, never looking back, but she doesn't. She thrusts her fork into the pie and cuts into it merrily. "So why do you think that?" she poses casually, the warm crimson filling sticking to her utensil.

Sighing, I know I have two options. I can either tell her the truth and risk the chance of losing my first potential friend, or I could lie and have the same outcome. I came here to start afresh and attempt to piece my life back together. So with that as my incentive, I exhale deeply. "I was involved in a car accident."

Lacey's fork trembles in transit to her mouth.

I realize I probably should have led with something a little less shocking. "Sorry, I'm still trying to figure out this whole social etiquette thing." I scrunch up my face and shake my head because that revelation isn't any better than my first.

Lacey chews her pie politely, waiting for me to continue.

"Six months ago, I woke from a coma." The fact still leaves me winded. "I actually have...amnesia. I have no idea who I am. I have strangers telling me about the person I once was, but I have absolutely no recollection of any of it." I toy with my fork, flicking my thumb over the plastic tines. "The doctors don't know if I'll ever remember. So far, nothing, but..."

"But what?" she asks, swallowing, utterly intrigued.

Pausing, I once again get lost in the gentle hum pulsating in the air. "But this place...something about this place feels so...familiar. It doesn't make any sense because I didn't grow up here, but I can't shake the feeling that I've been here before."

Sighing, I dig my fork into the flaky pie crust, needing something to shove into my mouth so I stop talking. I have no doubt I freaked Lacey the hell out. Talk about jumping into the deep end. The unintentional thought makes my stomach drop.

We're silent, both chewing pensively. As I deliberate what I just confessed, I find I can't read the blank look on Lacey's face. I wouldn't blame her if she kept her distance, but she said she was my neighbor, which has me wondering how long she's lived here.

Wanting a change of pace, I place my hand on the railing, shake out my hair, and strike my best model pose. "I don't suppose I look familiar?" I know I look ridiculous, but that's the whole point.

Lacey splutters up her pie, covering her mouth with her hand. "At the moment"—she's doing a poor job at hiding her smirk—"you kind of look like Donald Duck."

My pursed lips twitch before I burst into fits of laughter. "Well, at least I can rule out model," I manage to choke out between chuckles. Lacey cackles along with me.

"What are you doing tomorrow?"

"Tomorrow?"

"Yes, tomorrow." She nods animatedly.

"I have no idea," I reveal. "I have no idea what I'm doing. Period." I have no idea why any of this is funny, but being with Lacey is like gossiping with an old girlfriend where everything is funny.

"Well, in that case, I insist you let me help decorate this place. We can go into town and grab a few things." When something clatters loudly in my kitchen, Lacey's eyes widen before she bites back a smile. "Maybe a lot of things."

My heart swells at her suggestion because that sounds absolutely amazing. "Deal."

I feel an inexplicable kinship to Lacey. I have no idea why, but she's the first person I have met who I've been completely comfortable around. It could be because she has no idea who I was, and she's meeting the new Peyton Lane 2.0.

Whatever the reason, I don't question it.

"Let's look at the master bedroom and see what we need. Maybe we could put in a hot tub." She wiggles her eyebrows mischievously.

Her comment sobers me up somewhat. Looking over my shoulder, I examine the room behind me. It's the smallest room in the house, and the hideous retro wallpaper transports me back to the 70s, but for some inexplicable reason, it's perfect.

When I peer upward, a single glow-in-the-dark star pressed to the ceiling cements my decision.

"I think I want to stay in here."

"Here?" she asks, bearing her surprise.

I nod, chewing on my lip. "Yes. It's the room that needs the most work, but it feels…like home. Weird, right?"

"No, not weird at all," she replies a moment later. "It's perfect."

Silence falls over us, but this time, Lacey appears to be the pensive one. I don't have time to question her, though, because yet another bang and crash vibrate off my walls as the distinct sound of happy paws skating along my flooring comes to life. We both turn and are greeted with nothing but trouble.

Empire stampedes into the room and charges straight toward me. Before I have a chance to move, he's licking my face. Just like when I first saw him, a sense of happiness falls over me.

"Hey, Empire. Whatcha doing in here, boy?" I squish both his cheeks, laughing when his tongue licks me clean. "Is he always this friendly?" I ask Lacey, who is leaning against the railing, watching on in amusement.

"Yes, but only to the people he likes."

"Well, in that case," I coo, rubbing his floppy ears, "I'm honored. Maybe you could teach your owner a thing or two about friendliness. God knows he could use the training. Someone woke up on the wrong side of the bed, didn't they? Or maybe he's just born an asshole," I conclude, ending my tangent.

When Lacey straightens her back, I realize I may have overstepped a line. I have no idea exactly where she lives, but if she knows Empire, then she knows his master too. "Shit, I'm so sorry. That was really rude of me." I gently coax Empire down, who sits by my side.

Lacey waves off my apology, however. "I take it you've met Cayden, then?"

Cayden.

My stranger finally has a name.

Her question drips with innuendo. Maybe he's a notorious killjoy throughout the neighborhood.

Patting Empire on the scruff, I nod slowly. "Yeah, I think I offended him somehow."

Her curiosity is piqued. "What makes you say that?"

Shrugging, I think back to our encounter. He's undeniably handsome, but I have a sneaking suspicion he's hiding a secret behind those eyes. I should know. I recognize the look all too well.

"I don't know. Just a gut feeling, I guess. He practically ran away from me earlier."

"I'm sure he didn't run," she offers, attempting to play down the situation.

But I remember he couldn't get away from me fast enough. "He left skid marks in his haste."

Lacey's mouth twitches. "Don't take it personally," she says, turning serious.

It's now my turn for my curiosity to be piqued. "He makes a habit of running away from his neighbors then?"

She peers down at her scuffed sneakers, toeing over a crack in the wood before she finally replies. "The thing about Cayden is that he…" Her pause has me holding my breath, anxious to hear her explanation.

She chews her glossy pink lip, suddenly regretting saying anything. But I won't let this go. I raise an eyebrow at her hesitation.

"Is that he's really a nice guy but forgot he left the stove on?" I quip, wanting to lighten the mood. She smiles, but her struggle is visible.

I'm just about to tell her not to worry, that we all have secrets, but she inhales and exhales on a rushed breath as if she's afraid she'll lose her nerve. "The thing about Cayden is that he lost…"

But this conversation is bound to remain unfinished.

"Causing trouble again, I see."

Our heads snap to the doorway where Cayden stands, leaning against the doorjamb with his arms and ankles crossed. His stance may give the impression that he's casual and aloof, but the way his fingers are digging into his bulging biceps indicates otherwise.

Lacey instantly averts her eyes, gnawing on her lip, amplifying her guilt tenfold.

I don't know who Cayden is referring to—Empire, Lacey, or me. But regardless, Lacey's apparent retreat leaves me angry because I'll be damned if she feels intimidated in my home. "I have no idea who you think you are, but you can't just come waltzing into my room uninvited."

I don't allow his suffocating magnetism to intimidate me as I march forward and stop in the middle of the room, challenging him to reply. All he does, however, is infuriate me further when his wicked lips curve into a lopsided grin.

"Your room?" he asks, not concealing his surprise—or

disgust, I can't really tell.

"Yes, my room," I reply with defense. "Not that it's any of your business because this is the first and last time you'll ever see it."

My sass-infused comment deflates rapidly when Cayden deadpans me. I have no idea what he's thinking, but I'd give a penny for his thoughts.

"It's probably safer for you to stay in the main bedroom. This room has a leak, but that's just my opinion." He's giving me interior decorating advice now? Just who does he think he is?

"It does not have a leak," I argue, cocking a hand to my hip and lifting my eyes skyward. Sweeping my hand toward the ceiling, I attempt to prove my point but am verified to be a big fat liar when a bead of water with its own zip code splashes onto my upturned face.

Closing my eyes in humiliation, I wipe my waterlogged face and shrug it off. "What are you, some kind of building connoisseur or something?"

With that irksome smirk still tugging at his lips, he kicks off the doorway and flippantly replies, "Or something. You ready?"

I know he's not talking to Empire. Therefore, he must be addressing Lacey, who has remained awfully quiet during our exchange. Turning to look at her, I wonder why she looks like she's just been caught with her hand in the cookie jar.

A sense of dread suddenly engulfs me. Just who exactly is Cayden to Lacey? He's asking if she's ready to leave…with him.

Have I just put my foot in it?

Are they dating? Husband and wife?

My cheeks burst into flames. I am so embarrassed. "I didn't

realize you guys were…close," I settle on, fishing for the right word as I sweep my finger between her and Mr. Personality.

She nods, completely guilt-ridden, while Cayden scoffs playfully. "Not by choice."

"What's that supposed to mean?" I ask with bite, turning abruptly. I bump into a solid wall…of muscle, that is, as Cayden is standing right behind me.

His hands shoot out to grab my upper arms to steady me, and the moment we make contact, a hunger I haven't felt before consumes me.

I am beyond horrified by my completely inappropriate desire, but the thought of pulling from his embrace feels like I'm committing the ultimate sin.

Our eyes lock, his gaze scouring over every inch of my face as he tongues his cheek, deep in thought. He has the perfect poker face. I have no idea what he's currently thinking, but judging by the shit-eating grin slathered on his perfect lips, he can read my inner turmoil with ease.

"It means"—he dips low, leaving mere inches between us—"that she's my sister."

It takes a few seconds for the fog to clear my brain, but once it does, I can't shake my relief. He's trying to intimidate me, but all he's doing is riling me up. "Well, I suppose you can choose your friends but not your family. My condolences, Lacey."

Lacey snorts behind me.

My statement may sound big and brave, but beneath that façade, I'm trembling like a leaf in fall.

An amused hum fills the small space between us, and a darkened flicker consumes Cayden's pupils. Being this close to him, I'm enveloped in a fragrance that makes my mouth water. It smells like the ocean hit with a punch of dark spice.

My retort seems to have amused rather than annoyed him. Never breaking eye contact, he holds me captive as he declares, "I suppose we don't have a choice with a lot of things in life." His pause has my heart racing with anticipation. And what he says leaves me speechless. "But bad days build better days."

A small gasp escapes me because I can relate to his comment. It's one I relate to every single day. "And what happens if you're only surrounded by bad days?" I ask in a whisper, still engaged in a deadlock with him.

He sighs, the sound heavy and plagued, and I can't help but wonder why. "Storms don't last forever." He leaves me speechless yet again.

As we're silently sparring, speaking in innuendoes, I can't help but feel he somehow can relate to what I'm going through, which is absurd. But as I stare, losing myself in those eyes, I can't shake the feeling that Cayden wishes he had the luxury to forget…but forget what, exactly?

A niggle, the tiniest hint of warning, floats to the surface, and at first, I disregard it, too busy trying to interpret Cayden's demeanor. He looks angry, pissed off, but more so, underneath those layers, he just looks so incredibly sad and…lost.

"The thing about Cayden is that he lost…"

That small grumble, the insignificant twinge begins to *drip…drip…drip* ever so slowly against my skull. I quash it down, but the drip turns into a trickle, and before long, my head begins to fill with white noise. Slamming my hands over my ears, I squeeze my eyes shut because I know what happens next.

Deep breaths, just how I learned in yoga. Go to my happy place. But none of that works because before long, the static spills from my head down to my toes, and I'm drowning... always drowning.

Please no. Not again.

I prepare myself to be pulled into a vortex, which will leave me gasping for breath, but something suddenly changes. I'm no longer being sucked into a darkened abyss. No, I'm still swathed in darkness; however, those shadows are invoked because of dusk.

"Everything is always better after a thunderstorm..." The moment the raindrops fall onto my tongue, I taste cotton candy. I can also detect the trail of a fragrance that wraps me in a tight bubble. I smell the ocean. Just like I smelled minutes ago...

"What did you say?" I recognize this voice as my own. I just don't know if I've said what I thought I did aloud.

The world stops spinning, and I secure my breathing. My heart is racing, but I coerce my eyes to open, needing to confirm if what just happened is real.

It takes a minute, but I see Cayden and Lacey before me. Their mouths are moving, but I can't understand a word they say. All I hear are the words, *"Everything is always better after a thunderstorm..."* on repeat.

I pan over my thoughts from today when I longed to dance in the rain. I'm certain I didn't vocalize my thoughts out loud, but even if I had, that sentence was spoken by a male. Augusto barely said boo to me during the entire car ride down here, so who was it? Whose voice do I recognize but can't pinpoint?

"Peyton?" My name echoes off the walls in my head, bouncing and backflipping, leaving me nauseous. But I swallow it down and drag myself back to the present.

"I'm fine," I manage to wheeze, latching onto something hard to stop me from falling.

"You're not fine. Jesus Christ, you're hyperventilating." I don't fight it and allow myself to be led away from this nightmare, hoping wherever I'm going, it'll clear my head.

The moment I'm guided outside, and my gaze floats across the lake's edge and fixates on the tree, I exhale in relief.

It's a jumble of words, but among the chaos, I make out an intermittent string of words. "Shit. Just breathe. C'mon. Please, breathe…Snow." I'm cocooned in the most delicious warmth, and I never want to leave, but I claw my way from oblivion because I'm certain I just heard the word snow.

Tearing my gaze from the oak, I look upward and realize I'm draped in Cayden's arms. This is the moment I need to thank him for his chivalry, take a Valium, and lie down, but I don't.

I watch spellbound as the wisps of fallen hair over his brow sway in the wind. The way his eyes scan over every inch of my face, ensuring I'm not broken. But most of all, I remain still, listening to the hypnotizing rhythm of his heart as it beats in concert with mine.

"Are you okay?" he asks, and I'm thankful I can understand him. Nodding, I resist the urge to brush the hair from his cheeks and gently pull out of his hold.

"I'm fine," I finally manage when he continues to scrutinize me. I amble back inside.

He shakes his head firmly as he follows in hot pursuit. "The last time you said that, you almost passed out. I'm taking you to the hospital."

"No, I'm all right. I promise," I add when he doesn't look convinced. "I just need to lie down." However, when I look around at my bare surroundings, I realize that might be a problem. Cayden reads my thoughts and sighs.

"You can always stay with us," Lacey says, but the clenching of Cayden's jaw has me politely declining.

"Thank you, but the old couch in the living room will do just fine." I'm pretty sure I saw a family of raccoons nesting underneath it, but I don't plan on telling her that.

I'm suddenly embarrassed to meet Cayden's eyes, feeling completely damsel in distress-like. I want to ask him if he indeed said the word snow, but I don't. My head is already pounding. I don't think I can handle any more noise.

"Do you need a hand?" he asks, gesturing with his cleft chin to the living room.

I stubbornly shake my head, but I don't know why I bothered or why he even asked because before I know it, he's wrapped an arm around my waist and is leading me into the other room. Lacey's footsteps sound behind me, and I can't believe I've been here for less than an hour and have already fallen into a heap. So much for my newfound independence.

Cayden's hold around me is determined and dominant, and I can't help but think he uses these principles in his everyday life. But I can ponder that after I've slept this nightmare away because even though the discolored sofa looks like it's seen better days, I slump onto it the moment Cayden lowers me down. A plume of dust fills the air, but I settle into the cushions, surprised it doesn't smell or feel half bad.

"Thank you," I mumble, my eyes slipping to half-mast. This is normal after an "episode." Whether it's my body's way of coping with whatever the hell this is or my brain just wanting a time-out, I don't fight it.

The room falls silent. Even in my semi-alert state, I realize my guests have probably got the hell outta Dodge with the intent never to return. Not that I can blame them. My wisecrack came back to bite me in the ass because I suppose, in my case, Lacey can choose her friends, and after today, I most definitely won't be seeing her around here again.

A weight settles low because I really liked her, and I had a feeling we'd be great friends. As for Cayden, my exhausted body can't even begin to digest that can of worms. Falling deeper into a slumber-encrusted bubble, I begin to doubt everything that just happened.

My mind is playing tricks on me, and it's ridiculous to think I heard what I think I did. Why would anyone even mention snow in the summertime in South Carolina? And as for that sentence…it's all ridiculous. With that decided, I allow my weary mind the reprieve it so desperately needs and welcome sleep.

Lost in the silence and happy with my resolution, I succumb to my troubles and let everything fade away. As I hover on the cusp of slumber, I feel something soft placed against me, a heat warming the chill from my bones. I nestle low and sigh, drawing the material to my nose, and realize I'm burrowed under a blanket.

When my sense of smell catches a whiff of what I'm inhaling, my senses salivate while my mind, my once quiet mind, shakes its head and flips me off. Too tired to move, I surrender and stumble in the fragrance. I can deal with this shitstorm tomorrow because now, all I can smell…is the ocean.

THREE

When I wake, I don't know what time or day it is, but what I do know is that I'm somewhat rested, and my brain no longer feels like mush. Thinking back to what I can remember, I'm disappointed that my memory won't allow me to skip further back.

Sighing, I rise slowly, rubbing the sleep from my eyes. It's daytime, and the ache in my bones alerts me that I've slept longer than a few hours. Reaching for my cell from my handbag, I see that it's just after 8 a.m.

The wool blanket pooled around me reminds me of everything that occurred before I switched off from the world. Cayden and Lacey were here, and we were having a semi-decent conversation before I began hearing and seeing things.

My usual visions varied because it was no longer nighttime but dusk, and instead of drowning, I felt free. The smells and tastes—they were so real, but I have no idea what it all meant. I try to focus on the feeling, but all I'm faced with is a roadblock in my mind.

Pegging it as nothing but wishful thinking, I swing my legs and place my feet on the dusty floor. Taking a moment, I rise slowly, hopeful my jelly legs will hold me up. They do. Ambling through my home, I grab my backpack and suitcase and dump them into what will be my bedroom. The moment I step foot inside, that warm feeling surrounds me, and I instantly feel at home.

Dropping to a crouch, I hunt through my suitcase, turning up my nose at almost all of the clothes inside. They cost a lot of money—too much, in fact—and I'd trade every single garment for a comfy pair of jeans and a baggy sweater. Sadly, I won't find the likes of those in here, so I settle on a white summer dress instead. Grabbing my toiletries and towel, I make my way down the hallway and into the bathroom.

Peering around, I sigh because, once again, the photos did not do this place justice. The entire room is decorated in shades of green, and although it has all the essentials, I'm not sure how operational it is.

Undressing, I peer at myself in the cracked mirror above the basin. My snarled hair has seen better days, and we won't even touch on the topic of my smeared makeup. But that aside, I place my hands on the edge of the sink and lean forward, needing to take a closer look at just who is staring back at me.

I don't recognize this person because I don't know who this person is. I wish I could remember who I was because living in someone else's shadow is the most unsettling feeling. I have no doubt I'll make new memories—I already have—but a part of me is missing because I can't help but compare this Peyton to the Peyton everyone else knows.

Who is the better version? The past me or the me now?

I struggle with this question daily, and just like every other time, I'm no closer to uncovering the answer.

Not wanting to start the day on a downer, I step into the bath and turn on the faucets to hot. The moment the water hits my aching muscles, I forget my woes and focus on what I can remember, and that's my plan to renovate this place. I don't have a car yet because Stella thought it was too dangerous for me to drive, seeing as I had no idea where I was. But now that I'm determined to call this town my home, that's one of the first things on my agenda. That and ransacking a hardware store.

I have the money to buy everything I need, but I don't want to depend on Stella and Augusto's wealth. I need to find a job.

Maybe I could return to my profession as a marketing manager one day. One day, maybe, I can return to normal. That day doesn't seem likely to be coming anytime soon.

Switching off the water, I quickly dry off and dress. My ravenous stomach grumbles, reminding me I have no food and, more importantly, coffee in the house. I'll just add that to my list. As I finish applying a light face of makeup, I hear gentle rapping on the door.

Capping my lipstick, I pray to whatever God is looking over me that Stella isn't at my front door. Although knowing her, she wouldn't knock.

When I open the door, I am pleasantly surprised to see Lacey standing before me with two cups of steaming coffee in hand.

"Good morning," she singsongs when I stand mute. "Can I come in?" She wiggles the travel mugs, a bargaining chip to let her in.

Remembering my manners, I swiftly step out of the doorway. "Shit, I'm so sorry! Of course, you can. This amnesia thing appears to have messed with my manners, too," I tease as I gesture for her to enter. She laughs lightly, giving me a loose hug as she walks by.

The act catches me off guard because it feels so natural. The surprise shows, and Lacey is quick to apologize, mistaking my surprise for distaste. "Sorry, I'm a hugger. I forget some people aren't."

But I quickly wave off her apologies. "No, please, it's fine. I'm just happy to see you again." I close the door and follow her into the kitchen. "I'm really sorry about yesterday." She offers me the mug, which I gratefully accept.

"Don't be silly. There's nothing for you to be sorry about," she replies, jumping up onto the small counter, her legs swinging as she sips her coffee.

"Are you kidding me? I'm pretty sure as far as first meetings go, that went down as the worst in history. Not to mention the fact that your brother is kind of a smart-ass."

Lacey splutters up her coffee, thumping her chest in hysterics. "That he is. Cayden isn't really a people person. He means well, but…" She pauses once again, a common theme it seems when her brother is involved.

I don't push because the last time that happened, things went downhill, and I'd rather not relive that—ever. I nurse my coffee silently, indicating I'm listening if she wants to continue.

"It was just Cayden and me growing up. My mom split when we were kids," she explains while my heart grows heavy. "My dad 'raised us,' but he was no father figure for Cayden or me. It would have been better if he left too. And he did. One day, he just disappeared. I was eleven, and Cayden was days away from turning eighteen." The bitterness in her tone reveals no love lost between her and her father.

"I was such a little brat. The last thing Cayden wanted was to look after his little sister; I mean, he was in his prime. But not once"—she holds up her pointer—"not once did he ever complain. He came to every single dance recital. He picked me up without fail from every cheerleading practice. He was both my mom and dad. At the time, I resented him, but now, I realize everything he did was for me." Her voice turns sentimental, and I can't blame her. She's lived a tough life. Her comment from yesterday makes sense now. I know what Cayden lost…what they both did.

Discreetly wiping away her tears, she smiles. "So that's why I excuse his less than sociable behavior at times because my brother is a good guy. The best. You're trying to remember your past…but most of the time, I'm trying to forget mine."

Her statement strikes a chord within me because she's right. We all have our crosses to bear, and I've been looking at this the wrong way. If I want to remember, then I have to stop living in the past, so to speak, and focus on the future. By obsessing over what I can't remember, I'm shutting myself off from the things that I can.

Like right now.

"What are you doing? Right now?" Lacey pauses mid-sip, looking around her like she's been caught doing something wrong. I can't help but laugh at her response. "If you're free, maybe you could come into town with me? I could use the extra muscle." The sagging door from my pantry decides to strengthen my claim when it takes its last breath and gives way, crashing to the ground.

We both yelp, then look at one another and burst into unconstrained cackles. Once she can breathe again, she nods. "It's a date."

Unable to contain my excitement, I bounce from the kitchen and into the bedroom to slip on a pair of sandals. Just as I'm about to leave, I take a moment to appreciate what Lacey just shared. Cayden and I have only shared a handful of words, but I can't deny the overwhelming pull I feel toward him.

Even though tragedy taints our lives, we go on because that's what living is all about. I decide to make more of an effort with him—not because I feel sorry for him, but because he's the type of person I want in my life.

It doesn't hurt that he's incredibly easy on the eyes, but that's beside the point.

Shaking away such thoughts, I grab my bag and am ready to face the big, bad world. Lacey waits by the front door with a pencil and paper in hand. When I arch a curious brow, she smirks. "Just writing down a few things we need."

Standing on tippy-toes to peek at what she's writing, I quip, "Are you sure there are enough pages in that notepad?"

"It's a start," she replies lightly with a shrug.

She bounds down the front steps, humming to a tune in

her head as she taps her chin, looking at my nonexistent front garden. Once I've locked up, I stop beside her, wondering what she's thinking. "How about some roses? I love roses," she says, hand over heart.

I suddenly put two and two together. "You live in the amazing glass house with the beautiful rose bushes out front, don't you?"

"Yup, that's me."

"I admired your home and your roses when I first arrived. Your home is extraordinary. So different from any others around here."

Lacey looks like a proud mom, and I have no idea why. "Thank you. I love it. It's my dream home. I have Cayden to thank for that." The unconditional love she feels for her brother warms my heart.

"I think roses will look amazing. Add that to the list." She yelps in excitement, penciling it on her notepad. Her happiness is contagious.

She leads the way to her home. I didn't get to appreciate it in all its full glory yesterday, but now that I'm mere feet away, I shield the sun from my eyes and stop dead in my tracks.

The exterior is a dark woodgrain with large bay windows. The curtains are drawn back to let in the glorious sun. A balcony wraps around the upper level, providing Lacey and Cayden with views all around. Two glass doors sit dead center on the bottom level. I scan over the upper level, wondering which room belongs to Cayden.

This needs to stop. Now.

Quickening my step to catch up to Lacey, I give her my full

attention when she stops beside her car. "I know she doesn't look like much, but she's yet to let me down," she says, patting the roof of the rusted Volkswagen Beetle. In her heyday, she would have been a brilliant turquoise, but now she's a faded, rusty blue.

To most, she'd be sold for scrap metal, but to me, she screams personality, and I love her. "She is beautiful," I say in awe, running my hand over the metal. I can just imagine Stella's disgust.

As I attempt to open the door, it sticks, and I almost fall backward. Lacey chuckles. "It only opens from the inside."

"Well, I suppose that's a good way not to get carjacked."

Her laughter continues as she unlocks her door and jumps inside. Reaching across the middle console, she pulls on the door handle to grant me entry. The inside is just as impressive as the outside. Shaggy wool seat covers provide comfort for the front and back seats. A unicorn air freshener hangs from the rearview mirror. This entire car reflects Lacey's personality—fun, well loved, and vibrant.

Once I'm belted in, Lacey starts the car with a splutter, and I bite back my smile. After three coughs, she starts, and we're on our way. A pop song plays over the radio, setting a vivacious mood for the day ahead.

I take a moment to appreciate my surroundings because on the way down here, with Augusto behind the wheel and Stella bickering that he took the long way, all I could do was zone in and out, desperate to arrive. But now, with the wind in my hair, thanks to the windows being wound all the way down, I can fully admire my town.

The lake is never far from where we are, our gravitational nucleus drawing us back home if we ever stray.

Lacey isn't exactly driving the speed limit, and I reach for the grab handle, always a little anxious when riding in a car. The night of my accident, a wintry blizzard folded over the horizon, and it was bedlam on the roads. Stella told me I was on my way home from a New Year's party. The roads were slippery, slick with frost, and an oncoming car lost control and wiped me clear off the road. His blood alcohol was three times over the limit, thanks to the holidays—when it's a continuous party and the good times roll. What a way to start the new year.

I spent five days in a coma, and it was touch-and-go. If life was fair, I'd be out celebrating the new year with friends and family and maybe even a boyfriend. But Stella said I only really had one of the three. No guessing which.

"Are you getting car sick?" Lacey's concerned voice snaps me from my thoughts.

"No, why?" I ask, meeting her troubled stare.

"'Cause you look seconds away from throwing up."

Sighing, I slip on my sunglasses, worried I've ruined the mood. "No, I'm okay. Just thinking."

"About…?" she prompts me, and although I don't want to be a stick in the mud, it might be nice to talk to someone who wants to listen. And not just because they're waiting for their turn to talk, but rather because they're genuinely interested in what I have to say.

"About the night of my accident," I reveal, shifting in my seat, as this topic will always be a delicate one for me.

A shade of curiosity suddenly mutates into horror, and I

almost get whiplash when Lacey slams on the brakes. "Oh, my God. I didn't even think. I know these roads like the back of my hand, and I probably go a little faster than I should. I am so, so sorry, Peyton."

I realize that all Lacey and I seem to do is apologize to one another. As much as I appreciate her compassion, I don't want her to walk on eggshells around me. And I vow to do the same. "Let's make a deal," I offer, turning to look at Lacey, who is working her lip.

She nods, indicating she's listening.

"Let's stop saying sorry to one another and just accept the fact that I'm broken, and you're a…" My mind draws a blank because Lacey is pretty darn perfect.

She thinks otherwise. "A nosy neighbor who means well?"

A laugh erupts from me. "Okay, that seems fair. So how about from now on, we ask one another whatever is on our minds and make no apologies for it. How's that sound?"

Lacey taps her pointer against the steering wheel as if mulling over my suggestion. "All right. That's what friends do, right?"

She'll never know just how much I appreciate her choice of words. "Yes, that's exactly what they do. So go ahead…ask me anything."

Her head snaps my way before returning to the road. "Anything?"

"Yes, anything," I confirm. Leaning my head back against the headrest, I relish in this new sense of freedom.

The car is silent as Lacey contemplates which question to ask. "You really don't remember anything?"

I smile, thankful she's taken my suggestion and dived into the deep end. "No, nothing really solid…"

"Why did you move here? I don't mean to be nasty, but I could think of a million more exciting places to move to if I lost my memory and wanted to start fresh."

She quickly bites down on her lips as if she's overstepped a line, but she hasn't. "I honestly don't know. Yesterday, during my"—I search for the right word—"blackout, I thought I remembered something, but I don't even know what I saw."

"Has it happened before?"

I nod. "Yes. I have the same vision. It started not long after I woke up from my coma." The car is silent, the background music and our pensive breathing filling the otherwise still air. "I'm pretty sure I've been here before. I know that sounds crazy—believe me, I know—but that lake, that towering oak with the swing, I've seen it before." Goose bumps prick my skin, and I rub my arms to warm the chill.

Lacey swallows. Her sunglasses conceal what's going on behind her eyes, but I can sense her intrigue. "Lots of lakes have oak trees with swings, Peyton. I'm not trying to play devil's advocate, but what makes you so certain that this lake is the one you've seen?"

I know it sounds ridiculous, and she has every right to ask what she did, but her doubt only further cements my certainty. "Because I can clearly see the red ribbon in my flashbacks. You know the one. It's tied to the rope. It's so distinct." Lacey's hands tighten on the steering wheel, but other than that, she remains unmoving. "I don't know what it means, but I just have a feeling it's so important to uncovering all of this. I don't suppose you know what it means? Has it always been there?"

I give her the time she needs to reply because I know it's all a little confusing and weird. She inhales before shaking her head. "I haven't thought much of it, to be honest. I always figured someone found the ribbon and tied it to the swing in hopes the owner would find it."

I purse my lips because that's a very valid reasoning. But why would I remember it? Surely, it has to mean something for me to remember it so vividly.

"Do you remember anything else?" she asks, her tone grave. She knows there's more.

As much as I want to confess that I do, I shake my head. I need to wrap my brain around what I'm seeing before I confess to being a murderer because, deep down, that's what I think I might be.

She seems relieved that there isn't any more. "Well, I'm here to help. If I can help you remember in any way, then I'll do it."

"Thank you, Lacey. You'll never know how much that means to me. How long have you lived here?" I ask. I know she all but said I don't look familiar, but maybe she'll know of someone who might.

"All my life," she replies softly.

"Maybe you'd know of someone who might know who I am?" I know it's a long shot, but it's worth a try. She's quiet once again, which is probably my cue to shut up. She's being more than helpful, and I don't want to impose. "Anyway, I wanted to explain what happened yesterday, so if it happens again, you know to grab a coffee. I'll come to soon enough."

I jolt when Lacey reaches out to gently rub the back of my

hand. "Don't worry, it'll be okay. You've got me now. We can make new memories."

My earlier thought of living for the now crosses my mind, and I smile. Whatever happens today, tomorrow, next week, I know this memory is one I will never forget.

If I've ever had more fun than I'm having right now, then I don't want to remember because today has been amazing. After the awkward air cleared in the car, Lacey and I went to town, and I mean that in every sense.

The city hub may be modest in size, but it has everything a budding interior decorator needs. Lacey and I hit every shop in the small district. I'm now a VIP member at the local hardware store because I pretty much bled it dry.

We got one of everything, just in case, and before long, our carts were filled to the brim. Reggie, the store manager, couldn't believe his luck when Lacey rattled off a list of supplies we needed that weren't in stock. He said he'd order them in and give us a call as soon as they arrived. Lacey smiled as she placed a big red tick of completion against category number one.

The next stop was the furniture store. First and foremost, I needed a bed. I didn't care what it looked like. As long as it had a comfy mattress and was big enough for me to spread out and sleep like the dead, then I was happy.

I ended up buying a beautiful oak white French provincial queen-size bed. It was completely lavish and over the top with the silk upholstered headboard, but when I flopped onto the mattress, belly first, I fell in love. Lacey twisted my arm—and

I use the term twisted lightly—and coaxed me to buy the matching furniture.

Lacey sure has a way with words and people because she somehow managed to organize the delivery of my entire bedroom suite this weekend. I thought we were done for the day, but when Lacey revealed her list, I knew the day had only just begun.

As we shopped for groceries, Lacey let it slip that she was a chef. She worked as head chef at a notable French-inspired restaurant on the waterfront in Myrtle Beach. I had seen the place, simply called *Miam*, when I walked along the boardwalk. It was always packed, and one never simply walked in without a reservation.

I had asked Stella if we could reserve a table as the smells permeating the air had me champing at the bit, but of course, she declined. She didn't dine with the common people.

I couldn't get over the fact that Lacey had been feet away from me countless times, and not once did we bump into one another. Sometimes, the world really is a small place.

All our shopping worked up an appetite, but we were hardly able to finish the burger we shared because our mouths were busy talking instead of eating. We talked about everything; Lacey asked a million and one questions, which I really didn't mind. We did normal friend stuff, and for the first time in forever, I felt like I was learning how to live in the now and not worrying about remembering.

"Do you like lasagna?"

Lacey's random question, considering we're no longer eating and are in the cookware aisle in some retro homewares store, has me pausing from rearranging the supplies in our overfilled cart. "Yes," I reply suspiciously.

"Good." The silver spatula-looking apparatus sinks into the cart with its fellow contraptions when she tosses it in.

"Why do I need a spatula for lasagna?" I ask, so lost in translation it's not even funny.

She feigns horror. "It's not a spatula. It's a lasagna turner."

I burst into laughter but zip my lips shut when I see she's serious. "Maybe some things are better off forgetting," I playfully mumble under my breath, but loud enough for her to hear. She snorts so loudly that the couple next to us swiftly reaches for a can opener and exits the aisle in haste.

"Lacey, I don't think we can fit any more in this cart. Let's call it a day." Looking down at my silver wristwatch, I see that we've been out all day.

She taps her chin, peering at our loot and then at her list, which is massacred with red ink. "I suppose you're right. It should do for now." Shaking my head, I make my way to the registers with Lacey, and we wait in line.

While we're waiting, I notice Lacey standing on her tippy-toes to look over the heads of the three people in front of us. I too mimic her actions, wondering what exactly she's looking at. It's apparent she's looking out the window at the construction site down the road. Young workmen take advantage of the Southern sun, flashing their bulging muscles and showing off their strength as they carry pieces of wood over their tanned shoulders and move impossibly large building supplies with ease.

There is no shortage of eye candy, so I don't blame Lacey as she not so discreetly checks out the view. She is single, gorgeous, and absolutely amazing—quite the catch. She didn't mention a beau, so the world's her oyster. The thought has me wondering if maybe one day I'll find someone.

I don't even know what kind of a guy I'm attracted to. Sure, I've seen plenty of good-looking men, but none have given me butterflies or even remotely stirred a flutter. That is, until yesterday.

Cayden, although infuriating and not exactly a social butterfly, did have me emerging from my cocoon. I remember the way I felt in his arms and how he instantly, without a second thought, came to my rescue. I still don't know if he really likes me or not, but Cayden is someone you can rely on. Look what he did for Lacey. Not once did he abandon her, and she turned out to be so incredibly remarkable because of him.

On cue, a flutter takes flight, and I realize it seems to be the prerequisite whenever my thoughts wander to him.

Lost in a daze, I don't realize I'm staring until Lacey elbows me in the ribs. Before I have a chance to ask what's wrong, she gestures with her chin toward the front door and the man who just waltzed through it.

He is exceptionally handsome in a rugged, dirty kind of way. I say dirty because he's literally covered in dirt. From the state of his muddy clothes, it's safe to assume he's come straight from the construction site.

The way Lacey primps her brown hair and quickly reaches into her back pocket for her balm has me guessing she's sweet on him. I stand quietly by her side, wondering how this will unfold.

The moment his hazel eyes swing her way, they instantly light up, and he does some grooming of his own as he runs a hand through his snarled golden hair. He attempts to brush the dirt and dust from his work shirt but soon gives up that losing battle.

"Hey, Ace." The way he playfully addresses her has me thinking they're longtime friends. "Whatcha doing?"

"Just some shopping," she replies, her voice spiked with something I can't quite put my finger on. When she flutters her eyelashes, it dawns on me that I'm witnessing that mysterious concept of flirting.

I wouldn't even know where to start because I can't even remember how it's done. The only reason I know what it is, is because I've watched far too many reruns of *Gossip Girl*. It's beyond disturbing that the things which are foreign to me are innate to most human beings. But for some things, it's like learning how to walk once again. At the moment, I'm doing a very slow crawl.

"Some shopping?" he quips, examining our loot. "Looks like you bought half the store."

Lacey's lips tip into a slanted smile, her cheeks flushing a soft pink. "This isn't for me. I'm just helping out a friend." The moment she says the word friend, a small part of me cartwheels in excitement while the other wants to check her forehead to ensure she's not running a fever.

I haven't exactly been stellar friend material. I come with baggage, a lot of it, but Lacey doesn't seem to mind.

On cue, she tips her head my way. "Gunn, meet my friend."

Gunn peers over at me, nodding politely. "Hello, friend."

He extends his hand, which I shake with a small laugh.

"Hello, my name is Peyton."

"Nice to meet you, Peyton. I'm Gunn." I wonder if that's his real name.

Taking a closer look at him, I can see why Lacey finds him attractive. With blond locks bleached by the searing sun, a muscular body, and expressive hazel eyes one could get lost in if they stared for too long, he oozes trouble, and Lacey looks to be reveling in his wickedness.

"You should come over and say hi." I realize he means the work site. What I don't understand, though, is what he says next. "Coach would love to see you."

If this were a cartoon, a light bulb would be flashing over Lacey's head. I have no idea what she's thinking, but I know it'll end in trouble. "Sure, we will be right over."

Gunn nods, a dimpled smirk hugging his bearded cheek. "See you over there then. I'm just gonna grab something to eat." He makes no secret of checking her out, and I avert my eyes because I feel like I'm encroaching on a private moment. His heavy work boots thumping against the linoleum announce his departure.

When he's out of earshot, she latches onto my bicep and lets out a small squeal. "So Gunn and you?" I don't have to elaborate as she knows exactly what I'm implying.

"I've known him for years." When I wait for her to continue, she chews her lip, peering over my head to ensure he's not listening. "Nothing has ever happened between us. We've come close, but I don't know…the timing was never right."

Gunn's comment has me raising an eyebrow. "Who's

Coach?" I ask, wondering if maybe he's the reason the stars haven't aligned for them.

Lacey scoffs, raising her eyes upward. "Coach is a major pain in the ass. He thinks he's all mean and tough when, in reality, he's a puppy dog. He's…" When she abruptly halts and instead stares at me with a glint in her eyes, I'm almost afraid to ask what she's thinking.

The customers in front of us have a small basket of goods, so once the belt clears, Lacey begins piling our loot onto it. She's silent, clearly deep in thought, and I know whatever she's conjuring up can't be good. When the young checkout clerk scans over everything we have, she calls for backup over the intercom.

Twenty minutes and three hundred and two dollars later, we're pushing the loaded cart out the automatic doors. My skin soaks up every wave of heat from the blistering sun, and I stop for a moment, tipping my face up to bask in the warmth. It's a good day to be alive and spend it with a newfound friend.

"So…" the person in question singsongs beside me.

I risk a glance her way, a little terrified of what that mischievous smirk could mean. "So…?" I repeat, tilting my neck to look at her.

"There is no way all of this stuff will fit into my car." The loot stares back at me. She's right. In my excitement, I forgot a little thing called space.

"Crap." I purse my lips, pondering over our options. Lacey's VW is already jam-packed. There is no way we'll have enough room.

"It's okay," she pipes up. "I have an idea."

I don't have a chance to question what she means because she takes matters into her own hands and marches across the street with the cart. Her VW is parked in the complete opposite direction, so I have no idea where she's leading me, but I follow, intrigued.

The streets are quiet. It's everything you'd expect a small town to be. The storefronts are the essentials, providing the townsfolk with the necessities. I've visited most, but when my attention shifts to a small boutique, my curiosity is piqued.

I'm not comfortable in the clothes I'm wearing. My entire wardrobe back in Myrtle Beach consisted of expensive brand names and opulent materials, which look far too pretentious to wear down to the local store. When packing, I grabbed the least obnoxious outfits, so it goes without saying I left Stella's home with a half-empty suitcase.

"What's the matter?" Lacey asks, hoisting the cart onto the curb.

"Does this dress make me look like a…" I search for the right word. "Snob?" I finally settle on.

Lacey examines me from head to toe and tongues her cheek. "Is this a trick question?"

"Oh, my God!" I cry, horrified, crossing my arms around me to conceal my shame.

"I thought that was the look you were going for," she teases, which has me groaning. "I'm kidding. I think you look…nice."

"Nice?" I playfully chide. "Nice is such a noncommittal word. It's the word you use when you don't want to hurt someone's feelings."

"What about if I said very nice?"

In response, I blow a raspberry.

We continue walking, and just as I'm about to ask where we're going, Lacey heads in the direction of the construction site. I believe we're going to bypass it, so you can imagine my surprise when she walks through the metal gates, clearly searching the grounds for someone. There is a sign fastened to the mesh of the entrance: *Coachman Constructions.*

"What are we doing?" I whisper, smiling politely at the workmen around us. They are just as confused as I am.

"Saying hi to Coach."

"Now?" I ask, cursing my choice to wear white today of all days.

"Sure. You heard Gunn."

Brushing down the fragments of dirt from my dress, I don't bother arguing because Lacey makes it clear we're not moving a muscle until this notorious Coach graces us with his presence.

As I'm attempting to dance out of the plume of dirt swirling in the air, my attention is drawn to a tall man a few feet away. His back is turned, but his impressive shoulder span and confident stance have me wondering what his front looks like.

In jeans and a light blue shirt, he's dressed differently than the other men. Poring over a blueprint spread out on the hood of the truck in front of him, he has three men gathered around, listening intently to what he says. He's clearly the boss, and he clearly has a nice ass.

I chuckle to myself. I suppose when used in the right context, nice can be quite the descriptive word, after all.

"Are you looking at his butt?" Lacey whispers in my ear playfully, nudging me in the ribs.

"I most certainly was." I don't see the point in denying it. I mean, it's not like it's her...oh, for the love of all that's holy. I was going to say brother, but that's, in fact, who he is.

The hot guy, whose mere back leaves me drooling, is Cayden. *Please, earth, swallow me whole.*

"Let's go. We should go," I suggest on a rushed breath, my cheeks heating. And the blaze has nothing to do with the blazing sun.

"*Go?* We just got here. Besides, he's seen us now. That would be rude." She butters her tone with utter hilarity. I'm glad one of us is having fun because Cayden shakes his head, muttering something under his breath, before marching over to where we stand.

He is absolutely mesmerizing, all dominant, and clearly pissed off, and I need to look away, but I can't. The way he moves—he's all lithe and predatory, his movements mimicking a lion stalking his prey. When he stops a few feet away, and his fragrance catches the wind, I suddenly don't mind being game.

"Lacey, what are you doing here? I'm working." Yes, he's working that outfit. Wow, who would have thought a simple pair of jeans and a shirt could look that good.

"Hi, Coach." She waves while I almost gag on my tongue, transporting me to the here and now.

"*You're* Coach?" That was meant to be a silent question, but when he meets my eyes, all social grace goes out the door.

"Yes, my friends call me that. Why?" His bite shakes some sense into my hormone-fueled episode, reminding me that we're obviously not friends as I was not privy to such insight.

Before I have a chance to tell him to shove his friendship up his glorious ass, Lacey intervenes. "Our surname is Coachman." It takes me a few seconds, but I soon realize I've heard or rather seen this name before.

"*You're* the *boss*?" Again, I did not intend to vocalize that, but it appears my mouth filter is short-circuiting today.

Cayden's bowed lips twitch. "Yes, I am. I'll just take that dumbfounded look on your face as a compliment." His comment has me swiftly closing my gaping mouth while he chuckles.

My stomach frolics in response. Traitorous tramp.

"So care to explain why you're on my site with all that... stuff?" He gestures to the cart with his cleft chin, arching an amused brow.

Lacey's comment about her home and owing her gratitude to Cayden now makes perfect sense. The house is clearly different—a personal touch added to it because its owner is an architect. And a damn good one at that. Not just the house is witness to this, but I only need to look at my surroundings to see that whatever Cayden is building is going to be stunning.

All admiration is forgotten, however.

"Because my car is packed full, and you need to take Peyton home."

"He does?"

"I do?" we say in unison. While I ask in surprise, he is clearly opposed to the idea. I swallow down my disappointment.

"Yes, you do. You're almost done here anyway."

A dimple hugs his whiskered cheek. "And how do you know that?"

She scoffs, rolling her eyes. "You're the boss. Don't pretend you do any work." This is a fight he won't win, so he sighs. His reservations do sting, but I'm a big girl and read this for what it is.

Lacey's gaze wavers to where Gunn just happens to stroll past, carrying a plank of wood. His muscles bulge and ripple in just the right way to amplify every bead of sweat coating his golden skin. She doesn't stand a chance.

"Don't wait up."

Cayden turns, and when he sees Gunn, he shakes his head.

All amusement fades to the wind when Lacey's abrupt departure results in Cayden and me being alone. I don't know why, but it appears we're both uneasy around the other. Some may mistake it for chemistry or my hormones cavorting with an attractive man, but there is something underlying. And I intend to find out what.

"So…I have a few things to do. Here." He reaches into his back pocket, producing his keys. "My truck is just around the corner. Do you need help? I've got muscle I can spare." Of its own accord, my gaze drifts to his shirt and the way it clings to every hardened plane. I'm sure he does. "If you can tear Gunn away from my sister, he's yours."

Well, this is just going from bad to worse. The dusty air is clearly clouding my brain because he was obviously not offering his muscles. "No, I'm okay. I've got my own muscles." Even I cringe at how fucking ridiculous I sound.

But a strangled breath catches in my throat when a smirk tugs at his lips.

Reaching for the hard hat on his head, he removes it and steps forward so we're almost pressed chest to chest. I peer up at him, holding my breath as he places it gently on my head and roughly confesses, "I can see that."

He doesn't hide his admiration for me and my muscles as he scours every inch of my flesh. A wave of goose bumps licks at my skin, rippling across each section following his intense stare.

When he openly looks at me this way, I can trick myself into thinking he too feels this static bouncing between us, but as soon as the look of warmth passes him, it's outshined by vacancy. I can't deal with this emotional whiplash.

Cayden Coachman is bad news, and I need to stay away.

Reaching for the keys in his hand, I whimper when an electrical current of ten billion volts zaps me into near submission. A simple touch shouldn't have the aptitude to do this. But it does. Why?

Immediately, the need to escape overcomes me because I feel the walls closing in on me. I snatch the keys and dash for the gate. I know I've left the cart behind, but the darkened vortex is once again sucking me deep into the abyss of no return.

The disturbed earth kicks up from under my feet, but I continue sprinting until I make it out of the gateway. The manacles loosen, and I take a deep breath, but that is in vain because what I bear witness to, only feet away, has my blood turning cold.

A young girl, no older than eight, stands in the middle of the road; the pink ice-cream cone she held is now squelched in a puddle at her tiny feet. I come to a screeching halt, every fiber of my being screaming at me to stop.

We lock eyes, both in a daydream as we examine the other. That bothersome scratch rasps at my middle because she looks so…familiar. I get lost in her eyes…the color reminding me of the clearest blue water.

Water…

A guttural cry pierces the air, and I instantly cover my ears. But I need to fight. Every part of me is demanding I wake the fuck up and move. The reason is soon clear, and I quickly realize that death-curdling sound is coming from me because that little girl…the little girl who looks like she's just seen a ghost…is seconds away from being struck by a car.

Without thought, I let go of fear…I let go of this familiar burn, and I run.

FOUR

"Watch out!"

Adrenaline courses through my veins as I take off in a mad dash for the motionless girl. I can deal with the foreboding dread later because saving her is all that matters.

The driver of the Jeep slams on the brakes, a plume of smoke filling the air as her tires leave skid marks in their wake. I turn my back, prepared to shield this girl with my life as I wrap my arms around her middle and dive for the sidewalk.

My dismount is far from graceful, and I'm almost certain I've broken a rib when I slam into the concrete. But none of that matters. "Are you okay?" I breathlessly ask the little girl tangled in my arms.

It was an innate response to cocoon myself around her, and because of this, I think she is all right. But regardless, I have to be sure.

Disentangling myself, I sit upright, flinching when a shooting pain radiates all the way to my toes. But I ignore it.

"What's your name?" I ask the timid little mouse sitting on my lap.

Brushing the long brown hair from her face, I examine her closely, ensuring she is unscathed. She continues to stare at me, not saying a word. She looks so familiar, right down to the small freckle under her left eye, but the murky depths prevent me from seeking the memory out.

A crowd has formed, and I vaguely hear the onlookers calling the police or gossiping about what they just saw, but all that fades into the background when a voice drowns them all out.

"Ellie!"

Peering up, I see Cayden pushing through the bystanders, a wave of terror rippling within. This is the first response I've seen from the little girl on my lap, who finally tears her gaze from me. When she is ripped from my arms, a longing kicks me low, and I instinctively wrap my arms around my middle.

I watch silently and almost in a trance-like state as Cayden drops to a crouch, checking who I'm assuming is Ellie from head to toe. "Are you hurt?"

She shakes her head, sniffing back her tears. I instantly admire her strength.

"Are you sure?" He examines her twice, his thumbs rubbing gentle circles on the flesh of her tiny upper arms.

"Y-yes," she replies with a small nod. "I'm okay, Daddy."

Daddy.

That single word changes the course of everything and wakes me from my stupor.

Groaning, I slowly come to a stand, clutching my side. I hope nothing is broken, and I'm just winded from the fall, but my movement alerts Cayden of my presence. He looks me over before a fierce rage overtakes him. I instantly seek shelter, but I'm not fast enough.

"What did you do?" he accuses.

I recoil, utterly offended by not only his tone but also the fact that he's pointing fingers.

"Excuse me?" My tone is as fierce as his, which probably isn't wise because he comes charging over, nostrils flared and all crazy-eyed.

"What did you say to her?" When I hesitate, attempting to process the absurdity of his question, he steps closer, encaging me in his fury. "Peyton, answer me."

"I didn't say anything!" I finally manage to reply. "And I didn't *do* anything, thank you very much. So I'd appreciate it if you backed the hell off!" Instead of retreating, I advance and level him with a wrath of my own.

I understand he's just walked into every parent's worst nightmare, but I won't stand here and allow him to accuse me of being the bad guy.

"Buddy...she saved your kid's life." I have no idea whose voice this is because we're caught in a stalemate, and I'll be damned if I back down.

Cayden is the first one to look away. "What?"

The Good Samaritan continues. "Yeah. Your kid was standing in the middle of the road. That lady"—he points his finger my way—"she ran out in front of a car to drag her to safety. Pretty heroic, if you ask me," he adds, but instantly loses his bravery when Cayden clenches his jaw.

The small crowd looks back and forth, anxiously waiting for what happens next. But I'm done being a sideshow freak. No more. I came here to uncover who I was, but so far, all I've unearthed is a migraine.

Pushing past Cayden, I curse the internal butterflies which take flight the moment we touch and make a beeline for Ellie. Dropping to a squat, I keep my distance because she still appears terrified of me. "Maybe Daddy can buy you another ice cream for being so brave." Memories of the melted pink goo intermingle with visions of a watery immensity that have me shooting upright because I know what happens next. "Bye, little mouse."

Her mouth parts, and I see a flicker of recognition, but it vanishes a second later.

"Peyton." Cayden's tone has calmed, but it's too late. He attempts to reach out for me, but I almost wind myself a second time as I jump backward. He raises his hands in surrender. "I'm sorry, okay? I didn't know. I just thought…"

His pause fills in the blanks. "You just thought the worst of me? Is that it?" He lowers his eyes, clearly ashamed. "You know what, it doesn't even matter. Goodbye, Cayden." A pain slashes across his face, and I don't understand why. I don't understand any of it.

Pushing past the spectators, I steady my breathing because I'm on the cusp of passing the point of no return. I round the corner and press my back to the cool brick wall. I need a minute.

I can't keep up with the thoughts racing through my head, but at the forefront is why the nickname I used for Ellie rolled off my tongue with ease.

Just as I had no reservations about running out into the road to save her. It was almost…maternal.

Ellie is Cayden's daughter. But who is her mother?

Quashing down the darkness, I focus on finding out the truth because I don't know if this opportunity will ever present itself again. Taking three deep breaths, I peer around the wall, ensuring I remain out of sight. Cayden is comforting Ellie, and now that the show is over, the crowd has dispersed, giving me a clear view.

The air has calmed. That is, until a woman comes sauntering out of a clothes store, hands filled with shopping bags. She stops dead in her tracks when she locks eyes with Cayden. I know without a doubt this is Ellie's mother. Cayden's *wife*?

However, when Cayden appears as if he's just caught wind of something rotten, I retract my original thought. There is clearly no love here.

"Ellie? What are you doing out here? I thought I told you to wait for me in Patt's. I gave you enough money to stuff yourself full of ice cream." She is beyond pretty, and I would even go out on a limb and say she's the prettiest woman I have ever seen. But her exterior most certainly does not match her interior because her tone and the way she looks at Ellie like she is nothing but a nuisance is unsightly. I instantly dislike her.

"Great parenting, Hazel. I shouldn't be surprised," Cayden spits, half shielding Ellie with his intimidating frame. She looks even smaller when dwarfed by his malice.

"Oh, get over yourself, Cayden. You're hardly father of the year. Or have you forgotten?" The smug smirk tugging at her red-painted pout incites the white noise. But I push it down, refusing to lie victim once more.

Her words may as well have slapped Cayden's cheeks. His chest heaves, but he refuses to buckle. "I'm taking Ellie to the doctor. She almost got hit by a car. Not that you care. Yet another shopping spree is obviously far more important than your daughter's well-being."

The first sign of concern mars Hazel's perfect complexion. She pales. "*What?* Honey, is that true?" She looks at Ellie, who finally nods. The bags she's holding rustle, and I realize that's because she's trembling. It appears she's human, after all. "Ellie, I am so sorry. Are you okay?"

Cayden could continue this vicious cycle, but he stays silent because regardless of his strained relationship with Hazel, it's clear his daughter's welfare is all that matters to him. "I'm all right, Mommy. An angel saved me."

My heart stops beating.

"An angel?" Hazel asks, peering up at Cayden for clarification. I too stare at him, hoping he can shed some light on what the hell is going on. But of course, he doesn't.

"Someone pushed her out of harm's way before it was too late." I wait with bated breath for more, but there is no more. It's clear that's all I am to him. A someone—no one of importance.

"Where did she go? I want to thank her." Hazel takes in her surroundings, and when she peers over her shoulder, I withdraw lightning-quick, hiding behind the safety of the wall.

"She's gone now," Cayden simply replies. "Now, if you'll

excuse me."

Once again the voyeur, I peek around the corner to see Cayden loop his fingers through Ellie's as he attempts to lead her toward his truck, but Hazel stops him dead in his tracks.

"Never forget what you did, Cayden, because although I may be able to forgive, I'll never forget." Time stands still.

His shoulders rise and fall. His stance is menacing. I don't know what I'm about to bear witness to, but I'm scared. Although his back is turned, his anger is palpable, and I hold my breath. "I'll never forget. It'll always be...*she'll* always be... the biggest regret of my life."

The air hisses out of me like a deflated balloon, and I know I'll soon succumb to the demons. Before that happens, however, I hail a cab and tell the driver to take me home.

I wake, unsure of where I am.

It takes me a moment, but I soon realize I'm slouched in a weathered rocking chair on my balcony out back. Rubbing the sleep from my eyes as I sit upright, something tumbles with a thud to the rotted decking. Peering down at what made the noise, I see a white sketch pad. The intensity of its crispness contrasts with the weather-beaten decking. The distinct sound of a pencil rolling along the boards catches my eye. When it catches in the gap between the boards, I return my attention back to the open page because what stares back at me confounds me. It's a sketch of the lake, and the centerpiece is, of course, the oak tree.

Did I draw this?

Bending forward, I pick up the pad and run my fingertip over the lines sketched with precision, sketched by an artist's hand. Dividing my attention from the picture to real life, I'm overcome with my desire to remember, just like always.

Cayden's admission rubs me raw, and I don't know why. Who is *she*? Whoever she is, she has clearly pissed him off and is most likely the reason he's such an asshole. But underneath his bitterness, I can't overlook the ache in his tone. Whoever this person is, she undoubtedly hurt him. She got under his skin.

Thoughts of the mystery woman have me idly running my finger over the sketch. When I come to, I realize I have smudged the charcoal lines by applying too much pressure. My attention inadvertently focused on the swing and how the ribbon was tied with precision to the rope.

"Remember," I whisper under my breath, but I never do. These shadows are certain to remain with me forever.

Frustrated, I stand, tempted to throw this drawing into the lake. But I don't. It feels blasphemous, almost. Tucking it under my arm, I make my way into my bedroom, groaning because it looks worse than I remember.

Deciding to find my cell and call Lacey in hopes she's home and can drop off some of the supplies we bought today, I search the room, unsure how exactly I made it in here on my own. The blackouts are normal, according to Dr. Martinez. He's given me pills to take if ever they get too bad, but I refuse to live in a medicated haze.

Ambling down the hallway, I make my way into the kitchen and do a double take when I see shopping bags littering the floor. I can't contain my little squeal because this is exactly the distraction I need.

Dropping to a squat, I hunt through the bags, thankful when I see the cleaning products. I decide to bleach every surface until it's sparkling clean. Sleep isn't in the cards for me tonight because I'm on edge. Not to mention, there isn't really anywhere comfortable for me to sleep yet.

First things first. I decide to change into something a little more appropriate, which has me recalling my conversation with Lacey about the clothes I currently own. I'm tempted to light a bonfire out back, but as appealing as that sounds, I decide to donate my garments to Goodwill instead.

Settling on jean shorts and a tank, I slip my dress over my head, leaving me in nothing but my strapless bra and underwear. My reflection stares at me from the glass balcony door. Running a hand over my flat stomach, I'm hit once again with the emptiness I felt earlier when I first laid eyes on Ellie.

I'm twenty-seven years old. When I was younger, did I envision myself getting married? Or having children? Pushing out my belly, I'm overcome with happiness when I interlock my hands over the swollen bump. It surprises me, but I don't fight it. I can't.

I'm petite, and although I would waddle like a duck, the make-believe sight of being this heavily pregnant has me smiling like an idiot.

Unable to tear my eyes away, I turn from front to a side view, tilting my head and examining the vision before me. I imagine what my baby would look like. Would she have copper hair like me? Or would she resemble her father? What kind of a parent would I be? Nothing like Stella—that's for sure.

However, my fantasy ends as quickly as it began because I don't even know who her father would be. Would it be someone from my past? Or someone from my future? I suddenly don't like this game.

"Oh, fuck, shit, sorry!" The string of profanity shatters my bubble because what I see—or, more accurately, who I see reflected in the glass—has me yelping and covering my near-naked form. "I knocked," Cayden says, attempting to explain why he's standing in my bedroom doorway.

Dread weighs me down. How much did he see? Could he read my most treasured and unexpected thoughts? Beyond embarrassed, I cover my body as best as I can, reddening from head to toe. "Why are you here?" I demand, making a beeline for my clothes. But I fail. Miserably.

In my attempts to protect my modesty, I manage to stub my toe on the corner of my suitcase and tumble forward. I would have face-planted had Cayden not rushed forward and caught me. We look beyond ridiculous, poised and ready to break into a waltz if the mood suits us.

But all thoughts of dancing are put on the back burner when my traitorous body focuses on the fact that I'm enfolded in Cayden's arms. My heart begins to race, and it has nothing to do with my near miss.

Those mysterious eyes survey every inch of my face, leaving me with a stomach full of butterflies. I could lose myself in him, and that scares me because when these rare moments occur, I can almost pretend we don't get under one another's skin. I don't know what it is about him, but I'm drawn to him. His mood swings give me whiplash, though, and I need to put out the fire before it burns out of control.

Sanity returns, and the Cayden fog clears, making way for the fact that I'm draped in his arms in only my underwear. I could freak out, but bashfulness exited the room the moment my breasts were mere inches from his face. "Unless you're going to ask me to dance, can I please get dressed?"

My sassiness douses whatever electricity bounces between us, and he threatens to loosen his hold. I yelp, afraid he's about to drop me on my ass because our half dip pose would mean I wouldn't have far to fall. A lopsided smirk pulls at his lips, then he helps me to stand.

Ignoring the static, I roll my eyes, faking annoyance as I reach for my shorts. Stepping into them, I purposely face him as I fasten the zipper. Two can play this game—whatever this game is. His attention drifts to my fingers, his Adam's apple bobbing.

A wave of desire threatens to drag me under. Nothing good can come from this, especially since he all but accused me of pushing his daughter in front of the car. Pulling back my shoulders is probably not the best idea, considering I'm only in a bra, but he's seen it all anyway. "So are you going to answer my question?"

"What question? I got distracted," he quips, tonguing his cheek. No matter my comeback, he's always ready to outsmart me.

Deciding to embark on this war dressed, I slip on my tank and stand my ground. I pay no attention to the fact that my body is protesting, preferring to remain unclothed. "Why are you here? The last time I saw you, you made it clear you think I'm the devil reincarnate." I cross my arms, my anger replacing my hormone-fueled episode.

The playfulness subsides, and Cayden sighs, running his fingers through his snarled hair. "I'm sorry. I had no right to behave that way." I'm listening. "I am just"—his pause has my interest piqued—"I'm just an overprotective parent. Ellie's mom has floated in and out of our lives, so it's only ever been Ellie and me." He makes no attempts to mask his bitterness. "She is my number one priority in this world, and everything I do, every choice I make, I make for her."

A sinking feeling threatens to drag me under, but I quash it. It's time I laid all my cards on the table because I am done riding this emotional merry-go-round. "I appreciate that and admire you for being a good parent, but ever since we met, I can't help but feel like you have a problem with me." I decide to leave out the fact that on rare occasions, he appears to want to eat me alive.

I wait for him to deny my claims, but he doesn't. He merely lowers his eyes.

"I moved here because something about this town, this house"—I sweep my hand outward—"feels so familiar. It feels like home. These past six months, I've lived in constant darkness. I know that sounds melodramatic, but it's the God's honest truth. I don't know who I am, who I was, and coming here was the first time since I woke to this nightmare that I felt...something."

His head snaps up, but I don't know what it means. I don't know what any of this means.

"I'm sorry if me being here has somehow disturbed the peace, but I'm not leaving…not until I figure out what significance this place has. I know I've been here before…I just can't remember. I can't remember anything," I confess, the fight in me dying as I rub my temple.

"And what happens when you remember?" He finally speaks, but his tone is heavy with burden.

"I think the better question is *if* I remember." Shuffling my bare feet, I suddenly feel foolish for unloading all my personal shit on a mere stranger. But that's the problem—just as this house, town, and lake all feel familiar, so does Cayden. I just don't know why. "There's no guarantee I'll ever remember, but from what I can tell, giving up isn't part of my vocabulary."

A flicker of a grin tugs at Cayden's supple lips. However, it's gone just as quickly as it appeared.

"So I promise to keep out of your hair. You won't even know I'm here."

When a low chuckle slips past Cayden's lips, my olive branch gets completely shit on. "That's not possible," he explains. When I arch a brow, he continues. "Lacey likes you, and I'm glad she's made a friend. She doesn't have many. She works all the time, and when she's not, she's helping me with Ellie. I doubt she'll let you go without a fight."

Is he making jokes now? The mystery continues…

"Not to mention, my dog seems to adore you. So even if I wanted to ignore you, my nearest and dearest would probably make that impossible to do."

"So everyone seems to like me, bar you. And quite possibly your daughter." I need to lighten the mood because I didn't mean for that statement to come out so needy.

Cayden saunters toward me, that smug smirk a permanent fixture. Everything I just said is laughable, considering the closer he gets to me, the calmer things become. Staying away from Cayden is akin to denying my lungs oxygen to breathe. And when he reaches out to gently brush a stray piece of hair from my cheek, I need all the O2 I can get. "I do like you…"

Why does that comment please me?

His finger lingers as he appears transfixed by our connection. I remain still, not daring to move an iota. He eventually drops his hand, and while I attempt to mask my disappointment, I have to remember to breathe. "And as for my daughter, she is grateful…we both are. And to express my gratitude, I'd like to help you."

Now I've heard it all. "Help me?" I can't keep the suspicion from my tone.

Cayden nods. "This house isn't safe." I open my mouth in protest, but he quickly puts an end to my ranting. "Don't argue with me because it's my job to make these calls."

Annoyed with his bossiness, I smugly reply, "So…what? You're offering me a place to crash?"

He has the gall to laugh. "We both know how that will end." I don't bother arguing this time. "Let me help you get this place up and running. It's going to take a lot more than a fresh coat of paint."

"What's in it for you?" I ask, pursing my lips in distrust. Why is he offering to spend more time with me when he's been running in the opposite direction every chance he gets?

"I get to sleep easy at night knowing my new neighbor isn't

buried under ten feet of roofing." I burst into laughter.

Cayden's offer is tempting because he's right. This house is a death trap. But I don't know how that'll work. The thought of seeing him so often spells disaster on so many levels. But we're both adults, and he is offering, so I would be crazy not to accept.

"Okay."

His brows knit together. "Okay?"

A ghost of a smile tugs at my lips. "Yes."

He tilts his head to the side, clearly weighing whether I'm possessed. "You heard me, right? This means I'll be over here. A lot."

"I know."

"And you're okay with this?"

"I just said that I was," I counter, the banter a fun change. He appears satisfied with my response for now.

The air is heavy with unspoken silence, and I wonder if he's had a change of heart. Digging his hands into his pockets, he nods once. "All right then. I'll see you tomorrow." But he still doesn't budge.

I decide to take advantage of our civility because I don't know when it'll happen again. "So your daughter, Ellie…she's okay?"

Cayden exhales. "Yes. She is, thanks to you." His statement touches me.

There is no questioning his love for his daughter. I remember her bravery, holding back her tears when I asked if she was all right. No doubt she inherited her strength from her father. I'm still trying to decide what she inherited from her mother.

"She's a brave little girl."

He smiles, but there is something bittersweet about it.

The stilted conversation is giving me heartburn because there is still something underlying between us. I just can't pinpoint what. Taking a closer look at him, I wade through the quicksand in my mind and hope for something to emerge. Nothing does.

The disappointment rises, but I quash it down because Cayden is someone you don't forget. And besides, if he knew me, I'm sure he'd tell me.

Cayden steps back hastily, clearing his throat. "Well, night."

"Good night," I reply, unable to shake this sudden sinking feeling. When he turns to leave, my mouth has a mind of its own and spews out nonsense I have no control over. "Do you know who lived here?"

I have no idea why I just asked him this. But more importantly, why does it matter?

The silence bounces between us, and just when I think he's not going to answer, he nods. His broad shoulders rise to the heavens, and if I didn't know any better, I'd say I just hit a nerve. "I do."

I wait for him to elaborate. He doesn't.

I can't sleep.

After Cayden all but ran from my house in fear of me asking more questions, I've been left restless and wondering if he's Jekyll and Hyde reincarnate. I'm constantly left with more questions when in his company, which just leaves me even more intrigued by him.

If my day wasn't bad enough, Stella decided to add to the shit pile and call me. The conversation was short, but she was clearly checking up on me. She asked if I'd gotten over whatever this phase was and if I was ready to come home.

Her disregard for my feelings had me digging in my heels even more so, and I told her I wouldn't be offended if she didn't call me again.

Left agitated, I made good on my word and scrubbed the kitchen until it was sparkling clean. I only stopped because I ran out of cleaning products. I was hoping to clean myself into exhaustion, but no such luck. Which is why I'm tying my laces and placing my earbuds in.

Going for a run at two o'clock in the morning is surely the solution to force my body to switch off and give in to my fatigue. I select a rock song as I do some light stretching. Once I'm warmed up, I take off, hoping to sweat out this restlessness brewing within.

I enjoy the stillness as it appears I'm the only one awake at this ungodly hour. The gentle glow from the streetlights illuminates the sidewalk, and I allow the peacefulness in. There is a sense of liberation when my feet hit the pavement. Letting go has never felt this good.

Today has been a whirlwind, but I have a feeling this is just the beginning of things to come. With that as my motivation, I break into a faster pace, intent on running away from these demons constantly nipping at my heels.

I've only been here two days, and things are already challenging me in ways I never imagined. But more accurately, someone. I never expected to meet someone like Cayden. I actually wouldn't have imagined someone like him existed. Back in Myrtle Beach, I felt somewhat in control even though my life was frustrating. But now, everything is rampant.

I have no control over my reaction toward him, and I don't like it.

I push myself harder, refusing to lay victim to these irrational thoughts. He is just a man, an annoying man at that, but I need to remind myself why I'm here. Cayden Coachman is a complication I don't need. I have enough.

Not focusing on where I'm running, I turn right and realize I've reached a dead-end street. There are trees and bushes a few yards away, which no doubt contains a trail leading to the other side of the lake. I could run it and discover what's there, but the streetlights end abruptly, shrouding me in partial darkness.

Coming to a stop, I examine the scenery in front of me, wondering what it looks like in the daytime. Because right now, it looks creepy as hell. The shadows appear menacing, and my imagination runs wild. Just as one song ends and there is a split second of silence, the hair on the back of my neck stands on end. I snap my head to the left, certain I heard a branch crack in the distance.

Taking out my earbuds, I listen closely.

The rustle of the wind has me yelping, setting the stage for how every horror movie starts. I strain my eyes, attempting to make sense of the shadow that I'm certain looks like a person hidden among the dense foliage. I hold my breath as I make out their shape until the greenery shifts, and my imaginary creature turns into a tree.

Laughing to myself, I shake away such nonsense and decide to run back home. But as I reinsert my earbuds, I ignore the sudden feeling that I'm no longer alone. I have real monsters to deal with. There isn't any room left for the imaginary kind.

But as I turn on my heel, I can't help but notice that the journey back home is a lot quicker than when I began.

FIVE

"To have and to hold, from this day forward. For better, for worse, for richer, for poorer, in sickness and in health. To love and to cherish...till death do us part..."

The vibrant sunshine bounces off the jewels encrusted along the sweetheart neckline. The white silk is soft to the touch. It's everything a bride would want their wedding dress to be. Guests fill the garden, all cooing when the ever-important vows are exchanged.

The bride stands proudly, tears pricking her hazel eyes. She's marrying the love of her life. She feels beyond lucky to have found the other half of her soul. She can't see him clearly as the lace veil shrouds her view, but she knows he's handsome. She fell in love with him the moment they met. She can't wait until she's forever his.

"I now pronounce you..."

But darkness suddenly consumes the sunshine, and the clouds turn gray and angry. Horror soon replaces her happiness. Her groom becomes less distinct, his shape wavering and morphing into someone else.

Clutching at the pearls around her neck, she attempts to scream, but she's been robbed of breath. Night conquers day, and she is shrouded in darkness, wading through the confusion. She calls out to her groom, begging for him to explain. But she's only left with more questions than answers because the voice that fills the air is not that of a bride but of a young girl, no older than eight years old. The once fitted wedding dress now pools at her bare, tiny feet.

Her vision still cloaked, she wrestles with the veil, desperate to make sense of what's going on. The world spins in a kaleidoscope of colors as she clutches at something tightly in her hand. It's her safety net when times get tough.

However, through the chaos, she focuses on a soothing voice, which has always been her beacon in a weathering storm. *"Everything is always better after a thunderstorm..."*

Her universe centers, and she blinks back her fears. The boy who was once her groom stands before her in tattered clothes, but she doesn't care. He is her home. He makes everything all right. He steps forward, gently cupping her trembling hand. It's now she realizes that the silken object she holds is a red ribbon. Her SOS.

A crooked smirk paints the boy's full lips as he brushes away the tears from her cheeks with his thumbs. He only appears a couple of years older than she is. It's evident he cares for her deeply. And she feels the same way.

He is the only person who can explain to her why she can't remember. "What's my name?"

He laughs, shaking his head in humor. However, when he senses the gravity of her question, he turns comforting, her protector. He wraps her in a tight embrace, and she relishes in the way her heart does a tiny flip-flop. But that soon transforms to dread. "Snow…your name is Snow."

The red ribbon falls from her hand, *my* hand, and I pass out.

I wake, my heart threatening to spill from my chest.

Brushing back the mussed hair from my brow, I frantically seek out my surroundings, unsure what the hell just happened. A heaviness sinks to the pit of my stomach.

Muted voices alert me to my surroundings, and my brain finally plays catch-up. I'm home. I'm sprawled out on the ratty sofa in my living room, cocooned under a blanket. Now that my heart has returned to a semi-normal rhythm, I sit upright and ignore the thumping against my temple.

Finding my feet, I stand slowly, unsure if the room will stop spinning. It does.

Peering down, I see that I slept in my running shorts and tank—the ones I wore yesterday. Or today. I can't remember. What day is it?

"Hey. You're awake."

"Holy shit!" I yelp, almost winding myself as I spin around to see Cayden standing in the archway, hands raised in surrender.

"Sorry. I didn't mean to scare you. I knocked a few times. But you were out cold. You really need to lock your door," he adds as I attempt to catch my breath.

"I did lock it," I finally reply, or maybe I didn't. After scurrying home and ignoring the fact that I was seconds away from passing out from lack of oxygen, all I wanted to do was crawl under the blanket and tell my vivid imagination to chill the fuck out. I don't remember much after that. "What time is it?" The sunshine streaming in from the windows reveals it's daytime, but I have no idea of the time.

"Just a little past seven."

So I've once again blacked out and woken in a complete state of confusion. These missing chunks of time worry me. Instead of remembering, I seem to be doing the complete opposite.

"Where do you want it?" My house seems to be the budding hub this morning, so I overlook my crisis for now.

A deliveryman with a clipboard enters, looking at Cayden, then at me. I don't realize what Cayden is scowling about until the man stares pointedly at my breasts. During my blackout, I apparently had no problems unhooking my sports bra. I may not remember much, but comfort I remember quite well.

Quickly crossing my arms over my chest, I clear my throat, not at all impressed.

Neither is Cayden. "Front room," he orders while I forget my bashfulness and shake my head.

"No, hang on. Want what?" I ask, lost in translation.

The deliveryman sighs. Someone clearly forgot their morning coffee. "Your bed. Where do you want it?" Mention of my bed has my protesting muscles cheerleading in delight.

"Front room," Cayden repeats while I purse my lips, annoyed.

"The back room, please," I correct, attempting to point the way with my arms still folded.

It's visual ping-pong as the deliveryman produces a pen from the breast pocket of his faded blue overalls. "Look, I get paid to deliver the thing. Where it goes is not my problem. Now, who's going to sign for it?"

Cayden sighs, running a hand through his hair. A sure sign I've won this battle for now.

Accepting the clipboard and pen from the man, I sign as quickly as I can because I'm pretty sure he just sniffed me. When a grinding fills the room, the man snatches the paperwork and makes a beeline for the front door. Cayden's clenched jaw is the reason he ran from the room.

He's definitely throwing off some sort of alpha dog vibe, which calls attention to the fact that standing braless in front of him didn't even cross my mind. I suppose that was because he didn't ogle me like I was his next meal. It appears he can be a gentleman when he wants to be.

"So..." He rocks back on his heels. "You're insistent on staying in the most dangerous room in the house then?" I can't shake the feeling that he'd hoped I'd change my mind.

"What can I say? I like to live life on the edge," I quip while his cheeks puff out as he exhales. "Besides, what have you got against my bedroom?"

"Nothing." He raises his shoulders with a carefree shrug. "I just thought you'd want something bigger."

I can't help the cackle that erupts from me. I make no attempt to mask it either. "That's what she said."

Cayden's sculptured eyebrow lifts into his hairline, baffled by my humor until he finally catches on. When he does, the saints and all the angels break into song because I've never seen a sight more picturesque than right now. "Oh my God..." I cover my mouth, eyes exaggeratedly wide. "Did you just... smile? Holy shit. Is the world about to end?"

"Ha-ha," he taunts, clutching his side in mock laughter, but he can't take it back. I saw him smile, and it's a sight I won't be forgetting anytime soon.

The deliveryman interrupts our weird but amusing moment as he and a colleague attempt to wedge my mattress through the narrow doorway. I suppose I didn't really take the size of the house into consideration when I ordered this monster. But when I see the cushy top layer, I soon forget my regrets.

As they're fighting over whose left should go first, I suddenly realize the delivery wasn't scheduled until the weekend. Why are they early?

"I thought you couldn't come until the weekend," I say, but the delivery driver has other pressing matters to deal with—like walking the mattress down the hallway without taking out a wall.

Cayden's frustration catches in his throat before he grips the mattress and leads the way. Both men are all butterfingers as they clutch one side while Cayden carries his end with ease. The sight is impressive, to say the least, as he showcases what he's packing beneath that white T-shirt.

When he meets my eyes, I instantly avert my gaze and

scratch the back of my neck as if deep in thought. Deciding to freshen up, I wait for them to shuffle down the hall before I head to the bathroom, ensuring I lock the door behind me. Once inside, I take a deep breath. I seem to be out of breath a lot of the time when Cayden is near.

Reaching for my toothbrush off the edge of the sink, I brush my teeth, staring at my reflection in the mirror. There is so much to do, and I'm woman enough to admit I'm more than overwhelmed. I've bitten off more than I can chew with this house, and although finances aren't an issue, getting the house up and running is.

I'm fortunate Cayden offered to help because, without him, I would be lost. Selling is not an option, and I've learned I can be quite stubborn when I want to be. Therefore, I would have just roughed it until, like Cayden said, the roof caved in. So I am more than grateful he has offered his services. In return, I shall attempt not to annoy him and help in any way I can. I can't help my toothpaste-laden smile.

My toothbrush is a fire engine red. An innocent color on most days but today, it sparks a vivid memory or, more accurately, a dream. A red ribbon was wrapped around my palm, and that red was contrasted by white…a white wedding dress.

My cheek bellows from the toothbrush pressed against it, but I'm frozen, cataloging a nightmare that felt too real. *"Snow… your name is Snow."* A shiver passes over me.

Cayden called me this. I know I was fading between reality and questioning fact from fiction, but I'm certain I heard him call me Snow. His voice was my beacon, pulling me from the depths. But I'm unsure if my nightmare was a memory attempting to wade through the murkiness or if it was my mind filling in the blanks?

Frustrated, I finish brushing my teeth and washing my face. I need a shower, but I also need a change of clothes, so I open the bathroom door and make my way to my bedroom.

However, I pause in the doorway, needing a moment to process the sight in front of me.

Cayden is standing at the foot of my bed, hands interlocked behind his neck as he appears to ponder the position. But he's placed it exactly where I would have too.

I'm enthralled by the glow-in-the-dark star because it's now directly above my bed. I have visions of lying on that mattress and staring up at it for hours, but it's through a different set of eyes. Shaking my head, I clear the confusion and make my way into the room.

"Wow, looks great. You can add interior decorator to your résumé."

A ghost of a smirk plays on his lips. "It would look a lot better if you moved rooms." I'm prepared for battle, but when he turns around and crosses his arms, I'm suddenly left speechless. The wind gets ripped from my lungs because it's a vision that triggers…something.

I'm almost certain I've been in this room with him. Not once. But many times before. Images flicker faintly, but at the forefront, I see a boy and a girl lying on a single bed, staring up at the ceiling. The little girl's finger jabs at the air as she traces the star, humming a sweet lullaby as the boy sleeps soundly behind her. I can't help but notice his mismatched socks are riddled with holes.

Once again, I'm a secret voyeur, looking in at a scenario that feels so familiar that I can almost detail every distinct smell and sound. *"Twinkle, twinkle, little star. How I wonder..."*

"What you are...?" I gasp when the words are spoken in this lifetime and not the one in whatever era I was just lost in. What I do know is that what I just experienced...was a memory, *my* memory, which took place in this very room.

However, I don't know whether to be elated or burdened with grief because this memory was charged with sadness. Both children were the other's savior. Who are they? But more importantly, why do I want to embrace them and tell them it'll be all right? Tell them that...everything is always better after a thunderstorm.

"Peyton?" Cayden's voice once again cuts through the disorder, and I'm transported back to the here and now.

This room gives me the strength I need. And I fight the confliction within. "You said you knew wh-who lived here." He visibly holds his breath. "Who were they?"

Cayden's demeanor changes, and a wall erects firmly around him. "There isn't much to say. They were a family with normal family problems." But I don't believe him. "This house has been on the market for years. Over time, it may have suffered at the hands of Mother Nature, but the owners clearly haven't had the heart to sell because if these walls could talk"—he sweeps his hand around the room—"they'd surely have a tale to tell. She may not be all that much to look at it, but the memories are the glue that keeps this house standing. Why do you ask?"

Here goes nothing.

Toying with my bottom lip, I state, "Because I'm pretty certain I've...I've been here before." I'm waiting for any small flicker of response from Cayden to corroborate my story, but all I get in return is indifference.

Coolly placing his hands into his pockets, he asks, "So why this room? If you've been here before...why is this room so important to you?" I can understand his confusion because this doesn't make a lick of sense.

Shrugging, I raise my eyes, focusing on the star that triggered a memory I have no recollection of living. "Because when I'm in here, I feel...safe." I decide to leave out the fact that these fragments of a puzzle involving these nameless kids seem to float in and out of my psyche, sparking a sequence of events that evoke a deep-rooted sadness.

"What can you remember?" he questions. He's genuinely interested, considering this is the first time I've spoken so openly about this with him.

"I can't remember much of anything, but I do remember the lake. And the oak tree. It's what drew me here. But I haven't gathered the courage to go near it yet." He nods, gesturing for me to continue. "My mom told me it looks familiar because we vacationed here when we were kids."

He scoffs.

"I doubt you vacationed here. The residents on this side of the lake were people your mother wouldn't look twice at if she ran them over with her hundred-thousand-dollar car. The poor," he explains when he reads my utter confusion. "The other side, however, that's where you'd find your kind."

"*My kind?*" I ask, unable to mask my offense. "What's that

supposed to mean?" The mere mention of Stella instantly ruins my mood.

Stepping forward, Cayden roots my feet to the floor with a single look. "The rich. With a lake the only real divider, we kept to our side while the wealthy wouldn't dare pass the imaginary line and venture into the world of the impoverished." His bitterness makes clear which side of the lake he dwelled on.

"Lacey said you lived here your whole life." I watch for any signs that'll make way to another memory. But Cayden merely nods. "Do you...remember me?" I hold my breath because I know what his answer will be, but I have to ask it nevertheless.

Tilting his head to the side as if weighing what to say, he tongues his upper lip before replying, "No, I don't remember you. In case you haven't guessed, I grew up on *this* side of the lake. I don't belong in your world. I never have."

I cluck my tongue stubbornly. "I refuse to believe that I went along with such judgmental behavior. And besides, I'm here now. I don't remember that other side. I didn't even know there was 'another side.'" I air quote my point because it seems beyond ridiculous, but thinking of the way Stella looked down her nose at Cayden, I know that I may be the only one of *my kind* who thinks this way.

A tangible tension threatens to suffocate me, and I instantly seek out the ribbon in my hair, but there is, of course, not one there. Dropping my hand, I attempt to decode what the hell just happened. Why would I be wearing a ribbon? And why would a mere ribbon be able to soothe the ache in my chest?

I am clearly going mad.

However, when I lock eyes with Cayden, I see it—a flicker

of familiarity. I know he said he doesn't remember me, but I…I don't believe him. We *have* crossed paths. I know we have. It may have been for just a second, but I know he's seen me before. So the question is, why won't he tell me? What is he hiding?

Thinking back to Ellie's reaction when she first saw me, I felt like she'd seen me before. And she referred to me as an angel, and I called her the pet name of little mouse with ease. I have pieces of the puzzle, but the problem is, I don't have the whole picture.

I have snippets of information, and Cayden is hiding behind this bullshit ruse for a reason. There is a possibility that I'm wrong, but my gut is telling me I'm not. I intend to use whatever information I have as ammo and hopefully come out on top. "I saw Ellie's mom. Your wife?"

Cayden takes a step backward while I wonder if my guerilla tactics will work. "She is *not* my wife. When?"

"Yesterday. I saw your heated exchange with her. Is it safe to assume you don't see eye to eye with her?" I measure my words, not wanting to piss Cayden off. I will work any angle with the hope he divulges any small shred of evidence to sanction my suspicions.

"You assume correctly," he replies, swallowing deeply. "I've known Hazel since we were kids. She was always hanging around; the misfit, I guess you could say. But we all were." I allow him to continue even though the question lingers; who exactly are *we*? "My father"—he swallows down his disgust—"was never around. So my house was the local hangout, a haven for the outsiders to call home. I never liked Hazel like that… but sometimes, things never turn out how you expect them to."

So Ellie wasn't planned. And it appears Cayden never had feelings for Hazel. Could it be that a one-night stand or a drunken happenstance ended in a consequence binding them forever? Whatever the reason, I intend to dig, hoping it'll unearth some light on my past.

"And you're sure I wasn't one of those outsiders?" I know I'm pressing him, but I can't let this go.

Cayden nods as he leisurely walks toward me. With dangerously slow motion, he brushes a stray curl from my cheek. His touch lingers—just how it always seems to when we connect. "Yes. Like I said, you don't belong on this side."

"Well, I'm here now," I counter once again, trying my hardest not to lean into his touch.

"Yes, you are," he replies hoarsely, his eyes skimming over every inch of my face. This spark between us only seems to intensify with each exchange.

Taking a moment, I process what Cayden has shared. He may claim not to know me, but why does it feel like I know him? Yes, I come from an affluent family, but I refuse to believe I am anything like my mother or siblings. I may not remember, but surely, I wouldn't be drawn here if I was.

"Oh, my God! Sorry."

Cayden yanks his hand away from my cheek as if it's been burned as Lacey almost loses her footing when she enters my bedroom. Cayden instantly retreats, his hands clenching by his sides. Has touching me caused him pain? It appears so.

"It's fine. What's up?" Cayden says, making me feel like a pariah when he moves to the other side of the room.

Lacey examines his distance, which was the complete

opposite of what she just walked into. Clearing her throat, she holds up a tray of coffee cups and a brown paper bag. "I brought coffee and some donuts."

"Did someone say donuts?" My already small room grows claustrophobic when the deliverymen enter, carrying my dresser. "I'll just dump this, then. I don't mind if I do." He stands on tippy-toes, eyeing the bag Lacey holds close to her chest.

My digging for dirt is done for now, but for the first time ever, I feel like I'm where I belong. Which is ironic, considering this is contrary to what Cayden just said. "Seeing as you did such a good job with the bed, how about you take over?" I choose my words wisely, and it has the intended effect. "I trust you. I'm going to shower," I conclude while a stormy gray swirls behind Cayden's eyes.

Lacey looks back and forth, clearly confused, but Cayden reads my inner thoughts, loud and clear. He knows that I'm onto him. It's apparent he's hiding something, and I won't stop until I find out what that something is.

"Lacey, honestly, you have done more than enough. I'm just going to finish up in here and call it a day." But she stubbornly shakes her head. It appears pigheadedness is a Coachman trait.

"Never. No man will be left behind." She smirks from over her shoulder as she holds the putty knife in her hand.

For the past few hours, we've been busy at work in my kitchen, slowly peeling back the hideous floral wallpaper. We've stripped it as best as we could, but the backing and remaining facing won't budge. We've soaked the walls with hot water, attempting to soften the paste, but seeing as these walls have been coated since the 50s, it's proving to be a lot tougher than we originally thought when we started.

I have no doubt there is an easier way to do it, but seeing as Cayden has been avoiding me all day, I'm relying on Google to fill in the blanks.

Once I'd showered and changed, I went into my bedroom. The furniture transformed it into my own private oasis. That tranquility lasted all of ten seconds before Cayden came in, toolbox and sledgehammer in hand.

"The wallpaper needs to be stripped, and I need to patch up the hole in the ceiling. The whole roof will need replacing, but this is a quick fix for now," he said, intent on demolishing my serenity. But the thought of touching this room felt like he was taking that sledgehammer to my heart, especially since the hole would require him to cut out the plaster where the star twinkled brightly.

I objected quite fervently, using the precise words: *you'll touch this room over my dead body*. A tad overdramatic, but that's how strongly I felt. He produced a roll of plastic drop cloths, but the furniture was the least of my concerns. I had just moved in, and now he wanted to hack at it. Hell to the fuck no.

After our heated exchange, he marched into the living room, where he remained all day. Lacey and I took refuge in the kitchen, assuming the many tools on the floor were for us to use. We've done a good job, considering it has been the blind leading the blind, but neither of us wanted to get our heads bitten off, so we made do with the DIY videos on YouTube.

Our coveralls are covered in filth, but the sight is surprisingly rewarding. "Parts of my body I never knew existed ache," I say, only half teasing.

Lacey cracks her neck from side to side in agreement. "I think we should celebrate."

"Celebrate what?" I ask, scrubbing at a stubborn strip of paste.

"The fact that we're still standing."

Brushing away the hair from my brow with the back of my forearm, I can't help but laugh. "I suppose that's as good as an excuse as any."

Stepping back, I turn in a slow circle, examining our hard work. The walls, even though patchy and coated in paste, are a work in progress, and I can't wait to see the end result. A banging followed by a string of profanities has Lacey and me looking at one another, raising our brows. "Why is he so grumpy?"

Now is my chance to discuss my far-fetched hunch with her. Maybe she can validate my gut feeling? But I have already asked her, and let's face it, her memory is a lot more credible than mine. But I can't shake this feeling. The further Cayden retreated, the stronger it grew.

Chipping away at the wall like the chip on my shoulder, I reply as innocently as I can. "I think that's got to do with me asking him about Ellie's mom." Her pause hints at Lacey's surprise.

She expresses just how astonished she is a moment later. "You did *what*?"

When I sheepishly risk a glance her way, I see that her mouth hangs open. "It seemed like a good idea at the time," I reason with a small shrug.

Her tool hangs limply by her side, putting an end to our home improvements for the day. "What did he say?"

"He didn't say much. Just that he's known Hazel since they were kids. She lived on 'this side' of the lake. Just how he did." I can't help but roll my eyes. It seems so dramatic and petty.

Lacey pales, and she nervously licks her lips. "He told you?"

The devious side of me conspires to concoct a deceitful ploy to trick Lacey into telling me everything she knows. But as I'm drowning in her innocence, I know that I can't. "He told me that I don't belong in his world, but the thing is, why am I here?"

Lacey's gaze is riveted to the floor. She's clearly uncomfortable, and I suddenly feel like I've just kicked a puppy. But nonetheless, I have to know. "I know I've asked you this before, but I just…this place is so familiar. You're sure you haven't seen me before?"

Just as I did with Cayden, I look for any signs of recognition. Anything. But I get nothing. "Like Cayden said…you didn't belong in our world. Your place was across the lake." There is no malice in her words, only truth, which is why I don't take offense.

But she didn't really answer my question, and that gives me hope. "Let's just say for argument's sake that I did belong; would you know who I was?"

She finally lifts those virtuous eyes and meets mine. So many emotions reflect from deep within, swirling in chaos. But through the carnage, I see it. She's guarding a secret, but does this secret have to do with me?

"Holy shit. This place looks worse than it did before."

Cayden's sarcasm breaks the moment. Lacey takes a step back as if to sidestep her guilt. My frustration stabs at my temple, and instinctively, I clutch at my brow.

Cayden notices the sudden tension, his attention fleeting back and forth between Lacey and me. Just as he opens his mouth, Lacey exclaims, "We're going out."

"We are?" Cayden and I say at the same time.

Lacey nods animatedly. "Yes. We are. Let's celebrate a job well done."

Her zest for life is contagious, and I realize she's right. Why the hell not? When Cayden smirks, however, I know he's about to rain on my fun parade. "We're far from being done."

A lump forms in my throat. "How bad is the damage, boss?"

"You don't want to know." His filthy appearance hints at the fact that he's been elbow deep in it. He scrubs a hand through his hair, causing plumes of dust to take flight. "It's a miracle this house is still standing. If a gust blew, let's just say you wouldn't be in Kansas anymore." I'm thankful he's making light of something that is sure to end with me in tears. "The foundation is unstable. Everything holding this house together is either rotted or close to collapsing."

I exhale, my hair blowing out from the force. "So what's the good news?"

"That is the good news," he counters while I refrain from rocking in a corner. "But…"

"But?" My attention is piqued.

"But you're lucky I have an ace up my sleeve." I can't contain my excitement and clap animatedly. Lacey joins in too, and Cayden just shakes his head at our idiocy. "I wouldn't get too excited. This means I am going to be here a lot." His revelation has me missing my hands, and I end up high-fiving the air.

My heart begins to race, but I quash my inner cheerleader because he looks unmoved by the fact. "It's a sacrifice I'm willing to make." I mock sigh, hoping to hide my exhilaration.

I have no idea why the prospect of spending so much time with Cayden pleases me. We seem to forget about social etiquette and speak our minds, but that just adds to the appeal. Having someone I can spar with who isn't afraid to fight back excites me.

No matter my surname or my social standing and the ridiculous rules that come with it, it's evident that I belong on this side of the lake. I think I always have. Cayden and Lacey may claim that I don't belong in their world, but I'll be damned if I stop looking for someone who can tell me otherwise.

Cayden shrugs, but his grin reveals he likes the chase as much as I do. "Don't say I didn't warn you." This will end in a fiery mess, and I can't wait to watch it implode.

"Well, in that case, count me in, Lacey. God knows I need all the fun I can get because the next few months are clearly going to be hell." When Cayden rubs over his stubble, arrogance oozing from every pore, the word hell takes on a whole different meaning. It's going to be hell to keep my irrational feelings for him under wraps.

I've known him for all of five minutes, but those minutes have been the most awakening moments of my life—like right now. Every part of my body tingles as he's clearly sizing me up.

Lacey squeals and bounces on the spot, oblivious to my impending meltdown. "How about you, big bro?"

His gaze never wavers from me. "Maybe next time."

"Why, you've got someplace better to be?" she teases while he does a poor job of hiding his appraisal of me from head to toe. I'm certain I've just burst into flames.

I get my head back in the game when he ambiguously says, "I have something I have to do." Of course, there is no further explanation. I'm becoming accustomed to having more questions than answers when Cayden Coachman is involved. But this is good. I need to focus.

"Suit yourself. Girls' night!" Lacey exclaims, linking her arm through mine. That sounds incredible, and I'm beyond thrilled to let my hair down as Lacey and I get to know one another better. But I agreed for another reason.

If Cayden and Lacey don't want to talk…then I'll find someone who will.

SIX

Deciding what to wear was easy.

I'm now the proud owner of just a handful of clothes I'll happily be seen in public in, and this little red dress is one of them. The rest of my belongings sit in garbage bags in the corner of my room.

I'll donate them to Goodwill, so someone else can give them a good home because I'm not that person anymore. They are a part of my past I don't wish to remember because what do they say about my character. If I was okay spending that amount of money on clothing, maybe what Cayden says about me not belonging here holds some truth.

But I refuse to entertain such thoughts because I'm determined to find some answers tonight.

Slipping into my heeled ankle boots, I take one final look at my appearance. My copper waves are loose. I've washed my hair and applied a sea salt spray to give them a natural, windswept look. The red dress has a mesh and crochet top that comes in tight at the waist. Multiple layers of tulle shape the short, pleated skirt. I can't help but want to twirl in a circle to see the skirt ruffle in the wind. However, the main reason this dress survived the cull sits around my middle.

Fingering the red ribbon sash, I think about another just like it, which I have yet to see up close. *One step at a time,* I whisper, as I'll no doubt need all the courage I can muster to take that daunting leap. I know I'll have to eventually stop viewing it from afar. Tonight, however, is not that night.

I grab my clutch and switch off the light in my bedroom. As I pass the living room, I stop, smiling when thinking of what Cayden said. The thought of seeing him every day pleases me more than it should. This attraction I feel for him makes no sense, but I suppose none of this does.

I make my way down the front steps, excited to be hitting the town. Since waking to this life, I've been stuck in a rut, attempting to decipher who I was but discounting the person I am now. Yes, I want to uncover who I was and what part this town played in my past, but it doesn't have to be all doom and gloom.

With a skip in my step, I walk to the Coachman residence. Lacey told me to come over around eight. It's two past. I don't want to seem eager even though I am.

Now that my plans for the house are in motion, I can focus on other things like getting a job. I worked as a marketing manager, but I have zero desire to return to a role I think I would absolutely hate. I actually had to google the job description as I have no recollection of it. So that leaves the question, what do I want to do?

Remembering the mysterious sketch I woke to sitting on my lap has me wondering if maybe I have a hidden talent no one told me about. Like if the hidden memories only resurface in small fractions at a time, I wonder if my subconscious has done the same in this case. I certainly don't remember drawing it, but I suppose I don't remember a lot of things.

Lost in my head, I'm not paying attention to my surroundings until the hair on the back of my neck stands on end—again. The same thing happened last night. Instinctively, I pause to scope out my backdrop. Looking from left to right, I scan the night, struggling to pinpoint anything out of place.

Nothing strikes me as odd; this sleepy neighborhood has such a comforting feel that tonight is the first night I've locked my doors. Passing off my behavior as just jittery nerves due to what I might uncover tonight, I continue my walk toward Cayden's.

My quickened footsteps echo out here in the open, and the silence soon turns eerie when I can't shake the feeling I'm being watched. A shiver passes over me when I look over my shoulder only to be greeted with the gentle twinkling of the stars and the full moon. The distant, gleaming lights from across the lake play to my unforeseen anxiety because, for the first time since I arrived, I feel like I don't belong.

Squinting, my mind conjures up images of the bogeyman lurking in the shadows, but pushing aside such fiction, just as I did last night, I focus on the fact and breathe easy when I see that no one is there.

With the coast clear of serial killers and creepy clowns, I continue my walk but hasten my pace. When I'm feet away, I charge up the front steps, taking a deep breath. My heart is in my throat, which is absurd. I compose myself before ringing the doorbell.

Footsteps march down the stairs before the wooden door opens, and I'm welcomed by Lacey. "Hey! I'm running late. I won't be a second. Come in." She gestures for me to enter, but it suddenly hits me that I'm about to step into the lion's or, rather, Cayden's den.

My earlier suspicions of him knowing who I am float to the surface because stepping foot inside may confirm my hunch as fact. When I enter, I'm instantly hit with the smell of the ocean. It leaves me with a longing, but other than that, nothing else arises.

"Do you want a drink? The kitchen is just in there." She points to the left. An elaborate archway leads to what looks to be a living room with a deep blue-gray feature wall. Rustic wall sconces light up the room strikingly, giving it a warm, homey feel.

The crisp white walls set off the polished floors, eliciting the snoop in me. I wonder where those floors lead. The kitchen sits at the end of the hallway where I can see a black marbled counter. The house is sleek and elegant, giving way to my excitement. I have no doubt Cayden created this castle. I can't wait to see what he has planned for mine.

Realizing Lacey is waiting for me to reply, I shake my head. "No, it's okay. I'll just wait down here."

She nods, clapping in excitement. "Okay. Just give me a

minute." I watch with a smile as she takes the stairs two at a time.

Once she's disappeared upstairs, I take a moment to appreciate my surroundings because there's a lot to take in. The foyer is open, welcoming guests the moment they step foot inside. A low-hanging chandelier adds to the warmth, but it's not pretentious. It's smart. Elegant. The staircase is to the right. The black banister matches the black-and-white stairs.

Breathing in my surroundings, I focus, hoping something familiar will pop out and verify that I've seen it before. I don't rush it, and absorb everything with care. Tapping my boot against the polished flooring, I concentrate on the sound and the way it echoes throughout the foyer. Have I heard it before?

I wait for the headaches, for the blackness to drag me under, sparking a memory of being here before, but I get nothing. No familiarity, no confirmation. Nothing. This place is as foreign to me as any other.

I sigh in disappointment as a small part of me hoped that I was right. Surely, if I'd known Cayden, this house would hold some form of intimacy like the lake and the oak did, but it doesn't. Maybe it's just wishful thinking, and I'm grasping at straws, desperate to make a connection.

Beyond frustrated with myself, I blow a soft raspberry, suddenly wanting to turn around and go home. My mood has fizzled, and I doubt it'll revive anytime soon. Just as I'm thinking of calling out to Lacey to tell her I've changed my mind, all thoughts of speaking come to a screeching halt because standing feet away is Ellie.

She's emerged from the hallway with a cookie in one hand

and a stuffed toy mouse in the other. She freezes when she sees me, and I do the same. She's in pink pajamas dotted with white printed bows. Nothing but innocence radiates from her small frame, and all I want to do is…cry.

A guilt so heavy robs me of breath, and I hold the wall for support. Ellie remains unmoving, watching me with those wide, wise eyes. I need to talk to her, but I'm afraid of what I might say. I want to ask her why she called me an angel, but more importantly, I want to know if she knows who I am.

Clearing my throat, I smile. "Hi, Ellie. I'm Peyton. I didn't get to introduce myself." She continues watching me closely.

With a waver in my step, I stroll toward her, not wanting to scare her more than she already is. Stopping a few feet away, I drop to a crouch. She holds her breath. "Who's your friend?" I gesture to the tattered mouse she holds limply in her hand. Her fear of me is apparent, but I don't understand why.

And no matter how tempted I am to ask her, I don't. Regardless of my quest for answers, I would never draw her into my darkness. I am about to query what kind of cookie she has because it smells delicious, but I'm rendered utterly speechless when a whisper fills the silence. "I…know you."

It takes me three attempts to speak. "You d-do?" I finally manage to wheeze.

She nods, her ponytail bobbing in agreement. "Yes, you're an angel."

This is the second time she's referred to me this way, and I am still no closer to unveiling what she means. "An angel? I-I don't understand." The walls begin closing in on me, a feeling I've become accustomed to. But this time, I fight the shadows because I won't let them win.

Ellie's small fingers tighten around the stuffed animal as she appears to be as intrigued by me as I am by her. I don't move a muscle when she shuffles forward and thinks long and hard before offering me her toy. Not understanding any of this, I accept, but the moment I do, the air gets ripped from my lungs.

Closing my eyes, I run my finger over the bristly whiskers, then trail it up, knowing without looking that I will only find one eye. The other is missing. How do I know this? The fur has been rubbed away long ago, but the comfort is still there. Ellie feels it, and I do too.

With the slowest of movements, I open my eyes, examining Ellie from head to toe. The ache, the emptiness I felt when she was in my arms hits me once again, and I inhale sharply. A fierce urge to protect her overwhelms me, but protect her from what? Or rather, whom?

She smiles a gapped-tooth grin, her innocence too much for words. "It'll be okay, little mouse." Ringing blares loudly, and I resist the urge to cover my ears. But it soon vanishes when Ellie places her tiny hand on my cheek. "Remember"—I hold my breath—"you're the one who can fill the world with sunshine."

A tear trickles down my cheek.

"Ellie?" Cayden's curious voice sounds behind me, which is my cue to wipe away my tear.

When I think I'm composed enough, I hand Ellie back her toy. "He's perfect. Just like you." I run my fingers through her hair before rising to stand.

Ellie smiles, taking a bite of her cookie. I have no idea what just happened.

Turning slowly, I'm caught off guard when Cayden greets me with complete interest. I was expecting anger, but all I get is curiosity. That soon turns to interest of a different kind, however, when he examines every inch of me. This push-pull effect is sure to leave me with permanent heartburn.

"Sorry about that. I'm ready," Lacey announces, bouncing down the steps. She pauses on the second to last one when she sees me caught in a deadlock with Cayden. Brushing aside the disarray, I pray this is the moment I've been waiting for, for so many months—for me to remember.

I catalog everything I've learned, which isn't a whole lot, and attempt to piece together some sort of picture that makes a lick of sense. All I keep returning to is water and the red ribbon fluttering innocently in the summer breeze.

Clutching at snippets, I arrive at the same conclusion. The answers rest with the lake. All roads seem to lead me back there. Every time I dig too deeply, knocking on an invisible door, the walls my mind has erected pop up, guarding me from a past my subconscious clearly doesn't want me to remember.

But being here, close to Cayden, Ellie, and my new home, I know it's only a matter of time until things begin to unravel. And when they do, I won't be caught off guard. But this house means nothing to me. There is no warmth. No suggestion I've been here before.

Cayden narrows his eyes, examining me carefully. He seems to do that a lot when I'm around. Although this house is alien to me, Cayden and his daughter—who now stands by his side, looking as intrigued as her father—aren't.

Ellie chews her cookie, watching closely as Cayden steps

forward. I don't dare move. "Stay safe. It's a full moon tonight. Anything is possible."

Tilting my head and surveying *him* this time, I can't help but quip, "If I didn't know any better, I'd say you were worried about me."

A glimmer of a smile teases his lips as he shakes his head. "Just be careful." It feels like he's moments away from reaching out and touching my cheek, but then he changes his mind at the last second. Instead, he curls his hands into loose fists.

"You can take my mouse. He'll keep you safe." Only when Ellie's sweet voice rings do I break eye contact with Cayden.

Captivated by her innocence, I fight the urge to reach out and embrace her. "Thank you, but I think he'll miss you too much. And besides, I have your aunt Lacey to keep me safe."

"That's right, sweetie. And you're here to keep Daddy safe." Cayden's jaw clenches as his gaze drifts to Lacey.

Raising an eyebrow, I can't ignore my suspicion that Lacey has let something slip that Cayden clearly doesn't want me to know. But what?

Lacey nervously tugs at her gold hoop earring before descending the last stair. "We'd better get going. Raul is two minutes away."

"Raul?" Cayden barks, beating me to the punch.

Lacey rolls her eyes, waving her phone. "Yes. He's our Uber driver. Surely, you're not that ancient, and you know what that is."

"You're taking an Uber?" he asks, ignoring her wisecrack because it appears he has other pressing matters to deal with. "I could have driven you."

She scoffs at his suggestion, slipping her bag over her shoulder. "And have the fun police ruin my night? No, thank you. Bye, big brother." She kisses his cheek, silencing him.

She wraps Ellie in a tight hug, kissing her gently on the top of her head. "The chocolate fudge ice cream is in the back of the freezer. Don't tell your dad," she whispers loudly, and Ellie bursts into magical laughter. I can't help but smile. "Ooh, one minute." Lacey peers down at her phone, then she's out the door, hollering in excitement.

That's my cue to follow, but I don't.

The air turns menacing as if something significant looms just over the horizon. But I suppose that's nothing new. Clearing my throat, I ignore the innate response to kiss Cayden goodbye. "Good night, Ellie. Don't let the bed bugs bite." I ruffle her hair. I'm completely stalling because staying here suddenly is a lot more appealing than going out and socializing with a bunch of strangers.

But remembering why I agreed to go, I meet Cayden's impenetrable stare. "Well, good night, then. Don't wait up." My attempts at being humorous backfire when Cayden arches a watchful brow.

Following in Lacey's footsteps, I quickly turn to leave but am gently tugged backward and into a rock-hard smelling paradise. I soon realize I'm pressed against Cayden's chest. I can't see him because my back faces him, but I have no problem feeling him. "Call me if you need me. I meant what I said. Be careful."

His warm breath slides against the heated flesh of my neck, and it takes all my willpower not to sag into him. "Careful?"

"Yes," he hums, leaning in close and sweeping my curls to one side. He glides the tip of his finger down the slope of my neck. Every part of me trembles.

"Careful of what?"

"The Big Bad Wolf," he counters, his tone low and filled with innuendo.

My skin sizzles beneath his touch when he places his fingers on my waist and squeezes firmly. It feels like he's squeezing the air from my lungs. But I soon realize he's comparing my outfit to that of Little Red. What he fails to understand time and time again is that he's the wolf, and I'm constantly in danger whenever he's near.

All I want to do is throw caution to the wind and misbehave because Cayden's warning doesn't come without punishment. And right now, basking in his aroma and his heady charisma, I want to be so damn naughty. But I rein it in. "Lucky I packed my pepper spray then."

He chuckles, and it doesn't seem fair that even his laugh holds appeal. "Good to know."

When he releases me, I'm certain my cheeks match the color of my dress. I don't bother turning to see if he's as affected as I am because I've come to learn that Cayden Coachman has mastered the perfect poker face. I practically run out the door and am thankful I don't fall flat on my ass.

Even though it's a warm summer night, the heated air feels divine against my cheeks. Our Uber pulls into the driveway, and I've never been happier to flee. Lacey doesn't seem to notice my sudden meltdown, although she's most likely accustomed to my weirdness by now. We jump into the back seat of the Honda, the young driver giving us a wave hello.

Lacey rattles off directions while I take a much-needed breath. As we reverse out the driveway, I risk a glance at the front door, not surprised when I see Cayden's broad frame standing in the doorway with Ellie by his side. Their silhouettes stroke something deep within.

However, Lacey doesn't allow me to probe further. "Sorry about Cayden. Old habits die hard."

"That's okay. There's no need to apologize." I'm proud of myself for being able to string together a sentence. "You said he's always looked out for you, seeing as it was just you and him. What happened to your dad?"

When Lacey shifts in her seat and the mood turns sour, I wonder why. It's clear there is no love lost, which just makes me more curious. "I honestly don't know. Growing up, he was never really there. Cayden always made sure I was fed. Dressed. Safe." Raul turns up Taylor Swift on the radio as he clearly prefers her woes over ours.

When she bites her lip and gazes out the window, I wonder what memory holds her captive. "I don't really remember much of my childhood. Even my teenage years are a blur. So I can sympathize with you in a way. I know your situation is far worse than mine, but sometimes, it feels like I've forgotten for a reason. Crazy, right?"

She's seeking validation, but it doesn't sound that crazy. "Not at all. I can relate. Trust me."

She's still, and I allow her the time she needs. "Late at night, when it's dead quiet, I lie in bed with my eyes squeezed tight. That's the only time I really remember. And even then, I don't know if it's real. But the screams, the distinct sounds of someone being hit, the muted sniffles, I know I've heard them before…I just don't know who they belong to."

A sadness overcomes us both, and I offer the only comfort I can. Gently touching her knee, I sigh. "Sometimes, it's better to forget."

"Is that what happened to you?" Her question is innocent, but I can't help feeling like she's somehow ended up in my head. "I know you have amnesia because of your accident, but do you think subconsciously, your mind is saving you the pain?"

Toying with the ribbon around my waist, I reply without pause, "Yes." It's on the tip of my tongue to share my suspicions that I've met Cayden before. But even if I have, her loyalties will always lie with her brother, so I don't want to put her in an awkward position. "But I intend to get to the bottom of it. I have to."

She nods, finally turning to meet my eyes. Hers are rimmed with tears. It's the first time I've seen her sparkling personality dim. It appears we're all guarding secrets, ones we've clearly forgotten for a reason.

"Sorry for getting all heavy." She swipes at her eyes. "Damn Cayden and his chivalry."

A laugh escapes me. "I wouldn't go that far." She joins in, and the mood instantly settles.

Pop songs fill the silence as Lacey and I are content to watch the world pass us by. As I peer out into the darkness, I can't help but think about what Lacey shared. There's a reason she's unable to remember much of her childhood. It doesn't sound like one I'd like to remember either.

From the anger in Cayden's words when he mentioned his father, I know he doesn't have the same luxury as Lacey. He remembers, and I have a hunch she's forgotten because of him. He's saved her the torment of remembering and taken it upon himself to remember for them both. But the small snippets she can recall sound hideous. Just what did Cayden do to save her the heartache?

When Raul takes a sharp turn, I suddenly realize how winding the road is.

Taking in my surroundings, a hollowness cloaks me, and that familiar sense of déjà vu swallows me whole. "Is this the road we took to go into town?"

"No," Lacey replies, snapping from whatever memory she was lost in. She peers through the windshield. "We took the highway. It's *a lot* quicker." Raul turns up the volume on the radio.

Tapping my finger to my lips, I wonder why it feels like I've driven on it before. I'm almost certain we didn't take this route from Myrtle Beach. I'd remember these turns. On cue, I slide along the worn-out vinyl of the back seat, holding the seat belt across my chest for dear life.

"Are you all right? You're white as a ghost."

"Yes, I'm fine. I just…this road seems familiar."

"Did you take it when coming here?"

I shake my head, suddenly short of breath. "No." Looking into the desolation has me remembering the welcoming greenery when I first arrived. But now, all I feel is a guttural sadness.

Raul must sense my impending breakdown. Turning down

the radio, he meets my eyes in the rearview mirror. "This is a shortcut. Only the locals know it." His revelation has me rubbing a circle on my chest over my heart. It begins to throb and ache.

How could this road be familiar then? I'm not a local.

"Maybe it's similar to one you've driven on before?" Lacey offers kindly.

"Maybe," I reply half-heartedly. Clutching the seat beneath me, I recall what Stella told me about the accident. "Stella…my mom," I clarify, "said an oncoming car lost control and ran me off the road. My car rolled down an embankment. The roads were slippery, slick with snow and ice."

"Do you know who the other driver was?"

A sharp pain bangs at my temple, and I instinctively rub my brow. "No, I don't know. Stella said he was drunk, so I never really gave much thought to him. I was too busy trying to remember…anything."

Lacey nods, listening to me unload my madness.

Raul decelerates when we reach a snaking, steep hill. Even though he's proceeding with caution, I grip the door handle and steady my breathing. Bursts of color flicker brightly, a torturous rainbow of pain as I will myself to breathe.

I need a distraction because I feel like I'm going to burst into tears and switch off from what is turning out to be a disaster of an evening. "How long have you worked at Miam?" Lacey mentioned she worked as head chef at the classy French restaurant in Myrtle Beach.

"About two years. I love it there. You should come visit one day. I'll stuff you full of sweets."

When the white noise lingers in the background, I'm thankful the distraction is working. "I actually have walked past it a few times, but my…Stella"—I can't stomach referring to her as my mom—"refuses to dine anywhere but the country club." I curl my lip in disgust.

"So your mom is an asshole?"

Lacey's question has me loosening up and forgetting my meltdown. "You could say that. I have brothers and sisters, but they are nothing more than strangers. You, Ellie, Cayden… you're far more significant than they are."

She swallows, toying with the short hem of her black dress. I wonder what I said, as that was supposed to be a compliment. We ride the rest of the way in silence, both of us appearing to appreciate the quiet.

When Raul pulls up in front of a bar and Lacey unbuckles her belt, I know that we're here. The fluorescent sign reads Mustangs.

The moment I step out onto the sidewalk, the first thing that hits me is the noise. It's a Friday night, and everyone is in the mood to party. The line to get into Mustangs is long, but Lacey links her arm through mine and leads me toward two beefy security guards in black. When they see her, the taller one of the two smiles. "Hey, Ace. How have you been?"

"Good. Working hard, but tonight, we plan on letting our hair down. This is my friend, Peyton."

He, whose name badge says Justin, nods. "Hi, Peyton. Any friend of Ace's is a friend of mine. Is your brother here?" Justin looks over our shoulders, wading through the crowd in hopes of seeing Cayden.

She bursts into a sarcastic cackle. "You do remember who my brother is, right? Anything fun gives him a rash."

Justin laughs loudly, smirking at her sass. "All right then. Tell him I said hi." He moves to the side, permitting us entry. I feel guilty for jumping the line, but Lacey drags me inside.

"Thank you," I call out over my shoulder. "It was nice meeting you."

I'm not sure if he heard me because the moment we step foot into the luminous pink foyer, the noise notches up tenfold. Lacey hauls me down the long hallway, bopping to the live band playing on the stage.

When we enter the main room, I glance from left to right, taking it all in. The place is packed full of patrons drinking, laughing, and having a good time. There is a mix of people, but most are in ripped jeans, faded band T-shirts, and covered in tattoos. Stella wouldn't be caught dead in here, so that fact spurs me on to investigate further.

The band is deafening in the small place, but I understand what's on Lacey's mind as she leads me toward the bar. Everyone seems friendly enough as they move aside for us to pass. We wait in line, Lacey bouncing on the spot, her eyes rooted to the stage. I see why a second later. Sitting behind the blue drum kit and assaulting the cymbals is none other than Gunn.

The spotlight beaming down behind him ignites his kit and highlights his golden skin. There is no denying his good looks, but the memories of seeing Cayden on that worksite, exerting his control, have me wondering if anyone could ever compare.

I put thoughts of Cayden on the back burner, however, and focus on the patrons around me, hoping one face will stand out from the crowd. None do. I don't allow that to deter me because I'm not even sure if the pre-amnesia me would hang out at a place such as this. My clothes and upbringing certainly would point to that being highly unlikely.

"What's your poison?" Lacey shouts into my ear to be heard over the rock music.

"Whiskey sour," I reply without thought, shocking myself. That came so naturally, and I wonder why. "I may not remember much, but I sure as shit seem to remember what booze I like."

Lacey laughs, nudging me with her shoulder. "Whatever would Stella say?"

"Stella is probably why I drink," I counter, which has both of us cackling.

Lacey orders our drinks while I continue to survey our surroundings. The painted black walls have framed tour posters hanging around the room. There is nothing notable about this bar, but it appears to be well loved by many. When I take a sip of my delicious drink, I understand why.

Lacey pays the bartender, and we then make our way to the red leather booths in a small corner of the room. We take a seat.

"Cool place, right?"

I agree, nodding my head in time with the music. "It sure is, and the scenery isn't too bad either." When I wiggle my eyebrows, Lacey turns beet red.

"You caught me; although, Mustangs *is* the best bar in town," she says, defending her honor. "Cayden and I used to come here all the time. He snuck me in when I was underage." She drinks her beer with a smile.

That would explain Justin's comment earlier. It appears

Cayden has a fun side, after all. I don't want to pry, but I'm almost certain Lacey is aware that her brother gets under my skin in every way possible. "I can't believe he used to"—I pause for dramatic effect—"have fun." I slap both my cheeks and open my mouth wide, staging shock and horror.

Lacey almost chokes on her beer. "I know. He's a twenty-eight-year-old single dad who needs to let loose. But he won't. That's Cayden. Always looking out for everyone else."

Shuffling in my seat, I attempt to be as casual as I can. "He told me Hazel used to hang around your house when you were kids. That your home was kind of a haven for the outcasts of the neighborhood."

She nods but doesn't let anything slip. That doesn't deter me, however.

"He doesn't like her much, does he?"

"You could say that. Hazel didn't have the best upbringing, and Cayden, being Cayden, ensured she was looked after. I guess she took that form of kindness for something else. She lusted after him for years, but he was never interested."

"Why not?" I've seen her, and she is clearly gorgeous.

Lacey picks at the label on her beer. "He was in love with someone else." That thought doesn't seem too hard to believe. Cayden is protective, and I can imagine him cherishing and loving that person with all of his heart. "But the thing with Cayden is that regardless of what a huge ass he can be, he is selfless. Growing up, we all looked up to him, forgetting he was only a few years older than us. In some cases, even the older kids saw him as an authoritative figure. My brother grew up way too fast." The regret is clear.

"So it seems Cayden was the glue that held our neighborhood together." It feels right to refer to the neighborhood as mine.

Lacey lifts her eyes, nodding. "He was. Growing up in this part of town was tough. We all came from dysfunctional families and lived in poverty. But Cayden ensured we were looked after." There is no need for her to spell it out. For that to happen, Cayden would have lied, cheated, and stolen as I doubt their families would have offered a helping hand.

Suddenly, I'm quick to doubt myself. There is no way Stella would have allowed me to socialize with Cayden or his friends. And it's safe to assume by the clothes I owned and the life I led, I wouldn't be caught dead running with his crowd when I was old enough to make my own decisions. I'm so confused. Could it be that I am so desperate to remember that my mind is tricking me into believing these memories as being real?

Reaching for my drink, I throw it back in one big gulp, savoring the burn. I feel like I'm back to square one.

The crowd erupts into lively claps and whistles, hinting the band has finished their set. Lacey sits tall and joins in by clapping excitedly. I instantly harness my thoughts because we're supposed to be having a good time.

"How do I look?" she asks, straightening out her outfit. She looks stunning in a fitted little black dress. Her hair is tied back into a high ponytail, accentuating her striking features. Gunn doesn't stand a chance.

"You look beautiful. Does he know you're here?"

She shakes her head, interlocking her hands over her lips to hide her budding grin.

We both watch as he rises from the kit, beaming brightly

when his bandmates high-five one another on a great show. A group of scantily clad girls loiters by the side of the stage. Lacey sees them too, and instantly, her mood deflates. Her insecurities shine as her shoulders slump, and she slouches low.

But fuck that. There is no way that's happening. She can chastise me later.

Without a second thought, I shoot upward and put my fingers into my mouth, whistling. The noise is deafening, and I smile in response. Who knew I could whistle like a drunken Irishman?

"Oh, my God! What are you doing?" Lacey whispers, yanking on my arm frantically. She wants me to sit down, but hell no.

My tactics work because when Gunn looks over, I wave wildly, ensuring he doesn't miss us. When he sees me, I gesture for him to come over. He doesn't object and jumps from the stage, showcasing his impressive prowess, and bypasses his legion of fans. They immediately turn and glare at who dared to take their limelight. I wave my pointer in response.

"Sometimes…we just need a little push," I say, giggling when Lacey rockets from her seat and hunts through her bag for some lip gloss. This is happening, and she has no other choice but to be prepared.

"I'll remember that for next time," she replies, hinting I am so in trouble. But it's worth it. When Gunn approaches our booth and sees Lacey, the air turns electric. She stops mid-stroke of applying her pink gloss and quickly gets rid of the evidence by shoving the wand into her bag.

"Hi," he says, breaking the silence.

"Hi," she finally replies while I feel like the third wheel. "Great show."

"Thanks for coming."

I have the sudden urge to coo. But I don't. It's apparent this will probably advance past pleasantries if I leave them alone. "I need another drink. Lacey?" She barely hears me, too transfixed by the hulking rock star in front of her. "I'll get you a beer."

I excuse myself, giving Gunn a knowing smile. He merely smirks in response, wasting no time as he takes my seat and gives Lacey a tight hug. She looks at me over his shoulder, glowing in gratitude.

Now that the band has finished, the thirsty patrons are all lined up, ready to quench their thirst. I decide to visit the restroom first. The bathrooms are down a narrow hallway, and it's not hard to guess which line is for the ladies. The longest line, of course.

Overlapping faded stickers litter the hallway walls. Everything from obscure band names to smiley faces. Among the chaos are phone numbers written in marker, offering all kinds of services. I now know who to call if I'm looking for a good time.

Chuckling, I relish in the warmth within. It's not a feeling I experience too often. Being Lacey's wingwoman felt good, and it was fun to focus on something other than trying to remember. I may not remember the past, but I do remember now. Maybe if I lighten up, things may come quicker? Like when you stop looking for something, that's usually when you find it.

Happy with my newfound mindset, I decide to try to live by it because being a madwoman hasn't worked for me thus far.

Que será, será.

Peering ahead, I'm thankful the line is moving, but it's still about fifteen people deep. No one is behind me. Just as I'm contemplating whether to hit the bar and come back, I get the sense that I'm no longer alone, and that's because I am not. I'm about to turn and ask the person behind me to give me a little breathing room, but speaking is the last thing on my mind when that someone leans in close. "Wanna party? I have the good stuff. All the party favors you need."

The smell of menthol cigarettes is heavy on his breath, and I instantly have the urge to gag. But pulling back my shoulders, I spin around, not interested in whatever this scumbag has to offer. "No, thank you," I spit, glaring at him.

The man before me isn't what you'd expect your typical drug dealer to look like. Quite frankly, he looks like he should be playing college football in his varsity jacket and cream chinos. But regardless, he has two seconds to back off before I knee him in the groin.

"I know what you like," he presses, peering around, scoping out his surroundings, before reaching into his inner pocket and producing a clear bag containing a white powder.

I almost bump into the girl behind me as I recoil in disgust. "You know nothing about me. Now get out of here before I call the police."

His confusion reflects in his green eyes, but that soon turns to challenge as a shit-eating grin spreads from ear to ear. He crowds me further and purrs, "Oh, so it's like that then? I know what you want." I'm too shell-shocked to move when he lowers his face to inches from mine. However, when he pushes me up against the wall, rubbing his distinct hard-on into me, I retaliate like a caged raccoon.

"Let me go, you fucking jerk! If this tactic is meant to scare me, then I hate to disappoint. Although considering the pathetic excuse of wood you're sporting, I'd say you're used to disappointment. Now, fuck off." I attempt to break free but defying him only spurs him on.

"Don't be such a hard-ass. You never complained about my *wood* before. If I recall correctly, you begged for it." The fight in me dies the moment those vile words slip past his smug lips.

"*What?*" The world starts spinning, and the white noise rears her ugly head. I grow slack, and the asshole thinks it's because I've surrendered.

"Now, open up, baby. Daddy is coming home." He lowers his hand between us, walking his fingers up my thigh. His touch makes me want to be sick, but it's the wake-up call I needed. Adrenaline soars through me, and I act on pure instinct, kneeing him in the groin.

A satisfying sound akin to an orange being squashed by a bus fills the air, and the asshole topples forward, cupping his junk. "What the fuck is the matter with you?" he wheezes, turning a ghastly shade of white.

A crowd has formed, but I don't need any help. I can hold my own. "What's the matter with *me*? I'm not the one who tried to sell you drugs and then propositioned you for sex."

"You're fucking crazy! You never had a problem with it in the past." He's lying. There is no way I'd do the things he proposed I did.

But a small, irksome voice vibrates loudly. Why did he

choose me? Why did he speak to me like he knew who I was? There is only one way to find out.

Uncaring that he's in obvious pain, I grip his cheeks, forcing him to look at me. "Do you know who I am?" When he attempts to yank from my hold, I squeeze tighter, just as he did to me when he had me pinned against the wall. "Answer me! Have we met before?"

His wild exhalations sweep back my hair, and I'm suddenly hit with a memory of flesh upon flesh, writhing in utmost desire. But I refuse to believe it. There is no way. But I'm wrong. So. Fucking. Wrong.

"You're one messed-up bitch, Snow. I used to love that about you, but screw this. No woman is worth this bullshit." Pushing past his pain, he stands, eyeballing me. "Especially when everyone has had a taste of her pussy." He hobbles off, junk in hand, while I'm unsure if I'm still breathing.

It takes my mind a moment to catch up, but even when it does, I still don't understand what just happened. "Are you okay? Do you want me to call the police?" someone asks, but it's all background noise.

I'm on a merry-go-round with no sign of it slowing down. Round and round I go, images flashing before me, but now, I have a new piece of the puzzle to add. Bile rises, and I cover my mouth. The blackness threatens to drag me under, just like it always does, but I won't be stuck in this hallway when it does.

Pushing my way through concerned onlookers, I sag against the wall, attempting to regain my balance as I stumble toward the light.

You're one messed-up bitch, Snow.

No, this can't be happening. How does he know who I am?

You never seemed to have a problem in the past.

Past…

How that word has changed my life in ways unimaginable. It's been said that one shouldn't allow their past to define their future, but what kind of past did I lead?

Especially when everyone has had a taste of her pussy.

The further I dig, the more I understand why I'm in no hurry to remember. What kind of person was I?

I stumble out of the bar, hailing a cab and ignoring Justin when he asks if I'm okay. I know he will tell Lacey I've left. This is a total shitty move, but she'll be all right. Gunn is with her. When the cab driver asks me where I'm headed, I'm tempted to rattle off my parents' address, but I don't. I ask him to take me home. The only place I feel safe. The only place I can hide from the demons no longer silenced.

SEVEN

Tonight backfired—epically. I went out with the intent to find someone who knew who I was, but I got a lot more than I bargained for. The only positive thing I can be thankful for is the fact that I didn't succumb to the white noise.

Once the cab dropped me off, I staggered into my home, never needing the comfort of these four walls more than I do right now. My room has been my haven for the past few hours. Staring out into the lake from my balcony, I almost wish I could sink my worries to the bottom. But I can't. It's because of this lake that I'm here—in hell.

Tonight, I uncovered something about myself no person would want to know. But there is no denying the truth. It seems I was a drug user who had no qualms about sleeping with her dealer. If that isn't bad enough, I am evidently a woman with loose morals. But let's face the facts; I clearly didn't have any morals if what he says is true. I feel sick.

Groaning, I rest my cheek on my interlocked arms and stare out into the still depths. I haven't gathered the courage to go out and jump into the deep end, so to speak. I've been afraid. But after what I just uncovered, there isn't time to be frightened. It's time I make right the wrongdoings of my past. And I'm starting to realize I have a lot of offenses to reconcile. It's time to finally unearth what happened at this lake and why that red ribbon holds me prisoner night after night.

Without stopping to think or doubt my decision, I turn on my heel and march through the house and out the front door. My bare feet connect with the energy thrumming through the earth, and I take off in a sprint.

The air whips through my hair, cooling down the fire burning within. Even with my eyes closed, I'd know where I'm going, but I keep them open and focus on the tattered swing. A sliver of moonlight lights up the red ribbon, forcing me to run faster and harder, and to forget my fears. The closer I get to it, the easier it becomes to breathe.

Nothing about this makes sense, but I gave up on the notion of my life being normal long ago. I continue running, invisible manacles coming loose and setting me free. A maniacal laugh fills the still night, and although I resemble a madwoman, I couldn't stop myself even if I tried.

My legs burn from the intensity, and my lungs are screaming for a reprieve, but with the mysterious oak so close, I'm forced to push harder. The wind whispers inaudible warnings while the gentle currents of the lake caution me to go back, but when I'm feet away, I come to a sudden stop.

My chest rises and falls as I attempt to catch my breath, scoping out my surroundings and wondering why the air feels so invigorating out here. The grass feels softer, and the earth throbs with a pulsating vitality that kick-starts my heart. I take one step, then two.

From afar, the oak appeared enormous, so you can imagine what it now looks like standing feet away. Peering up, I marvel at its beauty. Flourishing green leaves cover the sturdy branches that are akin to strong arms welcoming me home. The swing is merely a wooden plank attached to the biggest branch of all. Thanks to the thick, weathered rope, which has frayed from the harsh weather and years of enjoyment, this swing appears invincible, like it could stand the test of time.

And I think that it has.

Inhaling, I take note of the sweetened scent emanating from the bright pink flowers that pucker on the lake's edge. I relish in the peacefulness, feeling like no one exists but me. This place is my paradise. This place is my home.

The red ribbon, my forever beacon, beckons me to come closer as it rustles in the gentle breeze. But I need to catch my breath. This is the very reason I'm here, but now that it's within reach—things aren't as scary as I once thought they were. I can do this.

I take my time, measuring my steps because something is almost sacred about this land. Reaching out with trembling fingers, I slowly wrap my hand around the rope. The moment I touch it, an innocence echoes around me. I thought I would recoil, but the complete opposite happens.

I run my fingers up and down the coarse texture, smiling

when the resonance of children's laughter sings to my subconscious. Unable to stall any longer, I caress the ribbon with the tip of my little finger as I would a long-lost friend. The energy surging through me backflips and somersaults in complete joy. There was never a time I was happier than I am right now.

Powerless to stop and with the slowest of movements, I slide my hand down and make a fist around the ribbon. My breath catches at the sight of the red silk contrasting the creaminess of my skin. It's perfect. Fingering the smooth texture, I continue my exploration, my fingers floating along the long strands.

The constant clamor fades into the background as the magnetism of this moment drowns out the noise. Unexpected tears prick my eyes, but something about them is cathartic, so I let them fall. The moonlight chooses this moment to ignite the lake—the perfect partner in crime.

Caught between reality and whatever this world is, the strands slip through my fingers as I round the swing and lower myself onto the wooden seat. A gasp escapes me because this scratchy surface suddenly feels like I'm sitting on a throne.

The view is breathtaking.

The vastness in front of me is a reminder of just how small I am in the grand scheme of things. My problems seem arduous as if my world is slowly coming to an end, but sitting out here alone in the beauty of silence, I know it'll be okay. Life is a beautiful mystery, one that sometimes remains unsolved.

I kick my bare feet into the ground and push myself to take flight. The swing rocks gently as I enjoy the slow ride. I finger the red ribbon, transfixed by the brightness of its color. This is the first time I've felt somewhat at peace, like my mind can take a respite. I may not be any closer to determining why that is, but for a few simple minutes, I let go and just be.

The swing sways with a sluggish speed as my feet connect with the ground each time I push off. My mind has finally found silence, and I continue my ride, staring into the darkness, mesmerized by the moonlight shimmering against the water's edge. The other side, "my side" of the lake, sparks brightly, and I wonder what it would feel like to peer in from that world. Would I still appreciate the beauty as I do now?

Lost in the silence, I fail to realize someone is behind me until he speaks. "Home already?"

"Holy shit!" I screech, my peace coming to an end. I know without looking who stands behind me. And it's probably better I can't see him because I am certain he'd be able to smell my depravity.

If Cayden does know who I am, I don't blame him for denying the truth. After my revelation tonight, it's no wonder he won't own up. I'm clearly trouble.

Groaning, I kick my feet, wishing to go higher. But Cayden takes matters into his own hands—literally.

"Here. Let me push you." He places his hands between my shoulder blades and gently makes good on his word. The moment he touches me, a shiver spreads like wildfire from head to toe.

A silence lingers, but I get the sense he's weighing what to say. He confirms my belief a second later. "How was tonight?"

I muffle my meltdown and shrug. "It was good."

"So good that you're back home already? What happened?"

"Why do you think something happened?" He's right. Something did happen; I just don't know what.

"Because everything about you looks different," he replies, pushing me as I come back down.

I suddenly wish I could take flight and fly away from this mess. But I know Cayden. He won't let this go, and he's currently in control of where I go. So with no other choice, I bare it all.

"I've been trying so hard to remember, but I can't help but wonder what happens when I do. What happens if I'm not the good guy? What happens if there's a reason I can't remember?" I've grappled with these fears since the moment I woke to this nightmare, and the small shreds of evidence I have uncovered point to a disturbing truth.

There is a secret so dark, so sinister, that it appears my body has gone into self-preservation mode and won't allow me to unearth just who I really was.

"Everyone has secrets, Peyton. Sometimes those secrets are there for a reason. They're there to protect. They're there to stop you from breaking one's heart." If I wasn't mid-swing, I would be frozen to the spot because it's evident he can relate. "We're all complicated. That's what being human is. No one is perfect. We all fuck up and make mistakes. But what's important is not the mistakes we make but, rather, how we correct them. That's what defines who we are."

Wow, this is the most he's spoken to me in three days. Maybe this place is cathartic for him too?

"Even you, the cool, calm, and collected Cayden Coachman, make mistakes? I don't believe it," I mock, needing to lighten the mood.

"I've made plenty of mistakes. Ones I will forever make amends for." His tone turns sorrowful, and I remember his admission to Hazel.

"I'll never forget. It'll always be…she'll always be…the biggest regret of my life."

Once again, a shiver passes over me. "Are you cold?" Cayden asks, unaware of my inner thoughts. He grips the rope, gently pulling it back to stop me from swinging. I end up cocooned in his embrace as he wraps an arm around my waist to stop me from falling. He doesn't let go of me or the rope. I'm suspended midair in his arms, but I've never felt more free.

His warm breath brushes against the side of my neck, and as always, I'm basking in the scent of the ocean. Normally, I would be able to mask my feelings, but a tiny moan slips past the floodgates, alerting him to the effect he has on me.

I expect him to let me go, but he doesn't. He draws me back farther as the lines where I end and where he begins blur. The contact shoots an electrical current straight through me, and I shamelessly rub my legs together.

How is it possible that he elicits this response from me every single time? My body has somehow always been in sync with his, and now apparently, so is my breathing. His usual cool demeanor is uncharacteristically shattered when his heaving chest reveals he feels whatever this is too.

I don't know whether to be relieved or frightened beyond belief. This can only lead to trouble.

Without thought, I clutch at the ribbon, its silky texture providing solace, but that soon turns to utmost yearning when Cayden slowly wraps his hand around mine. The warmth of his touch and the heat of his skin has me wetting my lips.

Leaning over my shoulder, he inhales softly, nuzzling my hair and the sweep of my neck. I hold my breath, never wanting more than to turn around and connect with those sinful lips. It would require just the smallest of movements, but nothing is easy about that scenario.

"You smell like a summer storm," he whispers, his heated breath causing goose bumps to prick my skin. "Just moments before the sky is about to open and wreak havoc, the air fills with sweet anticipation because everything is soon to be reborn. You smell just like that. An untainted tempest, washing away the bitterness and replacing it with clarity."

I can relate to every word he says because, isn't that how I felt when I first arrived—that storms clear away our sins and present us with a second chance?

"It's my new perfume," I whisper, attempting to steer the conversation away from wanting to devour him whole.

But he doesn't allow the derailment. Not this time. "No, Peyton"—he lowers his lips, severing my self-control when he places a single kiss on my racing pulse—"it's you."

This isn't normal behavior you'd share with a stranger, someone you only just met, but Cayden isn't a stranger. He never was. Not holding back, I confess my fears. "And who am I, Cayden?"

Not being able to see him makes this easier. It allows me to delve into depths I would usually be too afraid to explore. His grip on me tightens as he skims his fingertips up and down my side. "You're whoever you want to be. Don't you see…you're trying so hard to remember, but most of us, we're trying so hard to forget."

"What are you trying to forget?"

"Everything," he replies, stiffening. "But I don't have the luxury of forgetting." I know he isn't belittling my situation; I understand what he means. After tonight, I don't know if I want to remember who I was. But Cayden wrestles with his demons every single day.

We stay nestled, joined together in innocence as the air weighs heavily with an unspoken promise. Our hands are still linked, the ribbon our anchor. Remembering is suddenly not as important as it once was because I'm making a new memory, one I will never forget.

Eventually, he releases me but guides the swing and supports it, so it comes to a full stop. I miss his warmth, his smell, his connection, instantly. Instead of standing, I stay seated, skimming over the blades of grass with my toes. "I should call Lacey. I kind of bailed on her," I confess guiltily.

"I'm sure Gunn is keeping her company."

My mouth hinges open. "How did you know?"

"I know my sister," he replies confidently. I shouldn't be surprised. "I'll walk you home?" The thought of leaving has me tightening my hold on the rope, but I slowly let go. Now that I've crossed the invisible line, I plan on returning as soon as I can.

Standing, I take a breath, knowing I can no longer hide in the shadows of the night. Turning unhurriedly, I stand still when I finally lock eyes with Cayden. There is no denying his incredible looks, but that's not what I want. What's inside his heart is what sings to me the most. Cayden guards a painful past, but those secrets have shaped him to be the strongest person I know.

I don't realize I'm staring, lost in thought until he saunters forward, and I'm basking in his scent all over again. "Ready?" I nod, snapping from my Cayden bubble, and we begin a slow walk toward my house.

Cayden's hands furl into loose fists before he shoves them into the pockets of his jeans. I sigh because I thought we made progress. "I've ordered a few things for the house. They'll arrive tomorrow. Are you okay with me coming over in the morning?" He's asking permission, which is new. I'm so accustomed to Cayden ordering, not asking.

"Of course. I'll give you my keys and get another set cut tomorrow. It'll just make things easier," I clarify as flashes of tonight's conversation and me questioning my morals arise. I refuse to entertain the notion. I can't. Not with Cayden near.

"All right. That works. As long as you don't mind me coming over unannounced. I may need to let myself in while you're at work. Delivery guys come at all hours." His innocent comment has me falling quiet, and Cayden senses my retreat. "I'll make sure I call first then."

"No, it's not that." I shake my head as he has misunderstood my retreat. "I don't even know if I'll be returning to work. Well, not the job I was doing before this all started."

"And what was that?" he asks, staring straight ahead.

"I was a marketing manager." He nods, but the bright moonlight highlights his thoughts because they're mine too. "I couldn't think of anything worse. The thought of being confined to a desk, of rubbing shoulders with corporate players with no soul makes my stomach turn."

"Is there anything else you'd like to do instead?"

Pondering his question, I nod self-consciously. "Yes. I think…I think I'd like to do something that involves drawing." I'm waiting for a snicker, for a "go get a real job," but I get neither.

"Like an artist?"

I peer over at him, and he smiles, meeting my eyes. "Yeah."

"Are you any good?"

I can't help but laugh. "Honestly, I don't know. I think I am. I'm assuming the notepad I found in my lap with a sketch of this"—I sweep my hands outward toward our backdrop—"was done by me. If it was, then yes, I am damn good."

Cayden smirks at my confidence. "Then what's stopping you?"

My shoulders sag as I feel like a complete chicken. "Me. Stella…my mom," I explain, realizing I still can't refer to her as my parent.

His grin soon turns into a sour scowl. "I don't think she'd be happy with any profession you chose. The operative word there being choose, as in your choice and not hers."

Remembering the way she treated him when they first met, I sigh, embarrassed and appalled. "I'm sorry about the way she treated you. Don't take offense. She treats everyone that way. Even her husband."

Cayden shakes his head. "I didn't. I'm used to it." I raise a curious brow. "This side of the lake, remember?" he clarifies while my mouth forms an O in understanding.

"Seems ridiculous."

"It *is* ridiculous," he counters, tonguing his upper lip. "But that's the difference between my world and yours."

"It isn't my world," I state, hating that he sees this absurd distinction between us. "I may have been born into it, but that doesn't mean I went along with their barbaric ways." When he remains silent, I add, "Well, I hope I didn't."

My comment has the desired effect as a grin tugs at his full lips. "You could always ask Stella. Or your siblings, if you have any."

A laugh bursts from me, but it's not a happy sound. "I *have* asked Stella. Our argument the entire ride down here is an indication of what our conversations are usually like. And as for my siblings—" I pause, attempting to find the right words. "They're either afraid of her, or maybe they're afraid of me. The jury is still out on that one." I'm not looking for sympathy because it's the truth.

The moment I entered a room, they'd all scatter like mice. They all had somewhere else to be. Everyone except Isla. She knows more than she's letting on, but Stella made sure we were never alone for too long.

Only when I taste a sharp metallic taste do I realize I've bitten my lip hard enough to draw blood. "Hey." Cayden grips my bicep, coaxing me to a stop as he spins me to face him. "This will all come together. I promise." When I rivet my attention to the ground, he lifts my chin with two fingers. I expect him to release me, but he doesn't. Instead, he gently thumbs my bottom lip until it pops free.

Each touch sends me into a frenzy, and they just seem to be getting worse. I am so screwed. "I wouldn't be so sure," I state, hoping the waver in my voice doesn't reveal my utter delight that he's touching me yet again. He remains transfixed on my mouth as he traces a line from the middle of my bottom lip down my chin. He rubs over the small cleft before eventually pulling away.

It takes every ounce of self-control I possess not to pounce on him and sample if he tastes as good as he smells. As usual, I'm lost in a Cayden bubble, and it's not until his eyes narrow that I realize he's listening for something. I don't know what until I hear the clear sound of a branch snapping in the distance.

Goose bumps coat my skin once again, but this time, they're not the good kind.

Peering up at Cayden, it's clear he's attempting to wade through the darkness to make sense of any shape or sound. "I- is someone there?" I question, not game enough to look over my shoulder. He's quiet, still scanning our surroundings. The distinct feeling of being watched swarms me for the second time tonight. "Cayden?"

"Let's go inside," he replies, not answering my question. Just as I'm about to ask him again, I'm deprived of all air when he slips his hand in mine. I follow as he leads me toward the house.

We briskly march up my front steps. Cayden glances over his shoulder, and he's making me nervous. When I turn the handle and my front door squeaks open, he clucks his tongue. "Peyton. I told you to lock your doors."

On most occasions, I would tell him to calm down. I'd also remind him that I don't like being told what to do. But not tonight. Something sinister lingers in the air. "I know. I will. Promise." He seems satisfied with my pledge, especially when I hold up three fingers—Scout salute style.

"I'll see you in the morning."

"Okay. Feel free to make me pancakes." As usual, I hide behind my shield of humor because the constant undercurrent of awkwardness heightens. But instead of running away as I've done in the past, I embrace it. "Good night, Cayden." Before he has a chance to shy away, it's my turn to touch him, and I do—with my lips.

Standing on tippy-toes, I gently place my hand on one cheek, his scruff softer than anything I've ever felt before. The blue to his eyes spark bright in panic and something else, but I use that adrenaline rush to quickly smash my lips to the other cheek. I'm afraid he'll pull away; hence, the reason I captured him with my palm. But he does the complete opposite. He turns into my touch. He surrenders. To me.

Being this close to him, I want to lather myself in his signature fragrance. His flesh is hot to the touch, it almost burns me, but it speaks to the fire burning inside me. A kiss fills the silence when words are not enough, but this, right here, is more than enough.

Cayden hums, and my ears are close to climaxing. I need to leave. Committing this moment to memory, I swiftly break our connection and dive into the safety of my home. Locking the door, I lean against it to catch my breath. The butterflies have stolen my air.

Once I've calmed, I brush the hair from my flushed cheeks and decide to crash because I am suddenly exhausted beyond belief. As I take a step forward, the presence of a solid shadow on my porch alerts me to the fact that Cayden is still there.

The chance to see him once more is too tempting to let

pass, so I tiptoe to the window, hoping the lace curtain veils me from his view. But when I see him staring off into the distance, his attention riveted on the lake with his hand pressed to his cheek, the one I just kissed, I know his thoughts are elsewhere.

I'd give a penny for those thoughts because whatever they are…they take my breath away yet again.

EIGHT

I wake to the smell of pancakes, which has me second-guessing if I'm actually dreaming. Because why would the delicious buttery scent of pancakes be wafting through my home?

My confusion is most pronounced when I first wake, so I'm not a morning person. It takes me a few seconds to remember where I am and, most frightening, who I am. But this morning is different, clearer. And I know that has everything to do with last night.

I may not remember a great deal, but I'll never forget the look on Cayden's face as his stone walls finally crumbled. Swathed in quietude, he peered at the lake with a hand pressed to his recently kissed cheek. The sight made me feel at peace.

Cayden keeps his cards close to his chest, but on the rarest of occasions, when he lowers his guard and allows me in, what

I see rouses me in ways I can't explain. When my cell chimes on the nightstand, I realize I *am* awake, which means someone is making me breakfast. I can't wipe the smile clean.

Reaching for my phone, I don't bother to look at the screen and answer with a vigorous, "Hello." My mood soon sours when the caller speaks.

"Oh, you're awake? I thought you'd be unconscious after last night."

I take a moment to gather my thoughts. "Then why did you bother calling?"

Silence. A short, uncomfortable clearing of a throat. A small win for me.

"Because regardless of the decisions you make and the company you insist on keeping, I am your mother, and I love you."

Barely holding back my retch, I sigh because she doesn't need to spell it out. Stella is having me followed, which explains why I've constantly been looking over my shoulder. I should be surprised, but sadly, I'm not. "Call off your watchdog. I moved here for a sense of normalcy. That's hard to do when you've hired someone to lurk in the shadows, ready to report everything back to you. If you want to know something, all you have to do is ask."

"What would be the point? You don't listen to me anyway." She lets out a tiny sniffle, and I raise my eyes to the heavens. "Peyton, I know you can't remember...but, sweetheart, going to places in *that* part of town will only lead to trouble."

"I think you mean embarrassment for the Lane name. If anyone saw me venturing over to the dark side, God forbid, your membership to the country club would be revoked." Even though my comment is dripping with sarcasm, that doesn't deter Stella in the slightest.

"Why do you insist on hurting me?"

"This may come as a surprise, but my world does not revolve around you. Seeing as no one will tell me the truth, I have no other choice but to search for it myself. So I will come and go as I please." Rant over.

Stella is quiet, which is never a good sign. She can deny it all she wants, but I know she's picking and choosing what information she shares with me. She's hoping the things she doesn't want me to uncover, like my talent for drawing, will remain lost in a past I'll never remember.

"Come over for dinner next Saturday."

"Excuse me?" I can't keep the surprise from my tone because it's the last thing I expected her to say, especially after the earful I just served.

"I have a surprise for you. I was going to wait until you were ready, but it appears that is no longer an option. I'll invite your brothers and sisters. I'll see you then." She doesn't give me time to reply before she hangs up, making it clear this isn't negotiable.

Long after she ends the call, I sit still, wondering what exactly this surprise might be. An ominous heaviness lays in my chest as I can't help but think that any surprise from Stella can't be good.

The rattling of dishes in the kitchen reminds me that someone, who I hope is Cayden, is making me breakfast. Kicking off my blankets, I stand, wondering if I should put on a robe since my sleepwear doesn't leave much to the imagination.

He's seen me in a lot less, but I decide to slip into a pair of shorts and a tank. Even though it's early, the summer sun is already at a punishing degree. I'm in for a hot, restless few days, thanks to no A/C.

Throwing back my messy waves into a high bun after brushing my teeth, I walk into the kitchen but come to a sudden stop in the doorway at the sight I'm greeted with. Cayden is indeed the one responsible for the aroma drifting through my home, but all that sweetness pales compared to the fact he's not wearing a shirt while he's cooking me pancakes.

He hums a tune under his breath as he's working the stove like a whiz. When he shifts slightly to reach for the golden batter in the glass mixing bowl, he exposes his flank, adding to the appeal that is Cayden Coachman.

An intricate tattoo runs down his side, but there is no mistaking the image is that of a tree. An oak tree. He turns too quickly for me to examine it further, but my feet act of their own accord as I advance, desperate for a closer look.

My heavy footsteps alert Cayden of my arrival, and he looks over his shoulder. "Morning. I hope you don't mind." He holds up the silver utensil he's using to flip the pancakes with a smile. When he sees me moving toward him like a starved zombie—but instead of brains, I want answers—he cocks an eyebrow in confusion.

His expression stops me in my tracks because Cayden's being nice and letting down his impenetrable guard. If I continue beating a dead horse, these acts of kindness will stop, and after last night and now this morning, I feel like we've moved forward. And this feels nice. It feels normal.

So what, I reason with myself, *if he has a tattoo of a tree.* I'm sure a thousand other people do too. Just because it holds sentimental meaning to me doesn't mean it does to him. I need to chill the fuck out and eat my damn pancakes.

Pushing aside my insanity, I shake my head once. "Mind? Are you kidding me? If you're not careful, I'll be asking you to make me a roast too." Standing on tippy-toes to look over his broad shoulders, I can't stop the laugh which escapes me. "Are we expecting company? Like the whole neighborhood, maybe?" The mountain of pancakes on the counter is enough to feed a small army.

A lopsided grin lights up his handsome face. "I didn't know how hungry you'd be. And besides, it's force of habit, I suppose." There is no need for him to explain. He *is* accustomed to feeding a small army—his army.

"You won't ever hear me complaining when food is involved. Can I help?"

"You can grab a couple of plates. And whatever toppings you want."

Easy. I can do that.

He turns back around to tend to his sizzling creation while I stand on tippy-toes to reach into the cupboard. I grab the plates and then also pull out two mugs as he's brewed a fresh pot of coffee. We work in unison, respecting one another's space until we both turn around at the same time.

I take a moment. Actually, I need two.

He's standing before me, the absolute perfection of his chest stopping me in my tracks. I knew he was gifted in the muscle department, but holy shit, his muscles have muscles. But what transfixes me the most is that Cayden Coachman has scruff.

Dark hair is sprinkled between his firm pecs, leading downward like an arrow to his rock-hard abs. I could bounce pennies off those babies. The hair appears soft and not at all coarse. It's fine enough to see his tanned skin beneath it but thick enough to run my fingers through it.

My hormones get punched with another dose of hotness when my gaze lowers and I see that his jeans sit low enough to reveal the scruff leads down into the unknown. My cheeks instantly blister when I realize the top button is undone, emphasizing his glorious V.

Who knew? I like a man with hair. That, combined with the tattoo fanning his flank, leaves me a slobbering fool.

The scenery utterly engrosses me, but I quickly raise my eyes when I notice his chest ripple. He's exhaled deeply, reminding me that I am openly staring and doing a poor job of masking my feelings. "You really should put on a shirt. You're flammable with all that…fluff." I sweep my finger downward, unintentionally landing on his groin.

Oh my God, I sound like a freaking idiot, but it's better than voicing the perverse thoughts happily bouncing around my head. Cayden smirks, which does absolutely nothing to help my lewdness. He clearly took his shirt off because it's hotter than hell in here. However, when I see his delicious dimples of Venus, I may reconsider getting a new air-conditioning unit.

"Eat," he orders, using his utensil to point at the pile of pancakes. That sounds like a brilliant idea. Stuffing my mouth full will prevent the nonsense from spilling out.

Passing him the plates, I go to work on filling our mugs. The coffee smells delicious. The bitterness is exactly how I like it. A small blue cooler sits in the corner of the room, and when Cayden notices me gazing at it, he explains. "That's for you. I'm pretty sure that refrigerator is on its last leg." To confirm his claim, the rusted beast whines before spluttering out a cough.

I smile in gratitude, suddenly interested in what he's brought over.

Without thought, I pass him the coffee, and just as flippantly, he accepts. However, what we both didn't count on was that the mere brushing of our thumbs would leave us breathless. Thankfully, he has a hold on the mug because I yank my hand away like it's just been burned.

Cayden's chest begins to swell as he inhales and exhales heavily, which only brings attention to his sculpted chest and does not help my predicament in the slightest. I turn around, never more thankful for a distraction. I drop to a crouch and open the lid. He's brought over every topping one could want to decorate their pancakes with, but a simple bag of lemons is what holds me captive.

"See anything you like?"

The bright yellow of the ripe flesh has me wetting my lips as I can taste the zesty tang on my tongue. A bag of sugar on the counter is the next thing my eyes feast on. Reaching for both, I come to a stand with the ingredients in my hands. Cayden's brow furrows, and I wonder why.

"Thank you for bringing all that over, but for some reason, these two things seem like a match made in pancake heaven." He nods slowly, his look of bewilderment disappearing as quickly as it appeared.

He clears his throat before lumping a stack of pancakes on a plate. They smell delicious, and my stomach rumbles in delight. I hunt through the cupboard for the grater Lacey insisted I buy, which I am now thankful for, and go to work grating the rind from the lemon. Once it's skinned, I slice it in half, attempting to keep my cool under Cayden's scrutiny.

When he passes me the plate, it's clear we are both keeping our distance. Once again, we work in harmony as I spoon a dollop of butter on the top pancake, then watch hungrily as it melts and runs down the sides. Next, I squeeze the lemons, the citrus aroma mingling with the buttermilk pancakes and Cayden's signature fragrance. It's sensory overload, and I lick my lips.

Once they're coated in lemon juice, I open the sugar and dust my creation, the covering of white reminding me of a snowy winter morning. I'm transfixed by the sight, which is absurd. It's just breakfast. But when the heat from Cayden's flesh warms mine, I know nothing is simple about this scenario.

"Don't forget the rind. It's the best part." I watch mutely as he reaches across my immobile body and scoops up a pinch of the peel. He doesn't meet my eyes. It's like he's afraid to see if this connection runs both ways, but it does. It has from the moment we first met.

His long fingers work with precision as he sprinkles the final touch on my breakfast. The splash of yellow reminds me of sunshine on a hot summer's day, the perfect contrast to the white. A yin to its yang.

Reaching for the fork, I sever a large portion and forget

being ladylike as I stuff the entire helping into my mouth. The moment the tart citrus, the sweet sugar, and the golden butter hits my tongue, my mouth has a mini-orgasm, and I can't help but vocalize it.

"Yum," I groan, closing my eyes and savoring the taste. I thankfully remember to chew with my mouth closed, which is a miracle as my mouth is having a party and throwing social etiquette to the wind. Cayden's chuckles alert me to my pancake PDA, and my cheeks instantly heat. "You can cook me pancakes any day," I say from behind my hand as I continue chewing.

"Only if you promise to make that face when I do," he counters, which only has me blushing further. I continue to stuff my mouth in fear I'll say something I'll regret.

He shakes his head, grinning as he coats his pancakes with butter and syrup. It appears we both like our breakfast simple, but the same can't be said for the tension bouncing between us. We eat in silence, but the air is heavy with unspoken promises.

Cayden doesn't shy away from watching me, and although my cheeks must resemble tomatoes from the heat I feel in them, I do the same. Seeing as I have no table or chairs yet, we eat standing in my kitchen, cloaked in whatever this feeling is.

The hypnotic movement of his Adam's apple as he sips his coffee mesmerizes me. Of course, my eyes descend to his delectable chest and then land on his ribs. "I like your tattoo," I say, shattering the silence.

Cayden absentmindedly rubs over the ink. "Thanks." I wait for him to share the reason behind it, but he remains tight-lipped. Just as I'm about to press, he says, "So I've been thinking." I gulp. "You said you're good at drawing, and, well…"

Cayden Coachman is at a loss for words—wow, now I've seen it all.

He runs his fingers through his snarled hair, leaving a sexy faux-hawk in its wake. "How would you feel about working… with me?" I blink, stunned as I was not expecting those words to leave his lips. He mistakes my silence for aversion, though. "Or not. It's just—"

But I interrupt him. "I'm listening."

His relief is clear, which leaves me even more curious. "My main architect broke her arm, and I was wondering how'd you feel working with her to sketch what she can't. She would give you complete guidance." He quickly puts my mind at ease as I was going to remind him that I didn't have any experience. I don't even know if that sketch was a one-off, seeing as I haven't drawn anything since.

But the offer is appealing. The thought of starting fresh in a field that sounds fun and rewarding, and not to mention it's a job I think I'd actually enjoy, has me nodding animatedly. "What's the pay like?" I quip because I've already made my decision. I don't care what it pays. I'm in. But I can't give in so easily. My pride won't allow it.

"It's negotiable," he playfully replies, leaning against the counter, arms folded, which brings my attention back to the fact that he's topless in my kitchen.

I was doing so well with focusing on my job opportunities until he had to flaunt his chest my way. A thought suddenly occurs to me, which has me second-guessing my eagerness to accept Cayden's offer. Working with him means seeing him every day, which means I can count on reliving these moments of awkwardness daily.

"Change of heart?" There is a genuine curiosity in his voice. Is he testing me? Is that what this is?

Game on.

Pulling back my shoulders, I purse my lips, faking aloofness. "Not on your life. When do I start?"

Cayden accepts my challenge, the thrill exciting him as dark mischief readily replaces the blue in his eyes. "As soon as you can."

The fact that I don't have a car might prove a problem. "Can I walk there?"

He peers at me over the rim of his cup as he swallows down his coffee. "Not really. It's about a twenty-minute drive."

"I'll make sure to set my alarm early then." This is happening. I don't care that I'll probably swelter in the summer sun. I want this job, feet be damned.

Cayden smirks—always smirking—as he places his mug on the counter. He leans over until we're a hair's breadth away from touching. "Trying to impress the boss already?"

Technically, he *is* my boss, but there is no way I'm going to change my attitude and obey a word he says. Where's the fun in that? "The boss knows I'm not a kiss ass. In fact, I think he likes that I can hold my own."

Cayden nods, tonguing his upper lip. "Yes, he does." Digging into his back pocket, he produces a single key hanging off a silver keychain. "I don't doubt your independence, and I'm not questioning if you can make it to work on your own or not, but here, take my truck." I am about to object, but he silences me as he reaches for my hand. Unfurling my protesting fingers, he places the key into my palm. "I don't want you late on your first day." This is clearly not open for discussion.

Curling my fingers around his, I squeeze gently, ignoring the butterflies which take flight. "Thank you. It's only short term."

"I know," he replies, his voice hoarse. We're openly holding hands. Who knew holding someone's hand could be this exhilarating? But this feeling has nothing to do with the action and everything to do with the person.

"Wow, it seems today is full of surprises." That wasn't supposed to be voiced aloud, but it's anarchy within my mind as I'm flabbergasted that Cayden hasn't pulled his hand away.

He does the complete opposite and tightens his hold. "Why's that?"

With breakfast long forgotten, I decide to share the details of my phone call. "Stella called me this morning."

"Oh?"

"She invited me to dinner next Saturday. Apparently, she has a surprise for me." I shudder at the thought.

"A surprise?" he asks, his expression akin to mine. "She didn't say what?"

I shake my head. "No, but a surprise from Stella can't be good. She's the type of mom who, to surprise her child, would hire a clown for their birthday party. What type of sicko would surprise their child with a freaking clown? Deranged sociopaths, that's who."

Cayden's lips twitch, but I'm serious. Nothing good can come from this surprise. I can feel it in my bones. "Lucky you have my truck then." He squeezes my hand before eventually letting go. "You can leave whenever you feel uncomfortable."

"Thank you. I owe you. For everything," I add. He's just offered me a job and his truck in the span of a minute.

But once again, he amazes me when reaches out to brush away a stray strand of hair that has slipped free. "You don't owe me anything. Just come back home." His finger lingers, tracing along the apple of my cheek. I don't know when we crossed this line, but I'm not about to question it because this is the first time in forever I have felt rooted with both feet in this world.

"I promise." The fact that he has referred to this house as my home warms me beyond belief because I have felt like an outsider for so long.

My assurance seems to appease whatever worries he has. "Good. Now, let's finish breakfast. I have a feeling you'll need your strength."

"Why?" I drag out the Y, suddenly nervous.

"Because I have a few things I need to take care of at the office. Want to come with me? I could introduce you to Penny."

"But it's Saturday," I counter.

"I know, but this new project, the worksite you saw in town, is big, and time isn't on our side. My staff is just as eager as I am to see the back of it, and we're working around the clock to make that happen. So when Penny broke her arm, it goes without saying that we were all screwed. But now…I have you."

When he pins me with those eyes, I can't say no. And besides, the thought of starting a new job is exciting beyond words. "Yes, you do." I mean that in more ways than one. "Okay, I'm in."

His happiness is unmistakable, which has me smiling like

an idiot.

"I just have to shower. I wouldn't want to turn up on my first day looking like this." I sweep my hand downward. It was supposed to be a joke, but when Cayden licks his full upper lip, I suddenly wish I'd kept my mouth shut.

"You look fine to me."

I don't feel fine. Quite frankly, I'm anything but fine. However, I'll be damned if I let him know that. "Well, in that case..." I toss back my coffee, hinting I'm ready to leave whenever he's done. Just as I place my mug into the sink, he grips my wrist with a grin.

"Go get dressed." He rubs his thumb over my thrashing pulse.

Pouting, I feign innocence. "But you said—"

"Go," he interrupts, shaking his head at my brashness. "I'll wait for the delivery guys. They should be here any minute."

Sighing, I blow the hair from my cheeks dramatically. "Okay, boss."

I'm expecting Cayden to let me go, but he does the complete opposite. He tightens his hold. "Make sure you wear something"—my flesh chars when his gaze skims down my body—"more," he settles on before finally letting me go.

I stagger backward, the intensity of his look almost bowling me over.

His choice of words sings to my out-of-control fever. *More.* That's exactly how I feel. And what I want. *More.*

But now, what I need *more* of is a cold shower.

Afraid of what I'll say if I attempt a wisecrack, I instead steal Cayden's mug with a grin. He watches me, thoroughly amused as I sip my stolen coffee and coolly walk out of the kitchen.

Distracting myself, I hunt through my wardrobe, wondering what to wear. Now that I've culled my closet, I'm a little limited with my choices, but a striking peacock-colored summer dress catches my eye. Cayden did say more, and this is more...so much more.

I shower in record time, unsure if my excitement is due to the fact that I'll be spending the day with Cayden or if it's because I'm starting a new job. I decide to embrace both possibilities because each option is as exciting as the other.

Once my hair is dry, I decide to knot it into a low chignon. Reaching for the blue ribbon off my dresser, I fasten it tightly around the bun. As I peer at my reflection in the mirror, I suddenly wish the ribbon was red. But I shake aside such thoughts because today is about starting new.

My makeup is light as the dress is a statement on its own. I slip into a pair of sandals, then add a spritz of my favorite honeysuckle perfume to my wrists. Taking one last look at myself in the mirror, I almost don't recognize who I see. This person looks like me, but I've not seen the smile she's wearing before. She looks happy.

Not wanting to jinx myself, I stuff all the things I might need, including my laptop, into a bag and make my way down the hallway. The hem of my flowy dress floats behind me, adding to the sensation of taking flight and being free.

"Thanks, I appreciate it," I hear Cayden say to whom I'm assuming is a delivery guy. "Make sure you drop off the tiles tomorrow."

"It appears there really is no rest for the wicked," I quip as

I round the corner, seeing Cayden and a young deliveryman. "Monday will be fine." The stranger's eyes widen in appreciation of what he sees, and Cayden inhales sharply. I'm quietly saddened he's no longer topless.

Riling him up shouldn't give me this much satisfaction, but it does. "I believe this is something more," I casually say, running my palms over the soft material of my dress.

"It's something," Cayden replies, clearly affected. "I'll see you tomorrow." Cayden makes a point to look at the deliveryman, who is still gawking my way.

He registers a moment later, turning a beet red. "Oh, right. Yes, of course. I'll see you then."

Once the delivery guy leaves, I see my living room is now home to endless building supplies. Cayden mentioned tiles, so I'm guessing we'll be pulling the tiles from the bathroom tomorrow. But that's tomorrow because today, I have a new adventure to focus on.

"Are you ready to go?" Cayden shakes his head, appearing to need the mental slap.

"Sure. Ready when you are." He rocks back on his heels, hands digging deep into his pockets, and I don't realize why until he grins. "You have my keys," he explains when I stop with the ogling and get my head back in the game.

"Shit, I do. Sorry." With fumbling fingers, I split open my bag, frantically searching for the keychain. "I know they're in here somewhere." After hunting through my possessions and vowing to bring order to future chaos, I finally find them. "A-ha!" I exclaim, waving them in triumph.

Just as I'm about to toss them at Cayden, he says, "By this

rate, we should make it by tomorrow." He looks down at his imaginary watch while I chuckle. "C'mon then." Only now do I realize he wants me to drive.

"You're not driving?"

He folds his arms over his chest and shakes his head. "Let's see how you handle her."

"That sounds like a challenge." In response, he shrugs with a playful smirk.

Once I finally manage to get my fingers to work, thanks to Cayden's loitering, I lock up, and we make our way to his house. The closer we get to his truck, the more nervous I become. I knew she was a beast, but up close, she's intimidating, to say the least. But I refuse to allow my apprehension to show.

Using the control, I deactivate the alarm and unlock the doors. So far, so good. Cayden rounds the hood in silence, but if that smile is anything to go by, he so knows I'm shitting myself. His smugness spurs me on, so opening the door, I place my foot on the step and climb inside.

Taking a calming breath, I place my hands on the wheel and acquaint myself to the leather feel. Cayden reads my uneasiness, and I decide to tell him why seeing as I'm not in this truck alone. "I wanted you to know…I haven't driven since the night…of my accident."

"Oh, shit." His humor soon fades. "I'm sorry. I didn't think."

But I don't want him apologizing. That's not the reason I told him. "It's okay. I wanted to tell you in case you're having second thoughts." I wouldn't blame him if he was.

"Second thoughts?"

"Yes. I don't even know if I'm any good." Expressing my

concerns aloud should make me feel weak, yet I feel empowered that I'm trying. But his silence has me conjuring up the worst.

Just when I'm about to swap places with him, he surprises me—in a good way. Leaning across the middle console, he reaches across me, bathing me in his confidence while I forget to breathe.

My breasts are embarrassingly close to his face, but he's focused on the task at hand, and that's buckling me in. "You've got this. Take your time. I'm here." Once the seat belt clicks into place, he turns his chin to peer up at me. His words reflect nothing but sincerity, and his faith in me is the confidence boost I needed.

"T-thanks." I fumble over my words, his proximity short-circuiting my brain. With the grace of a bird of prey spreading its wings and taking flight, he leisurely pulls away and settles back into his seat.

I can do this, I repeat to myself over and over. Starting over entails taking risks and being free. I place the key into the ignition, yelping when the engine roars to life.

Cayden laughs hoarsely at my response.

"Wow." I run my hands over the wheel, marveling when I give her a little gas. I try out all the buttons and levers, familiarizing myself with what does what.

I take a minute to appreciate this moment. I'm back in a vehicle when I wondered if I'd ever drive again. Not only that, but I'm driving to my new job. So much has happened in four short days. But deep down, I knew that was inevitable by coming here.

"I'm ready," I declare, a swell of excitement taking over.

"The big pedal is the accelerator, right?" Cayden sits taller, a flicker of nerves passing over him while I wink. "Hold on." And he does just that when I put the car into gear and edge my way out of his driveway.

An excited shrill escapes me because I can't believe I am doing this. I'm actually driving.

"Take a right up ahead," Cayden directs calmly.

Even though I hit the wipers instead of the turn signal, I get the hang of it soon enough. "I can't believe it," I express aloud, never taking my eyes off the road. "Six months ago, the thought of getting behind the wheel had me breaking out into a cold sweat. But here I am." I may be driving slower than a snail, but I'm driving nonetheless.

"Here you are…kicking ass. Good for you. But I never doubted it."

I swallow. "You didn't?"

He's quiet, and just when I'm tempted to risk a quick glance his way, he says, "You're too stubborn not to fight for what you want. Just how you fought Stella coming here. When your mind is made up, it seems there isn't much anyone can do to change it."

I shrug, curling my lip in thought. He's right. "Thanks."

"Anytime," he replies playfully.

We ride the rest of the way in silence, and a small part of me is thankful Cayden didn't take the backroads like our Uber driver did. Riding those streets as a passenger was bad enough. I don't know how I'd actually navigate them.

When we pull off the highway and take a left into a busier part of town, Cayden points at a glass building on the corner.

"It's just up ahead."

The building he refers to is modern and chic. I follow the signs to the parking garage out back. It's small, but I find one reserved for employees of Coachman Constructions. I kill the engine, unable to keep the smile from my face. That was exhilarating.

"You okay?" Cayden asks as he unbuckles his belt.

"More than okay," I reply. "I can't believe that came so naturally to me. It appears I haven't forgotten everything." I turn in my seat to look at him and am surprised to see he looks as happy as I feel. I wouldn't want to share this with anyone else, and without thinking, I reach for his hand. "Thank you."

He peers down at our union, a bittersweet solace to his stare. "This is all you." His touch is comforting and reassuring. So are his words. "Ready?"

I look at the building in front of me and nod. "Yes. Let's do this." He squeezes my hand, then lets go. When Cayden reaches for my bag and shoulders it, I can't help but laugh. He better be careful—I could get used to this chivalry.

We exit the truck, and I take in my surroundings. The neighborhood is quaint but with a modern touch. I wonder just how much of this town Cayden has had a hand in. He hunts through his pocket for the keys to the back door.

When he opens the glass door and gestures for me to enter first, a giddy ball of excitement stirs within. My wedged sandals pad softly against the carpet as I walk the long hallway. I have no idea where I'm going, but when I reach the end of the corridor and see an enormous open workspace, I know I'm headed the right way.

There are two levels. The upper appears to be meeting rooms encased in glass, and there is a large room down at the end of the hall, which I'm guessing is Cayden's office. I return my attention to the lower floor, relishing in the hustle and bustle of what appears to be a very pleasant work environment.

The staff are standing around desks, discussing whatever project they're working on with their colleagues. I see an abundance of plans strewn across the long tables and a young woman drawing on her computer with some fancy-looking pen. I have a lot to learn.

A pretty brunette whose arm is in a plaster cast sees us first. The huge smile that lights up her face reveals she's happy to see us. Well, Cayden. "Coach!" she yells, waving her non-injured arm.

"Penny, I have a surprise for you." Cayden gently guides me out into the open by the elbow, coaxing me to meet my new partner in crime. "Penny, meet Peyton. Your new right-handed man—literally. Peyton"—he skims his hand up my arm, coming to rest on my bicep—"this is Penny."

I instantly like Penny. Her bright orange tights and blue pinafore dress covered in cats reveal she's a little quirky. I think we'll get along just fine. "Hi, Penny. It's so nice to meet you." I go to shake her hand but laugh when she quickly offers her non-plastered arm. "Boss man over here"—I hook my thumb over my shoulder—"has paired us up. But I want to warn you, I have no experience, like none when it comes to this field of work."

"It's fine. There isn't much to it," she quips while Cayden dramatically clutches his chest over his heart.

"I'll remember that when you complain about what a slave

driver I am."

"He's such a killjoy," she whispers loudly from behind her hand. A giggle escapes me.

"Okay. I'm clearly not needed," he teases. "Penn, can you show Peyton around? I have a few calls to make."

"No problem, boss." She mock salutes, and Cayden lifts his eyes to the ceiling. I like her even more.

He turns to me, and my heart flutters. "Have a good day. If you need me, my office is just upstairs." I appreciate the fact that he isn't lingering. He knows I need to do this on my own.

"Thank you." I want to reach out and hug him for giving me this opportunity, but that would cross a professional line. So instead, I extend my fist. He peers down at it while I chuckle.

"You'll fit in here just fine." He fist-bumps me with a drop-dead gorgeous grin. I notice a couple of young women looking our way, one in particular who looks about ready to jump over her desk and tackle me to the ground.

Heads turn when he makes his way to his office, but the thing about Cayden is that he doesn't even seem to notice the effect he has on people. He controls any room he enters, and being here, in a room full of his peers, confirms it. I'm losing an uphill battle.

"Ironic, isn't it?"

"What is?" I vaguely reply, my eyes still glued to Cayden's broad back.

"That someone who is such a pain in the ass has such a nice ass."

Penny's comment is exactly what I needed to hear to get my head back in the game. I can't stop my snort and loud cackle.

Cayden turns over his shoulder, untroubled that he's looking at me so openly. I would usually shy away but not now. I feel all woman as a lopsided grin tugs at his lips because I was the one who elicited such a response from him.

The woman who I noticed earlier giving me serious stink eye saunters over to Cayden, touching his forearm as she whispers something into his ear. Her closeness has him severing our connection. I immediately dislike her. The fact that she's wearing a tight white dress with a black thong adds to the loathing.

"That's Darla," Penny says, following my line of sight. The way she pronounces her name, it's safe to assume she doesn't like her either. "She's Coach's personal assistant. Although we all know she'd rather be something else."

My anger spikes as I watch her flick her long blonde hair over her slender shoulder. She's clearly flirting, and she's clearly my new archnemesis. "And what would Coach rather?"

I leave crescent moon indentions in my palms as I watch Darla and Cayden together. "Come on, I'll show you around."

Unable to stomach the sight of Darla fawning a second longer, I swallow past the lump in my throat and follow Penny, thankful she takes the long way around.

NINE

"**P**eyton, this is good. Like really good," Penny says, holding up the scribble I spent the past six hours on.

After Penny took me on the grand tour, she showed me to our desk, where we've remained. I ensured I was head down, butt up because the sight of Darla flirting with Cayden is still singed into my brain, and I'm not keen for a repeat performance.

This shouldn't get to me, but it does. A fierce wave of possession rolled over me, and all I could envision was ripping out Darla's red fingernails, one by one. But Cayden gave me this job to work, and work I did. I even surprised myself with how well I took to Penny's instructions.

I thought I'd be lost in translation, but I have never felt more in my element than I am right now. It could just be because Penny is a good teacher, but as I look at the sketch she holds up proudly, I know it's a joint effort.

"Are you sure you didn't go to Yale or something?" she gushes, shaking her head in awe. I told her briefly about my amnesia, but I spared her the gory details. I refuse to taint this workplace with my past. "We have to go out and celebrate."

"We do?" I ask, arching a brow.

"Damn straight we do." She thumps her cast playfully on the table to stress her point.

"We're going out?" says a voice behind me. Turning in my swivel chair, I see a handsome man packing up his desk. He looks smart yet casual in white trousers, a navy button-down shirt, and a light blue blazer. As he stuffs sketches into his tan leather briefcase, I figure he's an architect too.

"Yes, Ronnie, Peyton, and I are going out. I don't remember inviting you, though," Penny says, tongue in cheek.

"But who's going to hold your hair back after one too many gin and tonics?" Ronnie jokes, fastening the loops on his bag.

"Don't let this cast fool you." Penny holds up her arm while I bite back my smile, enjoying their banter.

Ronnie reaches across the space between us, extending his hand. "I'm Ronnie."

"Peyton." We shake, and he holds my hand a little longer than needed. "It's nice to meet you."

"Likewise. So where are you girls headed?"

I look up at Penny and shrug. "I don't know. I'm new to town…"

Ronnie's eyes light up, and Penny claps excitedly. "Are you thinking what I'm thinking?" Ronnie nods, and I suddenly get the sense this isn't up for negotiation.

I was thinking of going home and doing some serious cramming on everything there is to know about architecture. I really enjoyed today, and I figure the more I know, the better it'll be for me in the long run if I want to make this a full-time gig.

But when Cayden descends the stairs with Darla trailing behind, I suddenly feel like a martini. Or two. Ronnie notices me staring and scoffs when he sees Cayden. I don't know why, but I get the sense Cayden's charm is lost on him. "So you ready to have your world blown?" Ronnie says when Cayden is in earshot.

My cheeks instantly flush because I can't deny the innuendo behind his words. Cayden is by my side in a heartbeat. "Anyone would think I pay you to work. Crazy, hey?" he playfully says to the three of us. But the twitch beneath his right eye exposes a different picture.

I don't have time to dissect it, however, because Darla decides to add to the awkwardness when she addresses us. "Penny. Ronnie. New girl."

New girl?

Penny scrunches up her nose, appearing just as disgusted as I am. "My name is Peyton," I correct, coming to a stand. She's half shielded by Cayden, which annoys me more so than I already am. If she wants to be catty, the least she can do is do it face-to-face.

Speaking of annoyed. Cayden and Ronnie are having this weird, territorial pissing contest, and I have no idea why. "You ready?" Ronnie says, directing his question my way. When I make it clear I have no idea what he means, he clarifies, "For our date."

I actually recoil when Cayden steps forward, a low rumble escaping him.

"Did you want to come too, Coach? Ronnie and I were planning on taking Peyton out to celebrate her first day of work." Penny's quick to intervene as she too can sense something weird brewing.

Cayden is making zero eye contact with me because he's currently eyeballing the hell out of Ronnie. But Ronnie isn't intimated in the slightest. When Darla's glossy lips tip into a sly grin, I suddenly put two and two together.

Ronnie is sweet on her. Maybe they were once a thing. But she clearly has eyes for someone else. *My* someone else. A feral sound oozes from me. She has just become public enemy number one.

"Thanks, Penn. I'd love to."

I almost pull a muscle in my neck as I snap my head to look at Cayden. He folds his arms across his chest, daring me to argue. "I didn't take you for the...socializing type," I say, which is the truth. I'd imagine going out for drinks with work colleagues would be as appealing to Cayden as catching the bubonic plague.

But his rigid stance reveals he's not backing down.

The world is clearly on crazy pills because our foursome suddenly becomes disastrous. "Count me in," Darla says, flashing her toothy smile.

Well, this should be interesting.

"You can ride with me, *boss*." Who knew the words ride and boss when used in the same sentence could sound so dirty? I begin to wonder if this little crush stems both ways.

But Cayden puts my mind at ease for now. "I'll go with Peyton. We drove in together."

"Actually, *I* drove your truck." It's a complete immature move, but when a scowl replaces that arrogant smile on Darla's face, I can't help but want to shake my invisible pom-poms and chant *rah, rah, rah*.

I'm smug for all of five seconds, though, when Cayden arches a dark brow, clearly reading my irrational behavior. He steps forward, ignoring the fact that we're surrounded by people, and pins me with those captivating eyes. "Yes, you did. You know how to handle your own."

I gulp, certain the tips of my ears are on fire. With so much chemistry bouncing between us, I'm finding it hard to breathe. To add to the siphoning of oxygen, Cayden brushes his thumb across the apple of my cheek. The motion is quick, but goddamn, my entire body is a live conduit. "Let's go." I simply nod and collect my things, then follow Cayden as he leads me out the way we came.

The fresh air does nothing to soothe my burn, and when my cell chimes, I'm thankful it's Penny. She has sent me a text with the name of what I'm assuming is the place we're going. "The Loaded Cobra?" I question, hoping it makes sense to Cayden. I suddenly am not so sure if she's referring to a bar or Darla.

I breathe a sigh of relief when he nods.

I'm in no state to drive with the energy coursing through me, and I am thankful when Cayden holds his hand out, indicating he'll drive. I quickly find the keys in the side pocket of my bag and toss them to him.

We jump into the truck, not a word spoken, and when the engine starts with an angry roar, I can't help but compare it to its owner. Cayden puts the truck into gear, and although he's clearly annoyed, he doesn't tear out of the lot like an idiot. Although I have made progress, I'm still a little edgy when in a vehicle.

This sudden tension between us is soon to erupt. What I didn't anticipate was that soon would be right now.

"So…Darla seems like a bitch." I slap my hand over my mouth, mortified I allowed that to slip out. I have no idea what possessed me to say that. Although true, it's highly inappropriate. I just stooped to her level. "Cayden…I'm so…"

But when he bursts into husky fits of laughter, I recoil, wondering if he heard me correctly.

He slaps the steering wheel in delight, chuckling wildly like I just told him the funniest joke. Maybe I did. "Why are you laughing?" I ask, fearful my insanity has rubbed off on him.

"Because"—he takes a deep breath—"I was thinking the same thing about Ronnie. However, sly motherfucker was what I had in mind."

I knew there was a beef between them. "So what's the deal? Why was he eyeballing you like you were the devil reincarnate?"

Cayden sighs, his hands tightening on the wheel. "I don't get involved in office politics, but I think he and Darla were a thing. My staff work for me because they're good at their job. I don't care what they do after hours. As long as they show up, do their job, and don't fuck around, then we're good."

"I really think you should use another word when Darla is involved." I pale, tugging at the silver necklace around my neck.

Seeing Cayden caught off guard is a rare thing, so I can't help but gloat about my victory. "Darla may be a little…" He's clearly searching for the right word. I have a couple I could suggest. "Friendly, but she's a good worker. She's efficient, smart, and—"

"It doesn't hurt her boobs have their own zip code," I finish for him. Call the press. Cayden Coachman is left speechless, yet again, in the span of thirty seconds.

"I hadn't noticed," he replies while I playfully roll my eyes.

This playfulness among us has thankfully doused our earlier mood, and I settle back in my seat, enjoying the view. "Today was fun," I admit, deciding to share the details of my day with my boss. Still hard to believe he's just that.

"I'm glad. So you'll be coming back then?"

"Of course, I will be. I know this sounds insane…" He risks a glance my way, brow arched. "Okay, fine. More insane. But I really felt like I was in my element. Drawing came so naturally to me. Penny is fantastic, but it was like she was telling me things I already knew."

I'm waiting for Cayden to tell me I'm crazy, but he doesn't. He stares off into the distance, his breathing calm, smooth. "Looks like you're where you belong."

I spin in my seat to look at him, unable to mask my surprise. "I thought I never belonged on 'this' side of the lake." I air quote my sarcasm.

Cayden turns to me with a glimmer of hope in his eye. "I suppose maybe you did. Maybe this is where you should have ended up all along." I swallow past the lump in my throat. "But you're here now."

Pondering over his words, I nod with resolve. "I am. And

I'm here to stay." Satisfied, I settle back in my seat, content to watch *my* world pass me by.

When I see the flashing green snake a few yards away, I know we're here. Cayden reverses into a parking spot like a complete pro, and before I know it, we're exiting the truck and making our way to the bar. The sidewalk is filled with patrons enjoying the hot summer night.

A group of rowdy men is standing with beers in hand outside a bar. One of them doesn't see me coming and knocks into me as he steps backward. I almost end up in the gutter, but Cayden swoops forward and catches me.

"Th-thanks," I stutter, attempting to catch my breath. Being in Cayden's arms shouldn't feel this good, but it does. It feels fucking fantastic.

"Sorry," the man who bumped me says, but I can't concentrate on anything other than Cayden's smoldering expression. He finally lets me go, appearing just as bewildered as I am that a simple touch between us can provoke this response each and every time.

He wraps his arm low around my waist as he leads me toward the bar. When we reach the door, however, he loosens his grip and gestures for me to enter first. When I do, I admire the interior, which looks a little like the bar out of the TV show *Cheers*.

The place is quite full, but I suppose it is a Saturday night. The vibe is chill as patrons are happy to drink their beer and play a game of pool. There is a vacant red booth in the back, so I decide to make a beeline for it before someone else snatches it up.

I extend my hand behind me, hinting for Cayden to take my hand, and he does. We duck and weave through the crowd, making it to the circular booth before anyone else. I slide along the vinyl and think Cayden will enter from the other side. He doesn't.

He follows in after me and ensures our thighs are touching when I settle in against the cushioned back. Well, isn't this incredibly cozy. I'm about to reach for a napkin and fan away my blush, but Cayden isn't satisfied until I'm dead and buried.

Placing his palm on my thigh, he grins while a small intake of breath leaves me. "What do you want to drink?"

Ignoring the fact that my leg is currently on fire, I reply, "I think maybe a beer?"

"Maybe?" He cocks a brow, amused.

Jesus Christ, I need to stop babbling like a fool and order my damn drink already. "I was going to say a whiskey sour, but I thought I'd better start with something a little less...alcoholic."

Cayden chuckles. "Whiskey sour, it is." He peers overhead, watching the door for the rest of our party to arrive. But he does all this with his hand still resting on my thigh.

When I see Penny and Ronnie, I don't know whether to be disappointed or relieved. However, when Darla follows in behind, I suddenly wish it was just us. She flips her long hair over her shoulder, emitting her scent for all the hungry men to acknowledge her arrival. And they do.

She turns heads, and although she loves the attention, she only wants the attention of one man. She waves at Cayden in a flirty little way, and I instantly want to gag. "Hey!" Penny says while Ronnie eyes the closeness between Cayden and me.

I know what this is. Ronnie doesn't know me. I could be any girl, but I seem to be the girl Cayden can't leave alone, which makes me the perfect pawn in whatever beef he has with Cayden. But what he doesn't realize is that I'm not an airhead. I'm onto him.

Darla practically elbows Ronnie out the way so she can sit near Cayden. He clenches his jaw but settles in after her. Which leaves Penny and me facing one another on the outside. "Drinks?" I suggest, practically pleading her to come with me so I don't have to hear Darla asking Cayden what cologne he's wearing 'cause he smells *so good.*

She reads between the lines and nods.

Just as I'm about to slide out of the booth, Cayden's grip on my thigh tightens. "I'll go." Turning to face him, I get lost in the proximity of his lips to mine. They really should be illegal.

However, when Darla pulls out her cell and insists they take a selfie for the company's Instagram page, I welcome the excuse to leave. "I wouldn't want to photobomb you." He attempts to keep me there, but I slip from his hold with a playful grin.

"I'll have a Chardonnay," Darla says with a wave of her hand like I'm her own private butler. I bite the inside of my cheek to refrain from any lewdness spilling out.

"Beer for you?" Penny asks Cayden and Ronnie. Ronnie nods while Cayden shakes his head.

"Just a root beer for me. I'm driving us home." There is no questioning who us is. It shouldn't please me that Darla looks like she's about to burst into hysterics, but it does.

Penny and I make our way to the busy bar. As we wait in line, I can feel her watching me. I give in. "Do I have something in my teeth?"

Her mouth is slightly parted like she's just seen something that is jaw-droppingly amazing or scary. I can't decide. "No, but you clearly have something. What's going on between you and Coach?"

I recoil, pursing my lips. "Going on? You're going to have to be a little more specific."

"I mean, I've known him for three years, and I'm not even kidding when I say I thought he was asexual because no one, man or woman, has turned his head the way you have."

Her comments throw me for a loop, and I very ungracefully choke on air. Thumping on my chest to dislodge the bubble, I shake my head way too animatedly. "*Nooo.* Do you need new glasses? And besides, he has a daughter, so he can't be asexual."

Penny scoffs. "Please. That woman doesn't count. She was the reason I thought he turned asexual." I snort loudly and almost choke again.

But considering she's being so open, I decide to ask about Darla. "So what's the deal with Ronnie and Darla? It's pretty obvious he's into her. And she's…" I want to say into Cayden but opt for, "into herself," instead.

Penny bursts into laughter. "They hooked up at a Christmas party one year. He wanted more, she didn't, and he's been bitter ever since. You probably picked up on the tension between him and Coach? Well, that's 'cause he thinks Coach is standing in the way of them being together. It's all a little dramatic, if you ask me, which is why I'll just stick with my five cats."

As we wait for the drinks we just ordered, I think about what she just shared. She thought Cayden was asexual? It's hard to imagine, seeing as I have been getting nothing but the opposite kind of vibes from him since we met just four days ago. It's hard to believe it's only been that long because I feel like I've known him for…well, forever.

We place our drinks on a tray and make our way back to the table.

When Cayden is practically wearing Darla's boobs as a scarf, I know I can't sit back down there and play nice. Grabbing my drink, I tell Penny I'm going to play a game of pool. She looks at Darla and nods in understanding.

I'm not attempting to be dramatic, but I honestly am too old for this crap.

The two men playing pool are almost done, and when the bigger of the two sinks the black ball, it's my turn to play. I don't have an opponent, but when a handsome man with shaggy blond hair offers, I decide why the hell not.

He racks the balls while I pick my cue. As I reach for the chalk, I wonder why it feels like I've done this before. "Want to make a wager?"

"Sure," I reply, his arrogance instantly turning me off.

"Loser buys the winner a drink."

Seems fair.

Just as I'm about to agree, someone decides to up the ante. No guessing who. "One drink? Why not buy a round for the whole bar?" Turning slowly, I make big eyes at Cayden, wondering what on earth he's doing.

Before I can retract the offer, blondie agrees. "You've got yourself a deal. I'm Mason, by the way."

"She doesn't care what your name is. Now break." My mouth

hinges open and closed, incapable of speech. "You've got this," Cayden murmurs, just like he did in the car. His confidence in me is really flattering, but he's probably just cost me my first paycheck.

But regardless, there's no backing out now.

"Ladies first," Mason says, gesturing to the table. I ignore Cayden's sudden shade of the Hulk green and take my position. He stands on the other end, watching me closely, and sweat begins to collect at the small of my back.

I can't do this. I was stupid to think that I could. But when I raise my eyes to meet Cayden's, and he rewards me with a wink, I push aside my reservations because I can do anything. Being here proves that I can.

Lining up the cue, I bend low and familiarize myself with the wood. It feels so natural. With that approach, I move the cue back and forth, back and forth, my eyes never wavering from Cayden's, and then, I break.

The corner of Cayden's lips lifts as I blink twice to ensure I'm not seeing things. I'm not. I just sunk two balls. Speaking of balls…

"Looks like you're smalls." Cayden's tone is dripping with innuendo and humor as he addresses Mason, who rips off his blazer.

Shit just got real.

I sink another two balls before it's Mason's turn. He's good, but it appears I'm better. When he misses, I sip my whiskey, stalking the table like prey. The ball I want is directly in front of Cayden, who knows it as well. He doesn't move a muscle, daring me to squeeze in the space between him and the table.

Challenge accepted.

Penny, Ronnie, and Darla have joined the crowd forming around the table. Memories of her blatantly flirting with Cayden rise to the surface, stirring a different kind of competitive streak. I don't bother with pretenses; I walk over and squeeze in front of him.

Peering over my shoulder, I smile. "You're going to have to back up and give me a little room." He smirks, shuffling back a few steps, giving me just enough room to take the shot.

He wants to play dirty, then so can I.

Bending low, I give him a nice view of my ass. I don't bother trying to draw attention to it with a little jiggle or shake because I can feel his eyes surveying every inch. He wants me. And I… want him.

I focus on finishing the game because I can stew over this tonight when I'm in bed, alone. I line up the shot and am about to strike, but then I feel, smell, and taste Cayden at my side. His breath is warm along the length of my neck. "You've got this." But I suddenly don't know if it's just the game he's referring to this time.

He doesn't back up to give me room. Instead, he bends low and watches me. Not the ball or the game, but me. And if that's not the most exhilarating thrill, then I don't know what is. Openly marking me, in a way, as his, has my stomach not only filling with butterflies but with fireworks as well.

The game is over in ten minutes with me as the victor. Mason looks like he's been duped, and Darla's annoyed that the attention has shifted off her. But it's not their reactions I'm concerned with. It's Cayden's. He doesn't look surprised in the slightest. It's like he knew I would beat Mason. But not just beat. He knew I would whip his ass. He had no problem making the wager on my behalf because he knew I would win.

Which once again arouses my suspicions.

"Everyone kind of loves you right now," I say, looking around the bar as everyone throws back their free drinks. "Except Mason." Mason was a man of his word and paid up—literally. He and his group of friends now sit at the back of the room, nursing their free waters.

"That's his problem for underestimating you," Cayden replies casually. "Not my fault he's an idiot." I burst into laughter, sipping my drink.

I love this easiness between us, but I'm about to shatter it with my interrogation. "So…" Cayden peers at me over the edge of his glass. "How'd you know I could play pool?"

His Adam's apple bobs as he swallows his root beer. He's clearly uncomfortable, but tough luck. He runs a hand through his hair, a gesture he does when annoyed. He seems to do that often when I'm around. "I…" I'm on the edge of my seat, but the answer will have to wait for now.

His face twists into frustration when he reaches into his back pocket to retrieve his ringing cell. When he sees the caller, he stands. "I have to take it. It's Lacey. She's watching Ellie."

But there's no need for him to explain. "Go." I wave him off as I understand.

Before he answers, though, he lays a quick kiss on my cheek, startling me. I don't have time to process it because he's pushing through the thick crowd and exiting the front door to take the call.

My skin is ablaze from where his lips left a perfect kiss mark on my cheek. Without thought, I raise my hand to my face, rubbing over the spot in awe.

As I reach for my drink, I see that it's sitting to the left of me and not the right, where I thought I'd left it. I don't think much of it and toss it down. As I order another, I decide that I will lay all my cards on the table and tell Cayden what happened with the drug dealer. I can only hope that honesty will lead to more, and Cayden will eventually open up.

Tonight can't be another coincidence. It can't be.

As the bartender places a beer down in front of me, I notice the label is blurry. Squinting doesn't help. It only seems to make it worse. I reach into my bag for my wallet, but my arms are unexpectedly heavy.

I suddenly can't breathe.

"Sorree," I say, but it comes out slurred. The bartender impatiently waits for me to get my shit together, but it seems to get worse. He leaves and takes the beer with him.

Nausea builds, but I don't need to be sick. I just feel queasy. Deciding to go to the bathroom, I stand, but my legs won't hold my weight. What the fuck is going on? After three attempts, I finally find my feet and stumble my way through the crowd.

My vision is getting blurrier, and the background noise all converges into one. I'm clearly a lot drunker than I thought. Penny and Ronnie are playing pool, and I have no idea where Darla went, not that I'd want her help. After fumbling and bumping into people, I finally make my way into the bathroom.

It's a miracle there isn't a line, and I slump into the first stall, not even capable of locking the door. My heart begins racing, but I suddenly am so tired. I just need to sleep. My brain is yelling at me to wake the fuck up, but as each second ticks over, I'm gradually losing control of my body.

I cradle the toilet bowl, placing my head on the closed lid and allowing sleep to overcome me. It feels nice here in a sleepy bubble where I can forget. But self-preservation kicks in. I only had three drinks. Or was it four? Either way, I shouldn't be this wasted.

Something feels wrong.

But I can deal with that tomorrow because now…I just want to forget…

"Peyton!"

Everything happens in slow motion. I want to yell out to Cayden to help me, but my lips are slack. All I can manage is a pained groan. But it's enough. He's bursting through the door a second later, cocooning me into his arms.

"What happened?" He attempts to lift my face gently, but I'm like a rag doll and have no control over my limbs. I feel like overcooked spaghetti. "Fuck," he hisses, and I've never heard him so angry before.

His response scares me, and I begin to panic. What's wrong? "Cay…den…" I manage to mumble, but it's a jumble of words. Everything hurts.

"Shh…it'll be all right. I promise. I'm going to lift you up. Okay?" My head lolls to the side as I attempt to nod.

I've never been more mortified in my life, but when he lifts me gently and shelters me with his scent, I forget about my humiliation and finally surrender to the darkness.

TEN

My head hurts. No, it doesn't just hurt. It fucking throbs.

I have no idea where I am. Actually, I have no idea what the hell happened. The last thing I remember is… *think*. A shiver racks my body as I don't want to believe my mind has failed me again. But this is different this time. It's not amnesia…it's like I didn't exist.

"Peyton?" That voice is my forever beacon to this plane.

As I rub my nose into the smooth silk and am engulfed by the ocean, I know where I am. I'm safe because Cayden is here.

My surface becomes rocky, and only then do I realize I'm lying in someone's bed. It's not mine, so that can only mean it's Cayden's. "How're you feeling?"

I have severe cotton mouth, and I'm certain my eyes are glued shut, but other than that, I think I'm fine.

"What do you remember?"

Regardless of my pounding headache, I attempt to sit, but I abruptly realize I'm not wearing any clothes. That has my eyes snapping wide open. "Ow." I squint as the bright light burns. But I have other pressing matters to deal with like exactly where my clothes are.

With fumbling fingers, I keep the sheet pressed to my chest as I wearily lift myself into a half-seated position. The headboard is my savior and stops me from dropping back down. It takes me a few moments, but I'm eventually able to focus and see Cayden sitting at the foot of the bed.

His hair is ruffled, and he's topless. My stomach drops.

Lifting the sheet to confirm I am indeed naked, I slap it back down when I see that I am. Cayden watches me closely. Oh, my God. What have I done? "Did—did we…?" I motion back and forth between us, hoping he understands my gestures.

He's visibly stumped until he witnesses my cheeks burst into flames. "No. *No*," he says a little louder the second time around. "Of course not."

"Thank God." I exhale, my heart returning to a semi-normal speed. I don't understand why he appears a touch hurt, but then I realize my choice of words probably wasn't the best I could use when referring to us *not* having sex.

However, that doesn't explain why I'm naked in his bed.

"Where are my clothes?"

"They're in the wash."

"Why?"

"Because they were covered in vomit," he replies, never breaking eye contact.

This just goes from bad to worse. "Did you undress me?"

He threads both hands through his hair. "Yes."

I don't understand any of this. "W-why?"

He doesn't make a move, and I'm thankful. "What do you remember from last night?"

Churning through the smog, I grasp a memory that I'm certain is one I didn't fabricate. "Playing pool. You leaving to take a call." I attempt to dig deeper, but I hit a brick wall. "That's it."

Cayden grinds down on his jaw. This can't be good. "I found you semi-conscious in the bathroom. The moment I picked you up, you passed out. I was going to take you to the hospital, but I brought you here first. I don't know why. I just…" He shakes his head as if he's still questioning his actions. "I didn't want you to wake up in a hospital room again, not knowing what happened or where you were. I didn't want you to be alone." He lowers his eyes, clearly ashamed of his actions, but what he doesn't realize is that it's the kindest thing anyone has ever done for me.

"Where did you sleep?" I ask bashfully, focusing on one drama at a time.

"I didn't." He hooks his thumb to the chair in the corner of the room. It's pressed up against the door like he was keeping watch, ready to spring into action and protect me if need be. "I only took off your dress. I promise. In the middle of the night, you stripped off the rest. I didn't see a thing. I felt your forehead, and you were burning up. Just when I was about to call the paramedics, you settled and fell into a peaceful sleep."

Cayden is worried about my modesty. After everything he just told me, that's the least of my concerns. "I guess I should probably lay off the whiskey for a while."

It's supposed to be a joke, but Cayden isn't laughing. "I don't think it was the alcohol."

I turn my lip up, confused. "What? What else could it be?"

His chest inflates, deflates, just like my hope that this is a simple, innocent mistake. "I think you were drugged."

"Drugged? Like a…*date* rape drug?" I whisper, unable to say those ugly words too loudly.

He tongues his upper lip. "Yes."

The room starts spinning, and Cayden rushes over, gripping my arm. "That's impossible. Laughable, in fact. Who would want to drug me?" The moment the words slip past my lips, I remember my encounter with the shady drug dealer.

"What is it?" he asks, running his thumb along my bicep.

I want to tell him, but I don't even know what to say, so until I can figure this out, I decide to keep it under wraps. "Nothing. Oh, my God. I feel so violated. If you hadn't come…"

"But I did," he interjects, placating my panic. "I'm just sorry…" He abruptly pauses, smashing his lips together to stop anything further from escaping.

"Sorry for what?" There is no way I'm going to let him off the hook that easily, though.

He exhales and ardently cups my cheek, fisting my hair. "I'm sorry I allowed it to happen. I should have been more careful."

"Unless you're the one who drugged me, then you have absolutely nothing to be sorry for." His nostrils flare as he averts his gaze. He's angry with himself. "Cayden. Cayden, look at me." When he does, I say, "Thank you."

He scoffs, not wanting my gratitude. But I ignore him. "You

saved me from being a statistic. You've saved me since the first moment we met."

He hisses and instantly severs our connection. "I'm not the hero here, Peyton. Don't mistake me for something I'm not."

"I don't care what you think. You are to me." He forgets I can be as stubborn as he is.

"Thank you," he says, finally accepting my compliment as he looks up at me from under his long lashes.

My head is reeling because I still can't believe this happened. Over the past five days, I've uncovered some crazy shit, but this, this is something else. "Do I report it? I mean, the police should know this, right?"

The more I speak, the angrier Cayden becomes. The blankets twists in his fist as he claws at them like they're the only thing stopping him from punching a hole through the wall. "Yes, you should," he replies slowly, but there is hesitation in his tone.

"But...?" I prompt, flinching when he rockets off the bed and begins to pace. I follow his big, angry strides with my gaze, awaiting his reply, but after a few seconds, I get seasick with all the moving around.

Rubbing my temples, I groan. I'm frustrated and confused, and I really want a shower.

"But the cops won't do anything. It could have been anyone," he finally replies, continuing his laps around the bedroom. He's right. Who's to say Mason and his group of friends didn't want a little retribution for what I did.

A thought then occurs. Where was Darla? I vaguely remember staggering through the bar and seeing Penny and

Ronnie, but Darla was nowhere to be found. But I don't have any proof other than the fact that she makes me want to puke without being roofied.

All this thinking is adding to my monster headache. "I need a shower."

Cayden thankfully stops wearing tracks in the floor and nods. "You can shower here." I appreciate his hospitality, but I don't have any clothes.

"Thanks, but if I could borrow a T-shirt, I'll just go back to my house. All my stuff is there, and I can be less…naked." When a glimmer of a smile tugs at his lips, I'm tempted to rub my eyes to ensure I'm not seeing things.

"I'll come with you," he says while I press the sheet even tighter to my chest.

"Again, thank you, but that's really not necessary. I just want to shower, take some medicine for my headache, and go back to bed."

He is clearly opposed to the idea, and on any other day, I'd attempt to get to the bottom of the reason. But today, I barely remember my own name. "Peyton—" His pause has me sitting taller. "After last night, I really don't want you out of my sight."

I swallow, rooted to the spot when he strides over slowly and sits by me. A ray of sunshine streaming in from the window catches the elegance of his tattoo, and my attention drifts to the detailed linework. There is no denying Cayden's protectiveness over me since the day we met, but what happened last night really shook him up.

I shouldn't, but I just can't help myself. "Why not?"

He blows out an exhausted breath. "Because…I can't seem

to stay away from you."

I blink once. "O-kay," I murmur, measuring my words. "And why is that such a bad thing?" There is no denying our attraction, and we're consenting adults. So why is giving in to what we both want such a big deal? Cayden is torn, and I have no idea why. Yes, I come with baggage—a lot of baggage—but he doesn't seem so fickle as to allow that to stand in the way of something he wants. And by the way he's looking at me right now, all feral-eyed and possessed, it's fairly obvious what he wants. But what he says next steps up the ante.

"Because…I would ruin you."

A threat shouldn't sound this…wicked, but it does.

He can't say things like that to me when I'm naked. "No, you wouldn't…you can't ruin something that is already damaged. And that's what I am. Damaged goods." I'm not saying this because I want sympathy. Or pity. I'm saying it because it's the truth.

But he shakes his head animatedly. "Don't you dare say that." It seems to be an unspoken agreement between us that it's better if we don't touch. "You are brave. And strong. Don't you ever forget it."

His words hold so much passion that an unexpected sentiment overcomes me. But I don't give in. "Thank you," I whisper, my throat almost closing up.

We have so much more to discuss, but we're both beyond exhausted to delve into a discussion that demands our utmost attention. "So will you stay?"

He's pleading that I say yes. So I do. "Okay. But I need a change of clothes."

"Of course. Lacey can go over to your house and grab something. Or you're welcome to my wardrobe."

The thought of being wrapped up in his clothes really shouldn't be this appealing, but knowing they'll be about three sizes too big, I decide to settle on my own. "If Lacey wouldn't mind." I feel bad for asking, but I don't have much of a choice.

"Of course not. I'll ask her." He stands, his nakedness suddenly warming my cheeks. Averting my gaze, I tug at a loose thread on the blanket. "You can shower in here. Take your time." I appreciate his kindness because I will. After being told you were found passed out in a public bathroom, one has the urge to bathe themselves for a very long time in bleach.

I'm thankful he doesn't linger and allows me some time alone.

My muscles protest when I shift, and I take three deep breaths before placing my feet on the carpeted floor. I have no idea if they'll hold me up, but my shaky legs remain steady as I test my weight and stand.

The room starts spinning.

When it slows to a tolerable pace, I unwrap the sheet from the bed around my body and begin a staggered walk toward the en suite. I really wish I was in a better frame of mind to take in my surroundings as I *am* in Cayden's bedroom, but the hot water and soapy bubbles are calling to me.

The moment I open the door, I groan at the sight of the shower because it's huge. The glass screen highlights a large chrome showerhead which looks like it has some sort of massaging device attached. A small shelf houses all the products one needs to bathe their skin in luxury. There is also a small bench seat affixed to the marbled wall.

Without further ado, I step inside and turn the water to hot. It streams from the showerhead like a waterfall from the gods. When it warms to just the right temperature, I stand beneath it and tip back my head, gulping in lungsful of fresh air.

My tender body relishes in the warmth of the water as I simply stand beneath the spray and comb over everything these past five days have presented me with. Even though it's been far from smooth sailing, I've never felt more myself than I have by coming here.

I'm still no closer to uncovering what that ribbon or the lake means to me. Though I did get roofied and told I was some bed-hopping party girl, I'm starting to realize those moments, those things, don't define me.

Not many people get the chance I have to start over and make amends. I can dwell on incidents like last night, or I can focus on the now and hope the pieces aren't too painful when I finally gather them all.

With my muscles and my mind slowly unknotting, I reach for Cayden's shower gel and open the bottle. Unable to stop myself, I draw in a breath with it under my nose, expecting to smell the ocean—Cayden's trademark scent. But instead, I get hit with an aromatic cloud of woodsy and citrus undertones. It smells divine, but it reveals Cayden's comforting, rich scent is all him.

I lather myself in the gel and scrub my body until I feel every trace of last night gurgle down the drain. Cayden thinks he'll ruin me, and in some ways, he already has. But after last night—actually, after the first time we met—he's done nothing but the opposite. He's given me hope.

My breath catches just thinking about him, and I know that's because my heart is in concert with his. It's too early, not to mention completely absurd, to say something like I'm in love with him, but with these feelings, these persistent butterflies, and the constant need to seek him out in a crowd, what else can it mean?

I know he's hiding a secret. But sometimes, well, most of the time, I don't care. The reason being, I think he's doing it… to protect me. But protect me from what exactly? I hope to find out soon.

Switching off the faucets when my fingers resemble prunes, I reach for the fluffy white towel hanging on the rack. I dry off, feeling a million times better. The shower was exactly what I needed.

I don't want to be a snoop, but who knows if I'll ever have this opportunity again. So I stand in front of the double vanity and quietly open the mirrored medicine cabinet doors. There are three of them. I see what I would expect to find in any medicine cabinet—Band-Aids, mouthwash, aspirin. But when I look in the last cupboard, I see an orange bottle filled with pills sitting on the lower shelf.

This is wrong, and I am definitely crossing a line, but curiosity gets the better of me, and I turn over my shoulder to ensure Cayden isn't loitering. When I see that he isn't, with unsteady fingers, I turn the label and gasp.

The bright light confirms what I read is indeed correct. Cayden is on an antidepressant. There is absolutely nothing wrong with that, but I can't help but wonder why he needs them. He may be serious most of the time, but I never thought he was depressed. I suppose we all have our secrets, and just as Cayden has respected mine, it's my turn to do the same.

Turning the bottle to the way I found it, I gently close the door and rinse my mouth out with the minty wash, hoping to wash away my guilt. I use the matching white hand towel sitting on the vanity to dry my face. I close all the mirrored doors and peer at my reflection.

The bags under my eyes are a deep purple, the skin almost translucent from my fatigue. My hair hangs limply around my face, so I tie it back into a high bun. My skin is paler than usual, causing my freckles to appear darker and more pronounced.

My lips need a coat of balm because no matter how many times I wet them, they're still cracked and dry.

All in all, I look like shit, and I can only hope Lacey brought over some cosmetics as well.

Wrapping the towel firmly around my body, I make my way to the door and open it. I don't know what I expected to see, but Cayden planted face-first into the mattress was not one of them. A sudden panic rises because he looks dead, but when I see his broad back rise and fall gently, I know that he's merely dead to the world.

My clothes are draped over the back of the chair, and my toiletry bag sits on the dresser. It pleases me to see my belongings in here. For some reason, they look like they belong. Sighing, as I really need to stop with the fairy tales, I tiptoe across the room, not wanting to wake Cayden.

Biting my lip, I look over my shoulder out of modesty to ensure Cayden is still sleeping before dropping the towel. I'm standing naked in Cayden's bedroom. I feel above wicked and sexy.

As I step into the bikini briefs and fasten my bra, my eyes drift to Cayden's sleeping form. I wonder what he would do if I settled in behind him and pressed my body to his. Would he push me away, claiming we were just friends? Or would he welcome the contact and want more?

Cayden stirs and turns onto his side, snapping me from my very perverse bubble. I finish dressing.

Gazing back and forth from the bed to the doorway, I wonder what I should do. I did promise to stay here, but as a yawn escapes me, it's evident that the soft, comfy bed is calling my name. But can I do something so immoral? Can I give in to temptation and lie with Cayden?

Even though it's just to sleep, the innocence behind that sentiment seems a lot more touching than if we had sex. I don't know why that is.

As I'm wrestling with my decision, a small whimper escapes Cayden as he jerks and kicks his legs. Without thought, I rush to where he lies, carefully watching him and examining his pulled-in lips and the furrow lines across his brow.

Whatever he's dreaming about doesn't seem good, and the need to comfort him overthrows me. I place a knee on the mattress, careful not to disturb him, and then gently lower myself behind him. I'm lost in his musky scent. His heavy breathing. But most of all, I'm entranced by the familiarity of lying by his side.

When he mumbles incoherently, I shuffle closer and nervously press my chest against his back. His cries die instantly, and he inhales, finally at peace. The heat from his body is warm, almost too warm, but there is an underlying comfort in it, and my eyes instantly grow heavy.

On the cusp of sleep, I am a prisoner to this moment, but when Cayden sleepily reaches behind him and draws my arm over him to spoon him, I know that, truth be told…I am a prisoner to him. He sighs as he interweaves our fingers, with no intention of ever letting me go.

Before long, our breathing is in sync, and I have come home.

I woke the way I fell asleep…which is akin to heaven.

Cayden and I were a tangle of limbs, and it almost felt blasphemous to slip from his hold, but I really needed to pee. I feel recharged, no longer tired, which is a miracle in and of itself. I don't ever remember feeling this clearheaded. It's amazing what a good night's or day's sleep can do.

But as I bounced down the stairs with Cayden's scent clinging to my skin, I knew it had nothing to do with the nap and everything to do with who I slept beside.

Wanting to do something nice for him, seeing as he's saved my ass more than once, I decide to return the favor and cook him dinner as he cooked me breakfast. So that's what I'm currently doing with Empire sitting by my feet, happy to be my helper.

Lacey left a note on the fridge. It said she was taking Ellie out to the movies. I have the sneaking suspicion she did this to give Cayden and me some time alone. I intend on showering her with chocolates and wine.

This kitchen is every culinary master's dream come true. With ample cupboards, the blue-gray color and marbled countertops give this space a welcoming feel. No doubt, Cayden designed this with Lacey in mind. She *is* a culinary master, after all.

I can imagine many family meals were prepared in this kitchen. And I wonder if Cayden had a hand in cooking for his family. Or maybe even once upon a time, Hazel. I slice through a tomato a little too forcibly at the thought.

It's just after seven, and although Cayden hasn't come downstairs, I know by the running of the water in the shower that he's awake. The moment I heard the pipes whine, I shoved down the images of Cayden standing under that spray, glistening wet and very, *very* naked.

To quell my hunger, I devour one of the caramel cupcakes I baked earlier. I was saving it for dessert, but desperate times call for desperate measures. It isn't what I want, but it will have to do.

Thanks to the abundance of cookbooks Lacey has on hand, I followed an easy recipe for one-pot stovetop enchiladas. Everything I needed was here. Who would have thought I'd like to cook or that I was actually any good at it?

The smells wafting through the kitchen have my belly rumbling, and when I taste a spoonful of what's cooking, I can't deny that it's delicious. As I'm humming away to a tune on the radio and doing a little dance, I don't realize I'm no longer alone until I turn and almost give myself a heart attack. "Fuck. Me," I yelp, gasping on my raspy breath.

Cayden's brows arch into his hairline. I suddenly wish I'd opted for a different phrase.

"Are you hungry?" I nervously ask, brushing a strand of hair behind my ear.

"Starved," is his simple reply. There is nothing simple about the tall, dark, and handsome man in front of me, however.

He's in ripped jeans and a white V-neck, which has the blue in his eyes popping. His hair is still wet, with the longer strands flicked to the side. His feet are bare. On anyone else, this outfit sounds like nothing special, but on Cayden, he looks like he's ready to walk on any runway in Milan.

My gawking gets interrupted when he walks over to the fridge, noticing Lacey's note. The bottles in the door rattle as he hunts for a beer. "Drink?"

I helped myself to the pitcher of homemade lemonade earlier, and my glass is still full. "I'm good, thanks."

He closes the door with a Budweiser in hand and surveys the massacre I've made of his kitchen with an amused smile. "Whatcha cooking? It smells awesome." I'm elated he thinks so too.

I give the food a final stir before reaching for the bowl I found when I ransacked his kitchen. "It's a recipe I found in one of Lacey's cookbooks. I hope you don't mind, but it's a little spicy."

Slipping on the oven mitt, I'm about to remove our meal from the heat. But when Cayden sneaks up behind me and peers over my shoulder, I need a minute. "I like spicy," he says, his breath like a lover's touch as it slides down my neck.

My dinner is about to turn into a burned mess, so I forget

about how good he smells and turn off the stove. "Will you grab some bowls?" I don't think formal dining is really Cayden's scene, so I figure we could have a casual meal at the breakfast counter.

The moment he backs away, the air returns to my lungs.

I go about serving our dinner by placing everything on the counter. Cayden returns with two bowls and some silverware. "It's a nice night. Do you want to sit outside?"

Looking up at him through my lashes, I nod. "I would love that."

We work in silence, piling our dishes full. Either we are both clearly hungry, or it's our safety net in case things get awkward. So we can stuff ourselves full of enchilada instead of conversation. I follow Cayden and Empire as they walk out of the kitchen and up the stairs.

I look over my shoulder, wondering why we wouldn't sit out on the porch, but don't say anything.

When we enter his bedroom, memories of clinging to one another assault me, and a longing hits hard. I wonder if he remembers the way he reached for me, needing me as much as I needed him?

The bed is made with military precision, and everything is neat and put away. Now that I can see straight, I take in Cayden's room and appreciate a charcoal sketch above his bed. I didn't notice it before. I stop in my tracks, transfixed by it. It's beautiful.

However, when Cayden opens the balcony doors and a gust of warm air floats into the room, I continue walking, desperate to feel the breeze on my skin. "Wow." I now see why Cayden brought me up here. The view is breathtaking.

There is a small wooden table and chair set, which provides the perfect spot for one to eat their dinner and ponder on the beauty surrounding them. Cayden pulls out my seat, smiling and waiting for me to stop staring.

"Oh, sorry." I quickly rush over, but Cayden doesn't look bothered.

"It's okay. Take your time. We've got all night." His promise has goose bumps shadowing my skin. I slip into the seat and smile up at him, thankful for his chivalry. As I scoot my chair forward, he takes the seat beside me.

This isn't the first meal we've shared together, but the vibe certainly is new. I don't want to jinx it, but this kind of feels like a first date. And the awkward dialogue that follows confirms that fact. "Do you want to say grace?"

Cayden pauses mid-sip of his beer, his cheeks puffed out with the large mouthful he just took. I screw up my face, unsure what the fuck just possessed me to say something so absurd. His Adam's apple bobs as he swallows down his beer.

"Um, do you?" There is no judgment behind his question. Only curiosity.

Sighing, I look out at the remarkable scenery and decide that yes, I do because I've never been more thankful than I am right now. "I think I do." Extending out my palm, Cayden looks down at the offering and takes it without a second thought.

Another thing to be grateful for.

I've never done this before, but I don't think there is a right or wrong way. Expressing what you're thankful for should be something we do every day. It doesn't have to be religious or recited from rote memory. It should come naturally. Just as holding Cayden's hand and being with him are.

"I'm thankful for this delicious meal I managed to prepare without burning down the house. I'm thankful my roof hasn't caved in yet." Cayden snorts softly. "I can't wait for the adventures headed my way, like renovating and working at my new job. I'm thankful for Empire." He barks once, happy to have made the cut when I run my fingers through his mane.

As I list everything, I realize there is one common denominator.

Cayden.

He watches me patiently, and although my palm begins to sweat, I squash down my nerves and end on the one thing I am most thankful for. "But most of all, I'm grateful for you, Cayden. I'm grateful you exist."

He blinks once, as I've clearly caught him off guard, but I don't care. I want him to know because that's how I feel.

Neither of us speaks. The cicadas and the echoing wind fill the silence, only seeming to perfect an already perfect evening. Cayden brushes his thumb along my knuckles before gently squeezing my hand. "Amen."

I don't know why, but his response seems fitting to this entire situation.

We never break eye contact, our gazes dancing under the full moon. "Let's eat," he finally says, which sounds like a wonderful idea. Reluctantly, I release his hand, and we dig in.

I can't help it, but I watch in fascination as he takes his first bite. "This is amazing."

"Yeah?" I ask, swallowing down the spicy rice.

"Yeah," he confirms, scooping up a huge helping. It's satisfying to see the meal you made with your own two hands being devoured by the person you made it for.

We chew in silence, the conversation not strained, but rather, it feels like we're enjoying each other's company and appreciating the stillness around us. As I peer to the right, I notice my house and how the balcony extending from my room is visible from this angle.

I pause with a mouth full of food.

Cayden notices what has captured my attention but continues eating.

I sit taller, and without a doubt, if he were standing by the railing, he could see my room and my balcony. It's unmissable. He still remains quiet. I, however, do not. "Well, good thing I haven't decided to go skinny dipping."

He chuckles in response.

I can't tear my eyes away from my house and the red ribbon, which up until now, I hadn't given much thought to. But from up here, I have the perfect bird's-eye view of not only my home but the lake, the oak, and the ribbon as well.

"Have you been spying on me?" I can't seem to stop with the ridiculous questions, but when he clears his throat twice, I almost choke on my dinner.

"I wouldn't call it spying." I sigh, but it's in vain. "I was just making sure you were all right."

Pushing away my bowl, I try to focus on the positives like how Cayden was honest and didn't deny that he's a Peeping Tom. "So how often have you been 'making sure' I was all right?" I air quote, not believing that we're having this conversation.

He rubs his hand over his stubble. "Sometimes." When I raise a brow, he amends, "Every night."

I don't know whether to feel flattered or violated.

Looking over Cayden's shoulder, I see a number of beer bottles dumped in a small trash can. I also notice Empire's well-loved bed near the railing. Holy shit.

Needing to do something, I shoot upright and walk to the balustrade. I know I'm overreacting, but I can't kick this feeling that Cayden is watching me for a reason. If he wanted to keep it a secret, however, he wouldn't have brought me up here. "You wanted me to see?"

My gaze never wavers from my house and the lake just beyond it.

The chair slides along the decking, and I brace myself for what comes next. Cayden comes to a stand beside me but leaves enough space in case I'm overcome with the need to slap him. "Yes, I did. I wanted you to know that I won't let anything happen to you."

"What's going to happen to me?" I ask with nothing but curiosity as I rest my elbows on the rail and lean forward.

"Nothing, and I'll make sure of it. That's why last night…"

But I don't let him finish.

I turn sideways to look at him and find the mask of a defeated man. "Last night was a one-off. You have to stop thinking about it."

"But I can't," he presses, his voice wavering as he turns his back to the lake. "If anything ever happened to you…"

My heart begins a steady incline. "Cayden, I'm all right. And you want to know why?" He raises his shoulders limply with his chin drooped to his chest. "Because of this."

Pushing off the railing, I gently place my palm on his cheek, coaxing him to look over his shoulder toward my house. He does. "Because you're with me. Always." And I mean that both literally and metaphorically.

"You're not mad?" he sheepishly asks, leaning into my touch.

Searching his face for answers as to why he has made such a huge impact on my life, I answer the only way that I can. "No, I'm not mad. Curious, yes. But how can I be angry with you when you're sitting up here all night, losing sleep to make sure that I'm all right."

"It's not all night," he amends with a small smile. "When you turn the light off, I know you're okay."

Emotion fills me, and my heart, it hurts. It hurts because this man—this incredible, complicated, and damaged man—puts my needs and my comfort before his. I'm nothing more than a stranger. But we both know that I'm not.

This is the moment I ask him, beg he confirms my suspicions. But what happens when he denies me? Because when I look into those pained eyes, I know that's what he'll do. I may be ready, but he's not. Showing me this will have to do. For now.

The current flowing between us is electric, and I would only have to stand on tippy-toes and finally give in to what I've wanted to do for days. He licks his bowed upper lip, reading this for what it is. If we started, we wouldn't stop, and something about that is powerful and all-consuming, but it's damn frightening as well.

Cayden was right. He would ruin me. But in the best possible way.

Wrapping my hand around the back of his neck and toying with the hair curling at his nape, I surrender, but only halfway. I stand on tippy-toes and guide my lips to his. His eyes widen at the contact, but he doesn't pull away. His heart races wildly, which comforts me because so is mine. "It seems I ruin you too," I whisper against his mouth. His breath fills me with a life force so fierce, I almost crumple. But that's not what this moment is filled with.

Memorizing the softness, the taste, I leave a tender kiss on the crease of his mouth and pull away.

A kiss has the power to change the world...and I've just delivered one that'll no doubt change us both.

ELEVEN

One Week Later

This is a bad idea.

My week was spent working alongside Cayden as he exercised his notable dominant nature not only in the office but at home as well. Once our day finished, I was surprised when he came over after dinner to work on the house. I told him not to worry, as I saw how hard he worked during the day, but no matter how exhausted he was, he came over without fail.

Since that night on the balcony, the night of our sort of kiss, he's been a little distant, so I haven't spoken about it. Or the fact that I have my own private surveillance. I can't help but feel he's making himself scarce because he needs space, so I don't push. Instead, I enjoy his company and focus on work.

The deliverymen, who Cayden knew on a first-name basis, came with endless supplies for my home and weren't even bothered by having to make numerous trips back and forth each time. Most of it was wood, plaster, and roofing materials—the essentials to get this show up and running.

I did what I could, and I couldn't help but notice how pleased Cayden was when I asked continual questions. He suggested we work on the bathroom first. He noted that the plumbing could stay where it was, which meant it just needed a cosmetic renovation.

That sounds easy enough until we began ripping out the tiles, which was a backbreaking job. Even though I managed to use every swear word under the sun, it felt liberating to destroy something, knowing it was for the greater good. Cayden remarked that once we were done, I wouldn't recognize this place as the outdated, derelict shack it currently is.

He said it would take a week or so to get the bathroom back to pristine condition. In the meantime, he offered his home as an alternative whenever nature called. We only stopped to gulp down bottles of water as we were both eager to get back to our project.

As we were ripping out the sink, he suggested we do the kitchen next. This was going to be the most expensive room to remodel, he said. I told him he'd better give me a pay rise then.

We worked alongside one another as a dynamic force, and I was pleasantly surprised to realize I was a fast learner.

Everything was going great, better than great, but when he mentioned my bedroom, dread churned in the pit of my stomach because touching it almost felt sacrilegious. Like I was disturbing a holy place. The moment he saw my hesitation, we came to a compromise. His priority would be to fix the balcony after he confirmed my fears that it was seconds away from collapsing.

Even still. The thought of him tearing up the place I know every night for the past twelve days he's kept under watch punches a hole straight through me. But eventually, I agreed.

The day was turning out to be the best I'd had in a long time, and with my mind distracted, I didn't realize how late it was. So when it reached the time for me to get ready for dinner with my parents, both Cayden and I became tense, the easiness between us fading.

It was apparent that neither of us wanted this magical day to end, but curiosity got the better of me, and I was bidding Cayden farewell. He said he'd be back tomorrow, and the thought would be a nice one to come home to.

When he walked out the front door, his shoulders sagged with what appeared to be a sense of burden. As I watched him descend the first porch step, I was surprised when he stopped and turned over his shoulder. "Do you want me to come?"

I almost fell face-first onto my porch. "To my parents'?" I asked, in case I was lost in translation.

He nodded firmly, confirming my suspicions that he was also apprehensive about tonight.

But this man never ceased to amaze me. "You'd do that for me?"

The air fell still. "I'd do anything for you."

I wanted to say yes, please, come with me. Everything is always easier with you by my side. He read my thoughts, however, and settled on an alternative. "Call me if you need me. And make sure you lock this door." There was no further discussion.

I leaned against the doorway, watching him as he walked toward his house with a hint of frustration to his steps. Once he faded from view, I closed the door and locked it.

Taking a breath, I realize it was the first time all day I felt uneasy. Being around Cayden helps me forget, which is why... this is a bad idea.

I'm sitting in Cayden's monster truck, idling by the curb about a block away from my parents' million-dollar mansion. I have no doubt security, aka a police cadet reject, will be cruising around the corner in his little white car and asserting his authority any second now. But I need a minute.

I can't shake the feeling that something life-changing is seconds away from happening.

I know I'm probably overreacting because I don't have any fond memories of this neighborhood or my parents' home, but something big is looming. I peer into the rearview mirror, not recognizing the big, frightened eyes as my own.

I have no doubt my family won't recognize me either, seeing as I've tossed out the majority of the clothing I left this neighborhood with. When I opted for this bright orange bohemian dress, which sets the fire red to my hair alight, I knew Stella would be far from impressed that I wasn't decked out in couture. But she needs to get used to the new me.

So far, I'm happy with who I see.

Snapping from my funk, I run my hands around the steering wheel, finding strength in the fact that Cayden's hands have been here too. With a new lease on tonight, I put the truck into the gear, relishing when the beast roars through the gated community, disturbing the sterile peace.

The moment the tall, white gates come into view, I am hit with the memories of when I first saw them. It was the day Stella took me "home." Everything was so murky, and she spoke to me like I should have remembered all the information she relayed. But I didn't remember any of it. I still don't.

Looking at my parents' house, my childhood home, I am hit with nothing but dread. Memories of this place being my prison slam into me, and I'm instantly hit with the familiar feeling of wanting to flee. But sucking it up, I pull up to the gates and press the button on the intercom.

It doesn't surprise me when a mystery voice answers. No sane person could work for Stella for a long period. If you worked longer than six months in the Lane household, you were considered for sainthood.

"Hello?" says the nasally voice.

"Hi. It's Peyton." Silence. "I used to live here." More silence. "I'm the daughter who undoubtedly has driven Stella to have an extra Long Island iced tea with her quinoa and kale salad." No surprise when the gate opens.

I refrain from speeding down the driveway like a NASCAR on its final lap and cruise the drive, admiring the landscaped gardens, which were the only thing I ever liked about living here. Gardeners clip, prune, and mow, perfecting the greenery and ensuring the Lanes' garden is the best in the neighborhood. I have the urge to do a burnout on the front lawn but hold back, not wishing to throw anyone under the Stella Lane bus.

I purposely rev the engine, giggling when Cayden's truck roars like a lion, alerting my perfect family that their not-so-perfect kin has arrived. After I kill the engine, I reach for my bag and shoes.

Jumping from the beast, I decide to walk barefoot because the warm summer sun still heats the terracotta pavers on the driveway. The vast mansion in front of me would impress most, but I'm not most people. I know what lies inside. This house may have opulent possessions, but loneliness is what paints these pristine white walls.

I know this mansion contains eight bedrooms and six bathrooms, and I have firsthand knowledge of the costly things that have never been used. Every perfect surface has been committed to memory not because I am in awe of all my parents have, no, but because it is a reminder of what I refuse to become.

People like my parents crave more, more, more because more is never enough. Bigger houses, faster cars, trophy wives, scandalous lies—it all comes with the territory of being a part of this bullshit life. A life many crave, while me, I simply want to be happy. I have come to learn that in this world, it's either one or the other.

With a hesitant pace, I walk up the white marble steps, certain if I looked down, I could see the color of my underwear in the gleam of the polished floor. I wonder how long the workmen were forced to polish the stonework until Stella was satisfied.

The alcove is a white dome, completely superficial like the rest of this house. I press the doorbell, the chime akin to a sound one would opt for to announce the commencement of a death march. I hate this fucking house.

The door opens, and I'm instantly smacked with memories

I wish I could forget. When I walked through these doors after I arrived home from the hospital, I thought, by some miracle, all the answers to my questions would be uncovered. But as days turned into weeks, it was apparent that I wouldn't find solace here. And I doubt I ever will.

A man I've never seen before stands by the open doorway, waiting for me to enter. He looks to be in his early forties. He also looks like someone Stella would fire in an instant because he has kindness behind his green eyes.

"Good evening, Miss." He steps aside, welcoming me into my well-furnished cell.

Every bone in my body is telling me to run far, far away and not look back, but I figure the sooner I get this over with, the sooner I can go home.

He offers to take my bag, but I wave him off. I don't want anyone waiting on me. "Are my siblings here?" I ask, stepping into the lavish foyer. A grand staircase, similar to the one you'd expect to see in any Disney movie where the princess waltzes down to meet her Prince Charming, is feet away. I'm half expecting Stella to saunter down it in her designer threads and blinding jewels, as she's one to make an entrance. But I'm safe—for now.

"Yes," he replies, closing the door and sealing my fate for good.

"All of them?" I ask, astounded that Ursula, the Antichrist incarnate, could part from her luxurious lifestyle and mingle with the common people for one night. Her nanny most likely quit, which undoubtedly interrupted her plans to tour Europe for the summer. Looking at the kind man beside me, I empathize with him as he has no idea what he's in for.

"Yes," he repeats, his tone commiserating.

"Fucking great." A smile tugs at his lips, his full mustache joining in with the fun. I instantly like him. "What's your name?"

He peers around the room, almost afraid to speak. "Luis Lopez."

"Well, Luis Lopez…I won't bother asking you if you like working here because that's fairly obvious." Hunting through my bag, I find my checkbook and a pen. Flipping the book open, I casually ask, "Do you have any children?"

"Yes, I have three."

"Oh, that's lovely," I reply as I use my bag as a crutch and busily write out a check.

"Tonight is my youngest daughter's fourth birthday party," he reveals with a frown. Pausing, I shake my head and decide to add another zero.

Luis watches me closely, almost afraid as my determined strokes disclose my intentions. Signing my name, I tear off the check and hand it to him. "Here. Go buy her something nice." He backs away, shaking his head animatedly.

"If Mrs. Lane found out, she'd be very upset with me."

Scoffing, I wave the check, hinting this isn't negotiable. "Mrs. Lane will be very upset regardless of what you do. She was born with a stick up her ass, and that won't be removed anytime soon. Please, take it."

His dilemma is evident because what good father would miss their daughter's birthday voluntarily? I know he's a good father because that's the only reason he's stuck in that monkey suit, taking shit from Miss High and Mighty.

"What would I tell Mrs. Lane?"

"Leave her to me. Go spend time with your family." When he hesitates, I stuff the check into his palm with a smile. "Go before she realizes you're gone." He understands what that means for him if she does.

"Thank you, Miss." He clutches my hands in his and nods in gratitude.

My heart swells. It's the least I can do. This man deserves a medal for putting up with Stella. "It's quite all right, and please, my name is Peyton."

With one final nod, he stuffs the check into his pocket and opens the door. However, he turns over his shoulder, once again scanning his surroundings before divulging, "Miss…Peyton. Someone is waiting for you. Upstairs." My gaze immediately drifts upward, climbing the staircase with fear. "Mrs. Lane will surprise you before dinner. Be careful." He crosses himself like he does in church before slamming the door behind him.

I blink once, unsure how to interrupt his worrisome warning. Who is this someone? Is this *person* my surprise? It would appear so.

"Darling, were you robbed?" Stella gasps as she emerges from the living room, her hand pressed dramatically on her chest over her heart. She's decked out in a silky pantsuit with white studded heels. Valentino, no doubt.

I refrain from answering that yes, I was robbed of my sanity the moment I stepped foot inside. "No." I know she's referring to my less than acceptable dinner attire. She waits for me to elaborate, but I don't.

She purses her full lips, and I can't decide if she's smiling or scowling. "Where are your shoes?" When I hold up my gold sandals, a tiny giggle escapes me when I notice a wad of pink gum attached to the left sole. Stella, on the other hand, looks seconds away from spraying me with Lysol.

"Good to see you fit right in with your white trash neighbors."

Closing my eyes for the briefest of seconds, I can only hope whatever god is looking over me grants me the strength not to throttle my sister. She looks like a Christmas ham in whatever netted dress she's wearing.

"You do realize you've got lipstick on your teeth," I counter, amused when Ursula covers her mouth, horrified her perfect appearance is soiled. That should shut her up for five seconds. "I need a drink." I turn on my heel and head to the den, where I know Augusto keeps the good scotch.

Stella and Ursula whisper frantically, no doubt gossiping over my insubordinate attitude. They ain't seen nothing yet. Augusto sits on the white leather sofa, ankle crossed over his knee, reading the paper. He barely lifts his head when I enter. His detachment suits me just fine because I'm not in the mood for small talk.

Reaching for a crystal tumbler, I seize the decanter and fill my glass full. The amber liquid smells divine. It tastes even better when I toss it back in one large gulp. I refill my glass a moment later.

"Starting early, little sis." This stranger, named Lachlan Lane, is apparently my brother even though I don't see the resemblance.

He has thick blond hair and baby blues that I can only imagine would send unsuspecting women wild. However, men like Lachlan don't settle down. They use and abuse women because they can. It goes without saying that I hate his fucking guts.

"What can I say? This house drives me to drink." He raises his own glass in salute to my comment.

Augusto doesn't bother tearing his focus from whatever he's reading in the paper. His silver-rimmed glasses perch on the end of his regal nose as he clearly finds today's news far more interesting than his kids. This night can't end soon enough.

Taking my drink, I walk to the bay windows and peer out into the backyard at the acres upon acres of lush greenery. I can't help but wonder if I explored this garden when I was younger, spreading my arms out, ready to take flight as I ran down these rolling hills. I'd like to think that I did.

"Remembering the good days?" Lachlan asks, standing beside me. I wonder why he's so chatty.

Taking a sip of my scotch, I relish the burn. "I don't remember anything."

"Lucky you," he says. Leaning in close, he shocks me with his nearness.

Gasping, I snap my head toward him, hoping to read what's going through his mind. He's never said more than five words to me. I wonder why the change of heart?

Sadly, that's where my investigation ends because a tornado comes barreling through the room, disturbing whatever small amount of peace this house holds. "Give it back, Benjamin! It's mine!" screams Kyle, or maybe it's George; I can't really tell the bratty twins apart.

"No! It's mine!" retorts Benjamin, hugging the toy truck to his chest.

My three nephews are aged somewhere between five and ten. I can't really remember because Ursula and her husband, Roger, made sure I was not to speak to them for longer than thirty seconds. They're cute kids with red curly hair and freckles, but sadly, their futures are mapped out for them. With my sister and her jerk husband as role models, these kids are doomed to grow up being narcissistic assholes.

"It's mine!" screams maybe George. It saddens me that the word "mine" is apparently ingrained in their DNA.

Augusto doesn't seem bothered in the slightest while I'm seconds away from keeling over from the noise. "Hey, come on, you can share," I say calmly, hoping to pass my quietness onto them. It has the opposite effect.

Benjamin, who is the eldest, I think, looks at me like I'm a mere bug he could squish under his expensive shoes. "My mommy said you're a freak."

"Did she now?" I reply, tonguing my cheek while shaking my head. And the award for best mother goes to…

He nods with a dimpled grin. On anyone else, it would look cute. But on him, I'm fearful for my soul.

Maybe George and his twin, maybe Kyle, soon stop squabbling and decide to join forces. "Yes, my mommy said that you're a drama queen, and you're pretending to forget."

"That you remember everything but are embarrassed about what you did," adds his twin.

"Drama queen! Drama queen!" they both chant.

Insults aside, I figure maybe these two are my best hope at getting to the bottom of what exactly I did. "And what did she say I did?"

When Augusto lowers the paper, watching on intently, I know I'm onto something. "She said you…"

"Boys, that's enough! Go find your grandmother." It's the first time I've heard Augusto raise his voice or speak, for that matter, which only stirs my curiosity.

Dropping to a squat, I ignore his suggestion and pin my nephews with a stare. "You tell me what she said, and I'll give you twenty bucks." When George scoffs, I up the ante. "Fifty." Not my finest moment, but desperate times call for desperate measures.

His eyes twinkle at the prospect. "She said you brought shame to the family by laying with dogs. Did you really lay down with a dog?" he says in a rush, his eyes flicking between his grandfather, who has risen from his perch, and me.

"She also said…" Sadly, Kyle never finishes his sentence because a searing pain has me cursing like a sailor. The cause of the agony is none other than Benjamin, who is dangling off my arm by his teeth.

"This is how dogs play," he muffles from around my flesh.

"Get off," I demand, shaking my arm, but he only bites me harder. "Ow! You creep!" Shame on me for calling a kid a creep, but my discomfort has overruled my manners.

Kyle and George break out into diabolical chuckles before joining their brother and latching onto whatever body part of mine they can find. "You little turds! Stop it." I wiggle, trying to break free, but they only bite harder.

Lachlan raises his glass and grins. "Glad it's you and not me." Augusto attempts to pry them off. He fails and falls onto his ass, wailing when one of them kicks him in the groin.

Ursula and Stella decide this is the moment they'll enter.

"What is going on?" screeches Ursula, running to the aid of her children. "What did you do?" No surprise she directs her question at me. Stella screams hysterically, running to the aid of Augusto, who has turned whiter than a ghost.

"I did nothing," I spit, shaking off Kyle, but he has lockjaw. "Satan number one in training wheels just bit me. Then the other two joined in. No offense, but your kids are jerks." Again, not proud of my choice of words, but it's tame compared to what I originally thought.

"Mommy, she used a bad word!" says Benjamin from around my forearm. Taking advantage of this opportunity, I push at his forehead, and he thankfully lets go. Unfortunately, I had to use a little force, and he topples backward, joining Grandpa on the floor. The moment he connects with the carpet, I know what's going to happen.

He bursts into staged, over-the-top tears. And they call *me* a drama queen.

When the other two notice their brother is louder than them, they too decide to turn on the waterworks and fall theatrically to the floor. This means I am free from their razor-sharp teeth, but I am certainly not free from the wrath of their mother.

"I hope you're happy," she snarls, cocooning her kids into her bosom. They look at me from under their fair lashes, grinning a sinister smirk. God have mercy on their future wives.

"Happy?" I scoff, standing. "I'm covered in slobber and probably need a tetanus shot, so no, I'm not happy. But that's not the worst part. The worst part is finding out what your sister really thinks about you. So who is this apparent dog I've laid with? Maybe for once, someone in this fucking family can tell me what the hell is going on!"

Stella's eyes widen, and the whites almost look translucent. I've struck a nerve, but she's got another thing coming if she thinks I'm about to stop now.

"Oh, that's real nice. Showing your class right there by using such vulgar language," spits Ursula, attempting to shield her children's ears from my blasphemy. They only cry louder.

"Oh, please. That's nothing. If you want vulgar, I'll bring vulgar, you fuc—"

Ursula flies into a rage. "My children will need therapy after tonight!"

"They'll need something," I mutter under my breath, raising my glass in salute.

The mood is tense, and we're seconds away from starting something that is sure to end bloody and in tears. This can't get any worse.

"Peyton? Babe?" And just like that, things do get worse—a lot worse.

Babe? What right does he have to use that term of endearment?

Everyone's attention rivets to the doorway where a man stands, examining the insanity before him. Straightening out her outfit, Stella quickly rises, leaving Augusto to fend for himself. "Calvin, it's not time yet," she gently cautions. I've never heard her speak so delicately before.

The mysterious man, whose name is apparently Calvin, doesn't take any notice of her because his interest lies elsewhere. It's with me. He's attractive if you like the Abercrombie type, but he's way too straitlaced for me. And Stella seems to like him, which is an instant turn-off.

"I know, but I couldn't wait. I've waited long enough." He steps forward, arm outstretched like he's expecting me to run into his embrace. I do the complete opposite and take a step back.

His surprise is evident, and he stops, inhaling slowly. He's not accustomed to rejection.

I have no idea who this man is or why he has any right to be here when we're in the middle of World War III. Ursula is the first to break the silence.

"You wanted to know what is going on. Well, here's your chance." She sweeps her hand toward Calvin as if he's the key.

"Ursula!" scolds Stella, which only arouses my interest more.

Luis's warning sounds loudly, and I wonder if *this* is my surprise. The someone who was waiting for me upstairs. If so, I want a refund.

Lachlan clucks his tongue, rushing forward with a stagger to his step. It's clear he's had one too many scotches. But is there really such a thing in this place? "Peyton, meet Calvin."

"Lachlan, that's enough!" Stella's warning is fierce, but he doesn't care. The alcohol has given him a buzz, and he'll worry about the consequences later.

"She has a right to know."

My blood turns cold. "Know what?"

Lachlan turns to me with a look I recognize all too well—pity. "Peyton, Calvin is…"

"Is what?" I demand, on the verge of hysteria. Finally, the answers I have sought out are near. But I would have never guessed what Ursula reveals. Not in a million years.

She pulls back her shoulders with a smug smile. She takes great pleasure in my pain. I brace myself, but nothing can prepare me for what she says. "Calvin is your fiancé. He's here to take you home."

I could use all the cheesy clichés like my life flashes before my eyes or what doesn't kill you makes you stronger, but there is only one word to summarize how I'm feeling right now, and that word is FUCK!

Fiancé?

As in I was engaged to be married to this…to this tool? I can't believe it.

"No." I gasp, shaking my head in utter disbelief. "I-it can't be true." The walls begin closing in on me, and the darkness, which I've held at bay for days, begins to creep out of the shadows.

"It is true. Oh, babe. I've missed you." Calvin advances forward while I cover my mouth. I'm going to be sick.

"Stop. Right there," I manage to choke out, thrusting out my hand. If he takes one more step, I'll puke all over his Italian loafers. "Is this true?" It's a sad day in history when one is asking Stella for the truth.

She clears her throat before something that some would call a smile passes over her face. It's gone before I can second-guess it. "Yes. As usual, Calvin can't keep a secret."

He smirks, holding up his hands playfully. "Guilty as charged." His spirited nature just adds to the anger brewing within me. "It was torture waiting upstairs."

"Upstairs?" I whisper, calming my ragged breaths. He nods while I dig my fingernails into my palms. "What about waiting for the past six months? Was *that* torture because I know it was for me."

His mischief soon disappears. "Babe—"

But I cut him off, not interested in a word he has to say. "I am *not* your babe. If I were, you would have been by my bedside. You would have been the first face I saw when I woke up to this god-awful nightmare." The tremor in my voice displays my emotion, but I push it down as far as it will go because I refuse to show weakness. "But you weren't. As far as I'm concerned, you're a part of my past I wish to leave forgotten. Don't you *ever* surprise me again." I focus my seething anger on Stella.

How dare she do this to me.

"I think you need to talk." She and her suggestion can go to hell.

Laughing maniacally, I fear I've finally snapped. "And I think you need to stop telling me what to do. You gave up that right when you kept this"—I point at a cowering Calvin—"a secret. How could you? How could all of you?" I am done with this family. With this home. I am especially done with this stranger who thinks he has any right to touch me.

Calvin storms forward, but I recoil, holding up a single finger. "So help me God, if you touch me, I will break your hand." He senses my threat isn't empty and surrenders.

"I'll give you some time to calm down." But I am way past

that.

The more Calvin speaks, the more I want to throttle him. There is no way I was engaged to this man. Was I freaking crazy? Anything is possible, I suppose, because it seems I am constantly questioning my sanity. "I don't need to *calm down.* What I need is for all of you to forget me…just as I've forgotten you. Goodbye. Don't ever call me again." I turn on my heel, not caring that I take off in a dead sprint.

Only when I yank open the door and fly down the front steps do I allow the tears to flow. When I jump into Cayden's truck and speed down the driveway like the devil is at my heels, I permit the ugly sobs to overtake me.

My body shudders as I pull over to the curb, shedding frustrated, angry tears. I am furious at myself for allowing her to get to me. This was just another game to prove she is in control. She may have let me move, but tonight was her way of ascertaining that she is the puppeteer and I am merely her puppet. Here for her amusement only.

I slam my fists against the steering wheel, over and over again. I played right into her hands.

Wiping away my tears with my thumbs, I promise myself these are the last that will fall. Not one single tear will be shed for someone who doesn't deserve them. I put the truck into drive and make my way home.

The drive occurs on autopilot as I follow the GPS, my mind racing. I can't focus on a single thought. I kick myself for not gathering as much information on Calvin when I had the chance. But I know enough. His absence for the past six months speaks volumes. If he loved me, he would have never left my side.

I've never been happier to see my tattered home because it screams warmth. It's my safe place, and after tonight, I need all the safety I can get. Killing the engine, I breathe a sigh of relief when my feet touch the ground.

The constant energy that nourishes this magical place races through me, and I know there is only one place I need to be. I walk wearily, my heavy heart the compass as I make my way over the hill to the oak tree. The red ribbon flaps in the wind, waving me over and welcoming me back.

Being here soothes my demons, and it's no wonder it was the first place that ever felt like home. Ursula said Calvin was going to take me home. I can't imagine that being anywhere but here.

Taking hold of the coarse rope, I turn my back to the lake and lower myself onto the swing, wanting nothing more than to escape.

Cataloging everything I've learned, I've come to a conclusion that makes me feel a touch better. It's no wonder I was some sex-crazed, drug fiend. I needed the drugs and the random hookups to deal with the fact that I was engaged to a dipshit named Calvin. Even his name is stupid. What the fuck was I thinking?

But that's the problem—I don't think that I was. What event led me down the path that I took? What made me turn into the horrible person that I was?

"Peyton?"

How does he know I'm here? Like a moth to a flame—am I his true north like he is mine? It's time to find out.

"Hi." I keep my eyes lowered as I swing gently.

"How'd it go tonight?" Cayden knows; he can read my broken appearance for what it is. But he never assumes.

Swallowing, I muster the courage to reveal my dirty little secrets and don't bother with pretenses. "Apparently, I'm engaged to someone named Calvin." Silence. So I continue. "And if that isn't bad enough, the night Lacey and I went out for drinks, I found out that I was some bed-hopping adulterer who wasn't opposed to snorting a line or two. No wonder I can't remember. There is nothing good to remember." Tears threaten to break free, but I sniff them away.

I have no idea what Cayden is thinking. I wouldn't blame him for turning back the way he came. But he surprises me, just as he always does. "That's not true." His voice is powerful, my anchor in a punishing storm.

Finally lifting my eyes, I take him in, and instantly, the voices fade into the background. "What part? I'm not sure if you heard me, but I thought it was okay to be engaged to a man with no soul. Yet I also had no qualms about sleeping around on him. I apparently was some party girl who definitely did not live by the motto: say no to drugs."

"I heard," he counters, digging his hands into the pockets of his ripped jeans.

His cool composure irks me because I need to fight. I need to feel something other than this crippling, soul-shattering pain. Jumping from the swing, I storm over, adrenaline coursing through my veins. Cayden stands his ground when I close the distance between us. "Then tell me. Tell me how anything remotely good can come from what I just told you."

A rumble crackles, filling the starless night with power. A storm is brewing. Just as it did when I first arrived. Throwing everything to the wind, I press both my palms to Cayden's cheeks, desperately searching for the answers I know he holds. I promised to be patient, but I can't, not anymore.

The electricity threatens to burn us both. "I haven't even known you for two weeks," I confess, feeling beyond juvenile. I'm an adult woman with a schoolgirl crush. But I continue. "So why do I feel...this?" There is no need for me to explain what "this" is. He's felt it from the first moment we touched. But regardless, I can't help but question my sanity time and time again.

He closes his eyes, attempting to shut me out. I've ventured too deep.

The sky cracks with thunder, sparking the heavens like a sign from above. The storm is moments away from drowning us both, but it also has the power to baptize us from our sins. "I know I've asked you this before, but I need to know..."

A lightning bolt slices through the darkness, warning this is it. No turning back.

The wind turns brutal, the storm punishing anyone in its path. But I ignore it. "Please, I just need to know the truth. For once," I cry, my lower lip trembling. Cayden opens his eyes, and the color, the intensity, I know I've been lost in those orbs before. "Have we...have we met before?"

This is the moment Cayden tells me to stop with the conspiracy theories and drags me inside. The moment when he puts my uncertainties to bed once and for all. But when he draws his silence out, I know I'm about to receive a lot more than I bargained for. A simple word shouldn't have the power to change the world. But it does.

"Yes."

The heavens choose this moment to open with a downpour of punishing rain, which is ironic, considering I feel like I'm submerged. Even though the rain drowns us both, neither of us moves. We're caught in a deadlock. Cayden has just revealed what I always knew to be true. But now that he's confirmed my worst fears, I need to know why he lied.

I thought once Cayden told me the truth, things would become clearer, and maybe, just maybe, I'd remember. But now that I know the truth, I wish I didn't because now I'm faced with another dilemma. Why did he lie? It's been twelve days. Twelve whole days when he could have told me the truth. But instead, he chose to watch me suffer. To watch me question everything.

The truth was supposed to set me free, but it hasn't.

The rainfall is heavy, and I can barely make out Cayden's still form. But the steady rise and fall of his shoulders reveal my journey has only just begun. The need to flee suddenly overtakes me. The atmosphere ignites with a lightning strike, the sound spooking me, and like a wild horse, I turn and break free.

The muddy ground beneath me threatens to pull me under like quicksand, but I continue running. The lake has always been the magnetic force triggering this chain of events, so it only seems fitting I end it here now.

I sprint faster than I ever have before, slipping and sliding in the mud, but the closer I get to the body of water, the quieter things become. Cayden's death-curdling screams compete with the punishing rain, but his anguish wins out in the end.

"Stop! Peyton. Stop!"

But I don't. I want to shed my skin and be reborn, and no one is going to stop me.

I'm mere feet away, the water welcoming me with a soothing touch as a light mist cakes my face and my body. I'm almost at the finish line and spread my arms out wide, prepared for whatever fate throws my way.

As usual, fate reveals what a sadistic bitch she is because the smell of the ocean smashes into me before I'm knocked to the ground. The air is ripped from my lungs, and I struggle to breathe. But survival takes a back seat when Cayden wrestles with me, begging me to stop. But I will not surrender.

I fight him, clawing at his shoulders to let me go, but my attempts to break free only have Cayden pinning me down harder.

"Get off!" I scream, hysterical. "You fucking lied to me!" I wiggle my body and kick my legs, hoping to get in a lucky shot and throw him off.

I don't.

"Don't you dare do this to me again. Don't you dare!" he cries, yanking my arms above my head and gripping my wrists in one hand. His words have the desired effect, and I suddenly grow lax, the fight in me dying for now. What does he mean?

"I don't know what's real anymore," I confess, angry tears springing to life. I want to fight him, but I don't know who I'm angrier with—Cayden or myself.

His heaving chest presses to mine as he searches every inch of my face. "I'm real. And so are you. But most importantly"—

he nudges my nose with his, inhaling—"this is real. You are not alone," he says. It's an oath, one I believe to be true, but that doesn't chip away at the betrayal I feel, which is why he returns a little piece of my soul to me. "Everything…is always better after a thunderstorm…"

I gasp, blinking past the raindrops but also the tears. "Wh-why do you say that?" I whisper, not understanding any of this. Our bodies press together so tightly that not a single wisp of air can shift between us, yet this isn't close enough.

Cayden releases me, only to brush the soaked hair from my cheeks. The hypnotic gray of his eyes threatens to drag me under. "Because it helps us to remember that life goes on. No matter if we want it to…or not."

I don't have a chance to talk…think…breathe…because Cayden steals everything from me, and in turn, he makes it ours. He thumbs my bottom lip, coaxing me to allow him in. But he doesn't need permission. This man has been a part of me from the very moment we met.

His hair is tousled, and the rain darkens the strands to a deeper brown. A raindrop backflips from a dark lock that has flicked forward and lands on my parted lips. Without thought, my tongue darts out to taste it. To taste *him*. His groan cascades over my quivering form.

The rain thrashes down around us, but nothing else exists. "Did you lo-love me?" I boldly ask, my body undulating as he focuses on my mouth.

"Yes. Very much," he replies earnestly and openly. With a fingertip, he traces my features, lost in a dream. "But a single mistake cost us both."

"What does that mean?"

Cayden is unburdening his soul, but that doesn't come without consequence.

I feel every hardened inch of him as he crushes us together, threading his fingers through my hair. Sealing our fate forever, he once again thumbs my bottom lip, enticing me to welcome him home, and I do. He suckles my top lip. We're done for. "I broke your heart," he professes, nothing but sadness overtaking us both. But what he says next ruins me forevermore. "And for the next ten years…you broke mine."

Time stands still.

I want to say so many things, but no words could ever explain the chaos swirling within. So with no other choice, I end this once and for all. Lacing my hands through his tousled locks, I pull his mouth to mine, stopping a hair's breadth away. He waits, hovering over me, a mixture of rage, sadness, and frustration consuming him.

In no way am I gentle as I tug at his hair. I'm angry, so fucking angry, and at this moment, I don't know if I want to slap or kiss him. But then I watch as his tongue sweeps along his bottom lip, and I decide on the latter.

I devour him whole. Consequences be damned.

I don't have time to sample his taste because it's sensory overload, and I consume him like he is my last meal. Nothing is gentle about this kiss, and the fact our tongues are demanding the other to surrender is an aphrodisiac within itself. But I refuse to concede.

We fight for domination, but neither of us submits. I bite his bottom lip, but it only spurs him on.

He growls into my mouth, winding his fingers around my nape and holding me prisoner as we kiss like starved souls. We tease. We take. We give. I soften against him as he hardens and demands more.

He licks at the seam of my mouth, tasting me with long, elegant strokes. I'm panting and writhing beneath him because I know what comes next. I know because I could never forget Cayden's kisses. The sweep of his tongue, the softness of his lips, I remember. I remember because you never forget your first kiss…your first love.

Cayden was my first everything. I know that he was.

He sucks at my tongue, greedily drinking me into him while I bask in his scent. His skin smells of the ocean and sunshine, and I can't stop the whimper that slips past my lips. So many emotions crash into me. Kissing Cayden is familiar, almost innate, like breathing, because I need it to survive.

I am still angry. Betrayed. But I have an entire lifetime to wade through the bitterness. Now, I just want to feel.

Our tongues roll together in unison, as do our bodies, for a dance specially created for us. We fit together like two jigsaw pieces. Our flesh is slick from the rain, providing the perfect lubrication as I writhe and moan against him.

I cup his face, frightened he'll disappear because his admission demonstrates that our lives have weathered many hardships. Tears instantly surface. He senses my sorrow and slows the kiss down, gently and deeply making love to my mouth but, most shockingly, also to my heart.

This kiss comes in many shades, but my undoing is when love replaces his passion. He caresses and kisses me like I'm his world. Not just his moon. His stars. The sun. I am his everything. Without me, he will perish, and life is no more.

Tears break the floodgates, and I don't know when they'll stop. Cayden's sadness is palpable as he kisses me one final time. He kisses my cheeks, washing away my anguish, before lifting himself up. I miss his warmth.

Needing a minute, I lie still, peering into the heavens as the rain falls on me. "Why wouldn't you tell me this, Cayden?"

His breathing is heavy. This is about to break us both. "Because you asked me not to." I close my eyes, sealing away my tears. "You told me whatever the circumstances, I was to never speak to you again. That I was to forget you because you…had forgotten me." The hitch to his tone reveals he hasn't escaped unscathed from my demands.

"I've brought you nothing but pain. So when you told me if I ever loved you I was to leave you alone, I listened. You made me promise. And I did. It was the one and only time I didn't let you down."

Breathing in and out, I measure my breaths as I'm afraid I'm moments away from passing out. "What did we do?" I say, almost afraid to ask. I can't face him. Not yet.

Goose bumps prick my flesh as Cayden skims two fingertips down my forearm, circling over my racing pulse. This is what I've craved from the moment we met. For him to touch me openly like I'm his. But now, I know what this is. This is goodbye.

"You will always be my biggest regret."

"She'll always be…the biggest regret of my life." Cayden's admission to Hazel now takes on a whole different meaning

because it appears I am the cause of something so heinous, he will forever regret it and me for as long as he lives.

I am a monster.

"I don't understand. I don't understand any of this. But I'm s-sorry, Cayden. I'm sorry for whatever pa-pain I caused." My stomach turns, and the darkness is moments away from dragging me under.

Unlike anything in the past, this is a tsunami, the mother of all storms, and I know there is no coming back from this. I fight the blackness, but suddenly, it feels good to surrender, so I do. The white noise conquers the torture, and I allow it to overthrow me.

But when I do…all I can smell is the ocean. "I'm the one who's sorry. I'm the one who couldn't save you, Snow."

TWELVE

Three Weeks Later

"Doll, I ordered my eggs scrambled, not poached."

"I'm sorry?" My grip on reality flashes like a TV station's picture flickering in and out with the static. Blinking once, I return to the now.

The customer, a middle-aged man with kind blue eyes, points at his plate, where indeed sits two poached eggs, three strips of bacon, and a mountain of hash browns. It's apparent he feels guilty for pointing out my error, but I've grown accustomed to my oversight because it's happened countless times this week.

"I'm so sorry, Will. Here, let me fix that for you." I lunge for the plate, my cheeks blistering, but he gently wraps his fingers around my wrist.

"It's okay. Don't worry about it. I'll eat them." I smile, thankful he doesn't cause a scene.

"Here. Let me top off your coffee." Will, who I met on my first day of work, removes his hand and offers me his white porcelain cup. I pour in the dark liquid, sighing when my shaky hand overfills the cup, making a mess on his saucer.

"Not having a good day?" he asks, reaching for a wad of napkins to soak up my mess.

"You could say that," I reply, reaching into my apron pocket and placing a handful of creamers onto the tabletop. "Breakfast is on me."

On autopilot, I walk through my place of employment, the very cool 50s-themed diner, Nat's Place. This place serves good, wholesome food at reasonable prices. It's also open twenty-four hours. So it goes without saying that it's a hit with locals and tourists alike.

I pass through the retro layout, topping off coffees while remembering to smile. But that's a big ask, considering these past few weeks have been utter hell. I promised myself I wouldn't think of the night that kick-started my demise, but I've accepted the fact that I'm a complete masochist because before my life turned to shit, I was happy. For a single moment, I felt alive.

A simple kiss changed my world forever, but there was nothing simple about that kiss, nor the confession that followed. I swallow past the lump in my throat that forms when merely thinking his name. Cayden and I were in love. My heart warms. But a bitter cold soon replaces that warmth.

"I broke your heart…and for the next ten years…you broke mine."

His admission still chills me to the bone. What did I do?

What did *we* do?

The blackouts have been far more frequent, and the feeling of being watched is so overwhelming that I've begun taking the meds prescribed to me by my doctor. I vowed to never take them, but the line between fiction and reality is beginning to blur.

When I came to after passing out, I woke up alone in my bedroom. No doubt Cayden carried me home, but he didn't stick around. I gave him the space he clearly needed because I needed it too, but when dawn broke, I knew that space was endless.

Cayden lay low, as did I. I had to clear my head. His confession changed everything. It changed how I viewed myself. And him. After everything I've uncovered, one thing is clear—I wasn't a good person. How could I be? I made the man I loved promise to forget me because I had forgotten him. But evidently, I hadn't.

After two torturous days, I finally gathered the courage to knock on his front door. He never answered. I thought he needed more time, but as two days turned into three, four, five, it was apparent time wasn't what he needed. He needed me to leave him alone. Whatever love we shared was no more.

I still had Cayden's truck, so I left it in his driveway since he'd made it clear he didn't want to see me. The next day, it was parked in my front yard. He still cared, which just made things worse. I wanted to storm over to this house and demand he speaks to me, but I didn't. A small part of me was scared of what I would say. What I would ask. Everything is just so messed up.

I've replayed every conversation we've had, and each time,

I'm left more confused, angry, and wounded than the time before. I am furious that Cayden shut me out after everything he disclosed, but that rage soon disappears when I wonder what I did to him for him to look at me with such sorrow and regret in his eyes.

It appears he has stayed true to his word because, since that night, he's been MIA. Lacey too. I can't help but feel betrayed because she knew the truth this entire time. I made Cayden promise, but what about her?

Once again, I'm drowning in questions with no end in sight.

Cayden sent workmen over to the house to finish the job, which just made this entire situation all the more unbearable. His mixed signals confused me further. I wanted him, not them, and demanded they leave and never come back. Of course, they didn't listen.

Even in my times of absolute solitude, I've never felt more alone than I did in that house. Every noise was amplified in the silence. But even more so, *he* was amplified everywhere I looked. Late at night, while staring up at the single star, I came to realize why this house slowly became a home. It was because of Cayden. He gave me a taste of what I wanted…of what I had. But then ripped it out from under me—again.

Determined not to surrender, I educated myself as best as I could by making YouTube my best friend. I watched video after video on DIY home renovations. I also utilized the firsthand knowledge I learned from Cayden. However, after the stunt Stella pulled, there was no way I was going to depend on her for a cent. I may have my own bank account, but for some reason, using that money feels so wrong.

As I walked home from the hardware store one day, supplies in hand, I noticed a HELP WANTED sign in the diner window. As much as I loved working for Cayden, there was no way I could go back. So I applied and immediately got the job.

It's waiting tables, which I don't mind doing, and my boss, Nate, is terrific. This diner has been in his family for generations, and he's kept it the way his great-grandfather Nathanael designed it. Nate doesn't ask questions or say anything when I break yet another plate or cup when it falls from my forever shaky fingers. He rarely speaks, which suits me just fine.

I am happy to descend into anonymity.

Julia, a bubbly server from Texas, offers me a stick of gum as I round the counter and head for a coffee refill. I know she's just trying to be friendly, but I can't do friendly. The last friend I made vanished without a trace.

However, not wanting to be rude, I accept the peppermint strip and place it into the pocket of my mint green uniform. The dress is the traditional retro diner outfit with a white collar and white cuffed short sleeves. Thankfully, Nate drew the line at the white headband.

"Want to take a break?" Julia asks, standing beside me.

"No, I'm okay. I already took mine."

"That was yesterday," she kindly says. The glass coffeepot rattles in my hand.

She's probably right. Every day shapes into one giant repetitive loop, and the fact that I don't need more than three hours of sleep to survive has me working double shifts. I need the money and the distraction. It's a win-win.

Will appears, ready to pay his bill, but I wave him off. "Don't worry about it. I've got it covered." Reaching into my apron pocket, I attempt to sort through the wads of ones, prepared to pay for his breakfast out of my tips. But he reaches across the counter, gently wrapping his fingers around my wrist to stop me.

"No, you won't. Ring up the bill. I won't have you paying for my breakfast." The firmness of his tone affirms this isn't up for discussion. So I don't bother arguing.

He pulls his hand back while I nervously calculate the total. "That'll be ten fifty-four."

Will hunts for his wallet from his back pocket and gives me a twenty. "Keep the change, doll."

I hesitate to accept because it's too much, but Will seems like the type of man who doesn't take no for an answer. "Thank you. Have a nice day."

"I will. See you tomorrow?" he asks, pocketing his wallet before reaching for a toothpick from a container on the counter.

"Sure." I nod, not really knowing why he's suddenly making me nervous. He winks before turning and leaving me with a mouthful of questions.

When Will is out the door, Julia, who witnessed the weird scene, saunters over to where I stand, confused. "He's been in here a lot."

Pocketing the change, I shrug, hoping to come across as aloof. "I hadn't noticed."

But she doesn't buy it. "Oh, come on. Someone who looks like that. It's hard *not* to notice." I blanch because, yes, Will isn't unattractive by any means, but he'd probably be more suited for someone my mother's age. I can't help but chuckle at the visual.

My mother wouldn't be caught dead liaising with the likes of Will. They couldn't be more opposites. With his scruffy graying hair, Harley Davidson T-shirts, and faded tattoos, he'd give her a heart attack just by saying hello to her.

"He's sweet on you," Julia says, which has me almost pulling a muscle in my neck as I snap my head to look at her, paling. "Don't look so surprised. With all that fiery red hair and looks to die for, a lot of men are sweet on you."

This is news to me.

"Thank you, but I'm not interested. I'm here to do my job and then go home. I'm not looking for love or romance." That was supposed to be a hint for Julia to back off and leave it be, but I've come to learn she rarely takes a hint.

"Tell that to the hottie who just walked through the door."

Humoring her, I raise my eyes to see a sight I wasn't sure I'd ever see again. My memory has not done him justice because I don't remember him looking this good. But regardless of his good looks, I want to slap his cheek.

Cayden stands in the middle of the diner, openly looking at me. So many emotions smash into me, and I clutch onto the edge of the counter, afraid I'm moments away from losing my last shred of sanity.

I want to say so many things, but I'm afraid of what I will say. Seeing him evokes a raging anger because he lied to me, and then he just disappeared. I want answers. He owes them to me.

A betrayal tear breaks past the floodgates and trickles down my cheek. Cayden closes his eyes for the briefest of moments, wrestling with his demons as his hands curl into fists by his sides. I want nothing more than to speak to him, but I gave up that right when I broke his heart—not once, not twice, but for ten long years.

Although I told Cayden to stay away, it appears even amnesia wasn't strong enough to keep *me* away from him. I may have forgotten him, but it's clear my heart hasn't. Secrets and sorrows fill our past, and a small part of me believes I don't want to remember what we did.

But Cayden doesn't have the luxury. Whatever we did, whatever *I* did, he remembers, and every time he looks at me, he's reminded of those sins. He's reminded that despite the fact that he loved me, sometimes, love just isn't enough.

We commit one another to memory, unsure when we will see the other again because one thing is clear—it hurts. Unburdening himself hasn't set him free—it's only made things worse. Maybe it would have been better if he'd never told me.

"Julia, can you cover for me? I'm suddenly not feeling well." I barely recognize my own voice. Cayden and I are still caught in a stalemate, but I'm the one to end things once and for all.

"Of course. Take the rest of the day off." I don't bother arguing and quickly untie my apron. Reaching for my bag under the counter, I risk one last glance at Cayden because I don't know when I'll see him again. But he's already gone.

He's taken a piece of my heart with him as he escaped out the front door, so I decide to exit from the back. It's a beautiful summer's day, and on any other morning, I'd appreciate the sunshine but not today. I decide to walk home as I could use some fresh air.

I need to talk to Cayden, but today proved that neither of

us is ready to take that first step. Some may call me weak for not facing my demons, but the truth is, I don't know if I'm ready. I don't know if I'll ever be ready to hear the atrocities of my past. The small insights are enough.

Head down and lost in my own little world, I'm not looking where I'm going, that is, until I bump straight into someone. "I am so…" But my sentence remains unfinished because when I see who stands before me, I doubt I'll ever be able to speak again.

"You," gasps Hazel, blinking twice as if to ascertain that I'm really here. "You have some nerve showing your face here. How dare you come back."

There was a time when I was utterly desperate to uncover the secrets of my past, but now that I've been given a glimpse, I want nothing more than to forget. "I'm so-sorry." I stumble over my words, wiping my sweaty palms on my dress. The movement seems to alert Hazel of my attire, which she clearly overlooked.

She scans me from head to toe before her scowl is replaced with a smugness that has me wishing I'd just stayed at work. "Oh my God, I never thought I'd see the day Little Miss Perfect worked a job that was beneath her."

"Waiting tables isn't beneath me," I counter, not appreciating her tone.

Hazel folds her arms over her slender frame and arches a brow. She knows something is amiss. Sick of hiding behind my fears, I pull back my shoulders, refusing to allow the past to affect my future. "I know your name is Hazel." Wrath soon replaces her arrogance. She appears livid that I had the gall to speak her name. "I only know this because…Cayden told me."

"Don't you *dare* speak his name to me," she spits, her temper spiking. But I persevere.

"I don't remember you. I'm sorry. Six months ago, I was involved in a car accident. When I woke, I didn't remember anything, anyone." Hazel looks at me like I'm speaking Russian. So I clarify, "I have amnesia."

My admission throws Hazel for a loop. That much is clear. But that's all that's clear because I have no clue what she's thinking. She appears stunned, but there is an air of disbelief to her, which she confirms a second later. "Always have to be the center of attention, don't you? I've heard some bullshit stories in my life, but this one tops the cake." A sarcastic snicker follows.

"This isn't a story," I state, bitterness lacing my words. "It's the truth. What reason would there be for me to make this up?"

Hazel hisses a breath through her clenched teeth. "There are many reasons," she cries. "First and foremost is the fact that you ruined my life. Not only did you string Cayden along, you…" But she quickly seals her lips, appearing almost pained to continue.

"I what?" Whatever she has to say, I want to know.

She cocks her head to the side, really looking at me for the first time. "You're telling the truth, aren't you?"

I nod once. "Yes, I am."

"I'll be damned," she whispers, eyes wide. "This is my dream come true. That you'd forget this place ever existed. But here you are. Amnesia or not, you can't seem to leave him alone." No guessing who she's referring to.

"I'm sorry, Hazel, for whatever I did." I suppose I could ask her what exactly that is, but I don't know if I'd believe her or not. But thinking of Ellie, I realize she can't be that bad. Ellie is a great kid, and I want to believe that she had a part to play. "I was the one who pushed Ellie to safety. I didn't know she was your daughter…"

I have no idea why I decided to tell her that. I figured maybe she'd see I've changed and am not the person I once was. But my words have the opposite effect. I may as well have told her to go fuck herself.

She storms over, and time stands still as she slaps my cheek—hard. If not for the throbbing in my face, I'd have believed I spaced out. But I don't have that luxury. "You stay away from her!" she screams, and I cower, afraid she's about to smack the other cheek. "What did you do to her?"

"Nothing!" I exclaim, backing off with my hands raised in surrender. "I saw her standing in the middle of the road. She looked like she'd seen a ghost. So I acted on instinct and pushed her out of harm's way."

"*You* saved her?" she spits, voicing my actions like they're pure evil.

"Yes."

Cayden hinted that Hazel was a touch insane, but when she throws back her head and laughs maniacally, I think he may have gone a little light on her. "Oh my God," she says between winded breaths. "How ironic that *you* were the one who saved her. No wonder Cayden never told me who it was. But that's just like Cayden. Your forever protector." Her comment highlights the fact she knows Cayden and I have a past.

I gulp, refusing to address her crack. I know Cayden and I

have history. But when I grow a pair, that story will be his to tell, and not hers. "Ironic? How?" I am sick of her speaking to me in sentences that make no sense.

But what she says next has me wishing I'd been kept in the dark forever. She steps forward, invading all personal boundaries, when she snarls inches from my face, "Because, not so long ago, you were the one she needed saving from."

"No." I gasp, shaking my head, tears sticking to my lashes. "That's…that's not true." Cayden warned me of Hazel's poison, but this is just sick. What kind of a mother would use their daughter that way just to upset another?

But when I blink past my tears, I see it. Hazel is a mother scorned because I, Peyton Veronica Lane, hurt her only daughter, and Ellie is living proof that what she says is true. Ellie was standing frozen in the middle of the road because of me. I thought at the time it appeared as if she'd just seen a ghost, because she had.

Me.

Whatever I did…I did to Ellie.

White noise surrounds me, and flickers of the lake, of someone drowning, flash before my eyes. They are treading water, pleading for their life, but I…I do nothing. I simply watch them take their last breath before they sink to the bottom, forgotten to the world.

Hazel's insults fill the air, but I can no longer focus on anything other than fleeing and never looking back. I can only look forward as there is no other choice. It's time to strip away the guise and uncover the truth. Once and for all.

All plans of walking home were long forgotten. I hailed a cab and was thankful the driver wasn't a talker. During the ride home, all I could think about is what Hazel had said.

"Because, not so long ago, you were the one she needed saving from."

The thought is so heinous, but it explains so much. The way Ellie acted when she first saw me, down to Cayden's protectiveness over her when I was involved. I not only hurt him, but I hurt his daughter as well. I knew I wasn't in the running for sainthood, but this is just unfathomable. So many secrets color my past. No wonder my mind is in no hurry to remember. I can forget, but Cayden, he can't.

Which is why I step from the cab, give the driver a fifty, and look toward finally putting an end to this ordeal. Cayden is most likely at work, but I'm done giving him space. I need to know everything, regardless of the fact that it'll ruin me forever. I plan on changing, and then I intend to sit on his front steps until he comes home. I don't care how long that takes; this has to happen, and it has to happen now.

However, my bravery is all in vain because when I turn around, I'm reminded of life's sick sense of humor. "Please, let me talk." My walls must be erected ten feet high because Calvin raises his hands in surrender.

"What are you doing here? How did you know where to find me?"

Calvin descends my porch steps while I stand my ground. "There is no other place you'd be," he replies, which has me taking a deep breath.

"So it appears everyone is privy to my past but me."

"Can we talk?" Calvin isn't offering an olive branch. He simply wants a chance to explain. "I don't like how we left things. Stella assured me you'd be happy to see me again, but she was clearly mistaken."

"Yes, she was." I fold my arms across my chest, an invisible barrier to keep out the pain. My feelings on the matter are clear. If he wants to talk, he can do so out here. I don't want this conversation to taint my home.

"I stayed away because prior to your accident, you gave me back this." As he reaches into the pocket of his beige chinos, I hold my breath. The sunlight catches the ridged edges, showcasing the beautiful diamond I once wore. "We were engaged for one year, but we've known one another since we were kids."

I run a hand down my face because this is almost too much. "Why did I end our engagement?"

Sighing, it's evident the pain Calvin wears is real. "Because of the reason you're here."

"But that's the problem. I don't actually know why I'm here," I counter, but he doesn't accept my reason.

"You know why. It's always been the reason…since you were eight years old."

"What?" I question, completely lost in translation.

"Stella hasn't told you anything?" I shake my head slowly. "I stayed away, not because I didn't love you…but it was *because* I loved you. But you"—his regret is palpable—"you didn't love me. You never did. Your heart has always belonged to another."

"Who?" I ask in a mere whisper. I know the answer, but I need him to confirm it as the truth.

"Cayden." Even though I knew what his response would be, I still can't mask my shock. "It's why you're back here. You may have amnesia, but it seems your love for him knows no bounds. I was stupid for ever thinking we'd work."

"Please tell me our story," I say with nothing but sincerity. No matter what I thought of Calvin when we first met, his genuineness and apparent love for me have me hoping that maybe I wasn't such a bad person, after all.

He smiles, but it's bittersweet. "Our parents are longtime friends, so I'm surprised our marriage wasn't prearranged at birth. We vacationed here when we were kids. Our houses were the biggest. I used to admire the view, but I now know this was done with intent. We were looking down on the entire neighborhood—figuratively and literally. But that didn't stop you. Not only were you stubborn but you were also inquisitive. Not a good combination for an eight-year-old little girl." He takes a breath, clearly needing to compose himself, as do I.

"I knew I wanted to marry you. I may have been ten, and you eight"—he smirks at his naivety—"but I knew you were the only girl for me. But life doesn't work that way. The moment you met Cayden Coachman…everything changed."

My steady breathing fills the silence as I gather the courage to hear what he says next.

"I always thought you were with him as a fuck you to your mom, but it was just wishful thinking on my part. You always belonged to him. Even when you agreed to marry me, I thought that maybe things had changed. I knew you were still seeing

Cayden behind my back, but you had been long before we got engaged."

"What…what does that mean?" I ask, swallowing.

He pins me with his steel-blue stare while I remind myself to breathe. "It means we became a thing about eight years ago. But I use the term lightly. We were apart more than we were together, but I loved you. I accepted that Cayden was always going to be a thing of your past. But as long as he stayed there, I was fine with it. And he did stay there. For a while."

"For a while?" I wish I was a touch more coherent, but my head is spinning.

He nods, digging his hands into his pockets. "This place, it's always been your gravitational pull. No matter how settled things were, no place made you happier than being here. Even though I didn't want to accept it, I always knew a person, not the place, was what made you feel at home."

"Why did you stay with me?" I ask, ashamed.

"Because I loved you. I still do." He has no qualms about opening his heart to me, which just makes me feel worse. "We hadn't slept with one another for over six months. I knew it was coming, but the day you gave this back"—he fingers the ring, lost in thought—"I knew we were done for good."

Calvin's tale is just another proverbial nail. Just what sort of a person was I?

Regardless, it's evident that all of this, just as I knew all along, began with Cayden. So it seems fitting to end it with him too.

"What are you doing here?" The utter contempt in Cayden's question has me flinching, frightened of what comes next.

Calvin pockets the ring, appearing to treasure it and the memories it holds. But when his eyes narrow into mere slits, I dare say there are some memories he wished remained forgotten. "I'm here to tell Peyton the truth. Something you should have done a long time ago."

I'm afraid to face him because now that I have scattered pieces of this elaborate puzzle, I'm terrified of the image I'll see. But the reason I'm here gives me the strength I need to turn around. Everything Calvin just shared has me looking at Cayden in a different light. But underneath it all are the emotions I have associated with him from the first moment we met—home. Cayden is my home.

He can sense my change of heart. He knows that Calvin has fed me snippets, but now, I want to know it all. "What happens between us is none of your business. It never was. But you just can't help but be her knight in shining armor, can you?" Cayden spits.

The mood turns in an instant. "I don't make apologies for wanting to protect her."

Our gazes are locked in a heated exchange, and I am completely one with the phrase actions speak louder than words. At this moment, Cayden wants to devour me whole. "That's where you and I differ. You think she needs protecting. But she never did. I made that mistake once, and it ended up being the biggest regret of my life."

I am touched by his affirmation, as I like that he doesn't see me as some damsel in distress, because not once have I ever felt that way. I don't need protecting. All I need is the truth.

"You have *always* been your own strength," Cayden

confesses, and it's suddenly just him and me. "You are fearless. You are strong. You are Peyton Veronica fucking Lane." Tears sting my eyes because I have never felt more empowered than I do right now.

Cayden storms over, placing his quivering hand on my cheek. The moment we touch, I know that everything has changed. "Don't you ever forget it. Regardless of what anyone tells you, you are beautiful. You are wise, but most of all…you are mine. You always have been." I bite the inside of my cheek to stop the emotion. But he runs his thumb over the apple of my cheek, tearing me in two.

As I lean into his embrace, the noise transforms into silence because just as I knew they would, Cayden's demons appease mine. Sadly, Calvin's demons don't like being benched. I don't know why Cayden is shoving me aside, and when my butt hits the ground, I still don't understand his actions until I peer upward and see Calvin deliver an uppercut, snapping Cayden's head backward with a sickening crack.

I gasp, horrified, unsure if this is really happening or not, but when Calvin launches forward, armed with a war cry from hell, I know this nightmare is real. "Stop it!" I roar, finding my footing as I rise. But Cayden blocks me from harm's way, which puts him into the line of fire.

Calvin attempts to deliver another blow, but when Cayden ducks and serves a right hook of his own, it's clear that Calvin got in a lucky shot. He connects with his nose, and I immediately see blood.

They circle one another, fists raised, eyes sharp, but Calvin doesn't stand a chance. Each time he lunges forward, Cayden ducks and weaves. He is the true champion, but there never was any doubt in my mind that he was.

"The slate's been wiped clean. She doesn't remember," Calvin states. "So how about for once, you fight me fair and square. Or are you afraid she'll finally see you for what you really are?" I don't know what that means, but Cayden clearly does. The change in his demeanor is evident, and at this moment, I fear for Calvin's life.

Cayden growls, the low, graveled sound enough to warn me things are about to turn. His words inspire me, and I act before I think. Rushing forward, I wedge my way between them, thinking of the consequences later. "Enough!" I scream, resting my hands on Cayden's cheeks, beseeching him to stop.

Calvin is at my back, and the fact doesn't go unnoticed by him. The fight in him simmers. "Peyton?"

I don't know what he expected to happen. Did he think coming here all chivalrous would put him in my good favor? I appreciate his honesty, but any feelings I may have had for him are gone. I feel nothing. But from what he tells me, I doubt I ever did. "Just go, Calvin."

"Are you serious?"

"Yes, very," I reply, ensuring Cayden's gaze stays riveted to me.

Calvin hisses as I instantly feel the warmth from my back evaporate. "Nothing's changed. Even with amnesia, you still fucking choose him."

A rumble bubbles to the surface, and Cayden is seconds away from exploding. Unsure of what else to do, I do the only thing I can. "No, Calvin, you're wrong. I choose me." Without fears or reservations, I smash my lips to Cayden's, mindful that he's just been hit, but Cayden doesn't do things in half.

He threads his fingers through my hair, angling my head as he dominates me with a strength that takes my breath away. With our guards lowered, we kiss like starved animals, taking and giving all in the same token.

We sample one another, our tongues tangoing in a dance orchestrated especially for us. He suckles my bottom lip before breaking our connection and slides down the length of my neck over to my chin. His kisses are hot and frantic, and I want it. I want so much more.

A whimper escapes me, an unrefined sound that we have passed the line of no return, but who am I kidding; we passed that threshold the moment we met. I draw his lips back to mine, kissing him with a passion so fierce that I'm almost certain every part of me is on fire.

I'm unsure when Calvin left. It could have been two minutes or two hours ago because when lost this way with Cayden, no one else exists but us.

Although this kiss is dripping with raw hunger, there is an underlayer of softness, of longing as well. If what Calvin says is true, then Cayden Coachman has been entrenched into my very core since the beginning of time. I suddenly break free.

There is another side to this reunion, and that's anger. Acting on instinct, I slap his cheek. Hard. "That's for lying to me."

He rubs his cheek, accepting his punishment with a nod.

"I want the truth. All of it."

He inhales before nodding once. "Okay."

That was easier than I thought. But I know nothing about this will be easy. "I saw Hazel." Cayden closes his eyes briefly, clearly disturbed by my revelation. However, what I say next has him understanding this is just the start of things to come. "What did...what did I do to Ellie?"

He wrestles with what to say next, but the pretenses are over. He extends his hand, an invitation that offers me the strength I need. "Come with me, and I'll tell you everything. Are you ready?"

This is the moment I've been waiting for, for the past six months. Releasing whatever fear I have left to the wind, I slip my palm into his, never feeling more liberated than I do right now. "I'm ready."

THIRTEEN

The moment I enter Cayden's home, I know shit is about to get real.

Usually, Cayden is so guarded, and although he's still keeping his cards close to his chest, his confliction over what he's about to reveal is almost palpable. He leads me straight up the stairs and to his bedroom. When he closes the door, sealing us in, I know there is no turning back.

Taking a moment, I remember the safety this room brought me and hope that once this is done, it'll do so once again. Peering up at the abstract charcoal sketch above his bed, I now see that it's a naked woman. To the naked eye, one could guess it to be a million other images. But somehow, I know exactly what it's supposed to be. I'm transfixed by the linework, and the simplicity of being stripped bare this way brings tears to my eyes. But I'm not here to admire furnishings.

I stand at the foot of the bed, watching as Cayden paces, running both hands through his snarled hair. Whatever he's about to say isn't going to be easy—for either of us. "When I told you, you didn't belong here, I was telling you the truth. I met you when I was"—he takes a deep breath as he stops pacing and meets my eyes—"nine years old. You were…"

"Eight," I reply, almost lost for words.

He nods slowly, almost regrettably. "Yes. I remember the first time I saw you. Everyone knew who the Lanes were, but no one actually saw them because we weren't supposed to be in that part of town. That is, until one night, I broke that rule."

I inhale sharply, unbelieving his memories are mine.

"I needed to see what was so special about the other side of the lake. Rumors were rife, and kids who claimed they'd been to 'the other side' said it was like some magical fairy tale where the streets were flourishing with everything we lacked. I rowed my boat over in the dead of night and decided to explore the white house. The house stood out from any others around it. The house which was forever my beacon in the cruelest of times."

I pale, not understanding what that means, but I don't dare breathe.

"You had the most fruitful lemon tree growing in your front yard. And I began to believe the rumors. I had never seen anything like it back home because anything not bolted down was stolen. I don't know why I did it. I was only there to appease my curiosity, but it suddenly wasn't enough. I began to understand what Adam felt in the Garden of Eden. Those lemons tempted me in ways I never imagined, and before I knew it, I was jumping over your white picket fence, intent on picking the perfect lemon.

"I only wanted one, but then I thought of Lacey back home. If I picked a few, I could sell them and make enough money to feed us both for a few days. I couldn't remember when we had our last decent meal. So with that as my incentive, I took off my tattered T-shirt and used it as a knapsack as I picked your tree almost bare.

"I picked more than I could carry, so I decided to come back the next night to gather the rest. When I threw my loot over my shoulder, I felt like a true warrior as I'd come to the other side and survived. But I soon swallowed my bravery because when I saw you, I knew I'd never be the same again."

Cayden's tale is sad beyond words, but I suddenly understood why he looked at me like I was an anomaly when I opted for the simplicity of a lemon to garnish my pancakes.

"You had crept through the yard, catching me unaware. I didn't know if you were real or not because you radiated such life. With your fiery red hair and your dimpled smile, I was smitten from the very beginning. But I suddenly believed the rumors as true. I believed that I really was in a fairy tale because you were dressed as…"

"As what?" I whisper, holding my breath.

"As Snow White," he reveals while I blink once, processing what he just said. "I remember that night like it happened yesterday, but the one thing clearer than any other is the red… ribbon that was threaded through your hair."

I slump onto the end of the bed, unsure if my unsteady legs would hold me up a second more.

"You stood still watching me, unafraid. While me, I was

never more frightened in my life. I didn't know what you'd do. You had caught me red-handed. If my dad found out what I did…" Cayden's father sounds like a vile man, so he doesn't need to go into detail. I know he'd be skinned alive.

"So I did the only thing I could. I offered you a lemon. A sign of peace. But what you did next, it showed me that you were different. Regardless of our circumstances, you were just like me. You were clutching onto a toy mouse, which looked well loved, but when I offered you the lemon, in return, you offered me your mouse."

"Ellie's mouse?" I whisper, tears springing to life. They fall when Cayden nods.

"I accepted, as did you, and I thought it was over, but that was just the beginning. I never ran as fast as I did that day, desperate to get home, a place I loathed to be. But you stirred something in me with your innocence, and I was done for from that night forward.

"Two days passed, and the toy mouse was a reminder that you weren't a dream. That I had really encountered an angel with vibrant red hair. As Lacey and I devoured our mac and cheese, thanks to the money I made from selling your lemons, I wondered if maybe I should go back. I reasoned with myself that it had to do with the money, but deep down, I knew it was because of you.

"When Lacey was asleep, I slipped out of the house, excited by the prospect of seeing you again. But what I never anticipated was that you would feel the same way too. A flutter of red, waving me over in the still of the night, caught my eye because on our beloved swing—the only thing that provided our woeful neighborhood with any joy—was your red ribbon.

"You didn't know who I was, but I knew who you were. I knew this red ribbon was the only way you could communicate with a world you had no knowledge of. I ran toward the oak tree, the very same one that drew you here not only weeks ago but a lifetime ago as well. Beneath the swing was a bagful of lemons, the very same ones I was going to return for."

Oh God, my heart, it hurts. To know my past isn't filled with only atrocities has me hoping that there's hope for me yet.

"Another bag sat beside it, and inside was a bundled-up T-shirt and a pair of jeans. Both were brand new with the tags still attached. I had no idea how you obtained these, but the pricey garments would feed Lacey and me for weeks.

"This happened for the next two weeks. You left me gifts, alerting me to them by the red ribbon you left. If not clothes, you left food. Small offerings to show me you cared. One night, I decided to return the favor. I didn't have much to give, but I had bought Lacey a pack of glow-in-the-dark stars. She was and still is such a dreamer, so I wanted to give her a forever star-filled sky she could gaze into, wishing that all her dreams came true.

"I left a single star on the swing, excited that I was able to give you back something in return. As I went to collect my latest loot of a carrot cake and some cookies, I sensed I wasn't alone. I was filled with a feeling I hadn't felt too often. Hope. You emerged wearing your Snow White costume, but instead of hair as black as ebony, your red hair set my world on fire. So from that day forward, you were my Snow, placating the anger burning within."

Cayden is finally unburdening his soul, and each revelation is baring his beauty, exposing why I fell under his spell from the very first moment we met. It's nice to know I wasn't going crazy. That this place, the tree, the red ribbon, it all played a part in why I am here. But when Cayden sighs, I know our story is far from ending in a happily ever after.

"You told me your name, and I told you mine. You asked why I wasn't wearing the clothes you had stolen from your brother, and I explained my story. I told you everything, and you listened. And when I finished, then you told me yours.

"This happened for the next two months, and that summer was the best summer of my life. I had made a friend, but the secrecy surrounding our friendship just made it even more exciting. We'd speak for hours, sitting under that tree or me pushing you on that swing. However, one night, when I asked why you wore that outfit, your carefree demeanor changed. Your sadness was suddenly mine too. You shared with me that even though you lived in what appeared to be a castle, with everything you could ever want, you were happiest here. You wore that outfit in hopes that one day, your Prince Charming would wake you from your death-like sleep.

"No guessing who the villain is in your story or why you chose Snow White as the character you connected most with."

"Stella," I gasp, this tale woven from sheer woe. "The evil stepmom. Although, in my case, we are flesh and blood."

He frowns, saddened that I've come to learn a piece of my past he wished I never remembered. "You were looking for what every kid wants. To belong. It didn't matter that you had money or that your surname was renowned. You were lonely. So fucking lonely that you created a world in your head to escape that solitude. That was the moment I vowed to do anything to protect you. I didn't care what my father did; I promised you'd never be lonely again.

"But that promise was made by a naïve, stupid kid. Life doesn't work that way because once summer gives way to fall, the sunshine goes into hiding, just as you did. Your house, it was your vacation home, so it made sense that when vacation was over, so was your stay. We didn't even get to say goodbye.

"As the months turned cold, the memory of your smile, your laugh, was the only thing that saw me through. I had saved money from all the things I sold, but that soon disappeared, and I was back to stealing to survive."

"What about your dad?"

"What about him?" he replies quickly, his anger almost burning.

"He just left you and Lacey to fend for yourselves?"

Cayden's mood soon turns from nostalgic to murderous in seconds. "There is one thing you need to know about my dad. All he ever cared about was himself. We were nothing but a burden. He only stuck around for the child support, which he spent on his own dirty habits. He was a drunk. And a mean one at that. So it was better when he was gone."

"The screams, the distinct sounds of someone being hit, the muted sniffles, I know I've heard them before...I just don't know who they belong to."

Lacey once told me she remembered violence was rampant in her home. She just couldn't remember who the screams belonged to. I now know they were Cayden's pleas for help. I've never really hated anyone until now.

Cayden can sense my thoughts, and he violently shakes his head. "Don't. I don't want your pity. That's not why I'm telling you this." I understand completely and am quick to rein in my sympathy.

"Times were tough, but whose childhood isn't? I did what I had to, to survive. And soon, the memory of knowing you wasn't as clear as it once was. That is, until the next summer. Late one night, I was about to cross over the lake, and it appeared our worlds weren't so different, after all.

"I was a kid, dealing weed to kids with money to burn. They were happy to buy my drugs but wouldn't be caught dead talking to me in any other circumstance. But that was fine. I wasn't there to socialize. I was there to survive. I didn't want to believe the apple didn't fall far from the tree, but I knew what road I was headed down. I was angry all the time, and the only person who made me feel like I was worth something was gone.

"But when I saw that red ribbon tied to that swing, I just... everything changed. You had done the one thing no one in my entire life had. You came back for me. I was someone worth knowing." His chest rises and falls, and it's clear to see the effect this memory, that *I*, have on him.

"I know I should have stayed away, but I couldn't. And when I saw you, standing by that swing, hands filled with lemons, I knew I'd never let you go again. I knew what we had could only ever be a summer fling, but I didn't care. I would take anything you wanted to give.

"So that's what happened. For the next eight years, every summer, I waited, waited for you to come back to me. And every summer, you did. I knew our future could never amount to anything. A poor boy like me and a rich girl like you. But your life wasn't hearts and roses. You lacked the love you always craved, and that red ribbon was our SOS. I knew you were in trouble when it was there. Your mom knew you were sneaking off in the boat, and she grounded you countless times, but that didn't stop you. But that's all we ever had. Stolen kisses and covert touches. That's all I could ever offer you."

Cayden is incredibly still, divulging our secret in a rushed breath. I know there is so much more to our story, but our history is going to take a lot longer than a night to detail everything we experienced. He is giving me the essentials, so I understand just how important our love really was.

"What happened when I was seventeen? What changed?" Cayden once told me that he broke my heart, and for the next ten years, I broke his. Doing the math, something momentous happened when I was seventeen.

Cayden sighs, revealing from here on forward, our story turns. "You grew up and changed. We both did. We both couldn't live in denial anymore. It hurt. Too much. You told me you were going to college to study marketing even though your true passion was art. You were—you are an amazing artist. You drew me that." He gestures with his chin to the picture above his bed. "You told me it was a self-portrait of how you saw yourself when in my arms."

Turning slowly to look over my shoulder, I take in the beautiful artwork, unable to believe my hand drew something this perfect. I instantly felt a connection to this piece, and now I know why.

This picture is worth a thousand words. The vulnerability and the comfort of being stripped bare this way reveal that I felt then what I clearly still do now. "I loved you," I whisper, and it's not a question but rather a statement as I don't need confirmation. The sketch is all the answer I need.

"Yes, you did."

His saddened response has me turning back around to face him. "What happened?"

He's trying his hardest to stay strong. But when he walks to where I sit and drops to his knees before me, all the layers are peeled away. "I pushed you away. What could I offer you? I thought I was doing the right thing. You spoke of staying here once you graduated from school, but I couldn't let you waste your life. You didn't belong here. You deserved better. So I made sure you stayed away."

I swallow down my fear.

"You asked me to give you a reason to say…but I didn't have one. I wouldn't have you giving your life up for me. You didn't believe me, so you gave me one final test. You asked me if I loved you…and I…I said no. I broke your heart that day because no matter how beautiful or confident you were, underneath it all, you were still that lost little girl dressed as her favorite princess."

Blinking back my tears, I feel my heart break once again, just as it did ten years ago. To hear my life being retold this way is beyond words. In a way, I escaped the nightmares, but Cayden has had to relive them over and over again.

"Two summers passed, and just when I thought you'd forgotten about me and this place, you came back. It was the best day of my life. But just how I broke your heart, you were intent on breaking mine. You came in and out of my life, leaving for months, sometimes years at a time. One drunken night, I was alone and missing you so fucking much, and that was the night Ellie was conceived.

"When you came back, you saw that Hazel was pregnant, and I knew it was over for good. Our lives have always been a revolving door. One in, one out."

My relationship with Cayden has been a turbulent affair for so long. But I can't help but feel that something is missing. As headstrong as I am, and with the love I clearly felt, I know I would have fought harder.

However, remembering Calvin's comment about being on/off for eight years now makes perfect sense. Ellie is eight years old. Cayden did break my heart because it's breaking once again for the life we could have led.

He gently clutches the back of my calves, an almost plea that I listen to how this all ends. "But regardless of our past, of everything that happened, you still came back here time and time again. I knew you were seeing Calvin, but I just didn't care. I meant it when I said you were mine, Snow. You always have been.

"If circumstances were different, I would have married you the day you turned eighteen. But life doesn't always turn out the way you want it to." He lowers his head, clearly wounded that fate has once again reared her ugly head. "The night of the accident…you came here."

"I did?" I ask, gasping when he raises those poignant eyes and meets mine.

"Yes. You"—he blinks once, his lower lip quivering—"you

told me you were pregnant." The walls begin closing in on me, and I suddenly am finding it difficult to breathe. "You didn't know whose it was."

"Oh, my God." A tear slips from the corner of my eye as I sit frozen, unable to move. A flutter tickles low, but it's all a cruel trick—a taste of what I once had.

"You told me that regardless of who was the father, Calvin was going to raise the baby as his because you were going to marry him. You tore out my heart one final time, and I...I snapped. We had a huge argument. Ugly words were spoken. Years of repression burst the seams, and I knew at that moment that our love was toxic. I saw just how much when Ellie..." Cayden turns his cheek, pained.

After everything he's just shared, I have no right to ask, but this is why I'm here. "Tell me. Let me carry you for once." With a hesitant touch, I run my fingers through his hair, relishing in the rumble which passes his lips.

"Ellie loved you, Snow. And you loved her. You were more of a mother to her than Hazel. That's why she was so frightened the day she saw you. She thought you were a ghost because you were gone for so long. She'd carry your mouse everywhere, hoping that it held some magical power to bring you back to us."

She loved me, and in return, I clearly hurt her in ways unimaginable. "Remember, you're the one who can fill the world with sunshine. That's what she said to me. What does it mean?"

Cayden looks fatigued, but it's almost the end. I can feel it. "It's from Snow White. It's what you used to say to her instead of goodbye." I can't control my emotions, and a sob robs me of breath.

"What sort of a monster was I?" I cry, shielding my face, ashamed.

"You were never the villain in this story, Snow. Only the victim. Ellie hated us fighting, so she went outside. The dock was slick with snow. She just wanted to see the moonlight reflecting in the water, she told me. But she got too close to the edge, and she…she fell into the water."

My tears cease because I don't deserve to shed another one ever again.

"When I heard you scream, I knew something was very wrong. I ran out back and saw you wet, sobbing as you breathed life into my motionless daughter. You jumped in and saved her. The paramedics said if you hadn't…" He shakes his head, unable to complete his sentence.

"But seeing Ellie that way, I knew what I had to do. I ended it, and this time, for good. I told you to leave me alone. That I didn't…" He tongues his cheek, peering upward as if searching for the right words. "That I didn't want anything to do with you or the baby. I told you that you were the biggest regret of my life…and you were. I regretted being a coward for not having the balls to stop you from leaving when you begged me to ten years ago. But whatever we had, it was gone…"

"Which is why you haven't told me this until now. Wounded, I told you to forget me, didn't I?"

He nods once, heartbroken.

Still on his knees, I can't understand how an innocent love like ours ended in the twisted way that it did. There is something else, but I feel sick. I can't take anymore. I was pregnant, and I didn't know who the father was? I am disgusted by my actions.

However, a glimmer of light shines through, resolving a small part of my soul. Unable to stand to see him surrendering, I slowly, with weary bones, lower myself to kneel before him too. "The baby was yours." He opens his mouth, but I silence him as I place my finger to his lips. "Calvin told me we hadn't slept with one another for over six months and that the night before my accident, I gave him back his ring." That flicker of hope sparkles in Cayden's eyes, but that could be the tears we both will share for what will never be. "Why would I lie to you?"

This doesn't make any sense. I am missing something. Something vital that strings all of this together.

Cayden wraps his fingers around my wrist, stroking his thumb over my racing pulse. "Because we hurt the ones we love."

On our knees, we both need a minute to process everything. Cayden doesn't need to tell me what happened next. I left his house, distressed and hysterical, and one tiny mishap resulted in the loss of my—of *our*—child.

He's instantly on me, reading my thoughts. "Don't you dare. This is all on me. All of it. If only I had chased after you. If only I hadn't spewed such lies…" He clutches my biceps, shaking me to see reason. "You will always be my biggest regret." And now, I understand why. "In Ellie's eyes, you are her angel because you saved her…you saved us both."

I crumple, unable to stomach any more. However, the universe tells me she's listening when a rumble can be felt creeping over the horizon. "Everything is always better after a thunderstorm…" he whispers into my ear as I sag into his arms. "You used to love the rain…"

"What happened?" I say in a tone akin to his.

"Life," is his simple reply. "We used to lie in bed, holding hands as we peered up at the single glow-in-the-dark star—the one I gave you. We used to wish for a life where no one knew our names. We could just live and be happy."

The vivid image he paints…if I dig deep enough, I can almost see it, feel it. Feel him. I can hear his tender voice as he sings me "Twinkle, Twinkle, Little Star" to help lull me to sleep. I know my life wasn't smooth sailing, but a profound sadness threatens to drag me under into the murky depths.

I now know why that is.

Hazel had every right to be mad at me. What I did to Ellie, to Cayden, was inexcusable. I was a naïve, lovestruck teenager, and if I could speak to the seventeen-year-old me, I'd tell her to fight for him. He did what he thought was right, but everything is just so fucked up.

"Did you know the guy who insinuated I was some bed-hopping party girl?"

He clucks his tongue, angered. "Yes. That's Matt. He knows you because of me. We dealt together back in the day. I saw sense while he only saw dollar signs. Whatever you think of yourself, stop it. We smoked some pot, but what kid didn't? But Matt doesn't take rejection too well, hence him saying the bullshit lies that he did. He's always been flirty with you, and you've always shot him down."

I shouldn't be this relieved, considering I have a lifetime of sins I need to atone for, but at least I can still hold a small scrap of my soul.

"You can imagine my surprise when I saw you back here. I didn't know what to think. But when you told me what had happened to you, I just…I couldn't break your heart again." That tiny tickle kicks down low once again.

Gently breaking our embrace, I look at Cayden through different eyes because I am. I am seeing him for the first time, and what I see takes my breath away. "That's why you were so standoffish when we first met. You thought I was back to torment you?"

He animatedly shakes his head. "No. You coming back here was like I had a second chance. And when I found out you had bought my old house, which I finally had the balls to sell…it just confirmed that you and I"—he places his hand over my trouncing heart—"will always be unfinished business. I have loved you, Peyton Lane, since I was nine years old. And I still love you. I'll never stop."

Without a doubt, Cayden can feel the thrashing of my heart, but that's okay. I'm done hiding behind my fears. "I'm sorry for everything…"

But he doesn't allow me to finish as he places his finger on my lips. "You have nothing to be sorry for. I'm the one who's sorry for not telling you sooner. But if I could save you the pain, I would happily shoulder your heartache." He leaves the unspoken lost in the shadows because he doesn't need to detail the loss we both share.

Innately, I lower my palm to my stomach and feel the tremendous sadness sink low. I was going to be a mother, the mother of Cayden's child, but life had other plans for me. When

I ran off that road, I not only lost my memory, I lost a piece of me too. A piece I will never be able to regain again.

I finally know the truth. There are still so many questions, but for the moment, this will do. Now, I want to mourn the demise of the person I once was. It's time I let her go and learn from the many mistakes she made throughout her life.

"What are you thinking?" Cayden asks, interlacing his fingers through mine.

We've lost so much, wasted so much time. So without holding back, I squeeze his hand and only look at what tomorrow holds. "Nothing. I'm thinking nothing at all." He opens his mouth, and I do the only thing I can—I kiss him.

At first, he stiffens, and I reassess my decision to lead with my heart. But when he threads his fingers through the curls at my nape and angles my head to perfect our connection, I let go of everything and just feel.

The desperation for our touch only intensifies as we devour one another with fierce, carnal hunger. Our lips, our bodies, move in sync, and although I may not recall the memories he just shared, my body, my soul, does.

I have always felt a deep-rooted connection to Cayden, but at this moment, it almost feels like we're one. So without fear, I act on that emotion and turn it into our reality. Without untangling my lips from his, I begin unbuttoning the buttons on my dress. When I've popped two open, Cayden stills my shaky fingers.

"Let's not rush things. We just met." He grins against my mouth, igniting the out-of-control inferno.

He's right. A lady would wait. But I never claimed to be a

lady.

Shrugging from his hold, I declare, "This is happening with or without you. I would prefer with…"

A growl escapes him as his eyelids droop to half-mast. He is so damn handsome. I want this to happen. I want him. A nervous energy thrums through my veins, and I suppose that is what most people would call butterflies. But as Cayden pins me with those steel-blue eyes, it feels like so much more.

I have literally loved this man from the moment we first met—and not just the time I remember, but the one before it as well. Our love hasn't been easy, but what epic love story is? But I'll be damned if I make the same mistake again.

With two buttons left, I stop, fixated on Cayden's chest, which is rising and falling steadily. "Are you okay?"

He shakes his head. "No." He reveals why in the same raspy breath. "I'm…scared."

"Scared?"

He licks his lips, averting his eyes. "Yes. I'm scared you'll disappear again. The only thing harder than letting go is moving on. I can't lose you again."

"Hey," I coo, cupping his cheek. "I'm not going anywhere."

He nods but doesn't seem convinced. I need him to know that regardless of our past, I won't mess it up this time. I won't ever let him go. His uncertainty reveals just how much he loved me, and I make it my mission from this moment forward never to give him a reason to doubt us ever again. "I came back here because of you. And that kind of love withstands the test of time. I don't care about what we did or who we were. All I care about is you being my forever. Always."

"This isn't going to be easy." He leans into my touch with a heavy sigh.

"I've come to learn that nothing with you is." His smirk can brighten the darkest corner. "But who wants easy? Where's the fun in that?" I know we have so much more to discuss and that a secret still clouds us, but that can wait—we have forever to get to know one another again.

Cayden's walls finally crumble, and the simplicity is beautiful.

He turns into my palm, laying a single kiss in the center, before unfastening the last two buttons on my dress. The material hangs open, exposing my bra. Cayden licks his bottom lip before he surrenders. He runs his large hand down my neck, between my breasts, and over the curve of my stomach. When he reaches the band of my underwear, he skims his pointer along the elastic, resulting in goose bumps prickling my skin.

"Skin as white as snow," he says low, his eyes hungry as he feasts on my body before him. "I want to be gentle with you"—our gazes lock—"but I don't know if I can."

His threat should leave me apprehensive, but it doesn't. It only excites me further. "I don't want gentle." Reaching for the hem of his shirt, I yank it from his body, mewling when I'm engulfed in the sight and smell. "I just want you."

Those keywords make what we're about to do all the more real. I don't know who lunges for who first, but it's a flurry of hands and lips. The moment I press my chest to Cayden's, a sated groan leaves us both. He peels the dress from my body, his lips following in his fingers' wake. Every stroke of his tongue and glide of his lips have me desperate for so much more.

When he reaches the junction between my breasts, he gently nestles his nose into my flesh. "You smell like home," he whispers, bathing my skin in warmth. "You are the only woman I have ever loved. From the first moment I saw you, I was ruined. Our love has been messy, and it also has been cruel, but I wouldn't give it up for the world because you are my world."

An unexpected tear rolls down my cheek because his admission is bittersweet. Our journey has been anything but easy, but I want that to change. "Love me," I say, reaching behind my back and unhooking my bra. It falls to the floor.

My breasts are exposed, and a flush spreads over my pale skin when Cayden sits back on his heels, stroking his stubble in reflection. I wonder if I look different from how he remembers. Suddenly feeling self-conscious, I wrap an arm around myself, shielding my nudity, but he won't have it.

"No more hiding." He tenderly coaxes me to lower my shield. I do. "I just…I just can't believe how beautiful you are. No matter how many times we're together, it always feels like the first time."

He leans forward, running his nose down the length of my neck, his stubble a perfect abrasion to my heated skin. He cups my left breast, running his thumb over my budded nipple. We both moan at the connection. He wets his lips before sampling me, and I think I'm going to die right here where I kneel.

He tongues the underside while reaching up to gently caress my right. My head drops back. He circles my areola, kissing over the small, heart-shaped freckle. Wetness gathers between my legs, and shamelessly, I rub them together. The burn hurts so good.

With his mouth still working me into a frenzy, Cayden walks his fingers to the outside of my underwear. I know he can feel my arousal, so when he rubs two fingers in a sluggish circle, I open my legs wider, granting him permission to take it all. A grunt catches in the back of his throat.

"Please…" I whimper, not above begging. Cayden gives me what I want. He slips his hand into my underwear and cups my sex. "Oh…God."

Nothing should feel this good, nothing. But when he sinks one finger into me, I am done for.

We both hiss, and I surrender. Now and forever.

"I love you." His admission, coupled with what he is doing to my body, has me realizing that our love is the kind of love you read about in books. The all-consuming, soul-shattering obsessive kind of love that consumes your every breath. "You don't have to say it back. I just want you to know."

I want to say it back, but until I mean it like he does, I will show him how I feel rather than tell him.

Dragging his face to mine, I smash my lips to his, expressing my love for him through a kiss with the ability to change the world forever. We stand, our lips never breaking pace as we lower ourselves to the bed. We shift until my head hits the pillow with Cayden lying on top of me.

I explore his glorious body, my fingers drifting over to the tattoo on his flank. I remember when I first saw it, and I knew it meant more than meets the eye—just like him. Our relationship seems to have never strayed far from his thoughts. And that fact warms not only my body but my heart as well.

His abs ripple as I stroke over the hardened flesh. His

pleasure has me venturing farther down. I unsnap the button on his jeans, biting my lip when I slowly lower his zipper. I'm nervous, so damn nervous when I reach into his boxer briefs. But when I feel his hot, hard length, my wanton need steadily replaces those nerves.

He grunts, breaking our kiss to savor the feel of me reacquainting myself with his body. Bashful at first, I struggle with where to put my hands, but when he pulsates in my palm, all coyness takes a back seat. My desire gets amped to ten billion volts, and it's sensory overload as I want him slathered all over me.

I stroke his shaft while he lowers his forehead to my shoulder, an almost cry of relief that we've found one another in a ferocious storm. "I never thought I'd feel this again," he expresses his fears, unguarded. His honesty has me lowering my guard as well as I increase my rhythm.

He cups my cheek, kissing me fervently as he lowers his jeans. It's his turn to be in control. When we're pressed flesh upon flesh, he breaks the kiss, only to continue down my chin and over my pounding pulse. He tongues between the hollow of my throat before embarking farther. He devours my breasts while I remember to breathe.

When I'm a writhing mess, he descends lower. His lips score my skin as he kisses over my stomach and circles my navel with his tongue. His eyes set me on fire as he peers up at me from between my legs, then lowers his mouth to the outside of my underwear, kissing me gently. This is pure torture, which is exactly what Cayden wants.

Fisting the duvet, I squirm, wanting so much more. His

breathy chuckle just adds to the torment. He kisses my inner thighs, paying attention to the freckles which line my skin. I wonder how many times we have been entwined this way.

"Were you my first time?" I ask, threading my fingers through his hair.

"Yes," he replies against my thigh. "I was your first everything. Just as you were mine."

The thought is electrifying because it feels like I'm about to relive something that has always belonged to the man whose kisses are filled with nothing but utter worship and desire. "Help me remember."

Cayden lays one final kiss over my underwear, then sits back on his heels and visually devours me once more. He traces from my face downward, ensuring no part of me remains untouched. When he gets to the waistband of my underwear, I shiver because things are about to get real.

With a sharp tug, he tears them from my body, the final layer finally shredding its confines. My eyes drift to his length, which extends from his body proudly. His tanned skin complements his ripped physique. I love the scruff between his pecs that plunges down to the dark softness between his legs. I want him. All of him. I want it now.

Shyly, I shift, opening my legs, desperate to take the inevitable step which was always fated in the stars. Cayden hisses, then reaching into the side dresser, he hunts for protection. I watch mesmerized as he takes off his jeans and then sheathes himself. "You're sure?" he asks, stroking his finger along my bottom lip.

"Yes. It's time we make new memories." It's all the response he needs.

He presses us together, and the feeling is pure bliss. We kiss languidly, lost in the sensation of finding one another again. He's everywhere, robbing me of breath and replacing it with this life force that has me feeling reborn.

Even though I know where he's headed, it doesn't prepare me for the tremor that overrides me when he lowers his mouth to my sex. My back arches on its own accord as I have no control over my body, but Cayden does. He buries himself, sampling me in one hot lick. My eyes roll into the back of my head as he hums against my sex.

He suckles me while adding a finger, ensuring I'm primed for what's about to come. My ripened, slick center is pleading for a reprieve, and when Cayden flicks over the swell with his tongue, I'm more than ready. Unrefined sounds slip past my lips as I shamelessly chase my release.

He stretches me farther, and just when I'm seconds away from bursting, he lets me go. I cry out in frustration, but that soon turns into a low guttural whimper when he places his blunt head against my entrance. My eyes pop open as I peer up and lock gazes with him.

He's slathered with my arousal, and an animalistic possession overtakes me because I want to own him just as he owns me. Mind. Body. Soul. Letting go of the fear which haunts your every breath is a beautiful thing, but that's soon forgotten when I arch into Cayden the moment he sinks into me.

A gasp rips low as I'm filled full.

He stills, allowing me to accommodate his size, but the corded veins in his neck reveal he's barely holding on. He runs his hands along the top of my legs, squeezing and relishing in this sensation that is akin to none. "Are you okay?" he asks, just how he would have when we first connected this way years ago.

A tear falls free at the thought. "I wish I remembered."

Bending low, he places a kiss on my quivering lips. "All that matters is now." And he reveals just how much so when he moves slowly within me.

Wrapping my arms around his nape, I lose myself in his smooth rhythm, savoring what it feels like to be one with another. I may have forgotten the steps, but this dance is one I reacquaint myself with soon enough. To his pull, I push, a perfect yin to yang.

He scatters kisses all over me as his hips shift with a languid cadence. I tug at his hair, needing something to hold because I'm bursting at the seams. "Faster," I whisper, bucking upward to meet him stroke for stroke.

"I don't…I don't want to hurt you," he pushes out between clenched teeth as he's clearly holding back, measuring how deeply, how fast, he goes.

"You never could," I breathlessly reply. I don't know why, but my honesty has Cayden turning his cheek, ashamed.

He's suddenly lost to me, caught up in a memory that threatens to ruin something untainted and good. Refusing to give light to the demons, I dig my heel into the small of his back and coax him to take what I openly give.

He growls and shifts my leg, opening me up and deepening the angle, which has us both moaning in sheer delight. He sinks into me, the vigor bringing tears to my eyes, but it's exactly what I need.

The raw sound of flesh slapping against flesh heightens

my arousal, and a coil begins spiraling within. Cayden peers at where we're connected, a primitive growl overtaking him as he loses control. He isn't gentle, and nothing but unadulterated need exists behind each stroke. He is a true beast, a wounded warrior as he drives into me with a passion so fierce, I see stars. But I embrace it, knowing our story has just begun.

"It's okay," I whisper, barely holding on. "Let go." I mean that in every literal meaning of the word. Whatever secret Cayden is holding, I know it's to protect me from the pain. That's all he has ever tried to do. "I'm right here, and I promise I'll never leave you again."

My pledge is our undoing, and a rumble spills from Cayden as he sinks into me relentlessly. I grow lax, not in control of my body as it's no longer mine. Cayden punishes me with each wicked stroke, and when he reaches down to rub my clit, I scream, completely undone.

He doesn't slow down, however. It appears he was waiting for me to detonate first. "It was you, always," he reveals as he plunges into me over and over again. "Whatever I did…it was always for you." I'm too far gone to question what that means as I'm reaching another pinnacle, and this time, the downfall will be far worse.

The sight before me is my final tether, and I come so hard that tears leak from my eyes. Cayden is fierce and feral because it's evident his love for me knows no bounds. This isn't just sex; this is belonging to another. And whatever obstacles we face, bring it. I came back here to find him. He's always been my beacon of light.

He reads my thoughts because Cayden knows me. He owns

me. He always has. "Oh, fuck," he grunts, leaving fingerprints sunken into my flesh as he grips my waist, pistoning his hips. "I love you," he professes before letting go.

Seeing him this way, exposed and vulnerable, I understand why I cherished this man with every fiber of my soul. Running my fingers over his tattoo, I hope that one day, I remember that love because being loved by Cayden is something I never want to forget.

He presses us chest to chest as he kisses my lips, his skin prickling as I continue to stroke his flank. We're silent, our heavy breathing filling the space, but no one needs to speak—we both know this changes everything.

I'm finally home.

FOURTEEN

I didn't have the heart to wake Cayden. It was the first time since knowing him that he truly looked at peace.

My sore muscles protested as I scampered around his bedroom, attempting to find my clothes. My underwear sat in a ruined heap on the floor, so with no other choice, I decided to go home and change. I snuck out of his house with every intention of returning after a hot shower and some coffee.

The water feels wonderful against my heightened flesh, sparking memories of what I just did. I suppress a whimper. I don't know what happens now. Cayden may have told me the truth, but I know there is still so much more to explore.

With that thought in mind, I decide to dry off and wake Cayden with a kiss. I may have loved Snow White, but I don't need Prince Charming to save me anymore. I saved myself. Processing over everything Cayden shared, it's still hard to believe all that happened. But I don't doubt Cayden's retelling of events.

It pains me to know our relationship was so strained, and I can't help but wonder what exactly led to us hurting one another in the ways that we did. Cayden said the night of my accident, I came here, revealing I was pregnant. The thought is still too painful to fully comprehend. But why did I lie when I clearly knew the baby was his?

He said we fought and words were spoken? But what was so bad that I left here, resulting in me almost ending two lives? How I wish things were different. I rub over my stomach, a sadness overtaking me. However, I'm quick to dispel those thoughts. I need to get to the bottom of it before I can grieve.

As I walk into my bedroom, the hair at the back of my neck stands on end. I spin around, certain someone is standing behind me, but I don't find anyone. Tightening the towel around me, I disregard my frayed nerves as just my edginess from the past few weeks taking a toll.

Not wanting to be presumptuous but armed with the notion to better be safe than sorry, I hunt through my underwear drawer for the pair of black lace boy shorts I bought during my need for retail therapy. They are brand new, so I know they're not in the wash, but I can't seem to find them. Tossing aside the other pairs is to no avail because they're nowhere to be found.

Weird.

Dropping the towel, I step into a red pair instead.

As I'm fastening the matching bra, a creak sounds softly behind me. If not for my heightened state of awareness, I would have missed it, but I've come to learn the creaks of this house like the back of my hand. It came from the loose floorboard in my living room.

A shiver passes through me.

"Hello?" I call out, thinking that maybe Cayden has come to find me. But my voice echoes back.

Flight or fight instinct takes over.

I rip a summer dress down from the hanger and throw it over my head. I don't bother with makeup as I slip into a pair of flip-flops and race out of the room. However, a hallway has never looked more daunting as I peer down it, wondering how many steps there are to the front door.

I can't shake the feeling that I'm not alone.

Adrenaline rushes through me as I stand rigid, eyes focused down the corridor. It's peeking at dusk, so the shadows are settling over the horizon, wreaking havoc on my imagination. Blindly reaching for the light switch, I turn it on, hoping it'll settle my nerves.

The blood whooshes through my ears, and everything falls silent as I'm suddenly hit with a memory that I know took place in front of these very walls. Blood, so much blood. A fight. Someone hitting their head. I cradle my forehead, a scream ripping from my throat, but then the unmissable feeling drags me under once more.

I'm sinking to the bottom of the lake. Watching the world getting smaller and smaller. I'm running out of breath. Clawing my way to the surface, I smell the ocean. The glow from the star on my ceiling flickers brightly. I see the red ribbon...

"Everything is always better after a thunderstorm..."

What the hell is going on?

Gasping for air, I stagger down the hallway, using the walls as my guide to lead me through the house and out the front door. I don't bother locking it because the fresh air calms me somewhat, but when a malicious snarl vibrates around me, I almost trip over my feet as I run for dear life.

I tear down the road, only focused on the sanctuary of Cayden's front door.

My heart is in my throat when I dash up his front steps and bang wildly on the woodgrain. Whoever is at my back, chasing me, they're getting closer…and closer.

I bang harder, screaming, pleading with Cayden to let me in.

The moment the door opens, I throw myself into the safety of Cayden's arms, hysterical. "Peyton? Hey, hey, what's wrong? Shh, it's okay." He rubs my back while I sob a guttural cry. "Talk to me. What happened?"

He closes the door with one hand, ensuring the other is still wrapped tightly around me, and I take what feels like my first breath in minutes. "That's it, just breathe. It'll be all right. No one is going to hurt you."

His comfort is endearing, but alarm bells sound loudly at his choice of words. I've pulled myself from far worse situations such as this, so I steady my ragged breathing and refuse to give light to the demons. "Why di-did you s-say that?" I ask, still nestled in his arms. He stills, which just makes this looming premonition worse.

Untangling myself, I don't bother wiping away my tears because I have a feeling many more are yet to follow. "Cayden?"

He appears freshly showered, and when I see his truck keys

secured tightly in his hand, I wonder where he was off to before I blew in here like a storm. "What happened?" he questions, refusing to answer me.

But I won't back down that easily. "No, answer me. Why did you automatically think someone was going to hurt me?" My voice is still choppy, but I push past it, needing to get to the bottom of this.

When he sighs and runs his fingers through his damp hair, the wind gets knocked from my sails. "Peyton, I need to tell you something…"

Swallowing down my queasiness, I nod, indicating he has the floor. But his cheeks bellow as he blows out a deep breath. Whatever he's about to reveal, he's held on to for a very long time. It has the potential to change both our lives forever.

"Cayden…what did you…" I close my eyes for the briefest of moments, hoping to keep out the truth, but it's no use. "What did I do?" He hisses, and any doubts I ever had have just been put to bed for good. "Ten years are unaccounted for. Why?"

I may not remember my past, but this moment in time, I'll never be able to forget. "The reason is…" His sentence remains unfinished when Lacey enters the foyer, clutching a folder to her chest. From the browning of the paper, it's been in storage for a while.

She doesn't look her usual bubbly self. Quite frankly, she appears as if she's seen a ghost. She glances back and forth between Cayden and me, blanketed by sheer confusion. "Maybe you could explain why Peyton's mom bribed you with twenty thousand dollars to stay away from her."

I blink once, unbelieving of what I've just heard. *"What?"*

Cayden's gig is up. He reaches out to console me, but I immediately recoil, jarring out my palm. "No, don't you fucking touch me!" I don't understand what's going on. "Is that tr-true? Did my m-mother bribe you?" There must be some mistake.

But there isn't.

"Yes." His voice cracks while my entire world shatters before me.

But his next answer will cement our fate for good. "And did you take her money?"

He at least has the common decency to look at me when he splits my heart into two. "Yes." He peers down at the folder Lacey holds and pinches the bridge of his nose. "That was in storage for a reason."

"I can see why," she bites back. I've never seen her this angry with her brother before. "I knew there was a reason you told me to stay in Myrtle Beach. Now"—she waves the folder in one hand—"I know why." She meets my baffled stare as I play ping-pong between them, attempting to decipher what the hell is going on and hold back my tears.

She's been in Myrtle Beach? I thought she was making herself scarce because of the shit that went down.

"And now, she needs to know, Cayden. She needs to know it all." Our eyes finally lock. She looks fatigued and completely shattered.

"Wh-what's going on?" My falter betrays my utmost fear.

Cayden is riddled with whatever he's about to reveal. He thumbs the corner of his mouth, attempting to gather his thoughts before he speaks. With his face downturned and shoulders slumped, he finally delivers me the final piece—the piece which connects us all together.

"Everything I told you last night was true. But there is a common denominator." I gulp as the walls begin closing in on me. "My father."

Lacey's whimper has me rubbing the goose bumps from my arms.

"Us meeting when we were kids wasn't by chance. I knew who you were the entire time. Not just because your surname was notorious, but because my father told me about the white house and the woman inside."

"The woman?" I wet my lips twice, afraid I'm about to be bled dry.

"Your mom. Just like you and me, your mother and my father met here when they were kids. But unlike us, their relationship was one-sided. My father was smitten by your mom. But your mother saw my father for the parasite that he was, though he never took no for an answer. He saw her rejection as her playing hard to get. But there was no way someone like Stella Lane would be caught dead with someone like my dad.

"No matter how hard he tried, it didn't make a difference... until one night. Your mom knew he ran with a bad crowd, hell, he *was* the bad crowd, but she asked if he could score her some weed."

My eyes widen, and I pull back, stunned. "Are you sure you have the right person?" The notion of my mother smoking pot is just unfathomable.

But Cayden nods once. "Yes, this is what triggered a chain reaction that affected us all for the rest of our lives. In my dad's own twisted way, he loved your mom even though he knew he could never have her." I bite my bottom lip as this tale sounds a little too close to home. "But when she sought him out, asking him to meet her by the oak tree with some weed, he thought she'd had a change of heart."

"She doesn't have one," I bitterly counter, hating she has a part in every aspect of my life.

"And my father was soon to find that out. He wore his best shirt, which would have looked ridiculous to someone like your mom. He picked a bunch of flowers, hoping that night was the night the girl of his dreams finally felt the same way he did. I almost felt sorry for him because back then, I wanted to believe he wasn't the motherfucker he grew up to be."

Cayden's resentment toward his father has always been evident, but this hatred is something else.

"He waited, ready to lay all his cards on the table, but what he was greeted with affirmed his place in the world. It was and would always be us versus them.

"A group of guys your mother was friends with jumped him and stole his weed. They gave him a good beating, the message clear—stay away from your mom. Someone like him could never have someone like her."

"She set him up?" I don't know why this shocks me. I suppose I want to see the good in everyone. But Stella Lane is clearly the exception to that rule.

"Yes. After that, his love turned to hate. He resented her, but most of all, I think he resented himself. That single event was the proverbial straw that broke the camel's back. He grew to hate your mother and all that her 'kind' represented. She was a reminder of everything he wanted but could never have.

"In the crowd he ran with, he was the tough guy. No one said no to my dad—no one bar your mother—and he never forgot it. For as long as he lived, he promised to make her pay for everything she did."

Lacey and I stand mute, as there are no words to describe what we've just heard.

Cayden interlaces his hands behind his neck, peering up at the ceiling. "I was curious about your mom. I wanted to meet the woman my father would mumble about late at night when he was near passed out from the bottle of whiskey he drank. I was curious, but I should have just stayed away.

"The moment I saw that lemon tree…well, you know the rest. And that, like so many other events, is the biggest regret of my life. If only I stayed away, none of this would have happened."

I catalog over everything he shared. I knew I was missing the vital piece. I'm about to find out what.

"I tried to keep our relationship on the down low because, as you know, you're the spitting image of her. But when my father saw you, his lifelong obsession with your mother turned a corner. He no longer wanted her. He wanted…you."

He clenches his jaw, fists bunched by his sides. "If I'd known that, I would have tried harder to keep you away. But you were a bird, caged in that house. You rebelled, and look what happened. You met me, and your whole life changed. I tried pushing you away, but a selfish part of me was happy when you pushed back.

"One night, you had snuck into my bedroom, and my father caught us. I've never seen him like that before. Usually, he ran on pure anger, but something else was behind his gaze. A longing for what he lost? I'll never know. You introduced yourself, not knowing what you just did. But I leaped to your defense…I didn't want you anywhere near him. I told you to leave, and for once, you listened. But it didn't matter."

"And that's why he beat you?" Lacey's small voice draws us back to the now. "He couldn't understand why Peyton wanted you when her mother didn't want him." She has just connected all the dots, but we both wish she was wrong.

Cayden nods, standing tall. He doesn't want pity. He doesn't want to be a victim. But he isn't. This man is nothing but a warrior through and through.

I cover my mouth with a quivering hand while tears sting Lacey's eyes. "He beat you all the time. I remember. I thought they were just a dream, but they weren't. Oh God, Cayden. I'm sorry. I should have…"

"No, don't you dare." He charges forward, cupping her cheeks and leveling her with nothing but sincerity. "I would rather it was me than you. I'm your big brother. It's my job to protect you. To protect you both."

I can't listen to this without wanting to curl into a ball because there are so many layers. But Cayden withstood so much, and now, it's my turn to do the same.

"Every time Peyton was here…he beat you? Didn't he? As punishment or jealousy? Or maybe both?"

"It doesn't matter," he says, gently wiping away Lacey's tears before laying a kiss on her forehead.

"It does matter," I counter softly, barely holding it together. "You being hit because of me matters a lot."

Cayden sighs as he meets my eyes. "Being with you, touching you…it was worth every beating." Even now, just as he did years ago, he's protecting me, shielding me from a reality paved with sorrow. "The months my father went missing were the best months of my life. We did rough it, but we survived. All three of us. A family."

Lacey sniffs back her tears while I barely keep mine at bay. "What happened when I was seventeen?" I've asked him this before when he filled in the blanks.

Up until that point, even though our relationship was hidden kisses and stolen nights, we survived our messed-up circumstances together. Cayden tried to push me away, to protect me, but I didn't listen. But something heinous changed that.

The color drains from Cayden's face as he shakes his head slowly. This memory is one he relives every day, and it's the reason we're here. "It was the type of night when the earth crackled with electricity. The moon was full. I had just done a drop across the lake and was running late, thanks to some Ivy League assholes fighting over who would pay for their ounce of weed.

"I knew you were waiting for me. Just like you did on most nights. I tied the boat to the dock, hoping I beat you home. But what I heard next"—his Adam's apple dips as he swallows deeply—"you were screaming. It was a god-awful sound. It still haunts me to this day. I ran to the house, unsure what I would find. But not in a million years did I ever think I'd see what I did."

My heart begins racing, and bright flickers of white light flash behind my eyes.

"Just like always, you would sneak in through the balcony

door. It wasn't me you found that night, but my father instead. By the time you realized, it was too late, and he had overpowered you.

"When I found you, he had forced himself onto you and torn the front of your dress."

On instinct, my trembling fingers attempt to conceal my modesty. But it's in vain.

"He was touching you while you screamed over and over. For me." He turns his cheek, pained. "I have never, *never* been angrier. I wasn't thinking. I charged over and ripped him off you. He was stunned. His whiskey-soaked breath was an indication he was in no state to reason with. So the only way I had to talk some sense into him was the way he knew.

"I had never raised a hand to my father up until that night. I hit him again and again; I don't even know how many times. He tried to fight back, but he didn't stand a chance. I wanted him to suffer just how you did. And Lacey. And me. Only when he lay in a bloodied heap on the floor, unconscious, did I realize that ending his worthless life made me no better than him. That was the only reason I stopped."

I reach for the wall, unable to stand without support for fear of crumpling to the floor. Blood, so much blood. I can taste it lingering on my tongue. I may not remember it clearly, but the flashbacks expose I don't know if the amnesia is to blame or the fact that this memory is one I'm happy to forget.

"You were petrified. He took away your innocence, your ability to view the world through rose-tinted glasses, and suddenly killing him didn't seem like such a bad thing. I comforted you, thankful you didn't tell me to go to hell. You were aware of my father's fondness for you, but I never told you why. I was ashamed.

"You cried in my arms, and I promised that it would be all right. I would never allow him to lay another finger on you ever again. My father was never one for sentiments, however, and he suddenly came back to life. He caught me unaware, delivering a punch to my kidney, which had me dropping to the floor.

"He then proceeded to return the favor as he kicked and stomped on every part of my body. All I wanted was to protect you, but he made sure I couldn't do that when he shattered my wrist with the heel of his boot."

I flinch, unable to see clearly because my vision is cloaked in tears.

"I knew he had no intention of showing me the mercy I showed him, so I fought as hard as I could. I promise." He begs that I believe him, and not for one moment do I think otherwise. "But it wasn't good enough. He was intent on killing me, Peyton. Please believe me when I tell you this…it wasn't your fault."

Gasping, I attempt to break the surface, but I suddenly can't swim. The harder I push, the farther I sink. Invisible manacles secure at my ankles, dragging me down. Muddy water fills my lungs, and before long, it's all I can taste. I stop fighting and surrender…surrender to death.

This memory has plagued me for endless long months. I'm finally about to uncover why.

"You grabbed my baseball bat, the one I kept by the door, and proved to me that this entire time, I thought I was protecting you…but you were the one protecting me. You hit him, and he went down…and he…never got back up."

Lacey gasps while I'm unsure if I ever will be able to speak again.

Cayden walks toward me slowly, hands raised. He approaches me as he would a rabid animal. But I suppose that's what I am. I once thought I was a monster, and yes, that may be true. But there is another word for what I am, and that is a murderer.

With the tenderest of contact, Cayden wraps his fingers around my biceps. I need his touch. "You freaked out. Just like you're doing now. Regardless of the fact that he was moments away from killing me, you still saw yourself as the bad guy. When I checked his pulse, he didn't have one. I knew what this would do to your future if we called the police. I knew what would happen if your mom found out. If anyone ever found out, they'd take Lacey away and put her into foster care. At the end of the day, it was an accident. There was no other choice."

Lacey staggers forward, pleading he tell her the truth.

"I'm sorry, Ace. I wanted to tell you, but how do you explain to your eleven-year-old sister that you buried their father…at the bottom of the lake." She sobs while I just feel numb.

I always knew that the lake was the nucleus of my story. I just never imagined how. "I helped you, didn't I?" I know the answer as the visions, the ambiguous visions which made no sense, are memories that have risen from their watery grave.

"Yes. I fought for there to be another way, but you wouldn't allow me to do this alone. We were in it together, you said. But how I wish we weren't. That night changed us both. Days passed, and I knew what this was doing to you. It was eating you up inside. You couldn't look at the lake, my house, or me in the same way. I knew what I had to do."

"But I"—I need a moment—"but I bought your house. How could I want to go back there after everything you've just told me?"

"That house may represent heartache, but it also illustrates strength. And it was that strength that had me wanting to convert it into a shelter for kids. We talked about it not long before your accident. You may not have remembered, but a small part of you never forgot."

"What did you have to do?" I ask, referring to his earlier statement. I know what, but I hope, by some miracle, I am wrong.

"You got accepted into college, but as you know, you spoke of staying here once you graduated from school, but I couldn't let you. This place had ugly memories. I knew I was the only reason you wanted to stay, but I couldn't do that. I refused to allow you to relive that memory, and that's all you'd do by staying here. So I made sure you stayed away."

"That's the real reason you said you didn't love me when I asked?"

He nods, running the backs of his fingers along my neck with a hesitant touch. "Yes…but that's not the only reason you left."

Taking a deep breath, I prepare myself for what comes next.

"Your mother got wind of you staying here. It didn't take long for her to figure out who I was. I knew if she searched hard enough, she'd eventually uncover what we did. She forbade you to see me, but you never listened to her. And I knew you wouldn't start now. The harder you fought with her, the more determined you were to stay.

"We fought over your future, putting a strain on our already rocky relationship. You believed I was pushing you away because I didn't love you anymore. That when I looked at you, all I saw was what you did.

"One night, I found you sitting on the dock, peering into the lake, afraid and plagued by what we had done. You told me you couldn't stop thinking about that night. I was never more afraid than I was then because you had given up. And the way you looked at that water as a possible solution, I knew what I had to do."

"Don't you dare do this to me again. Don't you dare," he cried when I raced toward the water's edge. I had no idea what that meant, but now, I do.

Even though Cayden's dad was a fucking bastard, he didn't deserve what we did to him. But we were kids. We made a mistake. In times of crisis, one can be forgiven for not thinking how they normally would.

I was moments away from being raped, and Cayden was on the brink of death—it was an accident. But accident or not, we committed a crime, one which changes everything. "What happened?"

Cayden, although weighed with sorrow, has a sense of relief that shines through too. He's carried this secret for ten long years—it must be cathartic to finally unburden his soul. "You were in danger around me. My dad was involved with some shady people, and when he didn't show up for "work," they'd come around, asking questions. I couldn't involve you in that. I'd hurt you enough. You were my Achilles' heel. I couldn't risk them finding out how much you meant to me. You'd be collateral damage.

"I went to your house, intent on telling your mom how I felt. That although I loved you, it was in your best interests to stay away from me. And I was willing to strategize with her to find ways to make that happen. But what I never expected was for her to stoop so low. She offered me twenty thousand dollars to stay away. I was insulted she thought so little of me and my feelings for you. I was ready to tell her to shove her money, that I'd figure this out another way, but then I saw you, peering at me from the top of the stairs. You were waiting for me to tell her to go to hell, that no amount could ever be enough because you were priceless...but I didn't. I had exhausted every way I knew. I did what I thought was right. But it's the biggest regret of my life.

"I accepted, knowing what it would do to you in the process. I broke your heart, but if it gave you a real shot at making something of yourself, away from here, then I'd suffer the consequences. You already felt abandoned by your mom, and I did the same. I sold you out for twenty thousand dollars."

I blink past my tears as I've never felt more betrayed than I do right now. My mom's statement about everything she does is to protect me now makes sense because, in her warped way, she was.

"That's why I didn't fight harder. You...you broke my heart." My lower lip trembles, but I hold it together for now. "Why did you do that? You risked me telling everyone what we did. I'd hope I wouldn't stoop that low, but I can imagine the seventeen-year-old me was a woman scorned."

"I didn't care," Cayden reveals, showing me just how fearless he really is.

"But you didn't cash it," Lacey says, confused. She opens the folder and produces the check, the proof that Cayden is the man I thought him to be.

"Of course, I didn't," he spits, beseeching I understand why he did what he did. "There isn't a price tag on how much you mean to me."

Exhaling in relief, I can understand Cayden's actions. In his messed-up way, he was trying to protect me, but surely when I came back, when I was an adult, he could have told me the truth.

"I know what you're thinking, but you were happy," he says, reading my mind. "When you came back here, neither of us were the same people we once were. We grew up. You came here wanting to put a piece of your past behind you, but the attraction was still there. It always has been. Over the next ten years, you came in and out of my life. The first time, as you know, was a final fuck you. You claiming back your independence. But it only proved that what we had was real. But we were scared.

"Just how you did when we were kids, I'd wake late at night with you snuggled by my side. And in the morning, you'd be gone. You stayed for hours, sometimes days, but the common occurrence was you always left. You were torn between duty and desire. I had broken your heart, so your guard was up, but we have been a part of one another since we were kids, and it's hard to break that commitment."

The need to sleep beside him was overwhelming, and I now

know why. I have been doing it since I was a child.

"I wanted to tell you so many times that I never spent that money, but it was too late. I was happy to live in the darkness with stolen kisses and covert glances just like when we were kids because you were happy. You said Calvin was good to you and that your mother approved of him. That's all you ever wanted. To gain her approval. But one of the last times you came here, I couldn't stand it anymore. I had to tell you the truth. It went as expected. You were angry I'd wasted all these years. You left saying you needed time. And then I didn't see you until the night of your accident. You know the rest." His guilt is palpable because all Cayden ever tried to do was protect me.

I remember wondering what words we exchanged the night of our argument for me to lie to him about our baby. Now, I need to know. "What happened? Why did you push me away? I know you said we exchanged words. But what words? And why? I can't imagine after all these years wasted and the way I feel about you now, that I wouldn't have fought harder. I'm not seventeen anymore. And I don't need you to protect me. I never did."

"You're right. I said some awful things to you. You told me you wanted to forget everything and start over. Together. That it was finally our time."

"And in return, you told me you didn't want anything to do with me...or our baby," I whisper, putting the pieces to this ugly, ugly puzzle together.

Lacey gasps, tears shining brightly, while Cayden squeezes his eyes shut, hoping to dull the pain.

Why? Why would he do that?

I left here utterly broken. Although I loved Cayden, it was apparent we were intent on hurting one another over and over again. His comment hits home.

"We hurt the ones we love." And that's all Cayden and I have done for the past ten years.

"If I could take it back, all of it, I would. By trying to protect you, I did the complete opposite. What I should have done was tell you the truth because you could have handled it. You always were the strong one, and I was stupid for ever forgetting that."

He tried to protect me, but you can't protect someone from living, and that's how I clearly felt with Cayden—that I was living. That's why I came back here time and time again. On the outside, I may have seemed to have it all, but on the inside, I was still the eight-year-old little girl, smitten by the boy who broke my heart.

Lacey seems to be the only one able to make sense of what's going on. "Peyton." She steps forward apprehensively while I keep my feet planted on the floor. "The first time we met, do you remember I was going to tell you something?"

I retrace over everything we shared, and I know she speaks of the conversation when she was going to reveal something about Cayden, but she never got the chance. *"The thing about Cayden is that he lost…"*

I nod slowly.

She nervously wets her lips, looking at her brother, before confessing, "He lost you. I don't really remember you from when I was a child, but I remember how happy you made Cayden when you came back. It may only have been for a day, but it was enough for him. He was happy that you were free from this place. From the memories. That you'd worked your way to a powerful position at work. I told him to tell you to stay, but he always said that he couldn't. And now...I think I know why."

Cayden hisses, taking a step back.

"Lacey, why did you stay in Myrtle Beach?" I ask, remembering her earlier comment.

She swallows. "Because, for the past few weeks...I've felt like someone is watching me. All the time. And when Cayden told me to go and take Ellie with me, I knew something was wrong." She holds up the folder, desperate for him to confirm her fears. "Is it true?"

My blood runs cold when he casts his eyes downward. "Yes."

The terrified cry which leaves Lacey has me snapping into action, forgetting my fears. "What does that mean?" I latch onto his bicep, ignoring how good it feels to touch him.

"It means that I'm responsible for your accident. You left here hysterical, but I had to send you away. Please believe me."

But he has five seconds to tell me the truth once and for all because this is the final piece—the piece I was searching for all along. "Why did you have to send me away? What's the reason?" When he shrugs from my grip and runs a hand through his hair, I snare his wrist. He won't evade me. Not this time. "Tell me! I'm not seventeen. I don't need you saving me!"

My bravado dies a sad death, however, when he lets out an amused, frustrated laugh. "How I wish that were true." That look, I've seen it before.

My heart rate begins a steady incline while I measure how many breaths I take.

Gonna teach that mom of yours a lesson. You're just like her. A dirty whore. Sneaking in here. I know what you want.

I fight with everything I am, but he's just so strong. He kisses my neck, biting hard. I cry out. I'm afraid. *Get off! No, please no. Cayden, help! Please...help me.*

I smell whiskey. I can feel his blunt arousal. Oh, my God... his hands are everywhere...on me...in me. I can't breathe. But through the chaos, he's my anchor, refusing to allow the demons to drag me to rough waters.

"I will never let him hurt you ever again."

Cayden's promise, although gallant, doesn't make sense. The dead can't hurt me. Their memories, yes, but in the physical sense...a bright light flickers, a candle in a darkened room, and I suddenly strip back the past and focus on this moment, this very second in time.

"He's dead. He can't hurt me."

This is the time for Cayden to nod and tell me we're all safe, but he doesn't. He does the complete opposite. With a hesitant touch, he places his palm on my cheek, lending me some strength. "No...I don't think that he is."

There must be some mistake. Another cruel joke. But when I peer into Cayden's eyes, I see it—fear. My courageous warrior is afraid. "There must be some mistake?" I look at Lacey for assurance, but her tears only confirm my worst nightmare as true. "How? How do you know?"

Cayden swallows, brushing the tears I didn't even know I'd shed away with his thumbs. "The reason you came back here. The reoccurring vision you can't seem to escape." When he strokes over my hair, I stop breathing.

"The ribbon?"

Cayden nods, the world weighing heavily on his shoulders. "Yes. It appeared weeks before your accident. I knew it wasn't you...and that could only mean it was one other person. The only person who wanted to taunt me, to show me that even after all these years, he's still in control."

The world is spinning so fast, I can barely keep up. "That's why you said what you did the night of my accident? You knew I was in danger?"

"Yes. But it didn't seem to make a difference." This is all too much, but I stand strong. "What do you know about the person who ran you off the road?"

"I-I..." I falter, unable to speak. "I don't know. My mom said it was a drunk driver who was never found." When Cayden's jaw clenches, I shake my head, violently. "No, that's not...it can't be."

"I have no proof, but what Lacey holds, it's what I've been working on for the past few weeks. Your accident was two miles from here. The other car involved left the scene. They never located the driver."

My lower lip quivers. "Just like you, Lacey, since I arrived here, I couldn't shake the feeling that I was being followed. I thought it was my mom's spies, but oh my God..." That sentence is too horrifying to complete.

This entire time, I was led to believe that the accident was just that...but a small voice inside me is screaming that what Cayden says is true. Thoughts drift to earlier when I noticed a pair of my underwear missing. Gasping, I cover my mouth. I think I'm going to be sick.

"I need to go."

"Peyton!" But I shake my head and run toward the front door.

The fresh air cools my flaming skin, but it's temporary because the nausea continues to rise. I race for a tree and retch, desperate to purge up this bitterness within. But nothing will feel right again.

"Peyton?" Cayden's voice has me gripping the trunk, afraid I will crumple without the support.

"How is this possible? I…killed a man. And then, for the next ten years, I float in and out of your life with one foot in the future, and the other the past. Our love was toxic, Cayden."

"I know," he confesses sadly.

"And now you're telling me the reason I left is back and intent on, what…finishing what he started? Is that it?" I snap, spinning to face him.

He looks broken and defeated, but I march forward, enraged. But most of all, I'm scared.

"If he is back, then I probably deserve whatever revenge he decides to dish out. We…killed him," I whisper, still in disbelief.

"No, we didn't," he corrects, shaking his head angrily.

"We may as well have! We left him for dead! However you look at it, we're guilty." This isn't Cayden's fault, but I can't process this right now without wanting to scream.

"Come inside. Please."

But I can't.

I need to get far away from here, this place which I seem to have a gravitational pull to. But when I look into Cayden's eyes, I see that it has nothing to do with my surroundings and everything to do with him.

I came back time and time again because I loved him, but look what that love has done. Standing slowly, I will my knees to stop knocking. "Together, we're destructive. You know it."

He exhales in defeat. "I know, Peyton, I know, but I can't stop. I've tried, and so have you."

This isn't merely about us anymore. Until I can wrap my head around everything he's just revealed, I need to go. "Well, I'll just have to try harder." My heart thrashes about in protest, not wanting to leave him, but I can't keep doing this…to him.

I was selfish. For these past ten years, I floated in and out of Cayden's life, destroying any chance he had at living a normal life. I can't do that anymore. We need to set one another free.

"Don't do this," he begs. Storming forward, he grips my upper arms. "It's not safe with…him out there. That night, when you were drugged…I think it was him."

I gasp, tears stinging my eyes. "That's why you've been watching me, isn't it?"

"Yes," he confesses without apology. "He torments us and plays with us until we're ready to break. And only then will he strike. Look what he did to you! He tried to kill you, and he could have. But it was a sign, a warning of things to come. You know I'm right."

My silence says it all because he's right. But I refuse to stay hidden in the shadows. It's time I reclaimed who I am.

"I-I have to go."

"Where?" Cayden is desperate, desperate to save me once again. But he can't save me from myself. The only person who can do that is me.

"There is only one place." He doesn't need me to spell it out. I need to go back to where it all started.

FIFTEEN

Coming back here to Myrtle Beach is bittersweet.

Bittersweet because even though this is one of the first places I remember, I'm not returning of my own free will. I want answers, and I want them now.

Thumping on my parents' front door, I take a deep breath because shit is about to get real. Stella has some explaining to do, and I'm not leaving here until she gives me the answers I seek. When she opens the door, however, I'm not sure if she'll even let me into the house.

"Given your staff the day off?" I quip as she usually wouldn't be caught dead opening the door.

She folds her arms across her chest, pursing her lips. "I see you haven't lost this attitude. I refuse to speak to you when you're this way."

Tonguing my cheek, I shake my head, infuriated. "This

way? Have you ever thought I'm 'this way' because you've lied to me for so many years? No wonder I can't remember you. My brain has clearly gone into self-preservation mode because I've finally had enough."

When she opens her mouth, primed on telling me more lies, I strike forward, unable to stand here a second longer. "I know what you did."

"Did?" She nervously toys with her pearl earring.

"Yes, *Mother*." A word has never sounded so dirty. "I know you paid me out for a lousy twenty thousand dollars. How could you?"

She blinks once, caught off guard. "I did it to protect you." Her excuse didn't stick the first time around, and it sure as shit doesn't now.

"Oh, cut the crap. You did it to protect yourself and your precious reputation because, God forbid, I was seen with a Coachman. Cayden told me what you did to his...dad."

I gulp as I'm still coming to terms with what *I* did. I shouldn't be here condemning her, but I need her to know how her cruelty affected so many people.

"Come inside." She steps from the doorway. This isn't optional.

Desperate to find out the truth, I brush past her, hating that I'm stepping into the lion's den—voluntarily. She closes the door, sealing me in for good. "Let's go into the study. Your father doesn't know about this, and I'd prefer to keep it that way."

I follow as her heels click across the flooring, each step stabbing away at my resolve.

I am angry, so damn angry that everyone, including Cayden, has lied to me. I understand why he did what he did, but so much time has been wasted. And I lost my child…our child. I will never forgive myself for being so selfish. And I will never forgive Stella for playing a part in all of this.

We enter the study, the mood hostile. Stella makes a beeline for the liquor cabinet, which surprises me. She pours two glasses of top-shelf scotch. "Here."

I accept the offering as God knows this will be easier to stomach with alcohol running through my system. When Stella throws back her drink, her face twisting in pain as the burn hits her throat, it seems she feels the same way.

"It's true," she commences, taking a seat behind the large mahogany desk. I decide to stand. "I did pay that money, but I did it because I wanted you to have a chance in life. You were so…infatuated with Cayden Coachman. It was the only way I could save you from throwing your life away."

"You had no right to do that. None. It was my life," I cry, hooking my thumb toward me.

"Think of me what you will, but Cayden had no issues accepting the money."

Inhaling through my nose, I try to focus on why he did it, not the betrayal I feel. "Yes, he was wrong to accept, but you saw he never cashed that check. Yet you stood by and watched me change into you."

She purses her lips, shoulders pulled back. "I watched you do something with your life. Cayden was a deadweight around your neck, and whether you believe me or not, I did you a favor."

"I still went back to him!" I reveal, adrenaline coursing

through me.

"What?" she gasps, her mask finally slipping.

"For ten years. You may have come between us, but I always found my way back. And he welcomed me home because"—a sob escapes me—"the love we shared, it wasn't something we could forget. I'm sure I tried, but in the end, my heart won out.

"But because of what you did, I hurt him. I floated in and out of his life, hurting him how he hurt me. But he did everything, *everything* to protect me."

By the time I'm done, tears stream down my face.

Stella is out of sorts as I'm certain she isn't accustomed to such emotion. She no doubt sees this as a sign of weakness, but I don't. I see it as being human—something she isn't.

"I know how you ridiculed Cayden's father when you were children." She clears her throat, her cold eyes darting to the left, unable to look at me. "How could you do that to him? You have no idea what that did to him...to Cayden," I add, frowning when thoughts of what he endured as a child crash into me.

I dare not tell her about what happened between Cayden's father and me. She doesn't need to know because until I can figure out what exactly is going on, I won't tell a soul.

"He was nothing but white trash," she states very matter-of-fact. "And so is his son. You don't remember the tears, the heartbreak, but I do!"

I flinch, as her emotion is one I haven't seen before.

"People like us don't fall in love with the Cayden Coachmans of this world."

I was right.

Her reputation is what fueled her over the years. In

layman's terms—I was rich, and Cayden was poor, and nothing Cayden could do would ever have her seeing him as anything but unworthy.

"I was pregnant," I whisper, tears slipping into my parted lips. The room drops about a hundred degrees.

She covers her mouth with a wavering hand. "I know, the hospital told me. I never said anything because it was better that remained forgotten." Is she trying to label her lies as compassion? "Did Calvin tell you?"

Taking a deep breath, I confess softly, "No...because it wasn't his baby."

"Wh-what are you talking about?" she falters, clearly confused by what I'm telling her.

"The baby wasn't Calvin's. It was Cayden's. Looks like you would have been a grandmother to a Coachman. Your worst nightmare come true."

She turns her cheek like I've slapped her. "How could you? I raised you better than this."

"No, you didn't. You raised me to be a spoiled brat, one who was to look down on someone who you believed was lesser. But I'm glad I never did," I dispute, the fight in me dying.

She narrows her eyes, disappointed and also livid I would taint the family name. "Maybe it's best things ended the way they did then."

I step back, horrified. "How could you say that?" Is she *happy* I got ran off the road and lost my baby?

When she sits still, lips pursed, back rigid, I know I will never forgive her for being so cold and callous. Not seeing the point in dragging this out, I save us both the torture of talking to one another and turn on my heel and leave.

A tear scores my cheek, but I wipe it away with the back of my hand. I refuse to shed another one for someone who isn't worth it. I yank open the door, only to run straight into Isla, my sister. She's still in her scrubs, so she must be coming back from work at the hospital.

"Peyton? Is everything all right?" she asks, gripping my bicep lightly. She knows what the answer is. She only has to look at my face to see that no, I'm not all right. "Do you want to go for a walk?"

All I can do is nod because I need to talk to someone who knew me before this all happened.

She doesn't say a word and leads us down the stairs and toward the side of the house, where there is a small sunroom. I have no idea what this is used for because the wicker furniture in here looks brand new. But I suppose that's the norm for this place—it's more of a museum than a home.

"What happened?" Isla asks, sitting on the cream sofa and gesturing I'm to sit beside her. I do.

"Stella is what happened," I reply, tears of anger rising. "I cannot believe I'm related to her. Some days, I think maybe I can't remember because I don't want to. I don't want to remember the person I once was."

Isla casts her eyes downward, eyes so like mine.

This is the first time in so many months we've been alone, as Stella ensured this wasn't a common occurrence. Isla knows something, and I intend on getting to the bottom of what that is. "Was I happy?"

Isla works her bottom lip, weighing what to say. "Peyton…

you were…always living two lives. Here, with us, behaving how a Lane should behave, and back at that lake house with… Cayden."

A gasp escapes me. "You know about Cayden?"

She nods, the strands of her copper hair slipping free from her bun. "Yes. He was your weakness, but he was also your greatest strength. You loved him for as long as I can remember. And he loved you. You moved, he moved."

I sit motionless, finally understanding why Stella never wanted us alone together for too long.

"I thought when you got older, that love would fade…but it didn't. But Mom wouldn't allow it. So to keep her happy, you used to sneak off and see him. Sometimes for a day, other times, a week. But in the end, you always came back because you were torn between your heart and your head.

"So the answer to your question is, yes, you were happy… but only when you left to see Cayden. When you returned, it was like you were a different person, and I suppose in some ways, you were."

"Why didn't you tell me this?"

She shrugs, her guilt evident. "It wouldn't achieve anything. I was hoping that maybe you not remembering would give you a fresh start, but it seems you can't seem to forget some things."

And she's right. I can understand her reasoning. It's exactly why Cayden didn't tell me, but now that I know, the question is, where do I go from here?

"Mom never approved of Cayden, but he did something for you to stay away, didn't he?" I nod slowly. "You're too stubborn to only allow her disapproval to get in the way. I don't know what happened, but whatever it was, it changed you. You became…distant."

I wish I could tell her, but I can't. "I think there is something wrong with me," I confess.

She tilts her head, confused. "Why?"

"Because I tortured and punished the man I loved for ten years." I'm ashamed because after hearing the truth about who I really am, I now understand why my memory remains in the shadows.

But Isla places her warm hand over my clenched fist. "That's where you're wrong. You tortured and punished yourself, Peyton. For ten years, you went back to Cayden, knowing you could never stay. And each time you left him…you left a small piece of your heart with him."

A sob rattles my chest because, since hearing the truth, I was questioning just what sort of a person I was. But I like this version of events because the way I feel about Cayden now, it fits with the past.

"I love him…" I whisper, as I haven't been able to vocalize this aloud to him. But after everything I've just heard, it seems like I've never had a choice.

"I know, Peyton, and that's okay."

"Was I in love with Calvin?" I feel like he's the victim in all of this somehow. But I suppose we all are.

"I think you loved him…but in love, no. You settled because no one would ever be the man you really wanted."

By this stage, I have once again surrendered to the tears. "Thank you for being honest with me." I wanted honesty, and I've received it in droves.

"It's okay. I'm just sorry I didn't do it sooner." She squeezes my hand with a smile. "Do you need a ride somewhere?" I caught a cab here, so yes, I do.

Sighing, we both know there is only one place I want to be.

"Come on. I'll take you back home."

This is the first heart-to-heart I've had with Isla, but I'm going to ensure it's the first of many. "I hope I was nice to you," I say, unsure if I want to know the answer.

Isla smiles. "You always were. You may have had a tough exterior, but we all do…look at who our mother is."

Touché.

We go to stand, but I follow my gut and throw my arms around Isla. She freezes as I'm not even sure if this is a thing we do. But she soon reciprocates. "Even though you were always nice…I like this Peyton better," she whispers, hugging me tighter.

I smile because I couldn't agree more.

On the way back to my house, Isla and I catch up on everything. It seems now that the cat is finally out of the bag, she can talk freely, without fear of saying something wrong. Talking to her has made me see that I wasn't such an awful person.

Yes, I sounded like a hard-ass who had some serious baggage, but my past wasn't exactly what you'd expect from someone of my social standing to be like. I pulled away from the lavish lifestyle because here was always my home.

However, when Isla pulls up in my driveway, and I see Cayden sitting on my front steps, I know that it's him, not here, that always brought me back.

"Thanks. Let's catch up for coffee when I'm not a hysterical mess."

Isla bursts into laughter, but she isn't without tears. We bonded, and it seems like a weight has been lifted from her shoulders. I hope we can move forward from here. We hug goodbye while I open the door and take a deep breath.

It's time to face the music.

Cayden comes to a stand, watching me closely as I keep my eyes peeled to the ground. I don't know what to say. It's been information overload, and all I really want to do is curl up and switch off. But I owe Cayden an explanation of how I'm feeling. He too is lost and scared, and I need him to know that we're in this together.

"Snow...I'm—"

But I don't allow him to continue. I rush forward and throw myself into his arms. His surprise is evident, but he catches me just the same. "I'm sorry I left." It's on the tip of my tongue to add, *again,* but I don't.

"It doesn't matter. You're back now," he says into the crook of my neck as he squeezes me tight. "I know it's a lot to take in. I wish I had something less complicated to offer you, but this is us—a beautiful mess."

It sums us up perfectly.

We stay hugging for minutes, and I don't think I'll ever be able to let him go now that I know our past. I can't imagine how hard it must have been for Cayden this entire time, knowing what we shared. I hope my memories will one day return, but if they don't, I'm more than ready to make new ones.

"What are we going to do?" I whisper, savoring his scent, his touch.

"I don't know yet, but I won't let anything happen to you again. I promise."

"We can't go to the police, can we?" I know the answer, but I need to hear it all the same.

"No, we can't. I don't have any proof, and to tell them what I think means we'll have to tell them what we did."

He's right.

"So we wait?" It sounds so dismal, waiting for the Big Bad Wolf to come blow down our houses. But Cayden shakes his head.

"We don't wait. We live. We be vigilant, but I refuse to allow that asshole to take you away from me once again."

We break apart, and he gently traces the slope of my nose before fingering my lips. I can't help the moan which leaves.

"Can I kiss you?"

He's asking for permission because he doesn't know where we stand, a common occurrence between us.

But I will not succumb to the ghosts as I will live in the now. "Yes."

He swoops forward, slamming his mouth to mine, uniting us as one. I meet him with everything that I have, fisting his hair because I can't get close enough. Our tongues duel, fighting for control, but I eventually give in because it feels so good. Cayden doesn't just kiss. He devours, and I turn to mush against him.

Something is different about this kiss, and I suppose that's because we are kissing, full disclosure. I know everything, and although troubled, I feel closer to the man who I have loved since I was a child.

The thought leaves me heady, and I cling to him, his strength singing to my own.

"Let me take you out," he says against my lips, his breath hot and heavy.

"Out where?"

"Anywhere," he replies, suckling my bottom lip. "I want to show you how good we are together."

I whimper, almost sliding down his body with a quiver rocking me. "Okay."

He can't hide his happiness. "This is us, Snow, and I intend to remind you how we belong." When he wraps his hand around the back of my neck, robbing me of breath, I can't wait to uncover all the ways.

I'm nervous as I look at my reflection in the mirror.

I didn't know what to wear on our "date." The term seems absurd, seeing as I've known Cayden forever, but with my amnesia, it feels like I'm seeing him for the first time.

I don't know what happens now. In most circumstances, the truth is supposed to set one free. But for me, I'm left with this ominous shadow hanging over my head.

However, I keep such thoughts from my mind and focus on getting ready because Cayden will be here in fifteen minutes. I've tied my hair back into a messy bun and settled on wearing a red summer dress with brown sandals.

I wonder if Cayden is as nervous as I am?

Now that I know the truth, I wonder what happens next?

Will this new version of me love Cayden as much as the old me? A sense of dread fills me when the better question comes to mind—will Cayden love the new me? Or are his feelings for the girl I once was?

That girl didn't sound like a very nice or happy person, but he still loved her. What if this version is too different from the one he fell in love with?

Groaning, I massage my temples because these what-ifs aren't doing anything to help my nerves.

When there is a knock on my door, it's time to face these insecurities head-on because no matter how uncertain I feel, Cayden has always loved me and I have to believe in that love.

Reaching for my lip gloss and phone, I stuff both into my bag and take a calming breath. *I'm going to be fine,* I repeat over and over. It's Cayden. It's time I gave this love a real chance.

With that as my incentive, I march through the house and open the door with confidence. However, when I see Cayden, standing before me in blue jeans and a black button-up shirt with the sleeves rolled up, exposing his taut forearms, I hold the doorjamb to stop me from face planting.

"Hi," he says with a lopsided smirk.

"Hello," I manage to wheeze.

He is fucking incredible and knowing our past, just makes him all the more desirable. But I rein in my need to tackle him to the ground because I'm not the type of girl who puts out on the first date. Well, I don't think I am.

"Where are we going?" I ask when I think I can speak without gasping for air.

He steps forward while I tighten my hold on the doorjamb.

"We're going to where I should have taken you when you first arrived."

I gulp.

"Okay. That doesn't sound worrying at all," I quip, gathering my bearings and locking the door behind me. His bluntness has robbed me of my nerves, which isn't such a bad thing, I suppose.

However, when I turn and bump into a solid wall of delectable-smelling flesh, my nerves resurface. Peering up, I chew the inside of my cheek because every time I lock eyes with Cayden, everything falls into place. I can't explain it, but I guess what we shared is inexplicable.

"You look beautiful," he whispers, brushing a strand of hair behind my ear.

On instinct, I shiver as his touch has me catching my breath. "Thanks."

If he continues looking at me this way, I just may latch onto him and not let go. His grin reveals he's clued in to my thoughts. "Let's go."

He reaches for my hand and leads me toward his truck.

We're silent as he opens the door for me, as it appears we're both lost in thought. When the engine roars to life, I jolt in my seat. I turn to look out the window, but a warmth spreads from head to toe as Cayden places his hand on my leg softly.

I watch the world pass me by, just like I did when I first arrived. But now, everything is so different. I know why this place called to me because it's always been home, just how Cayden has been. Not remembering doesn't seem fair because what I feel for him...to experience a lifetime of that has me realizing that our love is something extraordinary.

"We're here," Cayden says, shattering my reflections.

Turning slowly, I peer out the windshield at the huge white house. A longing hits me, not because I recognize it, but because the blossoming lemon tree in the front yard reveals where we are. A breath hitches in my throat as I stare, transfixed at the sight which started this all.

Without thought, I open the door and jump from the truck, needing to get a closer look at my once home away from home. The closer I get, the harder it is to breathe. I'm waiting for my memories to return. But they don't.

Stopping in front of the white picket fence, I examine my surroundings and hate my surname even more. I can see why Cayden referred to this side of the lake as the "rich" because this house is heavy in riches. Compared to my modest abode, it's easy to understand why a distinct line was drawn in the sand between Cayden and me.

He stands beside me, allowing me the time to take it all in. Squeezing my eyes shut, I try to draw out the memories, but there are none. The only familiarity is through the story Cayden shared with me. "I wish I could remember," I say, unable to keep the tremor from my voice.

"I wish you could too," Cayden replies with regret. "But some part of me is glad that you don't."

Sighing, I allow the sun in as I open my eyes. I understand his reservations, but I don't want to be sheltered. That's all I've been this entire time. "Is this weird for you?"

"Weird?" he questions.

With my gaze still fixed on the house, I answer. "Yes. You

being here, with me, must bring up old memories, ones which I can imagine aren't all pleasant. Those memories have been wiped clean for me, but for you"—I rein in the tears—"they still burden you every day."

"I would do anything to protect you from that pain. So I happily take on the burden. All I ever wanted was for you to be happy and free. That's why I brought you here. It's time we let go of the past. No more secrets."

A tear slips free. "What are we going to do?" I ask again, as the question relates to the entire shitstorm we find ourselves in.

"I don't know, Snow." I'm terrified, but when Cayden reaches for my hand, it comforts me to know we can be unaware together. "But we will figure it out. Together."

Turning my chin, I look at him, and an unexpected rush of emotion drowns me. "I'm sorry for everything I did to you."

"Shh." He shakes his head, squeezing my hand. "It doesn't matter. What matters is now. This."

"I promise you, I won't make the same mistakes again. I wish I could—" However, I never get to finish my sentence because Cayden swoops forward, stealing the air from my lungs when he kisses me.

Instinctively, I turn into him, wrapping my arms around his nape. I lose myself to his touch, to the way he knows my body better than me. "I've always wanted to kiss you here," he whispers against my lips, his breath warm.

His admission has me standing on tippy-toes to deepen the connection. He moans into my mouth.

I know I should allow what he told me today to sink in and take some time to myself, but staying away from Cayden is impossible. His reasonings to why he didn't tell me the truth probably don't make sense to most, but I understand.

Cayden has always put me first to ensure my happiness before his. He believed saving me from the heartache was the right thing to do because that's what we do for the people we love—we sacrifice our soul to save theirs.

How can I be mad at him for having my best interests at heart? Our story is incredibly fucked up, but it's ours.

"Let's go," I pant, breaking the kiss. "This place is one memory I'm happy not to remember."

Cayden rubs his nose against mine and nods.

We walk back toward his truck, hand in hand. "Are you hungry?"

"I could eat," I reply, although my appetite is shot.

Cayden senses my worry and stops me from getting into the truck. "Did I make a mistake in bringing you here?"

"No." I shake my head animatedly. "I'm glad that you did. Thank you. It's helped me understand our past. I just hate that we've wasted so much time. That our lives have been shaped by others."

His shoulders rise as he sighs. "I know. Me too."

Will this feeling of remorse ever fade? When I think about what we did to Cayden's dad, I know the answer is no. How can it? Look what we did.

"Stop it," Cayden says, gripping my chin and pinning me with a passionate stare. "He isn't worth it. Trust me. It's taken my whole life to realize that."

I'll have to take his word for it. "Okay." Tired of all the doom and gloom. I peck his lips before getting into the truck.

"Do you feel like Chinese?"

"Yes!" I exclaim, bouncing in my seat. "I love Chinese. But you already knew that, didn't you?"

His smirk is all the answer I need.

When he starts the engine and drives away, a weight is lifted from my shoulders because this place has me thankful that I don't remember.

Needing to focus on something else, I decide to talk about my home. "You'll have to come over and look at the house. It's looking really good."

Now that I know my house was once Cayden's, it feels strange referring to it as mine.

"Maybe after we eat?" he suggests. "You can give me the grand tour."

My cheeks instantly flush because the moment we step foot inside the bedroom, I am going to replace the bad memories with only the good. But I attempt to remain passive. "Sure."

When he clears his throat, I'm privy to what he wants to ask. "How'd it go with your mom?"

I can't stop the scoff which escapes me. "It went exactly how you think it did. I told her I knew everything."

"And?" he prompts gently.

"And it's clear my mother is a heartless bitch," I reply without pause. "I told her"—I cast my eyes downward—"about the baby."

Cayden hisses softly, his pain evident. Nothing will ever take that heartache away, but I try to be strong. Even though I don't remember, that doesn't make this any easier to talk about.

"I'm glad she knows because she can remain a forgotten

memory. She's dead to me." I screw up my face, suddenly wishing I used another phrase.

The truck falls silent because sometimes, this is just too much for us both.

"I've been thinking about what our next step should be."

"I'm listening." I turn in my seat to face him.

His hands are tight around the steering wheel as he's clearly tense. I suddenly get the feeling I won't like what he has to say. "There was a guy, Benny, my dad knew—"

But I've already heard enough. "Okay, stop. Anyone that your dad knew is someone we don't want to know."

But Cayden shakes his head. "He wasn't like the rest of them. When he stopped by, he used to bring Lacey and me candy or some cheap toy. When I was older, he was the one who gave me my first dirty magazine."

"I stand by my earlier comment," I interrupt, shaking my head in disgust.

But Cayden ignores me. "I know it doesn't sound like it, but he actually seemed like an okay sort of guy." I cock a brow in disbelief but allow him to continue. "Anyway, just after what happened with my father." He swallows, while I steady my breathing. "Benny came around, looking for him. I of course told him that I hadn't seen him and that I was certain he split. But Benny knew I was lying. You can't bullshit a bullshitter, remember?"

"What happened?" I ask, rubbing my sweaty palms together.

"He told me my dad owed him a lot of money and that I was to call him when my dad returned. I never found out how Benny knew him, but it was evident Benny was someone you didn't want to mess with. I found out how much and googled him. I knew his nickname was The Owl, so doing a basic search, I uncovered that Benny was my dad's boss, I suppose you could say. He was caught and did time for extortion as well as some drug trafficking offenses."

My eyes widen as I don't understand where he's going with this.

"He got out," Cayden explains, filling in the blanks. "About a year ago. I'm sure he's got a score to settle. If I were to call him and tell him about my dad—"

"No, absolutely not!" I exclaim, sitting taller in my seat. "That is not going to happen. You're not involving yourself with someone whose nickname is *The Owl*."

"I know it's risky, but like I said, he never hurt Lacey or me, and he could have."

"Cayden, no way. I won't cover one crime with another. Two wrongs don't make a right."

"Sometimes they do," he rebukes, his jaw clenched.

"No," I repeat. "We will figure out another way, okay?"

His eyes are focused ahead, but I don't need to look into them to see the rage within.

"Well, I'm all ears because I don't know what else to do."

"Surely, we can explain to the police what we did. I mean, we were kids, and after what he did to us, they will understand." I know what that means. It will drag up old memories for both Lacey and Cayden, but resorting to crime to cover another crime just doesn't sit right with me.

"We could," Cayden says while hope rises. It deflates as soon as it appears. "But that'll mean my dad's old friends will know what we did. And trust me, they'll ensure we pay. No one likes a rat. We'll have a target on our backs. I can't do that to you. Lacey. And more importantly, Ellie."

I don't claim to understand the way of the crime world, but I know what Cayden says makes sense. And it makes me sick to my stomach. "Just, please, don't do anything just yet. Let's think of another way. There's got to be another way," I add, beseeching he sees reason.

I don't know what that is, but we will find a way. We have to.

The silence overcomes us once again.

My chest tightens, and I rub over my heart. I now understand why Cayden wanted to spare me this pain. If push came to shove, could I really do it? End Cayden's dad's life again? But for good this time?

The ringing of Cayden's cell is a welcomed distraction as the silence gives me the chills. He presses a button on the steering wheel to answer the call via Bluetooth. However, when Lacey's frantic voice spills from the speakers, that welcome turns to dread.

"Cayden! It's on fire!"

Fire? I spin to face Cayden, who looks at me, shrugging.

"What's on fire? Ace…"

"Come home!" she screams, and when I hear the distinct sound of sirens, I know the fire is there.

Home.

"Peyton's house is on fire!"

I blink once, not believing what I'm hearing because there must be some mistake. But when Lacey says, "I called 911, but it's bad. Please, come home," it's evident this is really happening.

"We're coming, Ace. Go someplace safe and tell Ellie I'm minutes away." He hangs up, and I slam into the door when he pulls a violent U-turn, flooring it.

The landscape passes me by in a blur, but even if Cayden wasn't driving like a madman, I still wouldn't be able to focus on the world surrounding me. My house is on fire? How is this possible? I turned everything off. I didn't leave any candles burning, and I doubt any of my new appliances would have surged.

That ominous shadow returns, and when I see Cayden white-knuckling the steering wheel, his jaw clenched tight, I know he feels it too.

"How did this happen?" I gasp, shaking my head in disbelief. "Cayden?"

"That piece of shit," he snarls under his breath.

"It's not possible." My mind has gone into denial because there is no way I can accept the possibility that something sinister is at work here.

Cayden slams his hand against the steering wheel, cursing. "It's very possible." He presses his foot to the metal. "I was afraid of this, Peyton. He won't stop, and this is why Benny—"

"No!" I shout as this isn't a solution. It's a tragedy. "Let's just get to the bottom of this before we talk about ending a man's life!"

"He's already dead," Cayden spits.

My stomach drops because deep down, I know there is no changing his mind. Regardless of my concerns, he'll do what he wants because this is the only way he can rid his father from our lives for good.

We travel the rest of the way in silence, but sometimes, the quiet is far more deafening than noise.

We arrive back home in mere minutes, but when we attempt to turn down our street, it's blocked off by the police. Cayden winds down his window. "Our house is down there," he says quickly, but the young officer shakes his head.

"It isn't safe, sir. One of the houses is on fire. We've evacuated the neighborhood." The sky is ablaze with streaks of blood red and a blistering orange.

Leaning over the middle console, I try to reason with him. "I know. It's my house! Please!"

I'm hoping he budges, but he doesn't. "I'm sorry. I can't let you down there. Not until the fire is under control."

"My daughter and my sister live a few doors down. At least let me see if they're all right!" Cayden is about to rip out this officer's spleen when he shakes his head.

"You need to move your vehicle, sir. This road needs to be clear for emergency vehicles."

Cayden opens his mouth, primed on telling the officer what he thinks of his suggestion, but I gently grip his wrist. "Let's park down the road and call Lacey, okay?"

It takes every ounce of his strength not to mow down the barricade, but he eventually nods. "Okay."

However, the officer isn't taking any risks and stands his ground, watching closely as Cayden reverses the truck down the road. The area is filled with neighbors and spectators, and when they see us, their eyes widen, and they whisper behind their hands.

I can only imagine what they're thinking. *It's about time*

that eyesore burned down.

Everything I've worked so hard for has just gone up in flames, and there isn't a damn thing I can do about it. Memories, ones which I can actually remember, have been taken away from me, but maybe this is my karma catching up to me. Those walls housed terrible secrets, and although my intention was good, maybe this is what was always destined for me and the house that changed my life forever.

"Ace! I'm here. Where are you?" Cayden has parked the truck and is jumping out before I have a chance to undo my seat belt.

As he frantically scans the crowd, I take a moment because what the actual fuck is going on? The more I think about my house, the harder it is to breathe.

No.

The familiar sense of drowning returns, which catches me off guard because it's been weeks since these dark feelings have surfaced. But the more I think about what has just happened, the quicker the darkness threatens to swallow me whole.

Burying my face into my palms, I focus on breathing deeply like I learned in yoga, but it's not helping. Each breath feels like my last. On the cusp of hyperventilating, I close my eyes and surrender, but when the door rips open, and I'm dragged into a warm embrace, the world slowly stops spinning.

"I've got you, Snow. Just breathe. Breathe with me." Cayden's soothing voice cuts through the chaos, and when he presses us chest to chest as I cling to him, I follow the steady cadence of his heart. "That's it."

I bury my nose into the groove of his neck, focusing on him

and not on the clusterfuck surrounding us. Gradually, through the clamor, I find silence and connect with the way my body and heart are in sync with Cayden's.

My arms are around his nape, and the closeness is everything I need. Before long, I return to the now and breathe. "Thank you," I whisper, slowly opening my eyes.

"Always," he softly replies, stroking my hair.

With regret, I let him go because we have far more important issues to deal with. Just as I'm about to ask if he found Ellie and Lacey, both cling onto me, squeezing me tight. It seems we all need the connection because this is beyond words.

"Are you okay?" I ask, wrapping my arms around them.

"Yes, we're fine. But your house, Peyton…"

"It's just a house," I say while Lacey hugs me tighter. "As long as you two are okay, that's all that matters."

As Ellie sniffles against me, I realize this is the first time I've seen her since I found out the truth. My heart instantly aches. "Are you all right, little mouse?" I gently run my fingers through her soft hair, holding back my tears.

She nods, squeezing me harder.

I meet Cayden's eyes, and without words, he knows what I'm feeling because he feels it too.

"Sorry to interrupt," says a stern voice, jarring us all apart.

When I see the tall, imposing man in pressed slacks and a white shirt in front of me, I know without a doubt he's a detective. And from his stiff upper lip, it's clear he's a detective who means business. "My colleague tells me it's your house that caught fire."

"Yes," I reply, keeping my arm around Ellie. "Lacey called

and told us what happened."

He nods, examining us all closely. "Who is Lacey?"

"That's me." Lacey steps forward with her hand raised low. "I live a few doors down. Cayden is my brother. He was on a date with Peyton."

The detective focuses his attention on Cayden, who steps closer to me. "Okay. I'm the lead investigator. I'm Detective Kyle Parks. When you've got a moment, I ask that you three come down to the station so I can get your statements."

"Statements?" I question, a shiver running through me. "We weren't here. You'd have more information than us."

"It's standard procedure," he explains, but nothing is standard by the way his steel-gray eyes narrow. "Besides, from what I can gather, this seems to be arson. I'm sure you'd want us to be vigilant in catching the perpetrator. So the more information we have, the sooner we can find the culprit."

"Arson?" I almost gag on the word while Cayden seizes up beside me. The action doesn't go unnoticed by Detective Parks.

"Yes, Ms. Lane." He digs into his pocket and retrieves a business card. "Please call me. I'll be seeing you all very soon." He gives Ellie's head a small pat before he bypasses the barricade and walks down the road toward the flames engulfing my home.

It's not until I see the back of him that I realize he called me by my name. He's obviously done his research. I look up at Cayden, who sighs, his jaw clenched tight. He nuzzles into my neck, and it would appear he's consoling me to onlookers, but I know better.

"Don't say anything. That cop will be watching. We have to be careful."

And he's right.

Although, isn't this our chance to tell the truth? We can tell him about Cayden's dad and how he is most likely behind starting the fire. But it's our word against a dead man's. There is no proof to support our claims, and if we divulge what we did, they'll scour this lake to ensure we're telling the truth. And from this cat and mouse game Cayden's father plays, I have no doubt he prefers to stay hidden.

I can only imagine what that would do to Ellie. She'd be ridiculed at school. Kids can be cruel. And so can their parents. Oh, God. This is a fucking mess.

With no other choice, we stand on the sidelines, waiting until we're given the all clear to go back home. Well, for me, to see what's left. We're far enough that I can't see what's happening, but the crackling alerts me to the devastating fire that has most likely consumed my whole house. The place that was once upon a time our sanctuary is now in flames, and I am certain I'm in hell because the heat I have no doubt will flay the flesh from my bones.

The flames are cruel. They blister a bright red, setting the sky and everything in their path on fire.

After what seems like hours, the crowd begins to disperse, and those who are left are my neighbors who just want to go home. They marvel at the sight before them. Things like this don't happen in a nice neighborhood such as this. Well, not anymore. But it seems with my arrival, I've somehow managed to awaken the ghosts of my past.

When the police remove the barricades, and the fire trucks begin to leave the scene, I know it's over.

Thankfully, Detective Parks isn't in sight, but I know if I don't call him come morning, he will be banging down my door, or whatever door I'm behind.

"Okay, folks. You're free to go home. Please call us immediately if there are any issues."

I don't even wait and practically run down the road, desperate to see what remains. But when my home, or what is left of it, comes into view, I stop dead in my tracks, blinking in disbelief. I thought I was prepared, but I'm not because before me stands a smoldering pile of ashes—remnants of my home.

The twisted black lumps of wood that once held up my house are barely recognizable. Was this space always so big? With no house, everything just seems so…empty.

"It's gone," Lacey cries, echoing our thoughts. Not only have I lost my home, but Lacey and Cayden have also lost it as well.

We stand on the outskirts, eyes never leaving the sad sight. But it suddenly becomes too much for Cayden. "You motherfucker!" he roars, turning in a circle, arms spread out wide. "I'm right here! Stop hiding like the coward that you are!"

"Cayden, stop!" I latch onto his arm, but he's furious, and I'm afraid his wrath will soon burn brighter than my engulfed home.

There isn't anything we can do. Are our memories going up in flames an omen of things to come? The heat from the fire still lingers, but it can't thaw the chill from my bones. I rub my arms, transfixed on watching everything I built go up in flames before my eyes.

Cayden eventually calms and stands by my side, watching helplessly once again. The savage stance of the man beside me can only mean one thing—this is war.

With the smoldering ashes as our backdrop, Cayden coolly links his fingers through mine. "What does this mean?" I whisper, numb inside.

He stands unmoving, but his stillness is far scarier than any violence he could inflict. "It means he's back to finish what he started. But this time…I'm ready."

If it's a fight my demons want…then I'll bring a war. No more hiding. It's time I claimed back what is mine.

SIXTEEN

I stayed at Cayden's as everything I owned was reduced to ash. All that remains is literally the clothes on my back. The materialistic stuff doesn't bother me. The memories that I made in the house sadden me the most.

I don't know where to go now because although I know the truth, I can't expect Cayden to just open his door, and honestly, I don't want him to. I need space to digest everything, and moving in so quickly isn't wise.

Going back to my mom's is definitely not an option, so I'm in limbo with what my next steps are. However, my immediate steps are clear—it's time to go down to the police station.

"We will go shopping after we give our statements," Cayden says, interrupting my thoughts.

Lacey has been kind enough to lend me some of her clothes, but the fact that I need an entire new wardrobe has me nodding slowly.

Cayden mistakes my restlessness for nerves. "Don't worry about the detective. You've done nothing wrong." He rubs over my leg kindly. I'm worried he will see straight through me.

Yes, technically I did nothing wrong, but if he begins to probe, I'm terrified I'll buckle under the pressure and tell him the truth. That might not be such a bad thing, but having to divulge it all…I gulp. How do I detail something I don't even know how to explain?

Cayden pulls the truck into a parking space and turns off the engine. He turns to face me while I take three calming breaths. "Are you okay?"

"Honestly, no," I reply, rubbing the perspiration from my brow. "I think he knows something is amiss."

"He's a cop. It's his job to be suspicious. It'll be okay. I promise." His assurance makes me feel a little better, but I can't shake the feeling that this is the start of things to come.

We exit the truck and walk toward the station, hand in hand. When we enter, I squeeze his hand. Everyone turns their heads to look at us, or maybe it's my imagination. But whatever it is, my stomach turns, and I think I'm going to be sick.

Just as Cayden is about to announce our arrival to the officer at the front desk, Detective Parks rounds the corner and pauses mid-step when he sees us. "Just the two people I wanted to see. Where is Ms. Coachman?"

"Lacey is at home with my daughter. She will be in later on. I didn't want to bring Ellie into the station," Cayden explains coolly, while I shrink into him, wishing I had his confidence.

Detective Parks nods. "Let's get started then. Ms. Lane"—

he focuses his laser stare on me—"I'll take your statement. And, Mr. Coachman, Officer Murphy will take yours." He gestures with his head that we're to follow him.

Cayden leads the way, never letting me go, but when Detective Parks goes left, I know I'm on my own. Cayden locks eyes with me, his expression saying so much. He lets my hand go, nodding once.

An officer indicates Cayden's to follow him, leaving us with no other choice but to part.

I don't look back and follow Detective Parks, who stands by a doorway. I presume this is where the interrogation is to take place. I brush past him, instantly shivering because something about this man leaves my stomach in knots.

"Take a seat," he says, pointing at a steel chair. Nothing about this room is inviting, but I suppose that's the whole point. Don't lie, cheat, or steal. Otherwise, you'll end up in a place like this.

"What's the matter, Ms. Lane? You look nervous," Detective Parks says, closing the door and sealing my fate.

I quickly take a seat and sit on my hands to stop from wringing them together. "I'm not nervous," I state, hoping he can't see through my lie. "I just have a thousand things to do today."

"I won't take up much of your time." He's unmoved by my current situation of being homeless and not wearing any of my own clothes. "Where were you from roughly six to nine o'clock last night?" He sits across from me, producing a small recorder from his pocket.

Shit just got real.

Internally counting to five, I shrug calmly. "I was on a date with Cayden. He picked me up around seven or seven thirty. We took a drive to my old vacation home."

"The one on Maple Avenue?" he asks while I cock my head to the side. He's done his homework.

"Yes, that's right."

"That seems like an odd place to go on a date." He leans back in his chair, stroking his mustache as he waits for me to reply.

I clear my throat as it feels like I've just swallowed lead. "I have amnesia," I explain, but by Detective Parks's impassive expression, it seems he already knew that. "Cayden wanted to take me there as it was where we first met as kids. He was hoping it would spark a memory."

"And did it?"

I shake my head.

"Then what happened?"

"Then we got into his truck and were on the way to get dinner."

"What were you going to eat?"

"Chinese," I reply quickly. I know what he's doing. He wants me to slip up, but this is a truth I can reveal.

"What time were you made aware of the fire?"

"I don't know. The time was the last thing on my mind." I can't keep the sarcasm from my tone, but he's pissing me off. He's acting like I was the one who started the fire. "Lacey called us, and we went straight home."

He nods, appearing to process everything I just divulged. "Have you noticed anything strange over the past few weeks?"

"Strange? You're going to have to be a little more specific." I sit unwavering, leveling him with a blank stare.

"Someone lingering around your home or work?" he explains, his eyes never leaving mine.

"No," I lie, my heart thrashing about in my chest.

He purses his lips, watching for any signs that I'm lying, but I remain perfectly still. "The fire was started deliberately."

"How do you know that?"

"The smell of gas was undeniable. And our team has confirmed it. It was as if whoever started that fire wanted us to know it was deliberately lit."

In and out. I steady my breaths, sitting tall. "Who would do such a thing?"

"I was hoping you could tell me," he counters.

Raising my shoulders, I state evenly, "I have no idea."

"There was no one you knew who held a grudge against you?"

"No, Detective." The perspiration gathers at the small of my back, but I keep my poker face in play.

I'm certain he doesn't believe me, and just when I'm about to buckle, he stands. "You're free to leave. I have everything I need for now."

I can't get out of this room fast enough, but I rise slowly. "Thank you."

I'm expecting there to be a catch, but when he opens the door, I can't believe I got away with...I refrain from thinking such a thought, especially when Detective Parks stops me in my tracks. "You know, Ms. Lane. You didn't look awfully surprised that it was arson."

And there it is. Proof he doesn't believe a word I've just said.

"It's all a little hard to process right now, Detective Parks." We are feet apart, and this close to him, he is sure to see through my lies.

"Of course." He steps aside, allowing me to pass. Just as I brush past him, he adds, "I will get down to the bottom of this. I will find out who set that fire, but most importantly, why."

Locking gazes, I swallow but keep it together. "I'm glad to hear it. Goodbye, Detective."

Before he has a chance to spring anything else on me, I quickly exit the room, sighing in relief when I march down the corridor. But I can feel the detective's eyes on me. I know this isn't the last I've seen of him.

I'm escorted to a lounge to wait for Cayden. Thankfully, I don't have to wait long.

When he enters the room, I stop myself from launching into his arms. "Ready?"

"Yes."

We leave the building, ensuring we play it cool because we both know Detective Parks is watching. When I get into the truck, I fumble with the seat belt, on the verge of tears. Cayden wastes no time putting the truck into gear and speeding away from the station.

After a couple of minutes, I let out a shaky breath and run a hand down my exhausted face. "He knows I'm lying," I say from behind my palm.

Cayden is silent.

But I need to fill in the static. "He is going to dig until he finds out the truth. He will know what we did. We should just tell him the truth."

Cayden's fingers tighten on the wheel.

I know how he feels about that suggestion, but I would rather we tell Detective Parks what happened than him probing and eventually finding it out himself.

"We can tell him, but without a body and the fact that my dad just disappeared, it doesn't look good for us. We don't have any proof he's back, but if we confess to what we did, there will be serious consequences for our actions." His eyes are focused straight ahead as he continues.

"But if you want to tell him, I have one condition."

A wave of terror overcomes me. "What is it?"

"You let me take the fall."

I blink once. *"What?"*

"I won't allow my father to ruin both our lives. I will take the blame. All of it. We don't tell anyone you were there."

"Cayden, no," I protest, my tone labored.

But he won't listen. "Yes, it has to be this way. I can't expect Lacey to look after Ellie on her own. She will need help. I don't want Hazel to be the only one Lacey can talk to about my daughter."

The more he speaks, the bleaker things become. "How can you ask this of me? I'm more to blame than you are. For you to do this...it'll ruin your life. I can't do that. I won't."

The truck swerves violently as he pulls over to the side of the road and drags me over the middle console and onto his lap. I go willingly with tears in my eyes. "You must," he pushes out between a deep exhalation. "Please don't fight me on this. I won't allow him to hurt you ever again."

"I won't stand by while you get persecuted for something *I* did."

His body trembles against mine as he threads his fingers through my hair. "These are my terms," he stubbornly argues, pinning me with a dogged stare. "You're right. It's better we tell the truth. Well, a twisted truth. But I won't ruin your life."

"But you expect me to ruin yours?" I whisper, defeated.

"Without a body, they won't have much to go on. But my confession will most definitely have me doing time. But he will be less likely to come out of hiding if I'm behind bars for his murder. Which means you'll all be safe. It's a sacrifice I'll happily make."

A tear slips down my cheek, but I have no right to cry. I'm not the one sacrificing my freedom. "I won't lose you again."

"Then what do you suggest we do?"

Sighing, I press my forehead to his, reveling in his scent. "Okay...we do it your way."

A hiss leaves him. "My way?"

He knows what I'm proposing, but he needs me to say it, just in case. "We"—I take a breath because what I'm about to say is immoral—"we talk to Benny. But...we avoid any violence if we can. Surely there is another way."

I know there isn't, but how can I sacrifice one man's life to save another? Regardless of what Cayden's father has done, doing this weighs heavily on my soul. And Cayden can sense my dilemma.

"I'll organize it all. You won't have to be involved. You won't know what I do."

"Cayden—"

"No, let me do this," he interrupts, his breath coating my cheeks. "It's my job to protect you. I want you to finally live the life you deserve."

I don't have time to protest because he slams his lips against mine, robbing me of breath. I wrap my arms around his neck and press my body to his, kissing him with a fierce need. I don't know why, but this kiss is heavy with desperation.

With salty tears on my lips, I kiss Cayden without apology because at this moment, I know that I love him. I always have. It seems so strange that such a strong emotion can exist after knowing him for such a short time, but I'm leading with my heart, and it feels good.

We kiss for minutes, knowing that once we stop, everything changes forever. But if Cayden thinks I will allow him to go into this alone, he's got another thing coming. This Peyton Lane will fight for what is hers, and Cayden Coachman is mine...he always has been, and I protect what's mine.

I only bought the essentials because I still don't know where I'm going to live. Cayden said I can stay for as long as I like. Even though I don't doubt my feelings for him, I still want to take things slow. Moving in together is definitely not doing that.

"Do you need me to move any more stuff?" Cayden asks as I pack my things into a drawer.

"No, it's okay. I've already imposed enough."

"You're no imposition," he says, coming up behind me and wrapping his arms around me. "I like having you here."

"I like being here." I melt against him, soon forgetting about rolling my socks into neat little balls. "But eventually, I will have to find a place of my own."

A sigh leaves him. "I know. Where will you go?"

"I don't know."

"Will you come back to work?" he asks, laying a soft kiss on the side of my neck.

"I like the diner," I reply, closing my eyes and arching my head to the side so he can continue his kisses. "Besides, what will everyone say if they find out I'm sleeping with the boss?"

I moan low when he bites over my pulse.

"Well, lucky I'm the boss, and I don't care." His breath heats my skin, and I sag against him, loving this openness between us. But the unspoken lingers.

When will he make the dreaded call?

Speaking of…

My cell chimes, forcing me to untangle himself from his arms. Reaching into my back pocket, I retrieve the phone, only wishing I let it go to voicemail. "What do you want, Stella?"

I don't have time for her bullshit because she's part of the reason I'm here in the first place.

"You didn't think to call to tell me you hadn't burned to death?" Most would expect their mother to show a fraction of concern if their child lost everything they owned to a fire, but lucky for me, I'm not most.

"I didn't think you'd care," I reply, turning around to face Cayden. My annoyed expression must give away who I'm speaking with.

"Don't you dare turn this on me. You were the one who left

here hysterical."

"That's because you are a heartless bitch," I counter with lightning-quick speed. When I think about how our last conversation ended, how she insinuated losing my baby was a blessing in disguise, I know I'm being kind.

Cayden's eyes pop open. He's clearly surprised by my bluntness, but I'm done with her.

"You can forgive everyone else, it seems, but not me."

"What's that supposed to mean?" I spit.

I'm suddenly scorching hot, so I brush past Cayden and yank open the balcony doors, needing the fresh air. The moment I see the vacant spot in front of me, the spot where my house once stood, I wish I had stayed inside.

"I'm assuming you're staying with Cayden Coachman." His name has never sounded so dirty. "You can seem to forget the fact that he lied to you, even forgive him, but you can't with me. I only did what I had to, to protect you."

"That excuse didn't stick the first time around, so I don't know why you'd think it would now." I should just hang up because no good will come from talking to her. But I can't help but wonder why she's called.

"You should come back to Myrtle Beach. It's not safe there." My anger soon simmers, and I steady my breaths. Does she know something?

"Going *back* to Myrtle Beach isn't safe," I correct. "I appreciate your concern, but it's come a little too late."

Cayden stands beside me, peering over the balcony ledge. We both seem transfixed on the emptiness.

"How did you even know the house burned down? Did one

of your spies tell you?"

What she says next, however, has my spirit soon waning. "A detective came by the house, asking a lot of questions about you," she reveals smugly as if that supports her claims of me returning home. "I told him you had amnesia and weren't yourself."

"What?" I gasp, gripping the railing and shaking my head. "Why would you say that?"

"Because it's the truth. You have uncovered so much. I know what you think of me, but I know you, Peyton, better than you know yourself. Sooner or later, you'll soon come to realize that I only want what's best for you."

"Yeah, well, don't hold your breath," I reply, so done with this conversation.

"I will prove that to you one day."

"Well, today is not that day." Before she has a chance to reply, I hang up as I don't need any more negativity.

Groaning low, I squeeze the phone in my hand, wishing it was Stella's head. How dare she call me like nothing happened, expressing concern. That ship has sailed and no matter what she says, I will never forgive her for what she did.

"Everything all right?" Cayden gives me space, but I know if I asked him to, he would wrap me in his arms and shelter me from this mess.

"I now know why Detective Parks knew so much about me. He spoke to Stella," I explain, shaking my head in disbelief. "She told him I'm not myself because I have amnesia."

Cayden sighs, just as horrified as me. "That detective is trouble. You were right. He will continue to dig until he gets answers."

The unspoken lingers.

Surrendering to defeat, I sag into his arms and rest my head against his chest. "I wish there was some other way. I know we can't go to the police, but two wrongs don't make a right."

He's silent.

"I don't know if I can live with myself."

"Shh," Cayden calms me. "You won't have to live with anything on your conscience. I promise."

Just as I'm about to protest because there is no way I'm letting him do this on his own, Ellie appears. "Hi."

On instinct, I'm about to break apart, but Cayden keeps a firm hold on me so we're facing Ellie together. His arm is wrapped loosely around my waist as he draws me into his side. It warms me to know he wants Ellie to see us this way.

After everything I uncovered, I want to say something, but I don't want to freak her out. A piece of paper hangs from her small hand, giving me the lead-in I need.

"What's that?" I ask her with a smile.

She bites her bottom lip. "I drew you a picture."

"You did?" I coo, my heart melting at the sight. Ellie nods and passes me the piece of paper.

When I turn it over and see what she drew, I gently untangle myself from Cayden and drop to a squat so I'm eye level with Ellie. She appears nervous. But I soon soothe her worries. "I love it. Thank you so much."

"It's a map of my house," she explains. "So you don't get lost."

Cayden mutes his laughter while I keep a straight face.

"This will definitely come in handy."

"This is my bedroom," she says, pointing at the biggest, pinkest room of all on her map. "Daddy snores sometimes. So we can have a slumber party."

This time, I'm the one who can't contain my laughter. "That sounds like an amazing idea. Thank you, little mouse." I tenderly brush her cheek.

Hoping I'm not crossing a line, I tuck a lock of hair behind her ear. "I promise, I won't leave you again, okay?"

I didn't just drift in and out of Cayden's life. I did from Ellie's as well. No wonder she was so frightened when we first met.

"Okay," she says, but I can sense her apprehension.

"I'm really sorry for ever hurting you." I'm on the verge of tears, but I hold them back. "But I'll never do it again."

Ellie nods, her intelligent eyes taking everything in. I don't expect her to say anything, but I need her to know I'm here to stay.

"So it's okay for me to stay here for a little while?" I need her approval because she means as much to me as Cayden does.

"Yes." And who knew a simple word could feel so good.

She throws herself into my arms and squeezes me tight. I do the same to her.

Feelings of nostalgia overcome me. We are one little family, and when I peer up at Cayden, I see it in his eyes. He would do anything to protect our family, which leaves us no choice. Sometimes, you have to sacrifice something to save another. And in this case, sacrificing our souls seems like a small price to pay to save the ones we love.

Nodding slowly at Cayden, he knows what to do.

He leaves me hugging Ellie while he digs into his pocket to make a call that will change everything forever. But I'm ready.

SEVENTEEN

Three Days Later

I've managed not to break anything today, but the day is still young. Wiping down table five, I keep my eyes glued to the door in case Cayden walks in, declaring today is the day. Just the thought has my shaky hands knocking a fork to the floor.

Quickly retrieving it, I go about my business as I don't want anyone clueing into my inner turmoil.

Three nights ago, Cayden made the dreaded call. Although I didn't want to know the details, I wanted to know the essentials, and that was when we were going to meet. Cayden was adamant that he'd do this on his own, but there is no way that's happening.

Cayden got ahold of Benny, who said he'd be in touch soon. I didn't ask if Benny was clean, but the fact he was going to call us has me guessing his stint in prison didn't curb his immoral ways.

So now we wait.

My boss isn't here today, so I'm able to hide my cell in my apron pocket. If Cayden calls, I need to be ready. I've let Julia know that I may need to rush off for a family emergency. As far as excuses go, it's beyond lame, but she knows better than to ask questions.

"I'm pretty sure you can see your reflection in the tabletop," Walt, the busboy, says as he passes me with a grin.

I nudge him in the ribs playfully, rolling my eyes. It's the kick in the ass I needed to join the land of the living and attempt to act normal.

The lunch rush means the diner is packed, so it takes my mind off things for a little while. I can almost pretend I'm not looking over my shoulder every five minutes. However, when my apron vibrates, I can't pretend a second longer.

Reaching for my cell, I see it's Cayden calling. "Julia, can you cover for me?" She's taking an order, but I don't wait for her to reply as I dart out the back door.

Ensuring the coast is clear, I say in a rushed breath, "Hello. Is everything all right?"

I hate this seems to be the norm these days for answering a call, but I can't sugarcoat it. I need this done now.

Cayden inhales before replying. "Everything is fine." But I can tell otherwise.

"He's called, hasn't he?"

The weighty pause before his response answers the question for me. "Yes. I'm on my way to see him now."

"What?" I take a step back, shaking my head. "Now? Are

you coming to pick me up on the way?"

"Peyton—"

But I cut him off, furious. "Are you serious? We agreed we'd do this together."

"I know, but it's easier this way," he reasons, but all I hear are excuses.

"Easier? How? You don't know what you're walking into."

"Well, that's a risk I'm willing to take. On my own. I can't do this with a clear head if I'm worrying about you," he presses, but he just infuriates me further.

"So we're back here again? You trying to protect me? You remember how that ended, right?"

He sighs, clearly frustrated, but there is no way I'm letting this go. "You can hate me from there where it's safe."

"Cayden!" I exclaim, angered.

But he won't hear a word. "I've got to go. I'll call you once it's done."

"Once *what's* done?" I press, ripping off my apron and yanking open my locker door. There is no way I'm going to stay put.

"It's time I make amends for all the wrongdoings and to be worthy of your forgiveness."

I pause from ransacking my locker, mouth agape. Is that why he's doing this? "I forgive you, Cayden," I press, my heart breaking when I read between the lines. "But you don't forgive yourself, do you?"

"I never will, which is why I have to do this. Besides, Benny remembers me. He wouldn't do anything."

He's basing this on blind faith.

"I've got to go." I don't have a chance to get a word in edgewise because he concludes the call with, "I love you," then hangs up.

I stare into thin air, blinking in disbelief. What just happened?

Cayden's guilt just may be the death of him, and I mean that in every literal sense of the word. A lot of time has passed since he last saw Benny. Not to mention, Benny has done time. That changes a man, especially a man who was already a bad seed.

I can't let him do this alone.

Thinking on my toes, I call the only person who can help me. "Lacey! Do you know where Cayden is going?"

"Peyton?" she questions, because I sound like a hysterical banshee. "What's wrong?"

Cayden has tried to keep as much of this to ourselves, as he didn't want to involve Lacey as well, but I'm desperate. "It's Cayden," I explain, quickly gathering my belongings. "He's gone to see someone who used to know your dad. Someone who he thinks can help." There is no need for me to elaborate.

"Help? With what?" I allow her to figure it out herself. She does a second later. "Oh, my God. No."

"I'm sorry we didn't tell you. We just wanted to...protect you." Saying it aloud, I can understand why Cayden has done what he has. We just want to protect the ones we love.

"I knew something was going on," she says, and I can just picture her shaking her head at our stupidity. Before I can beg for forgiveness, she displays just who is the brains of this family. "Which is why I put a tracker on Cayden's phone."

I pause, not even sure what that means.

"It's an app," she reveals. "It traces his steps. As long as his phone is on, I can see where he is."

I lean against the locker, sighing in relief. "You're a genius, Lacey."

"You can thank me later. I'm leaving work and will text you where his location is. Ellie is with her mom today, so she's out of harm's way."

"I'll organize a ride and meet you, as it'll take too long if you come and pick me up. As long as one of us catches up to him, the other can catch up."

"Okay, sounds like a plan. I will be in touch as soon as I leave here."

We hang up, and by some miracle, I was hoping a cab would be idling by the curb, but no such luck. When I call an Uber and see the wait is eighteen minutes, I curse loudly. That's a lifetime, especially when you're in a rush.

With no other choice, I stare at the screen, waiting for Lacey to text or call.

I'm seeing double, so when I hear my name being called, my head snaps up, and I blink twice to see who it is. "Will?" I question, shielding the sun from my eyes to see him in his pickup.

"Hey, doll," he says, confirming I'm not seeing things when he winds the window all the way down. "Whatcha doing out here?"

Will is a regular customer who has been nothing but nice to me. All the women at work gush over his good looks, and even though he's old enough to be my dad, I can see why they find him attractive. "I'm just waiting on a ride, but my Uber is ages away," I explain, unable to mask my annoyance.

"Where you off to?"

"Ah," I pause. "I don't know."

He arches a brow.

"I'm just waiting on a friend to text me the address," I explain before yelping because, on cue, my phone pings. It's Lacey. She said Cayden is headed for an address about an hour from here. This app must be able to tap into his GPS or something.

So I have an address. I just don't have a means of getting there asap. Or do I?

"Do you need a ride?" Will asks.

On any other day, I would have said no, but this is an emergency. "Coffee is on me. Forever."

He chuckles, gesturing with his head that I'm to get in.

I do.

Running to the passenger door, I open it quickly but get the sudden sense I'm being watched. Gulping, I launch into the truck, exhaling deeply. I rattle off the address, which Will punches into his GPS.

As I buckle up, I say, "Thank you and, Will, feel free to step on it. I won't tell if you don't."

"Yes, ma'am." Will gives in to my suggestion as the truck roars to life and races down the road.

Lacey's text says she is on the way. She is closer than I am, so she will be there before me, so I text back and tell her to be careful. We both know not to mention calling the police because it's easier this way until we know what we're walking into.

"So where're you off to?" Will asks, snapping me from my

thoughts.

The less he knows, the safer it is for him. "Just helping a friend," I vaguely reply.

Will peers over briefly and smiles. "Is that code for it's none of my business?"

I can't help but laugh.

"I know the look of someone who guards secrets, believe me," he says, piquing my interest.

Turning in my seat, I look at him, wondering what that means.

"Love is usually the reason for secrets," he says, which is true. "Love makes us do crazy things."

"It sounds like you're speaking from experience."

"I am," he replies, keeping his eyes peeled on the road. "But love comes in many different forms."

My skin breaks out into goose bumps, and I don't know why.

"What one person considers love, another may consider obsession and turn something beautiful into something horrible. Love has the ability to make someone do something they never would."

My heart begins to race as my blood whooshes through me.

"Has love ever made you do something you never would?"

It's an innocent question, but I suddenly can't breathe. I reach for the handle to open the window, as I need some air, but it's gone. It's an old truck, I reason with myself, but something isn't right.

"Doll, is everything okay?"

Gripping the chair, I measure my breaths, inhaling slowly

through my nose. "I'm fine. Sorry. This happens sometimes." It hasn't happened for a while, but now, the blackness lingers close to the surface, threatening to drag me under.

The GPS spits out directions for Will to turn left, but he turns right. "I know a shortcut," he says, when he notices me look at the GPS.

When I look into his eyes, I get kicked in the solar plexus and a hiss of air leaves me. I clutch my stomach and attempt to catch my breath. What's going on?

"I…can't breathe," I gasp, on the verge of hyperventilating. "Can you pull over? I need air."

But he doesn't. He just drives faster.

"Not a nice feeling, is it? Struggling to breathe. Makes you feel sorry for a fish out of water, gasping for air. A sport for one means death for another."

Muddy water fills my lungs, and before long, it's all I can taste. I stop fighting and surrender…surrender to death.

The visions blindside me, and I squeeze my eyes shut. But Will doesn't seem privy to my impending breakdown.

"So this friend? Do you love him?"

"Yes, very much," I whisper, and it's the first time I have confessed it aloud. I don't know why I feel the need to defend my feelings for Cayden, but the skepticism in Will's tone has me dragging myself from the abyss and into the now.

Opening my eyes slowly, I turn my chin to focus on Will and just how it's happened before, a flash of recognition hits me…I've met him before. But my mind seems to have forgotten him for a reason because when I attempt to dig deep and uncover how I know him, a guard arises and a shooting pain stabs my temple.

It's like self-preservation mode has kicked in—again.

"And you'd do anything for him? Say, even kill for him?"

I blink once, confused to why he would ask that. But I reply, "Yes," without question, desperately attempting to piece together how I know him.

He whistles. "He's one lucky man. I wasn't expecting that answer…not from a little whore."

My mouth hinges open slowly. "W-what?" I stutter because I must have misunderstood him.

But when he turns sinisterly slow, a reptilian grin spreading from cheek to cheek, I know that I haven't.

"Let me out," I exclaim, yanking on the door handle, only to find the door is locked. When I attempt to search for a lock, I see that there isn't one. I'm trapped. "I don't understand what's going on."

The screen on my cell lights up, and when I look down at it, my entire world comes full circle because it was always bound to end this way.

> I'm not far. He's the reason for all of this. I wish he was at the bottom of the lake because my father is dead to me. Damn William Coachman to hell.

I never once asked Cayden what his father's name was, but I should have. If I had, I wouldn't be in the predicament I'm in.

Frantically, I type out a reply to Lacey, detailing my suspicion that I'm currently experiencing hell on earth, or more accurately, in this truck. But my finger hovers over the send button as tears sting my eyes. "Ellie is such a pretty thing. Looks like my son has similar taste in women to his old man."

What does that mean? Ellie is...

The world begins spinning as bile rises. If I send this text, I know Ellie will be in danger, which is exactly the reason we've done what we have, only to have it backfire epically.

"No." I gasp, shaking my head. This can't be possible, but it seems the devil was a lot closer than I thought him to be because sitting beside me is Will...William Coachman. Cayden's dad.

"What do you want?" I spit, trying to keep my cool. But Will sees straight through me.

He simply smiles and continues driving.

A million thoughts crash into me as adrenaline soars through me. Every fiber of my body demands I text Lacey and then call the police. But if I do, I have no doubt I'm endangering Ellie because Will has been planning his revenge for ten long years. She's his bargaining chip, and I have no doubt he'll use her any way he can.

I'm on my own.

I'm disgusted I once thought he was kind and admired his good looks. But on closer observation, I see the reason I thought he was attractive was because he looked like Cayden... his son.

"I don't remember you," I cry, hoping that'll change the course of his actions.

"Then I'll just have to remind you," he deadpans.

"Did you run me off the road? Are you the reason I can't remember?"

He inhales in victory.

"Why?" I plead. "Why after so long have you done this? Yes, what we did was wrong, but we were kids. And you were hardly a saint."

"Because, doll, revenge is a dish best served cold."

And that's it.

He doesn't offer any other explanation other than the fact that he's a deranged psychopath, hell-bent on making everyone who wronged him suffer.

When we turn a corner and a familiar neighborhood comes into view, it seems fitting that he's taken me here because this is where it all started. And when he pulls the truck up near my old vacation home, I'll give him credit for raising the bar on being a creepy fuck.

He kills the engine and turns to me slowly. I instantly shrink back. Even though I don't remember him, I will never forget the retelling of the vile things he's done. "Now, if you do what you're told, no one will get hurt."

I find that very hard to believe.

"We clear?"

With no other choice, I nod. "Ellie is okay?"

"For now." Will smirks, but it's lacking warmth as he opens his door and rounds the hood. I wait for him to open my door seeing as I'm locked in. When he does, the contempt rolls off me. He laughs in response and offers me his hand.

Peering down at it, I compare it to a live grenade. But this isn't an option.

Slipping my hand into his, I recoil and swallow down my nausea. His touch is cold and calculating as he leads me through the gate and onto the grounds of my old home. From my understanding, my parents still own the house, but from the unkempt appearance, it's safe to assume they haven't been here in a while.

Will leads me around the back, which has me speculating how he knows the layout so well. When he drags me to the door and opens it, I wonder what in the ever-living hell is going on. Even though my parents haven't used this place in a long while, there is no way they would leave this place unlocked and without an alarm.

He shoves me inside, and I see that we're inside what looks to be a sunroom. Furniture is covered with dusted white sheets, but the farther I venture, I see that this is not the way for the rest of the house. When I enter the enormous kitchen, it's apparent from the pile of dirty dishes and the endless takeaway containers that someone has been living here for a while.

No guessing who.

"What are we doing here?" I ask, so done with his games as I yank from his hold. "If you're hoping that I'll remember by bringing me here, then I'm sorry to disappoint you. It won't."

I know I should be afraid of him, but that's the thing about amnesia—I don't remember all the reasons. Yes, Cayden has told me what he's done, but being told and experiencing it are two totally different things.

Will leans against the counter, arms and ankles crossed, while I search for a weapon. There has to be something under all this junk.

"We're here because it's time I'm given what I'm owed."

I gulp. "I don't know what that means."

Reaching into his pocket, he offers me his cell. I look down at it, then back up at him, baffled. He soon clears up any confusion. "Call your mom."

"My mom?" I repeat, my pitch an octave higher than usual. When I take in where we are and the fact that he believes he's entitled to something, I snort in humor. "If you're going to hold me for ransom, expecting a hefty sum for my return, you're in for a shock. My mom won't pay you a penny."

But he soon reveals I've strayed way off the path. "Your mom knows I'm here. Who do you think gave me the key?"

I stumble backward, eyes wide, wishing I didn't believe him. But I do.

"So call her. I know you're *dying* to know how this ends." His emphasis on the word dying has me accepting the cell with shaky fingers.

I hate that he's right, but I don't understand any of this and the fact that Stella is somehow involved has me dialing her number. "I told you not to call me on this number, you..."

"Stella, it's me."

Silence.

"Peyton? Oh, my God." And for the first time, I hear fear in her voice and it makes her...human, terrifying me. "Where are you?"

With eyes fixed on Will, I reply, "At our vacation home... with Will."

I'm waiting for surprise. For her to challenge his claims. But I get neither. "I'll be there as soon as I can."

"You knew he was here?" I question, my stomach dropping.

"I—"

"Answer the question!" I yell, not in the mood for excuses.

Will smiles happily as my pain seems to please him.

"Yes."

Tears of anger sting my eyes as I shake my head, disgusted. She sits on a throne of lies. I hang up, refusing to listen to another word because one word has amounted to ten.

I pass Will his phone, the fight in me dying because I don't know what to believe anymore. Stella has said she's done everything to protect me, but protect me from whom?

"Does Cayden know you're here?"

Will grins as he pushes off the counter and walks toward me. "That's the thing about amnesia. You have no other choice but to believe what people tell you. I mean, you can't remember, so you're taking their word that what they tell you is the truth."

"No," I argue, shaking my head violently. "I don't believe you. Cayden wouldn't lie to me."

"He has, and he would," he contradicts. "I wonder how his meeting with Benny went?"

Oh, God. The walls close in on me as I wrap my arms around my middle. How does he know about Benny? And what does that mean for Cayden? Benny and Will, it appears, just may be on the same side.

"Stop it!" I cry, my lower lip trembling.

"You were always running after him like a pathetic little puppy. You were merely a plaything. When he got bored, he pushed you away, but you kept coming back for more because you're weak," he spits, lowering his face inches from mine.

I stand my ground, however, challenging his claims.

"He got Hazel knocked up because he was sick of you.

He didn't have to try hard because that Hazel sure loves the Coachman cock." He reaches down and cups his junk while I almost gag in horror. "The truth is, Ellie could be either of ours. Or anybody's really. But I suppose Cayden is a better man than me and took care of her."

"No! You're lying." I cover my ears because this filth is not true. There is no way it's true.

But a niggling voice, down low, scratches at the surface. I've been presented two contradictory stories, and Will, no matter how much it pains me to admit, is right. With amnesia, I have to believe the retelling of my life because I can't remember. I can't remember who I was. Or if I was the person I want to believe I was.

A tear scores my cheek, a tear which Will sweeps up with his finger. He samples my sadness and relishes the taste. "You always tasted so sweet."

I blanch, horrified. How would he know of my taste?

He's messing with my head, I reason with myself. I can't let him see weakness. "Did I really throw your body in the lake?"

His nostrils flare, hinting I have hit a nerve. "Yes, you did."

I cover my mouth, disgusted. I have so many questions, but the truth is, I can't believe anyone. "Where is Cayden?"

"You'll see soon enough."

A door slamming outside has both Will and I riveting our attention to the front door. When he grins, it's clear he thinks it's a friend and not a foe. I use this opportunity to desperately search my surroundings for a weapon.

I'll settle for anything, but when I see a butcher's knife tucked away under a Chinese takeout box, I don't think twice and lunge for it. I've caught Will unawares, but I'm not quick enough to inflict any injury because before I have a chance to use it, he punches me in the face, winding me.

I stagger back, stunned and gasping for air as I cup my bleeding nose. The knife drops to the floor with a miserable thud.

"Don't make me hurt you," he warns, eyes wild.

He grips my biceps and drags me through the kitchen and into the living room. I try to fight him, but it's no use. I'm pretty sure he just broke my nose, so if he doesn't call that "hurting" me, then I'm frightened to find out what's the worst he can do.

He forces me to face the entrance so whoever is about to enter can see me bleeding all over the white Persian carpet. When Stella rushes through the door and sees me cupping my bloodied nose, she stops dead in her tracks. I should be angry with her, but honestly, I'm relieved, something I never thought I'd ever be.

"What did you do to her?" she exclaims, running to my aid. But when Will quickly reaches behind him and produces a gun from the small of his back, both Stella and I freeze.

"That's far enough," he snarls, waving the gun at her.

"What do you want, Will? I've done everything you wanted. You promised you wouldn't hurt her." If I wasn't delirious from being punched in the face, I'd think I heard concern in her voice. But that's impossible.

"And I haven't. Well, not much." He snickers, clearly loving the limelight. "I'm here to settle old scores."

Stella swallows, tugging at her pearl earring. "No, don't. I beg of you."

Stella Lane begging? I never thought I'd see the day.

Will steps forward, hurling me with him as he pins Stella to the spot where she stands. "It's time she knows the truth. The real reason you wanted her to stay away from Cayden and me."

"Wh-what's going on?" My attention bounces between Stella and Will, beseeching someone to tell me what the hell is going on.

"You really are an asshole," Stella spits, knowing that her secret is moments away from being revealed.

"Sticks and stones, Star."

"Star?" I utter, confused. But when Stella averts her gaze, I've finally uncovered the truth.

"Cayden told me Stella ridiculed you. Is that true?"

The grinding of Will's jaw confirms that fact. "Yes, Little Miss Perfect wouldn't be seen dead with scum like me. But when no one was looking, that was another story, wasn't it, Star?"

My nose has stopped bleeding, but I still feel unsteady on my feet because an epiphany hits. "Oh, my god." I gasp, eyes wide. "You *liked* him?"

Stella's chin snaps up as the truth has whipped her into submission. "I was young. Stupid," she says, defending her actions, which confirm my claims. "He tricked me into thinking he was a good man."

"No one tricked anyone, sweetheart," Will argues smugly. "You slummed it voluntarily. I even think you liked it."

"Shut up!" she cries, running a hand over her flawless hair. It seems she needs to ensure her outer mask isn't crumbling, just how her inner one is.

"People like us don't fall in love with the Cayden Coachmans of this world."

Stella's words ring loudly because, at the time, I thought she was referring to me, but in reality, she was referring to herself.

"You fell in love with him?" I ask even though I know the answer. "But you couldn't get past him being poor. So you ridiculed him so no one would suspect you had feelings for him."

I wrap my arms around my middle, shaking my head in disbelief. "I'm just like you," I whisper, tears filling my eyes. "But I saw past the superficial shit and loved Cayden for him, not his social standing. I didn't care what his surname was."

"It was different for me," Stella cries, emotion filling her for the first time. "I would have been disinherited. A laughing stock. My parents would have disowned me. Where would that have left me?"

"So money was more important than happiness?" I question, unable to understand.

"You rarely can have both, Peyton," she says regrettably, but I disagree.

Will is sick of standing on the sidelines as he rushes toward Stella, gripping her biceps and shaking her like a rag doll. "I loved you, but you used me. All I was, was someone to make you feel good. To tell you how pretty you were. How special you were. And you were, until you tore out my fucking heart!"

"You knew what we had. It never could have been anything more," Stella says, and it's hard to believe these two felt an iota of love for each other.

"You turned me into the man I am today." Will shoves her

backward.

She's unsteady on her feet but soon recovers. "Don't you dare pin that on me. The choices you made were yours alone. I never forced you to turn into the sick individual you are!"

He narrows his eyes. "You just fed the beast, Star. All of this is your fault."

It's evident Stella hurt Will beyond repair, resulting in Cayden and me paying the price. "You left this place and forgot about me, but I never forgot." Will points the gun at Stella, and kudos to her, she doesn't flinch. "Your daughter falling in love with my son was poetic justice. But she looked so much like you…"

I gulp as his faraway tone reveals he's transported back to another time.

"And it turns out she was *exactly* like you. A tease." He turns slowly, training the pistol on me. I could cower, but I don't. I stand unbending, refusing to show weakness.

"Leave her out of this," Stella pleads, which stuns me. It's still hard to accept her as anything but the ruthless bitch I've come to believe she is. But seeing her this way…I don't know what to think. "I've done what you wanted. For ten long years, I was a prisoner…to you."

"*What?*" There must be some mistake. She *knew* he was alive this entire time? "What's going on?" I manage to spit out.

Stella sighs as she unburdens her soul. "Will told me what you'd done." I blink once, the walls closing in on me. "He said he was going to the police. There was only one way I could stop him," she confesses wretchedly.

I cover my mouth, sickened. "No."

"Oh, yes," Will declares with a grin. "And she loved it… every single time. She gave up what you wouldn't."

"You bastard!" I launch forward, intent on killing him with my bare hands, but he waves the gun, stopping me dead in my tracks.

"Once he got what he wanted, I thought he'd go away. That was the agreement," Stella says, glowering at Will. "I was to… sleep with him, and he would leave you alone. But it wasn't enough."

"You owed me, Star. Money was so important to you, more important than what we had. So it was time I took it away from you."

I watch on in disbelief.

"So I paid him a lot of money to stay dead. But I didn't doubt for a second, that he wouldn't go back on his word, which is why I had to pay Cayden to keep you safe. If you stayed far away from here, there was no way he would find you. You would be safe. You'd never have to pay for my mistakes ever again," she confesses, her eyes filling with tears.

The sight is too much, and I curl in on myself, heartbroken. "All this time, you were protecting me from *Will* and not Cayden?"

"Yes."

What a fool I've been.

Everything falls into place, and even with amnesia, one thing is clear. "Cayden isn't his father. He's a good man. But he was a reminder of the past. One you wanted to forget."

"I couldn't trust Will wouldn't come back. I had to keep you apart. I make no excuses for wanting to keep you safe. But I never knew you came back here over the years. If I had, I would have told you the truth. Will told me Cayden used you out of spite for what I did. Which is why I was so opposed to you being together. I thought he was just like his father. But I'm beginning to think I was wrong."

Pieces of the puzzle are forming a picture, but there are still so many questions.

"If you got, what I imagine, was a hefty sum of money, why did you come back?" I ask Will, hating I can now see the visual similarities between him and Cayden because Cayden is nothing like him.

Will appears thrilled to finally be the center of attention. "Because Star is right. Money can't buy happiness. For a few years, having all the money at my disposal kept the demons at bay. But I grew bored. Idle hands and all that," he says casually while I shake my head at his flippant attitude.

"I decided to pay my son and daughter a visit, but I never intended on seeing you. I was certain you'd moved on, just like your mom, but there you were, just as much in love with him like when you were kids, and that fucking…pissed me off. You all had moved on, happy to have me gone. And well, that didn't seem fair."

I stare at him, stunned at how pathetic he sounds.

Wetting my lips, I squash down my nerves because I have to know. "Did you…run me off the road?"

Stella inhales sharply while I dare not breathe.

"I couldn't let you leave. You were the only way I could make sure Star would come back here."

"You're sick," I gasp, horrified. "I was pregnant, pregnant

with your grandchild," I reveal, tears stinging my eyes.

His mouth parts, and just when I think I'll see a sliver of humanity, he shrugs. "An eye for an eye. You killed me. Well, you thought you did."

A fierce anger spews from me, and I can't stop myself as I storm forward, intent on slapping that grin from his cheeks. But he reminds me who's in charge when he points the gun in my face. "I dare you, doll."

At this moment, I don't care, let him do his worst, but Stella is my voice of reason as she cries, "Peyton, no! Don't. Just tell us what you want, Will."

He inhales deeply, briefly closing his eyes in satisfaction at hearing her beg. "Always so impatient," he tsks, smirking. This is clearly a joke to him. But I shouldn't expect anything less. Cayden told me what he did to him growing up.

Will is a monster—a deranged, delusional monster who is back to settle old scores.

"I want everyone to know who you really are," Will says, pinning Stella will a stone-cold glower. "I want all your country club friends to know about us."

"What?" She gasps, taking a small step back. "Why? They don't even know who you are."

"I want you to change that," he explains, and I finally understand.

Will is sick of being an outsider. Of always looking in. This is Stella's punishment for making him feel like he was never good enough. Will had money, but money and blackmail? What a potent cocktail for a lover scorned.

"You can't be serious. This will ruin me," she says, shaking her head.

Which is exactly why Will has asked her to do this. "I also want you to tell your husband what we did."

"No, Will. Please, no. You can't expect me to do that. He will never understand. He will never forgive me."

Pleading with a psychopath only evokes insanity. "I had money, and I thought that would appease the beast within, but it didn't, and that's because I want something more."

"And what's that?" Stella asks, her lower lip quivering. The sight breaks me.

"Revenge," Will replies simply. "I want you to feel what I did, Star. I want you to lose the one thing which always meant more than me. Your precious reputation."

If she does what he wants, it will ruin her because the social circles will have a field day, tainting the Lane name. It shouldn't matter, but to Stella, it does. The Lane name would forever be stained, thanks to a young Stella Lane falling for the wrong boy.

"I can't," Stella cries, and seeing her this way has me wanting to go to her, but I don't. And that's because I know there is more to come.

"You will because if you don't, I will forever be a constant presence in your life. I will haunt you. All of you," he adds, glaring at me. "And I will put in an anonymous call to the local police about the body at the bottom of the lake."

"And when they drain it and find no body, what then?" I challenge, because his story has a major plot hole.

But he reminds me whose show it is. "Who said there wasn't a body?"

My stomach roils, and I cover my mouth, fearful I'm about

to be sick. "They'll do DNA testing. They'll discover it's not you."

"The only thing that lays in the bottom of that lake is some sad, old bones. Good luck if they find a trace of DNA after ten long years. You did me a favor. Being dead allowed me to escape the debts I owed, and with all my money, I was able to build my own empire."

This is too far-fetched to believe, but I don't doubt him for a moment. I say a prayer for whoever's bones lay in the watery grave. "When Cayden finds you…" I snarl, measuring my breaths. "He's going to kill you…for real this time."

"I wouldn't be so sure about that."

My blood turns cold.

"What did you do?"

"I commend Cayden for his creativity. Too bad Benny is one of the bad guys…like me."

"No." I stagger backward, my heart in my throat.

"What's going on?" Stella asks, but I can't speak because I knew, deep down I knew it would always end this way.

Will couldn't appear happier as he says, "Oh, you didn't know? Cayden was attempting to rat me out to a dear old friend. He's indebted to me after I got his sorry ass released from prison early. It's amazing the good your money can do, Stella, because a lot of people would turn a blind eye when bribed with a substantial sum of cash."

I shake my head slowly, not believing this is happening right now. Will was in control. We were stupid to think there was ever another way. "Where is he?"

There is no need for me to elaborate who.

Will peers down at his leather cuff watch. "I think right about now, Benny is teaching my son what happens to snitches…they get stitches," he adds with a humored chuckle.

This man feels nothing for no one, and he can blame Stella all he wants, but Will Coachman was born bad. He only needed a reason to ruin the lives of so many to add value to his.

"No," I sob, rummaging for my cell in my pocket. My hands are sticky with blood and fumbling with nerves, so the phone ends up plummeting to the floor.

When I dive for it, Will traps it under his motorcycle boot. I peer up at him with nothing but hatred. "You asshole. You won't get away with this."

He bends low, leveling me with his smugness. "I already have."

"No!" I launch forward, ready to kill him with my bare hands. But it costs me. It costs us all.

Will twists and grabs my arms, dragging me into his chest. He threads his fingers through my hair and yanks hard. He cranes my neck back as I grunt in pain.

"Maybe we can come to a compromise then, Star." When he rubs his groin against my back, there is no need for him to draw a diagram. "I'll let you go. You can live your perfect life while I live mine with your daughter." His wet tongue laps at my cheek slowly as he jerks my head back farther.

"Get your hands off her, you bastard!"

"The choice is yours. Will you sacrifice everything for the life of another? Can you really be that selfless?"

"Of course! She is my daughter. My own flesh and blood! I will do anything to save her. What do you want?"

This entire time, she's proven that she would. I owe her a thousand apologies.

Will exhales, the waves of anger rolling off him. "That's real admirable, but there isn't really a choice. It's time I taught you Lanes a lesson. You think you're better than me?" he spits into my face, his spittle coating my cheeks. "Well, I'll show you because this is just good, old-fashion revenge."

And that's far scarier than some elaborate plan.

As Will bites over my racing pulse and fondles my breasts, I close my eyes, unable to look at my mother. I know she didn't call the police. She didn't know what Will had up his sleeve. We're alone. There is no one here to save us.

I hear her heels race along the floor, a war cry splitting the air, but when an ear-piercing shrill bounces around the room, she sobs. "Don't make me use this, Star."

I can only assume Will has fired a warning shot because, deep down, I can only hope his obsession for my mom saves her. For me, however…I know there is no reprieve coming my way.

He continues fondling me while Stella's weeping tears me in two. I have no doubt he will use that gun on me because Will doesn't strike me as a person who needs a willing participant, but it'll be a cold day in hell before I submit to his filth.

With adrenaline soaring through my veins, I thrash wildly like a caged animal as I try to fight my way to freedom. I flail madly, kicking and screaming, but the aggression only seems to turn Will on further.

He jerks my head farther back, the angle threatening to snap my neck. But I don't cry or beg for mercy. I won't give this asshole the satisfaction.

"You know, you really are the spitting image of your mom," he snarls into my ear, before suckling my lobe. "Maybe I'll just let her go and have my fun with you. You owe me anyway, you bitch."

I know he's talking about me throwing him into the lake.

Will seems to blame everyone for his predicament but himself. It's easier to point fingers than to take a good, hard look at oneself.

He's too busy fondling me and grinding himself up against me and releases his grip for a moment, but that's enough slack for me to stomp on his foot and rear my head backward and connect with his nose.

"Bitch!" he shouts, letting me go.

"How do you like it?" I roar when I see him clutching his bleeding nose.

I'm about to knee him in the balls, but apparently, he's been playing nice because he strikes out, pistol-whipping me in the temple. I'm taken off guard and stagger to the left, attempting to find something to clutch onto before I pass out.

I'm surrounded by blood, pain, and fear, and I'm certain nothing can ever make any of this better, but when I hear a voice, a voice that seems to be my forever anchor, I allow myself a small reprieve and sob in relief.

He's here.

"You motherfucker…what did you do?" Cayden rockets through the room, his arm raised as something shiny catches the light. It takes my groggy brain a moment to process what that is, but when I focus, I see he's gripping a gun.

It happens in seconds. One moment, my eyes are locked with Cayden's, and the next, the world is tipped on its axis as I'm spun around and trapped in the arms of Will, yet again.

"You bas—" My words die a quick death, though, because Will shoves the barrel of his gun into my temple, robbing me of breath. Cayden skids to a sudden stop, eyes wild, but doesn't lower his gun.

"What the fuck?" Will snarls, but his tone is laced with utter shock. "You're supposed to be dead."

"Yeah, well"—Cayden shrugs, his attention never wavering from me—"you should never trust a con, especially a con who can be easily bought. There is no loyalty to someone like you."

He inhales through his nose heavily when he scans me from head to toe. I can only imagine what I look like. "Are you all right?" he asks, pained.

I nod in response, not trusting my voice.

"Let her go. This is between you and me." Cayden tightens his grip on the gun, ensuring it stays trained on his father. The only issue is, is that I'm his shield.

"I don't think so. Drop the gun." When Cayden doesn't waver, Will cocks the trigger, and I have no doubt he'll pull it. "Don't do anything stupid. Doll is counting on you."

Cayden's jaw clenches. "She is *not* your doll."

His anger is palpable, which has me wondering why the nickname irks him so.

"She was once upon a time," Will says smugly before leaning down and licking my cheek slowly. I'm trembling in rage but also in fear. What does he mean?

I attempt to pull away, but he pins me to his body as

he presses his forearm against my stomach. I'm not going anywhere. I focus on Cayden, wondering how in the hell we're going to get out of this alive.

"D-doll?" I stutter, ignoring the wrath coming from Cayden because I need to know.

"Oh, yes. With all this fiery red hair"—he lowers his nose and takes a whiff—"and porcelain-smooth skin. You're perfect like a doll." When he presses his arm firmer across my stomach, I wheeze for air. "But deep down, I always wanted to ruin that perfection. To see you break. Maybe I can finally see my wish come true."

Cayden roars, storming forward as anger radiates from every pore. But with wide eyes, I shake my head and cry, "Don't! Ellie!" My safety is the least of my concern, but if Cayden doesn't submit to his father, I fear Ellie will fall victim to this sick man's games.

Cayden comes to a screeching halt, his gun wavering. "What?"

"I think he knows where Ellie is," I reveal, not needing to spell out what that means.

"I don't believe it." Cayden shakes his head violently, but I can see the uncertainty beneath the surface.

Will hums happily before rattling off an address. When Cayden pales, it seems any reservations have been put to bed. "That Hazel hasn't changed a bit. Always so eager to please. It didn't take much for me to find out everything I needed to know."

"You piece of shit! Stay away from my daughter." It doesn't seem to surprise Cayden that Will is implying he and Hazel are a thing, which has me wondering about Will's earlier comment.

"He said you got Hazel pregnant on purpose. But that Ellie might even be his." In the grand scheme of things, I know this is insignificant, but if I'm moments from my death, I want to know the truth.

Cayden blanches, horrified. "And you believe him?"

"I-I don't know," I reply honestly. "He knew you were going to see Benny. He said you knew he was here. I'm so confused."

Saying it aloud, I know what my heart wants to believe, but my head…I have been lied to by everyone.

Cayden frowns, and the sight is filled with pure heartache. "I'm sorry I've given you reason not to trust me," he says, shaking his head slowly. "That's all on me. I should have been honest from the beginning. But I do love you, Peyton. I always have. That's the reason I've done all of this. To end this once and for all."

Tears spill down my cheeks because his words are nothing but genuine. I want to tell him that I love him too, but I don't want that memory to be tainted by this.

Cayden focuses his attention on Will, who is still pressed to my back, holding me prisoner. "And as for Ellie," he snarls. "She *is* my daughter. There is no doubt about it. You really are fucking pathetic, you know that?"

Will tenses while I hold my breath. Why is Cayden provoking him?

"Your whole life"—he commences a slow walk toward us—"is filled with nothing but greed, lies, and you're so miserable, you have to involve everyone else in your unhappiness because you're lonely. And by doing all this, it makes you feel powerful.

But in reality, you're weak."

Will's breathing grows deeper as it's clear Cayden has touched a nerve.

"I would feel sorry for you, but in reality, you've got no one to blame but yourself. When Lacey and I were kids, you had the opportunity to change your life, regardless of what happened in your past. But you didn't. You chose to dwell on someone breaking your heart." He scoffs, grinning. "And that shows how weak you really are. It takes a man to face his problems. But you've proven time and time again, you're a coward."

"Coward?" Will repeats angrily. "Let's see who's a coward."

When he removes the gun from my temple and instead points it at Cayden, I understand why Cayden has baited him this way. He would rather be killed than watch me suffer. And this confirms what I always knew deep down—Will said all those things to mess with my head. To have me doubt Cayden because if Benny did what Will had asked him to, then I never would have known the truth. Cayden would be dead, and I would be left to believe he lied to me and never cared.

"Go on then," Cayden goads, stopping a few feet away. "Take your best shot. I should have made sure you were dead when I threw you in the lake, you worthless piece of shit."

"No!" I cry, attempting to wiggle free. Cayden may be comfortable calling Will's bluff, but I'm not. "Let me go!"

My struggles are futile because Will's hold on me is firm, but if he wants to take Cayden up on his offer, then he will have to loosen his hold because he can't have both—he either lets me go or he shoots Cayden. Cayden won't make it easy for him, and Will knows he will have to use both hands to take his son down.

Frantically, I search the room for something, anything that'll help us, but when I lock eyes with Stella, I know she is our savior. "I remember the first time we met. You were wearing that Pepsi T-shirt you loved so much."

Something in the air shifts.

"I knew you were trouble, but I didn't care. I was spellbound by you."

Cayden turns over his shoulder slowly, mouth parted as he watches Stella advance unhurriedly.

"You remember the Pepsi T-shirt?" Will asks, his tone heavy with surprise.

She nods, smiling timidly, but I know there is nothing bashful about Stella Lane. She nods subtly at me, and if one were to blink, they'd miss it. But I've seen it. It's her cue to tell me that shit is about to get real.

"Of course. How can I forget? You were thirteen going on thirty. You were such a bad boy. Didn't care for rules. You did what you wanted. I admired that."

Will's exhalations are deep, as he no doubt is attempting to work out what Stella is playing at because playing him, she is. She runs her fingers over her pearls, drawing attention to her plunging neckline, thanks to the three buttons she popped open on her silk shirt when no one was looking.

"If you admired that, then why did you deny what we had?" he asks, his grip slackening. "You let those assholes steal from me! You stood by as they beat me up and stole my shit."

As Will is reliving their history, Cayden meets my eyes, and without words, he's telling me to bide my time. When Will is fully under Stella's spell, I'm to fight and break free. But not a second sooner.

"I know, and I'm sorry. I was scared," Stella says in a docile voice, one I've never heard before. "I never meant to hurt you. If I could take it back, I would. But now is the time that I can. You have always wanted me. So come get me."

"This is a trick," Will says, but his uncertainty is clear.

Stella shakes her head. "No, it's not. I want you, William. You want me to tell Augusto about us? I'll call him. Right now. I will tell him everything. You will never be forgotten ever again."

The room is on tenterhooks as we wait for Will to make his move. Will he see through her? Or will he fall for her lies? Stella stands unwavering, using the only thing which will get us out of this—herself.

Just when I think it's useless, something remarkable happens—Will lets me go.

I instantly sag forward, tempted to push Cayden and me to safety. But I don't. I don't want to spook Will as he's still holding a gun. So I shift to the left, out of reach as I watch from the sidelines.

"You want me?" Will asks, eyes wide as he seems to be under Stella's spell.

"Yes. I do. I'm sorry for everything. Please forgive me."

I am just as transfixed as Will because I can't believe this is happening. Stella is dancing with the devil, but it seems she would happily do so if it meant I was saved.

This can't be the way our story ends. I refuse to accept it. But as Will walks toward Stella, I don't know how she'll get out of this unscathed. Cayden's gun is gripped tight in his hand, but he isn't anything like his dad. He can't shoot him in cold blood.

"Call him." Will digs into his back pocket and produces his cell. "Tell him you're leaving him for me." Stella accepts the phone and dials a number without a pause.

A nervous energy is thrumming through me as I watch Stella make the call. "Hello, Augusto. I'm leaving you. I don't love you. I never did. I love William Coachman. I always have." She keeps a straight face, listening to what my father says.

Will watches on, grinning in victory. He's delusional, however, if he thinks she means a word of it.

"I'll be waiting at the lake house. Call me when you're gone."

She hangs up, unruffled that she just broke up with her husband over the phone. Even though Augusto is nothing but a mere stranger to me, I can't help but feel bad for him.

Stella hands Will his phone, unwavering. "He'll be gone in a few hours. We can go back to my house then."

Will tips his chin upward and inhales in triumph. Stella quickly risks a glance my way, nodding that it'll be all right. I don't know how.

"The call is yours, Will."

She could suggest he let Cayden and me go, but that would arouse suspicion. Stella is one smart cookie. She allows him to think the ball is in his court.

"Yes, Star, it is." He finally lets on to what he is thinking as he saunters over and grips the lapels of her shirt. As he draws her into him, it's clear she is trying to fight the need to recoil. "You don't know how long I've waited for this moment."

Before she has a chance to speak, he brutally slams his lips to hers, kissing her roughly because there is no love. This is about possession. About winning. And it's clear he's won when he breaks the kiss and levels her with a sinister stare.

"But you're not that good of an actress. Just to think I once called you Star because you were the only light in my darkness. Now, I see it would have been better to remain in the dark."

I don't understand what he means until he presses the redial button and the voice of Michael Robb can be heard—Stella's attorney. It seems the call is literally his to make. "Stella, I don't know what's going on, but I've called the police. They're on the way."

Will isn't stupid. Although he wanted to believe Stella, it's too late. He doesn't want her to repent. He just wants revenge, and he won't settle for anything less.

He hangs up the phone, jaw clenched as he glares at Stella. "Things could have been so different for us. But you'll never change. You'll always be the spoiled rich girl who broke my heart."

Stella pales. Her ruse is up. "William, please, just let my daughter go."

But that was never an option. And Cayden knows it too. He storms forward, gun raised, shoving Stella to safety. This is going to end how it was always destined to—in bloodshed. "You will never hurt her again!"

Everything happens in the blink of an eye.

One minute, I'm standing on the sidelines, and the next, the room explodes into pandemonium. Cayden roars, but that is nothing compared to the deafening boom when Will fires his gun. The scream that erupts from me is unlike anything I've heard before, and on instinct, I rush forward, desperate to save Cayden. But the move is one I will regret for the rest of my life.

"No!" The pained cry echoes and rattles my core.

Bang.

Bang.

I don't understand what I'm seeing because all I can see is blood…so much blood. Another gunshot rings out, but I can't focus on anything other than the lifeless form in front of me, twisted in a sad, bloodied heap.

I open my mouth, but not a sound can be heard. What I see is too horrific for words. So I run over and drop to my knees, cradling the limp body in my arms. "No," I whimper, blinking past my tears because there is no way I'm seeing what I am.

But the warm blood coating my hands cements this as truth. In my arms lies Stella Lane. And she is dying.

Cayden races over, kneeling beside me, ensuring she'll be okay as he dials 911. But when I look into her eyes, eyes so similar to mine, I know she won't.

I don't even know where Will is, but the fact that we're not facing the same fate as Stella has me guessing Cayden finally ended what should have been done ten years ago. "The police are on the way."

But it doesn't matter. By the time help arrives, she'll be gone. "Pe-Peyton," she wheezes, flinching as she tries to raise her hand.

"No, don't talk. Save your energy," I say, trying my hardest not to break down because it's my turn to be strong for her.

If it wasn't for her selfless act, I would be the one lying on the floor because, without thought, Stella jumped in front of me and took a bullet intended for me. I owe her my life.

"Help is coming, okay?" I try to make her comfortable, but

it's in vain. "You can stay awake."

"I can't feel my legs," she says, staring up at me, her hollow breaths rattling loudly.

Peering down, I see the gaping hole in her stomach is the reason for that. But I simply brush back her hair. "It'll be okay."

Cayden squeezes my arm, and the simple touch denotes that I'm not alone. I never was.

Stella's eyes follow the movement, and a ghost of a smile plays at her bloodied lips. "I'm so-sorry, Cayden. I thought I was protecting her."

"Shh, it's okay. There is no need for apologies."

But even nearing death, Stella Lane is stubborn as shit. "Look after h-her," she stutters, a tremor overtaking her. "I'm sorry, Peyton. I'm sorry for everything. I would have lo-loved to be a grandmother. Be happy, and don't look back."

The tears I've attempted to keep at bay break past the floodgates, and I sob violently. "It's okay…Mom."

"You…you just called me…Mom." Stella blinks past her tears and smiles, which is how she will be remembered, which is how she takes her last breath.

Even though I know what I'm seeing, my brain can't seem to process that she's gone. "No. No!" I cry, rocking her, but her limp body is just that—a vessel. Her soul has gone.

Gasping, I attempt to break the surface, but I suddenly can't swim. The harder I push, the farther I sink. Invisible manacles secure my ankles, dragging me down. Muddy water fills my lungs, and before long, it's all I can taste. I stop fighting and surrender… surrender to death.

The walls begin to close in on me, and I can't breathe.

Cayden's voice floats into the background, but this time, it can't be my anchor. I'm already drifting out to sea.

Will's hollow sobs reveal he's still alive, and knowing he will have to live with killing the love of his life on his conscience forever gives me an iota of comfort. The room spins, and the blackness tackles me by taking hold of my feet, dragging me under.

I gasp for air, as this feeling is one I've become accustomed to for months, but this time, I don't fight it. I surrender because, just like Will, I have to live with what I've done.

"Snow, no! Don't you dare! Come back to me." Cayden's cries cement the fact that I'm floating farther and farther away.

Other voices are suddenly mingled with his, and I feel a sense of comfort knowing he'll be all right. I should have stayed lost because finding myself has cost so much. So I accept my fate and embrace the darkness. I lived in the light, and all it's done is destroy.

My head hits the floor, and I yield because there is always solace in the darkness. But soon, that blackness bursts into an assembly of color, and moving pictures flicker behind my eyes. I can't remember these images because they were lived in another lifetime.

I see myself as a young girl. Toothless and innocent as I run around the vibrant greens in what appears to be a Snow White outfit. Flashes of moving pictures flicker so quickly that I can barely keep up, but at the forefront is one image I can never forget—Cayden Coachman.

I see him as a boy, us together as teens, and then finally, as adults. I feel his kisses. I can hear him tell me that he loves me.

He's forever been my protector because he has loved me since the first moment we met.

Reality and the past intermingle, and I don't know what's real or not. But when Cayden presses his lips to my unmoving ones and breathes his life into me, I remember...I remember everything.

Be happy and don't look back...

That's what my mom asked me to do, and I won't let her down ever again.

"I love...you," I manage to spit out before I get lost in the memories which sparked this journey to begin.

So it seems fitting I end it here.

EPILOGUE

One Year Later

"A little to the left. Okay, stop. No, just a little more."

Cayden turns over his shoulder, a dimpled smile punching me in the guts with its cuteness. You'd think I'd be used to it by now. I'm not.

It's been one year since my life changed forever—again, because it seems my life has been filled with nothing but milestones that had the capability to shake my world up beyond repair. But remembering who I was…that was a game changer.

The day my mom, Stella Lane, sacrificed her life to save mine is nothing but bittersweet. I finally remembered, remembered everything, but it came with a price. Her death triggered my demons to resurface and this time, they were intent on taking me down for good.

But I wouldn't allow her death to be in vain because somehow, through the darkness, I remembered. The doctors said that to regain one's memory, sometimes, nothing extraordinary has to happen, but in my case, something so heinous helped me remember.

The shock of what I saw had me shutting down, as I was unable to cope with seeing my mother die in my arms. But even in death, Stella Lane showed me that everything she did, she did for me.

Be happy and don't look back.

Those words helped me wade through the darkness and live the life Stella wanted me to live.

It turns out those voices I heard were the police, well, more specifically, Detective Parks. He turned up at the crime scene first as he was never too far away. His suspicions were right. We were hiding something, and when he saw Will bleeding out on the floor, we could no longer hide.

Cayden had wounded Will, but he's no killer, no matter how badly he wanted to be. They took us all into custody and after weeks of investigating, Cayden and I were free. Will, however, got what he deserved.

A jury of eight men and four women found him guilty of the murder of my mother and sentenced him to life in jail—a place where he belonged. The punishment could never bring back my mom, but knowing he lives with her death is all the reprieve I need.

That bullet was intended for me, but my mom saved me, and now, even though this can't come close to what she did for me, it's a way for the world to remember what a great woman she was.

"You know, you could always do this yourself," Cayden

says, holding the hammer.

"I could," I quip, batting my eyelashes playfully. "But I like looking at your ass."

He opens his mouth, primed on a smart-ass reply, but closes it quickly. Who is he arguing?

"That's perfect," says a bubbly voice, a voice which I fondly remember. Lacey's hands are filled with trays of homemade pizza, reminding me that we're on a deadline.

"Let me help." I offer my empty hands, while Cayden raises those stunning eyes to the heavens.

"So you'll help my sister, but not me?"

Lacey and I attempt to mask our smiles as we love seeing him riled up. "I'm pretty sure she helped when you barked orders at us to apply a third coat of paint. Or when you made us assemble that weird-ass ergonomic desk, which screams old man, by the way."

"Okay, enough," Cayden replies, grinning.

"You should know by now, two against one, you'll never win." Lacey smugly walks up the front porch steps and into the building we all built with our bare hands.

Like I said, this is one way I can honor my mom. She may not have been in the running for mother of the year, but she did what she thought was best. And that's all I could ever ask for.

"Lacey is right. That's perfect," I say with a nod, looking up at the porch where Cayden holds a wooden sign.

"Are you sure?"

"Yes, no more stalling. Let's do it."

Cayden's smile is filled with nothing but love as he positions the nail and with one simple strike, he secures the wooden sign in place. When I see it hanging by the door, my chest fills with pride.

Stella's words will never be forgotten, not just by me, but to everyone who passes through this door. They saved me and now, I hope they can save the world.

Be happy and don't look back.

That's what the sign says, welcoming those who need this place as Cayden and I finally saw our dream through because before me is a sanctuary for anyone who needs it. We built our shelter, but it's a place for everyone. A place that unites the neighborhood, for we are all equal. We always were.

"Are you okay?" Cayden asks, descending the stairs and coming to stand by me.

"Yes," I reply, and I mean it.

A piece of me will always be lost, but this place will help me heal. The Stella Lane Community Center was erected in her honor. It reminds me that every slither of darkness can be eclipsed by the light. Through tragedy, we refuse to lay victims and will try our best to change the past by making the future the best we can.

"The press should be here soon." Cayden looks down at his watch.

Once the media heard of our story and what we intended to do, everyone wanted to help. Cayden being the owner of one of the biggest construction companies in South Carolina didn't lack the tools he needed. But it seemed everyone wanted a small part in making a difference, and we have.

This place will help people see that they're not alone, no matter their circumstances. History won't repeat itself, and that's thanks to Stella Lane.

"What time will Ellie be here?"

Cayden wraps his arms around my middle, and I bask in the memories—new and old.

"Hazel said around four."

Cayden's kindness knows no bounds because he forgave Hazel for siding with his dad. But I suppose she was a victim, just like we were. Which is why a place such as this is needed. History won't repeat itself. Well, we will try our hardest for it not to.

"We better go inside then and make sure everything is ready." But neither of us moves.

I don't know what the future holds, but I know my past has shaped the way, and with Cayden, Ellie, and Lacey by my side, anything is possible. I have loved this man for as long as I can remember. And it seems knowing one another for as long as we have, has us in sync with each other's thoughts.

"I'll push," he playfully says, laying a tender kiss on my cheek.

His touch, his smell, the way I feel when in his arms are the reasons I'm here. We both turn to look at the swing, which has taken us high into the clouds and brought us back down to earth, just how the red ribbon tied to the oak has.

Cayden slips his hand into mine, a gesture that touches my heart because he has never let me go throughout all this. My forever Prince Charming. His forever Snow White.

My fairy tale may not be perfect, but it's my story…and it's a tale I'll never forget.

Again.

Subscribe to my Newsletter: landing.mailerlite.com/
webforms/landing/b4j1v6

Someone Else's Shadow Playlist: tinyurl.com/5n9y6ywt

ACKNOWLEDGEMENTS

My author family: Elle and Vi—I love you both very much.

My ever-supporting parents. You guys are the best. I am who I am because of you. I love you. RIP Papa. Gone but never forgotten. You're in my heart. Always.

My agent, Kimberly Brower from Brower Literary & Management. Thank you for your patience and thank you for being an amazing human being.

My editor, Jenny Sims. What can I say other than I LOVE YOU! Thank you for everything. You go above and beyond for me.

My proofreader—Rumi Khan, you are amazing!

Sommer Stein, you NAILED this cover! Thank you for being so patient and making the process so fun. I'm sorry for annoying you constantly.

My publicist—Danielle Sanchez from Wildfire Marketing Solutions. Thank you for all your help.

To the endless blogs that have supported me since day one—You guys rock my world.

My bookstagrammers—Your creativity astounds me. The effort you go to is just amazing. Thank you for the posts, the teasers, the support, the messages, the love, the EVERYTHING! I see what you do, and I am so, so thankful.

My ARC TEAM—You guys are THE BEST! Thanks for all the support.

My reader group—sending you all a big kiss.

Samantha and Amelia—I love you both so very much.

My fur babies—mamma loves you so much! Dacca, I know you're hanging with Jaggy, Dina, Ninja, and Papa.

To anyone I have missed, I'm sorry. It wasn't intentional!

Last but certainly not least, I want to thank YOU! Thank you for welcoming me into your hearts and homes. My readers are the BEST readers in this entire universe! Love you all!

ABOUT THE AUTHOR

Monica James spent her youth devouring the works of Anne Rice, William Shakespeare, and Emily Dickinson.

When she is not writing, Monica is busy running her own business, but she always finds a balance between the two. She enjoys writing honest, heartfelt, and turbulent stories, hoping to leave an imprint on her readers. She draws her inspiration from life.

She is a bestselling author in the U.S.A., Australia, Canada, France, Germany, Israel, and The U.K.

Monica James resides in Melbourne, Australia, with her wonderful family, and menagerie of animals. She is slightly obsessed with cats, chucks, and lip gloss, and secretly wishes she was a ninja on the weekends.

CONNECT WITH
MONICA JAMES

Facebook: facebook.com/authormonicajames

Twitter: twitter.com/monicajames81

Goodreads: goodreads.com/MonicaJames

Instagram: instagram.com/authormonicajames

Website: authormonicajames.com

Pinterest: pinterest.com/monicajames81

BookBub: bookbub.com/authors/monica-james

Amazon: amzn.to/2EWZSyS

Join my Reader Group: bit.ly/2nUaRyi